CW00517305

# PREFACE

## The Heart of the Dragon.

This fantasy series is my first published book series ever! I'm very excited about this. Creative writing and reading has been a lifelong passion of mine. This book series is about a young woman's hero development story; a journey that every person takes to make sense of their own inner world. The Heart of the Dragon continues where Polly and the Tome of Herne ends; where Polly is guided to find a dragon's egg, in a long forgotten Pagan temple underground. This is foretold in an ancient prophecy.

A quick recap: Polly was gifted powers on her sixteenth birthday by a pagan witch. The natural world and the universe are at risk of being annihilated due to an imbalance. A secret society called the Inner Circle, who is supported by a clandestine black operations organisation, The Company are trying to use this imbalance for their own gains. The Tome of Herne is a powerful book of magic. Written by a sect of monks wishing to defy the Dark Lord and restore balance to the universe. The Tome foretells of an ancient prophecy to save all living beings and restore all. Polly is destined to be the hero that the universe needs - she just doesn't realise it yet and she also needs to conquer her own demons.

The Heart of the Dragon book aims to draw its readers from the everyday world around them, into a magical world that exists within our own world. Ancient fables come to life through Polly meeting a vast array of witches, wizards, dragons, demi-gods, Goddesses, High Priestesses. Through her journey, she encounters warrior tests, ancient relics, talismans, a deranged Horn God, and a whole lot more. But…although this is fantasy novel, it asks of its readers to reflect on some serious issues that are impacting our society today and human existence itself - our purpose and our contribution to the legacy of this planet we call Earth ( I have always wondered what other civilisations – maybe even other species - called the Earth before our civilisation were the custodians of it).

Polly is the main character and her start in life is not ideal. Her hero journey is based upon both an external adventure and an inner journey of transformation. An odyssey every individual embarks upon in their lifetime - the quest to understand self, to seek meaning and to find a place we feel at home in. In book one, Polly was beginning to understand herself and the second book is about seeking her life's meaning and finding her a place where she belongs. The third book, the final one, will be about her new found confidence and sharing her gifts.

I wanted to tell a story about a person who is a survivor of hard circumstances and incorporate the changes she experiences, as she embarks on her own transformation. This book focusses on empowerment of women of all-ages (there is more than one powerful female in this story too) and learning to navigate life's obstacles with one's own self-belief and compassion.

The aim of this book is to return to the tradition of imparting teachings through the telling of fables; the handing down of life's often hard-won lessons and sharing of experiences from one generation to the next. Ancient tribes and civilisations have used stories and folklore for centuries to impart and hand down valuable life lessons, so that humans that come after will not necessarily have to make the same mistakes time and time again. Something that I wanted to leave behind and share with young and older adults alike, is my own learning throughout my journey through this wonderful life. My own sister died in March of 2023. Sorry to bring up something so sad and I know that many of us have lost a great deal during the pandemic and post-pandemic, but the reason I am sharing this with you dear reader is that on the day she was dying, she wanted to share so much of her life experience with me and to share some of her life-lessons. She run out of time. Don't run out of time…share all of the brilliant, weird and awe-inspiring things about you that make you unique, especially with your loved ones and those you care for.

This book is about exploring meaning, grief and sharing with the people that are most important to you. That is what really matters in life, that we care for our loved ones, we look after the earth and all the creatures who live with us on it and we leave behind our legacy – a planet that is thriving in this great big universe of magic and wonder.

I hope you enjoy my writing and I hope you experience the same joy and excitement reading about the characters in this book, that I do when writing stories for them. Peppa x

# Meet Pollux. Kind. Caring. More than what she seems. Expert in multiple forms of arm-to- arm combat, Mother of Dragons and Destiny awaits her....

On Pollux's sixteenth birthday last year, the young woman discovered that she has special powers. Our protagonist, better known as Polly, was taught how to use her new magical gifts by a powerful and not to mention very assertive, pagan Witch, Eleanora and a scholarly Wizard, Prof. Timothy Rothschild. A mind-boggling experience: Polly was shocked at first about the existence of a magical realm in the United Kingdom, but soon got used to the idea of magic. Being confronted by the daily reality of it through the discovery of ancient prophecies, magical books like the Tome of Herne, a High Priestess who set warrior tests, Pagan mystical swords – Polly's very own Sword of Hestia. Talking and wise Trees, Pagan temples with hidden treasures and to top it all, the Goddess revealed the location of a sacred Dragon Egg for Polly to guard.

The adventure continues with Polly as the Chosen One of legend, fighting one of history's most Evil Dark Witches, to protect her friends and her family, while seeking the seven sacred objects of the Goddess to try to stop Armageddon. Chris and Toni, Polly's closet friends, are also learning to navigate the magical world alongside her and to learn how to use their own gifts.

The Inner Circle are hot on Polly, Chris and Toni's heels and will stop at nothing to obtain the magic to start Armageddon on earth and find the key to extend life and obtain superpowers, all for their own evil gains.

This year is different, this year is darker, and the stakes are higher, and Polly must learn to lose before she can rise again even stronger.

# The Heart of the Dragon

by Peppa Aubyn

The Heart of the Dragon – Book Two on Amazon.com:

A fantasy story about a girl with magical powers who uses them to save the planet, humanity, and all living things from total annihilation.

ISBN: 9798867421984

EAN

Fiction > reference > Independently published / self-publishing.

**Other books by Peppa Aubyn**

Polly and the Tome of Herne -  book one

Who are the monsters – a short story on Peppa's Goodreads Blog

# Contents

To my children, Ry Ry and Secret. I will love you for all eternity. I carry you with me wherever I go. Always remember, I am yours and you were mine, as the children of the stars that you both are.

*In the midst of hate, I found there was, within me, an invincible love.*

*In the midst of tears, I found there was, within me, an invincible smile.*

*In the midst of chaos, I found there was, within me, an invincible calm.*

*I realised, through it all, that….*

*In the midst of winter, I found there was, within me, an invincible summer.*

*And that makes me happy. For it says that no matter how hard the world pushes against me, there's something stronger - something better, pushing right back.*

*By Albert Camus*

# The Sect of the Oneness – the Prophecy of Restoration

The master's will drive the children to maim and destroy nature in the 21st century. The planet weeps and no one hears her. She is in darkness; her pain goes unheard. The creatures of the world are dwindling and those that are meant to be their caregivers; put greed first.

Her tears will rise and all land will be consumed by fire.

One hundred years of drought and famine

Followed by one hundred years of floods.

And one hundred years of ice will swallow the world.

To right the wrong that has been done onto the universe.

The children of the forest are loved. The Goddess will send forth a champion with extraordinary gifts, when she is needed. The protector of the Earth and the Universe she is. Two dragons' eggs will open to save the twin planets: all will start anew with rebirth within ten days. Mother Goddess will cover her children, who are the embodiment of the celestial forest, in sunlight. Within them, the children of nature, of balance. They will be with The Chosen One, giving her strength to save all of The Goddesses' children of Herne, great and small. The seven sacred objects and the Heart of the World will be sought and brought together at the High Seat of the cosmos. The Light and the Dark will flicker, intertwined. One will remain seated and the universe will be a reflection of the victor. Darkness and Light will combine and the Universe will be restored under the Oneness. All will be saved, unless He sits upon the Throne at the Seat of the Cosmos, then all will fall to Darkness and ruin . . .

## Chapter one - The Birth of the Chosen.

We all hear the thrum of this beat. It is and has always been a part of every living being on this planet - we are all connected by its pulse. This rhythm, this dull thud in our mortal ears. To be alive is to hear this beat. There is no life without it. This is the sound of the universe, calling out across time and space. We are gifted to hold it within us and guard it for our own for a while.

To be alive. To experience. We hear it from the first consciousness awakened in us, in our mother's womb – we are connected in this truth. Fluttering and banging against our ribs throughout our lives.

Upon the day of our death, the good in us all takes time to reflect on three things; how willingly we have used it, how openly we have shared it and how connected to others with love we have been - to exist is to hear this rhythm. The Rhythm of Life.

*** 

In the dark space underground. In the chamber made by the roots of the mythical Willow Tree, the scaly egg nestles in the bones of the earth. Waiting for the warmth of the touch of The Chosen to ignite it into being. The pulse is getting louder, stronger and bringing life into the world. A life that will change the path of all living things. The living legend will eventually awaken and be the Bringer of Myth, of fable and rebirth. A creature older than time, older than the foundations of the earth. But for now, it waits under root and tree, nesting. Quiet. Waiting for the other of its kind – the twin.

It is a time on earth when wild forests and abundant jungles cover the planet's lands. Where scorching desert plains and treacherous seas are in dominance over this vast inhospitable environment. Animals roam freely in their natural habitats, unencumbered by the race we now know as humans.

An early form of homo sapiens is running through the treacherous snow on a cold winter night. A female. She halts, doubled over; her knees crash onto the frozen ground still clutching her swollen belly. The impact causing her full breasts to leak. Through clenched teeth she yells into the stillness of the night, then finds the strength to push herself up from the ice and starts running frantically, once again. Knees stinging but numb from the cold. The mother fears she is being pursued - eyes wide and darting, with pupils dilated in her panic. The bitter taste of phlegm at her throat and nostrils. She dashes out of the interior of the densely wooded area of the forest and crosses the clearing, into the space where the golden leaved silver birches grow - they are all bare and offer no protection from the predator at her back. A reminder of the bleakness of the winter months.

Toughened fur and animal skins cover her sweat glistening body, and she is stumbling forward with animal hide bound to her feet. Tied across her back is a handcrafted weapon - a spear made from a filed down tree branch. At its tip, a piece of jagged flint is appended. The stone of her Tribe and one that is only found in the clear streams that provide drinking water to her people and the animals that graze on her protected lands.

She is losing the last battle, willing her flesh on. Leaving fresh tracks in the fallen snow - her footfalls crunching as she runs by. These are easy to spot but she does not try to hide them this time from hunting animals, which will naturally follow her – eager to feed. The lone woman is not afraid on this occasion. Knowing her time is running out. On her arm is a deep bite from a predator and her blood is oozing downwards, droplets forming onto the white snow. Her breath can be seen in front of her face, like a frozen mist collecting in the chill night air. She staggers on trying to find somewhere warm and safe to give birth before her passing. Panicking, she knows she does not have long now before the eternal rest takes her for its own.

The large grey wolf is following her, staying back out of sight and in the shadows. The Grey One of Legend is waiting on the edge of the light of the full moon - its haunting eyes are seen as glowing disks of light in the dark. Its mighty claws channel great grooves in the ice floor. The harsh scratching sends out a warning across the silent woods and small mammals tremble in their dens.

The mother furtively looks at the frozen ground, desperate to find a space under the canopy of the trees. Drawn here under the safety of the foliage, away from watchful eyes. Nostrils flair, inhaling the comforting smell of spring grass here. A calm descends and she lays down. To pant, to heave and push with the rhythm of the coming pain - the swell of the ultimate beginning. Drifting in and out of consciousness from the amount of blood she has lost. The luminous amber eyes look on and the she-wolf places a paw forward on the freezing snow. The claws of the wolf tunnel a grove in the icy floor.

The mother gives one more almighty push, screaming into the uncaring cold night, and the baby slithers out. Onto the snow-covered grass bed of the forest. The newling starts to cry and grizzle, shock is the first memory, laid there in the perilous snow. In its small, bunched fist, a sapling of the willow tree. Sacred tree of the Goddess. It is a sign.

The High Priestess steps out of the shadows, with her helmet made from starlight gleaming and her white tunic flowing in the wind. Called forth to this place due to the vibrational pull of Destiny. Fate whispers in the chill air. The snow is heavy with magic, announcing the fate of us all. Its imprint shapes each snowflake that crests the ground on this Night of Nights.

The snowflakes drift lazily to the floor, in the same pattern. Announcing the birth of the Kaidaluminere line, in the shape of the Dragon.

The High Priestess bows down before the infant and cuts the cord of the baby, brutally separating her from her mother.

Picking the startled baby up. Arms splaying out, the infants survival instincts heightened. The High Priestess holds the baby girl in her arms, gazing upon the child's beautiful angelic face and then the warrior-Priestess gently wraps the newborn in some fabric torn from her own tunic – a makeshift blanket, swaddling the child's form.

The High Priestess removes the sapling from the infants bunched fist – it is not given freely, then starts to speak "The Chosen One must be born of blood. I am sorry to say, destiny foretells the warrior must endure a hard life. It must be this way, to forge the spirit and demonstrate the power of the heart, even when little good has been experienced by it. Be brave my little youngling, long will you be known as the bringer of the beginning. You are the first of your line."

With this knowledge imparted, the tall and gamine High Priestess takes long strides over to where the She-Wolf sits waiting. The High Priestess greets the she Wolf as an old friend and  hands the baby to its new mother. "Your cub, your life, your own."

The She-wolf bows and takes the swaddled form gently in her teeth. Turning away with her precious load, to cover the distance to her cave, where her cubs are waiting to feed on their mother's milk and welcome their new sibling.

The High Priestess watches with kindness, as the she-wolf descends the winding path, up deep into the hills. The lone figure of the wolf cuts a shadow-form against the background of the forest, under the pale eerie light of the full moon.  A fable, a living inkblot drawn on a page, committed unto the memory of Time.

The Priestess turns, with regret marking her face, to the task at hand. Her tunic flowing out behind her, turning back towards the lifeless body of the mother. Walking forward into the space where the amniotic fluid and the mother's blood are seeping slowly into the cold forest floor. A ringlet made of the purest of gold,  is placed on the mother's head. A gift from the High Priestess to honour the young woman's life. She recites a prayer, giving thanks for the offering of one to save many. The ringlet turns into a halo and the body starts to rapidly decay and decompose into the frozen earth - returning its borrowed energy from whence it came.

The High Priestess holds up the sapling in her hands and blows life into the seed before planting it in the ground. On the spot  the baby's and mother's fluids are forever united with the Maternal one - the Earth.

An ethereal shaft of light from the full and glowing moon beams down onto the sapling. The light is marking the tree as distinct. Signifying  The Willow Tree is now bonded into the story of the Kaidaluminere line. The sapling shivers, naked in the ground – set apart from the forest. Destiny marks it out, so it must be alone in its quest for reaching the sky. Striving to take hold of the moon,  yet still to remain as tender as a tree.

The High Priestess sets an enchantment over the area and then exits the place that in centuries will be referred to as The Old Wood, but for now it is part of the newness of the world.

The Kaidaluminere lineage is established on that night and so is the first human line to be gifted magical powers to host The Chosen Ones. The One's with the magical powers and abilities of nature, given to protect the planet, the Universe, and all living beings.  The rest of the developing homo sapiens at this time, will grow as part of humankind's evolution on this planet. The Kaidaluminere line will be the first magical beings and will go on to create the first generation of magical humans – their DNA structure is different, gifted. Unique.

***

Centuries upon, centuries have past, another mother has been brought to the sacred space of The Old Wood to give birth.  She has been laid down on her back under the watchful gaze of the fated Willow Tree. The moon is full, and the She Wolf is in the shadows at the edge of the forest - Guardian of the Chosen One's birth.

There are other eyes in this forest, which go unseen this night.

Some distance away, the High Priestess looks out from afar from a hilltop. The shadowed hazel and golden flecked eyes of the child's father are

16

watching the scene as it unfolds. He is circling like a tiger, pacing the perimeter to keep the mother and baby safe during this very special, yet perilous and vulnerable time. The two women acting as midwives for the mother, do not know of the father's presence, and yet, they can feel his male energy in the air - protecting the birthing circle and his line.

"Push Tabitha and breathe my girl. That's it", Eleanora says encouragingly then casts a look over at her sister, Esme known, as The Lady. The two pagan witches look at one another, concern etched on their kind faces.

The mother is haemorrhaging and does not have much time left. They are placing spells on the young mother, trying their best to save her, protecting her giving birth. They know this is a futile effort, due to the prophecy, but still they try anyway. Legend foretells that when The Chosen One is born, the baby is brought into this world through the sacrifice of blood, and that is the way of it. How it must be. As brutal as life is, there is still love within this act – within the act of birth.

For what is purer than the love of a mother? To put oneself in danger to give your child life when you risk your own. To breathe new life into the world - to risk self for love.

Tabitha screams in pain, clutching at her swollen belly. Catching a glimpse of the concerned exchanges between her midwives' faces and understands in that moment what this means – what this means for her. A calmness descends over the mother, and she accepts her fate with grace. Her last messages are given in a whisper, as her life is ebbing away. She searches out the eyes' of the women aiding her birth and utters these words in little more than a whisper, in this the last space she will physically occupy "Tell her I love her, tell her she was mine and I was hers. Don't let her be alone in her destiny. Show her my love and tell her to come to this space and I along with all the mothers of our line, will be here bonded to the willow tree and to her." The young mother says this while looking up at the branches of the Willow Tree wistfully, hoping there is a way. Eleanora's tears run like branching rivers down her cool face. The witches throat is constricted with emotion, and she cannot respond, and does not have the heart to watch the end. Eleanora turns away.

The Lady draws her strength to her. Being used to nursing the dying and greets the sense of the profoundness of the passing of another living being, like an old friend. The Lady goes beyond herself to offer comfort in this time before death - the remnants of the glory of life's last embers as they gently come undone.

"Your child will be drawn here to this place. She will know you and you will be in the trees, immortal and unending, bonded in love."

With a smile on her pale face and comforted by these kind words from The Lady Esme, Tabitha the young mother, sucks in her last breath, then bears down and Pollux is born onto blood. Tabitha slumps forward after this final act. Eyes open, glassy and unseeing, the stars above are reflected in her iris.

As is part of the Rite, the cord is cut. The baby is swaddled in a white linen tunic and laid down under The Willow tree. The she wolf steps forward into the light of the full moon. It is a blood moon - another portent. The she-wolf is anxious and whines, stamping her paws on the ground, sensing a change upon the wind, sniffing around - unsettled. Eleanora brushes the tears from her own blue eyes and her cheeks with the back of her hand. The wolf has attracted her attention. Eleanora walks over to the she-wolf, whose teats are swollen and heavy with milk. Eleanora bends down on her heels to be at eye level with the wolf. "You have come, and we are grateful, but the world has changed. Your baby will be placed with a family this time."

The She-Wolf whines with sorrow and bows its head confused by this turn of events. It snarls and jumps majestically forward and goes to try to take her baby by force - the animal instincts in her are strong to protect her young at all costs.

The Lady places her staff in front of the She-Wolf blocking her path. "The world has changed", she says more forcefully but with kindness "You can see her when she comes here and you will be with her again. You are bonded in destiny, and you know it, look into your heart, Mother Wolf." The Lady bends forward and balances in a squat position, to hug the She-

Wolf, who is mewing sorrowfully. "Next time a Chosen One is born, hopefully, the world will be in balance again, brought forward by this warrior, your cub." The Lady sweeps her hand towards Polly. "The next Chosen One will go with you, as a wolf, as nature will be restored but not this time, Mother-Wolf. Not this time."

The She-wolf places her head in The Lady's lap and licks the tip of the witch's hand and then at her face. "Go and enjoy your cubs, Mother. Pollux will be back here, and you will be reunited again with The Chosen One." The she wolf turns and at a run, follows the path through the forest up to the hilltop and as she is about to disappear, turns one more time to glance at the baby. Silhouetted by the fullness of the blood moon, the she-wolf lets out a primal howl so the Chosen will know her as their guardian and that seals the bond, the wolf is letting The Chosen know that she will be here when needed. The She-Wolf turns and disappears into the interior of the forest, but not forgotten.

Eleanora and The Lady Esme turn to the body of the mother. As is tradition, they place the ringlet of gold on the mother's head and a halo appears. The flesh starts to rapidly decompose, returning its burrowed energy back to the earth. The baby is gurgling, and a few moments pass. Suddenly, the Willow Tree of the eternal, springs to life. Holding Polly with its branches and touching the baby with its leaves. The Willow Tree is weeping no more.

Eleanora lifts her head to study the edge of the woods, she senses something - the Father is kicking up and stirring the leaves with the pounding of his feet. The male, in his nakedness, strides into the clearing.

Eleanora and The Lady do not know what to do. This is unusual, but they dare not engage him. In nature, the male tiger, at times, senses a threat in its own cub and returns to the birthing circle to kill its offspring. The two women rush forward and place their bodies in front of the baby to protect her. The Father, standing tall, looks past the witches to gaze at his baby. His long chestnut brown hair is fluttering in the cold air. To him, his human form is colder than the animals he inhabits. Shrugging on a tunic conjured from his large hands and he removes from his neck a gold chain with a circle within a circle and the letter "*G*" inside. Moving lightly, with a refined grace and majesty; over to his offspring and places the large chain on the baby's swaddled form - it drowns the infant. His large hands holding the baby up and looking deeply into her large, almond-shaped hazel eyes and they are his own. He kisses her forehead and gently places her back down on the leaves before The Willow Tree. The resemblance striking, like a copy was made of him. Lifting his face to the tree. He looks confused and with his eyes, sweeps the ground, as if looking for something "where is my son?" The Willow Tree stirs and shivers, rolling its long branches towards him, being lifted on a gust of wind. The Willow Tree sheds new leaves, with a tinkling sound, which echoes like tiny bells in the stillness of the forest. The leaves then float over the Father and land on the ground near a patch of tall grass - silently and without being observed by the two midwives, a bundle appears on the forest floor. The Father lovingly rubs one of the leaves between his fore finger and thumb, caught up in a memory. Coming near to tears holding the fresh rubbery leaves in his hand and then slowly lets them go. Dropping them onto the grass. He walks away. In the distance, the wolf pack awaits Him and when he reaches them, he transmogrifies. Changing from human form into that of the primal spirit, The Wolf. Howling as he runs with his pack. Desperately seeking to slip into animal form, to embody it. Letting it consume him, to escape the emotions of the world of humans.

Eleanora is stunned, mouth agape, left wondering what it all could mean . "Why did he appear? What did he come for?" says Eleanora but not really expecting a response. The father is a demi-god and who knows what his daughter, Pollux will become or how this will manifest in the fate of us all. Only time will tell.

Later that same night, when all had left the clearing, the She-Wolf comes back, returned secretly and by stealth. She is sniffing the ground with her large snout. Eventually, finding what she is looking for hidden in the long grass and starts digging at the ground. Picking something up gently in between her teeth, furtively looking around before carrying off the precious package, away with her. The Willow Tree shivers, capturing the light of the moon on her sparkling leaves. The High Priestess watches the revenant tree and whispers to the wind "Well, Eleanora, I think that we are going to find out what having a demi-god as a father means."

## Chapter two – Of Loss

Three years come to pass and it is July once more. A young couple that we will come to know as Mother and Father, Polly's adopted parents, have arranged a corporate picnic for their employees in the Old Wood of St Albans. They are holding a BBQ in the sprawling woods today for their employees and their families. It's a corporate sports day with lots of games and tournaments arranged throughout the afternoon, to keep their staff and families entertained. Both Mother and Father feel pretty good about the event they have planned - giving their workforce this one perfect day. Next week the two of them have hired an organisation to deliver some pretty bad news - the plan is to announce that they are selling the company and there will be a down-sizing of at least thirty percent of the workforce to cover the merger costs. Mother and Father have sold one of their companies for an eye-watering sum, so they happily throw this soiree for the unsuspecting workforce -the very least they can do really. The reason that the company has to be downsized to this extent is that the two demanded way over the asking price.

Mother is wearing tight red capri pants, a striped nautical box shirt, Gucci sunglasses and the latest Stella McCartney shoes. Father is in a casual, stone coloured linen suit with a crisp shirt and white converse shoes. Their stylists wanted to achieve a causal, yet empowered look, so they both appear more 'approachable' to the workforce at the event. Polly is dressed in a Gucci dress with matching bracelet, shoes, and hairband. She has a piece of apple in her mouth and is chomping away quite happily. She takes the pulp out of her mouth and mushes it into her little toddler-sized fingers, wiping it on her new dress. "Polly, really! You are disgusting. Don't you know that there are starving children who would give anything to have a pretty dress like this and you treat it like it's a tea towel." Mother shouts, in one breath barely taking in oxygen while she rants.

Polly giggles at the funny woman who is mostly always screeching and going red in the face.

"Father, do something. She's ruining our day, again. She is really selfish, and I just don't know what to do with her." Father comes round to the side of the buggy to peer in at Polly, who is covered in mushed up apple. "Yuck, yes, it's awful. Do you think she is a bit slow or maybe there is a behavioural issue of some kind?".

"Yes, a behavioural issue of some kind." says mother repeating it so it seems true "I bet that's it. Genetic or something, maybe?" Father has lost interest; his eye being caught by a pretty young woman, Mother observes. She looks round upset and unclips Polly from the buggy harness. Putting her on the ground, being careful the whole while not to let her own hand touch the mulch of the apple. The thought of it repulses her "Go and wash yourself off and clean up, Polly. Its each for their own round here". she says, giving the toddler a nudge in the direction away from her.

Polly stands there looking forlorn and confused, at first. She scrunches up her cherub face and holds out her arms, fingers clutching for a hug. When it does not come, she places her arms back down by her sides and a deep, dull ache blooms inside her belly. She is glum, eyes cast down, but senses that crying will not result in comfort being given. A large butterfly flaps its delicate wings before her, brushing its wing tips on the top of her little nose and her attention is immediately drawn away from her sadness. The wing tips brush her delicate cheeks, and she starts giggling and twirling round happily - her love of nature shines forth "Wings of da budderfly" she squeals.

Polly runs after the butterfly on her little legs, out of the clearing and onto a quieter path. She follows the twirling butterfly into the woods, onto the denser parts of the forest. Stumbling over thick roots and through hedgerows, she continues to follow the beautiful butterfly. This place feels warm, soothing and is familiar to her somehow. Polly pauses to look around her and sits down "Mama" she asks the stillness of the Woodland. Pushing herself up from the ground, her feet can be heard in the stillness of the woods. She no longer needs the butterfly to guide her on - she knows this place. The air smells different here, like home. Her small toddler sized feet are treading the path where they have been before. Polly enters the clearing and immediately sees the Willow tree. It stands separate from the other trees and is proudly splendid, covered in a midsummer haze. The smell of summer and of nature, of life and birth is wafting through this clearing and Polly smiling, ambles over to touch the wispy leaves and is ready to be swept up under its branches. The baby rejoices in the dappled light that dances across the blades of grass and on the trunk of the tree. Following the sunbeams that glitter and light up the clearing, she makes her way over and lays down amongst the roots. Falling to sleep feeling cherished, loved, and cared for. "Happy birthday dearest one" sings the Willow tree,

"Happy Birthday" says Eleanora the pagan witch in that space.

The She-Wolf scratches at the earth and lays a briar crown on the ground,

The Father watches from a distance, through the eyes of a woodland animal, unseen.

Polly is bathed in a green glow. The particles lift off of her and float up into the fragrant air. Evaporating, as they touch the trees, the great expanse of woodland. The ancient wood bathes in the presence of The Chosen One and the wood and all of its inhabitants, can see the wonder of the cosmos in the baby, fast asleep in the clearing – covered in a summer haze.

Later that same day, the picnic is being packed up by tired catering and entertainment staff. The last of the families are getting into their cars and putting sleepy children in the back, while they are yawning and pretend not to be sleepy at all. Mother and Father waste no time in talking about the event they had just hosted. Cases of unopened champagne, caviar, and canapes strewn on the grass, leftover. "Brilliant event darling. I really felt it was a fantastic last supper for the Oiks. You should be really pleased" says Father. Mother replies "Yes but look, I ordered all this caviar and lobster canapes and the simpletons wolfed down the Godawful hotdogs and burgers like it was the food of the Gods. Actually, probably too good for them too". A crack of thunder overhead snaps across the sky. Mother peers suspiciously upwards, towards the heavens. Confused as the sky still looks calm and a vibrant shade of the brightest blue. With not a single dark cloud in the sky - the rumbling had been rather menacing. "Oh well, there's no accounting for taste", agreed Father, nodding his head and sweeping his fringe from his eyes, trying to look foppish.

The event coordinator comes rushing over. She is a finicky, slim, pale looking woman and of late, not eating too well, being kept rather busy by the demands of the Hanscombe family. "Ahhh, Mr and Mrs Hanscombe, are you off then? We can pack up and then drop the rest of the food and champagne round to you?" Mother smiles too quickly, "ok, but anything that I won't like I don't want delivered to the house, got that?" The event coordinator smiles sweetly and gives a quizzical look, adding "... but I won't know what you don't like unless you tell me."

"What the hell, so I have to do everything, do I?" Mother replies, fizzing waspishly, like a buzzing insect, angry at repeatedly bouncing off a windowpane. The false smile slipping from her face.

Father clucks his tongue, puts his briefcase in the back of his car. Beckoning to Mother to get in. She spins on her heel, corkscrewing the pointed tips of both shoes into the soft mud in her temper and gets into the passenger seat of the silver Bentley. The interior is cream leather and plush, and Father curses at the mementos of nature being wiped on the floor of the huge car.

The event coordinator peers into the back of the car with a smile. She reels back, head whipping from side to side and around Mother "Ahem, where is Polly? Where is your baby?"

Mother turns around slowly in the passenger seat and looks with alarm at the empty baby seat in the back. Visibly turning pale, blinking rapidly. Only remembering now that she hadn't seen the baby since the 'Mushing-behavioural-incident' earlier in the day. Mother goes to say something and before she can utter a word, Father leans forward, over her to reply to the assistant. "Oh, her grandmother collected her a while ago, she was getting fussy" says Father with a charming smile and a flash of his brilliant white veneer, tombstone teeth.

"Oh, okay." says the event coordinator, not quite believing him but she could not imagine that two parents could misplace a baby for hours. Could they? Impossible to think anyone would be that cruel. She stared ahead, the sudden realisation that she did not have a very high opinion of her two customers. Remarking to herself how easily the doubt had crept in.

Father presses a button and the window slides shut on the passenger side of the car. He mutters out of the corner of his mouth "not a single word until we get out of here". He slams on the accelerator, mud flying up and over the event coordinator. The car is out on the road in no time at all. They argue all the way home, bickering and battling, backwards and forwards, over who is to blame, who is the better parent (and who is the worst) and how this is Polly's own fault "Always running off" Father boils. In the end they agree out of protection for themselves, that they will have to report this to the police in the morning and they concocted a story together. They would say that she had not been in the cot when they awoke. Father would "fix" the scene like someone had broken in. They could not bear looking at each other for the rest of the ride home. An uncomfortable feeling settles over the two of them, coating them with a greasy unease and silently questioning and prodding at their belief system and what type of people they truly are.

The two parents are subdued when they open the door to their large and expensive house, in Winchmore hill. They gratefully slam the door closed on the outside world. This is where they can finally be themselves. Mother walks into the hallway, lost in thought. Father lingers for a little longer, resting his hand on the doorknob. Leaning down heavily for a while with his full weight on the door. Bowing his head. He let out a strangled sigh. Reflecting on the unpleasantness that is to come when they report their child missing. They are stuck, spiralling. Left imagining the newspaper headlines. Mother is sobbing, thinking about prison and the confines of an unflattering boiler suit - and sobs louder. Hysterical, she trembles as she pours herself a drink. The grip of her hand barely able to clutch the chinking glass. Father musters the courage to walk through and join his wife in the lounge and throws himself down on the chair. The balls of his hands resting neatly in the sockets of his eyes. Wondering what is to become of him.

Strangely, they both have not given a second thought to where Polly *actually* is. Wallowing in their own self-pity.

The pagan witch, Eleanora, dressed in a woollen cape and travelling attire, walks into the room holding the baby, Pollux to her closely, as if coveting a most precious treasure.

"Who are you? What the hell are you doing? Why have you got Polly?" Mother and Father both say in unison, flabbergasted looks fixed on their gaunt faces.

The Lady Esme follows close behind her sister, Eleanora, with her staff outstretched before her and casts a spell to freeze them both in that moment in time. Both Mother and Father caught with an indignant rage across their faces.

"They are worse than we thought, Eleanora. A difficult life does not mean abuse, cruelty, and neglect" says The Lady Esme, the words come out coated in disbelief and she is choked on the words.

"Let's give her the amulet from her father now." Eleanora says this while placing the piece of jewellery around Polly's neck. "It will protect her physically as well as her heart and her head" Eleanora continues, while glaring at Polly's supposed parents.

"We will need to place a spell on these two though, so they don't see the magic of the amulet" With that statement, The Lady raises the staff once again and a pale pink smoke emits from the end. "That should do it. I also, think she needs to be able to escape to the Willow Tree whenever she needs to", says The Lady, knowing the child would most likely need to spend every waking hour there, with these two as parents.

"The amulet will take her there and then transport her back here, whenever her heart is heavy. It will be fine, sister" Eleanora says with a look of hope rather than certainty. "You know there is nothing else we can do. This woman" Eleanora gestures towards Mother "is a distant relative of Polly's on her birth Mother's side and we know that blood magic is the strongest form of protection there is while she is growing. You know what evil is trying to find her. Hunting her, haunting her steps. She must be protected at all costs, even if it means living with these two selfish, obnoxious, pieces of...."

"Okay, okay, I understand" The Lady interjected with a forlorn look on her face, before Eleanora would change her mind and go against Destiny, which she has been known to do in the past.

Both women gazed sadly yet adoringly at the baby. "Let's put her to bed and tell her a story of the Old Elf Queen and her courage, then we can leave but stay watchful. We are not supposed to interact with her, but we can watch her and keep her safe from a distance.". They carried the baby upstairs to her cot, in a small corner of the palatial house and put her in, covering her with a blanket and wished for her heart to remain strong.

## Chapter Three - The Witches in the snow

### July fifteen years later

Polly pops open the lid of one of her almond-shaped hazel eyes, long dark lashes cresting the outer edges. Her lush and thick brows currently knotted together, in a type of frustration not usually seen upon her kind face. Awakened abruptly, with a start. She can't quite put her finger on what woke her. It wasn't the loud beating of her own heart vibrating loudly in her ears, nor the red throbbing sensation over her eyes. There is a dread that clings to the air because of a background sound she can hear in the distance. A thudding difficult to describe *"where is it coming from and what is it? A warning perhaps?"* whispering to herself. Concentrating hard with her eyes closed, she tries to catch it once again and glean the direction. The infuriating rhythm has no source that she can determine, and it is slower than her own heartbeat. Duller, thudding on the edge of sound.

*thrum, thrum, thrum, thrum, thrum, thrum, thrum, thrum, thrum,*

Sitting up, holding her breath, and straining to catch the sound in the stillness of her tent. Admittedly, she has been hearing this thudding sound sporadically over the last year. Of late, the thrumming has been a constant companion.

Slamming her clenched fist down, on the sleek nylon, she lays back once more in her sleeping bag, but she cannot shift her focus away from constant thrumming. Her teeth clenching. Maddening it is.

Closing her eyes again, she starts to slow down her own breath. To drift. To match the slow rhythmic beat that only she can hear. Her breath is a soft rhythm. Her head is lolling and at last, she achieves synchronicity; her heartbeat perfectly matching the thrumming sound. And there, in that perfected, deep steady thrum, a psychic vision comes into view:

Polly is transported to an ancient, whispering forest. The smell of grass and fauna like mushrooms and cabbage leaves. She finds herself walking under the dappled sun-drenched canopy. Warmth touches her cheeks in the dappled sun light and a chillness in the shade. The splendour of the wall of trees is beautiful. A hidden paradise, that makes her heart slow down. Her hand brushes rough bark. The leaves under foot are a mixture of crunchy and slippery wet underneath. There are old, gnarled trees and soft wisps of spiders webbing between the trunks – hooking across her face. Pathways of fallen crispy leaves. There, in the distance, is a cave and she is drawn towards the enclosure. Inside the cave is a thick black darkness, blanketing all from view. Impenetrable to her sight. She hesitates, holding her hand on one of the moss covered, jagged rocks of the outer wall of the cave. It's cool, wet even and hard under her touch. Her long, slender fingers grip on to the wet moss, as she leans into the dense blackness. *"The cave I fear to enter holds the treasures that I seek."* Polly whispers to herself. Shaking her head like emerging from a dream, not knowing why she had suddenly said this to herself. Placing one foot inside the cavemouth and starts moving forward, onto the jagged stony and earth ridden path – comforting to her weary feet. The air is hot in here and a tangy smell of sulphur clings to the space - it has a primal taste. Yet, terror is far from her mind. In the distance, deep within the cave, Polly can make out two great balls of light in the darkest point at the back of the cave wall. The yellow flames points are coming towards her. Drawing nearer and nearer to where she is standing. Hovering more than twenty feet in the air. Swooping down on her and moving side to side, getting larger and larger, hungrily coming towards her in that hot space. She lets out a gasp of recognition, they are not balls of fire at all but…

"Polly. Hey, are you okay?" Chris, one of Polly's oldest friends in the world, is leaning his long lean body through the opening of her all-weather and highly technical tent. He is doing this while trying to rile her awake by shaking her foot vigorously. Polly's body and feet are toasty warm in the confines of the sleeping bag she is currently cocooned inside. She is instantly irritated by being shaken out of the vision.

Polly groggily peers down, along her body towards her feet to where Chris is crouched low. For the briefest of time, she manages to hold on to the image of the large amber balls of fire in the cave and then, the memory vanishes, drifts out of her mind like a puff of smoke. Smacking her lips. The taste of sulphur lingers on in her mouth.

Chris looks at her with a deep concern in his large green eyes. He has a very legitimate reason to be worried. This considering Polly was gifted superpowers last year on her birthday and it is her seventeenth birthday today - who knows what will happen this year. Chris is knocked to the ground by a sudden freezing gust of Siberian wind, circling the outside of the tent. He scrambles back up, to right himself against the blistering gales of icy wind and crouches over once more.

"You were thrashing about in there just now. Groaning quite a bit. What is it? Is it the biting cold or is it anything to do with that half rotten, manky vegetable you found and ate for dinner last night. I bet you had terrible wind" Chris says, laughing at his own joke. He is crouched low, rocking backwards and forwards on his long muscular legs, trying to keep the blood flowing in his cold limbs. He has on a thick woollen balaclava, rolled up like a hat over his light brown curly hair. A humongous feather-down, navy blue technical winter coat over his tall, filled out frame. He is wearing extra-large waterproof trousers to accommodate for how tall he is and size eleven snow boots to keep out the ice and the cold.

"Happy seventeenth birthday, Polly. Not long until you're as old as me. I can't wait until next year when I hit my twenties" Chris says, chuckling to himself again. He's easy-going disposition showing in his open, kind chiselled face. He leans further inside the tent, peering in at Polly, wondering why he is being met by silence.

Polly pauses, her throat constricted from the warm, tingly feeling that she experiences in his presence these days, but she finds it all rather confusing. They have been friends since they were little kids. She sighs in frustration and tuts. She lost the vision to listen to bodily function jokes, just great.

"Why are fart jokes so very funny to men?", Polly snaps, taking her frustration out on Chris. She had lost the vision, which might have given them a clue to the whereabouts of the White Hart, the mythical beast, that they have to find to help them cast a spell to stop the apocalypse. Polly feels like she is the only one on this expedition taking it seriously at times.

Chris scrunches up his forehead to reflect on Polly's question, like it was a serious point of view being expressed "Just, well, I suppose, it might have something to do with…"

"The smaller brain thing?" Polly interjects flippantly, with a mischievous grin.

Chris widens his eyes "*Polly*, that's a bit much. You'd tell anyone else off for saying something like that, right? What's got into you lately?"

Polly narrows her eyes and chooses not to respond. She is either very irritated with Chris these days or absolutely fawning over him and she finds it all very confusing, and annoying. Her mouth involuntarily bunches into a thin line. He is right of course. The remark was sexist and that irks her even more. She thrusts her arm out of the double lined sleeping bag to unzip it. Immediately feeling the goosebumps prickling under the freezing weather conditions and dips her arm back under the sleeping bag for warmth against the elements.

Polly, Chris and Balan are in Oymyakon, Russia in July. The Professor had researched the last whereabouts of the legendary and mythical beast, the White Hart. The last recorded sighting was in this place, up in the highlands, where the larch and other conifer trees and pines grow. A forest of larch is hard to miss. These trees tend to grow up to a staggering height. The bright yellow pine needles cover the floor of the forest here, like a prickly thick mustard carpet. This is a cold, desolate place, permanently covered in ice and snow. Where no food source can be found apart from mammals living in the wild. Chris and Balan have been living off deer meat and Polly has been eating energy cakes and freeze-dried vegetables to sustain her - being a vegetarian here is a bit of a drawback but Polly is doing remarkably well under the circumstances. Her stomach rumbles under the sleeping bag and her taste buds ache for some real food. She pulls her belt tighter and moves the notch up another hole. It helps a little.

Chris realises he is being ignored, his smile slightly fades, and he attempts to cover the sadness in his large green eyes when he says "Anyway, Balan and I have a surprise for you when you get up. When you're ready come up to the communal hut. We'll be waiting for you.". Polly pops one of her eyes over the rim of her cover and watches Chris. He hesitates before he slowly turns around and walks out of the tent. Leaving the opening flapping in the freezing wind. A stream of freezing cold air is rushing towards her face and Polly decides to brace herself and get up to face the day.

Although it is miserable outside, there is a kind of excited at the prospect of it being her birthday, despite the terrain and deathly biting cold. It is so cold here that she hasn't been able to feel her nose, and fingers and feet in days and she has been miserably frost bitten in places – lucky for her she has healing powers. They touched down in this part of the country a few days ago, ready to look for the White Hart.

Polly can't quite believe it is her seventeenth birthday. A lot has changed since this time last year, which is when she had gained her powers and become the chosen champion of The Goddess. Whenever Polly thinks about the Goddess, that she has not yet seen, she feels this excited kind of dread. What if she doesn't live up to The Goddesses standards or worse still, she makes a complete fool of herself in front of the ethereal being? Shoving that thought to the back of her mind for another day.

Polly rises to get ready, pulling her slender but strong frame, out of the sleeping bag. Thinking about the last year with a smile to herself - she has found a new contentment in life. There are so many things that are different. Firstly, she has not returned to the place she had previously called home. In Winchmore hill, London. Living with Mother and Father was starting to feel like a horrible distant memory. Or a better way to describe her home life with her adopted parents, would be to describe it as more like a living nightmare. Home for her is now the sprawling castle estate in the highlands of Scotland, living with her peers and the magical community. Eleanora, the powerful pagan witch, and her mentor in all things magical, has given Polly, her very own wing of the castle to live in.

Polly enjoyed decorating her piece of the world, her sanctum and filling the shelves with her favourite books and trinkets. Most importantly, she has been finally able to get her own rescue animal to live with. A gorgeous, slinky black and white tuxedo cat, called Indiana, named after her favourite action hero. Mother had always insisted that she was allergic to pets with hair so Polly had always admired cats from afar but couldn't have her own, until now that is. Indiana is a very clever cat and both wise and devilishly charming - he visits everyone individually in the castle, giving feline head butts and kisses freely. He is well known to the kitchen staff, who lovingly save him special treats and scraps, feeding him as he does his companionable rounds of the castle.

Polly had taken some time to learn more about the origins of her powers, needing to understand them better. The secret society called the Inner Circle are aware of her now, since her mission to retrieve the Vessel of Life last year and she is proud to say that they are having to make precautions against her – she is their number one threat. Trying not to dwell on the Inner Circle for too long and what they are capable of, she has taken to studying the ancient texts of the Grimwald. A set of history books written by priests, on all things magic, mythical, and legendary. The works are heavy going at times and the descriptions quite clunky and overly detailed - The Professor speculates that this is because the Priests had lived in a harsh and remote part of Finland, where there were no visitors, women or other men, or mead. Therefore, little else to do and not very much to enjoy. Part of the Grimwald is a journal and very dull to read.

Polly usually found a great deal of pleasure in books, but reading this set was more of a punishment than anything else. Rather frustratingly, the content did not venture into the Chosen One's origins or abilities. When she had asked, the Professor and Eleanora had told Polly that the Tome of Herne held this information, and that she was not ready to read these pages quite just yet. Finding this a little irksome, feeling left in the dark, because in all other respects she is encouraged by the two of them to seek knowledge and grow. Her two mentors did, however, encourage Polly to train more and learn about her powers through the practical application of magic rather than read the Tome. The book of magic had to be kept safe and locked up in the lower chambers of the castle - lest it fall into the wrong hands. The Inner Circle still need the book to start the apocalypse.

Learning how to use her powers and magic in general, has been a full-time job. This had taken her a good few months of focussed attention and a great deal of trial and error - plus there had been lots of accidents. Often finding herself in the healers' quarters of the Castle. Luckily, she has the ability to heal rapidly, which has come in useful, particularly during those first few months of training.

Polly's discovered her amulet has a magic all of its own and is not connected to her powers at all. The golden object autonomously offers protection and guidance in an unspoken way - she is strangely fond of the piece of jewellery like it is a living, breathing being.

Today, she finds herself reaching down to hold the amulet in her two hands, cradling the intricate casing. The amulet begins to twinkle at her like a thousand glittering stars, glowing under her touch. The necklace lights up the underside of the tent, forming into a replica of the night sky – Mars is aglow with a brilliant red light. Polly becomes quite emotional, and the twinkling lights reflect in the welling of her tears, in her orb-like hazel eyes. The light gently rescinds, and Polly kisses the necklace, as a way of saying thank you for the gift of lights. Somehow, the amulet seems to know it is her birthday.

The gift of lights had distracted temporarily from how cold the weather is outside. Standing there in her thick thermals and trousers, she blows on her hands to heat them up. Making a grab for her clothes, pulling on her wool-lined waterproofs and then heaves on her huge winter coat. Topping it off with a gigantic bobble hat, then covering that with a down-filled hood - packing her long chestnut brown hair into the sides. Her mittens so thick that she cannot bend her hands, and this makes it pretty impossible to pull on her googles, but she eventually manages to do it. She looks in a small mirror fastened to the top pole of the tent and giggles at how utterly ridiculous she looks, but not regretting a single layer of clothing she has on - her cheeks are rosy from how extraordinarily cosy she feels. Usually, when she feels this way, Polly curls up with a good book and a cup of steaming hot cocoa. This wouldn't be happening today, there is too much to do.

Chris, Polly and Balan are in this inhospitable land to find The White Hart and return with a piece of its bone. This search is crucial in the battle against evil. The white hart's bone is one of the seven sacred objects, needed for a spell to stop Armageddon.

Letting out a long sigh, watching her breath freeze in front of her face before she musters up the courage to walk forward through it. Chilling her nose in the process. Shuffling out of the tent sideways under the weight of her clothes, she moves away from the snow-covered tents pitched close to one another and carefully treads the long icy snow path to the communal building. This is a fancy name for one of the small log cabins that the trio had acquired - small is the word. It is in fact one square room. They rented it so they have somewhere to store equipment and keep some essentials dry, food fresh and a fire always burning - this is essential to keeping them alive in this treacherous, hostile terrain.

Polly reaches the large door of the cabin. Tugging it open with a force, finding it stuck under the thick paint, and sticky, deep coat of lacquer to seal the heat in. Instantly, Polly is hit with the warmth from the fire and the smell of baked beans cooking on a hot stove. There are big chunks of leaven bread on sticks, toasting over the fire. Polly's cosy feeling explodes in her chest.

"Happy birthday, Polly" shouts Balan, turning with a great big grin on his handsome face away from the stove. Polly smiles back. Removes her hat and hood and shakes out her long chestnut coloured hair. Deeply inhaling the familiar, distinctive tomato rich smell of Heinz baked beans. Her mouth starts involuntarily watering. Tears prickle at her eyes, this is one of the kindest things that anyone had done for her birthday in a long while. Not quite knowing who to thank for this meal, Chris or Balan? She doesn't want to ask. At times there is an awkwardness between Chris and her if she makes a fuss of Balan's kind gestures.

"We don't have any plant butter so you'll have to do with deer dripping or sunflower oil, which would you prefer?" says Balan in a teasing way, knowing Polly is vegetarian. Her love of nature and care for all living beings is her number one priority, especially now she is The Chosen One, sworn protector of the planet. Or was that the Universe? She wasn't quite sure.

Polly pulls a face. "Sunflower oil, please!" she bellows and smiles. Balan teasingly winks at her. The pair have bonded instantly, relaxed in each other's company. Chris is watching the exchange from where he is sitting near the fire, shoulders rolled forward and chewing his lip.

"Sit down and let me serve you, m'lady" Balan says, with a jaunty smile. His perfect teeth on display and warm brown coloured eyes, twinkle slightly. Balan is a tall, handsome, and athletic, twenty-something young man, with a confidence that had people mistake him for much older than he is. Chris is much taller than Balan, with rich, creamy caramel skin and is very handsome too, but looking quite worried at this moment in time. Polly's gaze drifts over to Chris and she can see he is unsettled, watching her and Balan intently. He does not seem to like their relationship for some reason and keeps questioning Polly about the dynamic, trying to figure it out.

Chris is sitting. Subdued, knotting his thick eyebrows together, biting his lip and then catches himself in the moment. He moves swiftly forward and automatically pulls out a chair for Polly and starts to help her take off her coat, which takes a great deal of effort, time, and grunting. Polly's upturned face is directly above Chris. His attention is elsewhere. His chin lightly touches her nose. Avidly concentrating on unclipping her buttons. He misses her pupils dilating and her face warming with a pink blush, that spreads across her cheeks. This is not due to the sticky steam from the cooking. Chris turns to face her "you're done now, let's eat" and then he looks into her eyes and they both smile at each other, and the blush turns to a warmth that surely he can see.

Hastily, they sit down to eat breakfast together, made in honour of this day - the birthday of the Chosen One.

After they had breakfasted on baked beans in plenty of piping hot tomato sauce, the three joked a great deal about the effect of beans on the human anatomy- led by Chris, of course. With plenty of eye rolls from Polly. They clear away the breakfast dishes and cutlery, to make space at the table and pulled out maps of the surrounding area. Poring over these, the group start plotting a path to the Larch Forest on the Northern point of the land, referred to as the Siberian bowl, which is famously, at times, -60 degrees - sub-zero temperatures.

This is where the White Hart had last been spotted by a group of scientists. On an expedition to record climate change in the area. Unbeknown to the group of explorers at that time, they had recorded the strange sighting and phenomenon; of a glowing white hart with diamonds for eyes and a strange fur covering it. Unaware, the White Hart is a creature of immense magic and revered by the magical community, as a deity of Spring. This account of the sighting detailed that the great beast was three times the size of a stag and in the wake of the animal, grass sprouted up from the ground. The report was instantly dismissed by world experts. They had questioned the validity of the claim, calling it preposterous. This intelligence had later been picked up by the magical community, who declared it as a sighting of the White Hart, a mythical beast of legend with great powers to guide the seasons and call forth Spring during Winter. The White Hart has immense powers and is one of the celestial beings who are protectors of the rhythm of time. This sighting was recorded back in 1982. The Professor had advised them all to seek out the last location and talk to the locals about the incident. The Village of Oymyakon is currently in lock down due to the severe weather conditions and snowstorms, there is no way in or out of the small network of villages in the area. The weather should improve in the next day or so.

Polly, Balan and Chris had agreed to wait out the snowstorm but were becoming restless, so the three adults decided to change their plans and see if they can climb the hill, adjacent to their settlement. To scout around the site of the last sighting of the White Hart. Maybe see if they could find some more clues about the creature's whereabouts. The trio are wrapped up in layers upon layers of warm clothes and technical gear. They had finished up their breakfast, content and full, with gurgling bellies. They pack some essentials, ready to leave for their expedition. Polly pulls back on her huge coat before she wrenches open the door, which is stuck fast with ice in between the crevices of the door frame. The dense snow and strong Siberian winds howl through the doorway, leaving a pile of snowdrift to rapidly build up inside the cabin. The icy gusts whip through the small enclosure, knocking them over like skittle balls. They are thrust backwards under the force of the icy, frigid wind.

Getting back up is a task. They determinedly nod to each other and brace themselves. Driving muscles forward, forcing their bodies out and into the ice filled snowy landscape, all the while, their wills of steel are being tested. They start to wend their way up the hill, by the side of the cabin. Slowly, wading through four feet of packed snow covering the path. Further and further, they go. Each step is hard and pure agony for Chris and Balan. Every step is like wading through freezing, setting cement. They find that their sight is obscured by the denseness of the falling snow. Its morning, but quite easily can be mistaken for night. So very thick is the grey cloud and sky overhead, that it obscures the top of the hill with a frozen vengeance. Balan and Chris are using all of their strength to push through the snow. They head towards Polly, aiming to walk behind her. She alone, is able to walk unhindered through the snow, using her legs to kick a path through the heavy deluge for her friends. But she could quite as easily walked lightly on top of the freshly fallen snow, like if the Chosen One is made of wisp and summer breeze.

Further on they go. Walking onwards and upwards against the Siberian winds. The ledges are treacherously icy. Balan and Chris are struggling to stay upright. Exhaustion is setting in; the way ahead is becoming far too dangerous. They stop to put ice tracks on, clipping them onto the underside of their boots and stamping to test the grip before they continue on.

The sky falls, the wind howls in small circles around them, and the chill wind is whistling in their frozen ears. The sky is bleak. Bitter tears of exhaustion freeze upon Chris and Balan's faces. Up ahead they can see the yellow needles of the Larch firs. Branches thick, full of holding a ton of weight of snow. They start heading with a new-found hope towards the yellow trees. Chris and Balan relieved, they will be pausing soon at the edge of the forest, before they continue into the unknown. Ten feet away from the tree line, they are, when a tinkling sound above them can be heard. Gazing upwards, they are alerted to a large array of frozen icicles, glistening threateningly as sharp javelins. The icicles are hanging precariously from the smattering of trees sprouting up into view. Suddenly, the icicles start moving, slowly creaking and ominously cracking. A sound of snapping, suddenly wrenches the frozen air. Polly charges forth with her sword drawn, she heads to protect Chris and Balan. Springing upwards, Polly cuts straight through the middle of the icicles, flying downwards, through the air. She pushes Chris out of the way and onto the ground. He could not get up again without assistance, due to the weight of his clothing, he resembled a turtle that was stranded on its back.

Balan rushes forward to the space where the icicles lay on the floor, smashed to pieces. Balan starts to feel the air with his gloved fingers. Testing to see if magic had been performed - spells tend to leave a solid residue of sorts that resembles a change in atmosphere - practically, it feels like an invisible waterlogged sponge. He found what he was searching for. Removing his balaclava, he frantically waves them on and mouths "Polly. Quick, quick. Get us out of here" he communicates this as quickly as possible before his lips freeze solid in these sub-zero temperatures. Chris manages to roll himself onto his feet, both of them following Polly and they make a slow dash towards the Larches - with all their strength, they move forward. Towards the safety of the canopy of the conifer trees.

Once they step under the canopy of the trees and have their feet on level ground, a strange thing happens. The ice covered interior of the forest vanishes, the atmosphere changes drastically to that of a fine summers day. The land changes shape and not a snowflake can be found anywhere. It is warm in here. The air is sweet and filled with the fullness of the perfume of a thousand flowers. Calm and lush, with sweeping fields of long grass that are dancing in the warm wind. As tranquil and as swelling and ebbing as an inviting sea. The sun ripples and glints in this space and the sky is a brilliant shade of blue. They very quickly become sweltering hot. Uncomfortably so and their layers are sticking to them in the heat. They get the urge to remove some items, leaving their base clothes on. Folding their clothing in a pile on the edge of the forest, marking the place with a stone circle as a reminder for their return, they continue on. They are looking around, raising their eyebrows towards one another.

Some way ahead and in the distance, they can see an old woman with an open and smiling face. She is dressed in a rattan straw hat. It is secured with a scarf made into a pretty bow under her chin. She is busily scything wheat grass and packing the long stems into bundles, placing them in a woven basket. Working the scythe with a poised skill like a farmhand. The blade is at least three feet long, but she holds it in a practised way and slices the chaff with precision.

Polly senses something is off about the place, immediately. Placing her hand on the hilt of her sword, drumming her fingers lightly on it. Closing her eyes, listening intently to her surroundings. There are no bird's song or humming or chirruping from crickets. Also, the rhythmic heart that had been following her for the last year could not be heard in her ears. She hadn't realised what a constant it had been - until the sudden absence of the thrumming. Doubt blooms up in her, a sickness is on this land, and it is growing heavy upon her mind. Without looking round, she says rather loudly "be careful in this place, we are not in Kansas anymore."

Balan nods his agreement and takes out his dagger, long as his forearm. Sweeping left and right for any potential threats in this strange place "A spell of some kind I think, and quite powerful too. Let's keep our wits about us" Balan shouts out. Conjuring a shield charm and holding it out before him – his training bears witness to the skill of his handled blade.

Chris looks on. Confused and keeps looking behind him at Polly and Balan. He didn't see anything wrong with the place. He is gleefully happy and admiring the utterly beautiful fields and he feels carefree. Deliriously free and happy. Happy, happy, happy. What is he doing here again? He thought to himself.

41

Polly watches Chris for a while, dancing on the spot with his eyes closed, moving his hands wildly in the air. "What is this enchantment?" Polly says and then her gaze is shifted to looking out over the field. Polly calls out to the older woman and another person steps out from behind the woman in the field . The second woman has rosy cheeks and curly, shiny brunette hair. "Hello, we are lost in the highlands, and we were just walking through a snow blizzard, when we fell into this place. Can you help us, please?" Polly asks, sweetly. She does not step forward.

"Of course, dearie. This happens a lot to travellers in these parts." The first old woman stands up, straightens her back while putting down some corn ears and wipes the sweat from her brow "The climate rapidly changes the further you move up the hill, m'darling. It's all ok. Trust us. It's nothing to worry about. Come with us, come with us. We want to help you" one of the older women replies. Both women start to walk across the field towards the farmhouse, some distance away. Balan stretches out his arm and holds his dagger aloft, feeling a dread settle into his stomach. It's all too clean, all too perfect, yet it felt foul.

"What sweet old women" says Chris, in a daze and his eyes are oddly distant. Balan looks at Polly, raising his eyebrows and she shakes her head behind Chris's back, something is very wrong in this place.

"let's go with them, they are being very helpful. What lovely old women" Chris continues to say, dryly, in a strange high-pitched voice. In addition to his dagger, Balan pulls out a large sword, the sheath, of which he carries on his back.

"You lead the way, Chris. We will be here with you". Balan encourages, gently nudging Chris forward. Chris with a rictus smile affixed on his face, leads them on through the fields of golden barley. Chris playfully sweeps his hands over the heads of wheat, and then he leads them on through more farmland, which is picturesque and all a bit too wholesome. Sheep in their brilliant cream wool coats, are frolicking in the hazy summer fields. Chris makes his way through the grasslands and follows the path the two older ladies tread, practically running and skipping to be in their presence.

"Please wait for us dear sweet peasant women" he croons, while Balan sniggers behind him.

"Shall we put away our weapons and see what happens?" says Polly.

"Good idea but let's stay vigilant. It may seem harmless but this is a powerful spell. I think we are still wandering in the snow, and this is an enchantment of some kind. Whoever is behind this might know something about the White Hart, so let's play along for a while" suggests Balan and Polly nods in agreement. The sound of the steel of their blades being sheathed rings in the air, as they both put away their weapons with precision. Balan places a spell of concealment about their persons. There is no need to place a spell on Chris, it's a bit too late for that. He is clearly, and rather entertainingly, already enthralled.

Walking cautiously behind Chris, Polly and Balan enter the courtyard of the farmhouse. Their boots gently squelching on the mud and cobblestones. Tall, proud geese waddle by and donkeys bray sleepily in the sun-drenched backyard. Chickens peck at bits of seed in between the cobble stones. The farmhouse is covered in a wall of wisteria and there are forget-me nots and poppy flowers all around the borders of the cottage-style picturesque house. It looks idyllic and evokes a sense of tranquillity to the untrained eye - it's been designed to disarm wary travellers, quite expertly so.

The two rosy cheeked women are joined by a third now and all three smile and wave at the travellers. While leaning out of the stable doorway of the farmhouse. There is a distant whispering on the breeze, urging them to take shelter and come inside. Into the quintessential working kitchen for something refreshing to eat and drink, and to take rest in the comfortable building after their perilous journey over the icy hill.

All the while the three travellers continue to walk forward, a large silver windchime on the porch, is lazily spinning in the breeze. There is a mirror inside and it is catching the light of the sun. Its glint is blinding. Causing Polly to scrunch up and close her eyes. It is dazzling each time it streaks across her face. The wind picks up and the chime is spinning faster in the breeze. When it starts to slow down, the group and their footsteps start to slow down in unison with the blades of the chime. The glint becomes more and more pronounced, flashing across each of their eyes like a strobe light flicking in and out of view. Chris is behaving oddly; he begins moving in slow motion ahead.

Polly watches the scene unfold before her, sensing the danger of the situation, they are in. She must act fast or die in the enchantment. Her eye is drawn to the windchime, taking in the impression of the object – it stands out solid from the rest of the scene. This is at the core of the enchantment she would bet anything. In one motion and without making a sound, Polly unsheathes her sword and takes a running leap in the air towards the mirrored glass object. Her whole body is spinning through the air, slowly rotating in a circular motion. She lifts up the Sword of Hestia and starts driving the blade downwards and smashing, deeply penetrating the mirrored surface of the wind chime.

A sonic "BOOM" resonates through the air, sending shockwaves outwards. The fine dust from the mirror turns to a desert of sand, blowing all over them - the enchanted object is shattered. The trio flinch and reel backwards, their eyes automatically close as the sea of harsh fragments of glass and sand hits their faces with a gritty force. The curtain between the world and the enchantment is no more. The temperature drops to below freezing point. When they are ready, they open their eyes and look at the horror surrounding them. The sand on the floor gradually turns to a fine white powder, drifting in circles in the gale force winds all around. Everything returns to how it was before.

Polly opens her eyes and adjusts to the Siberian climes once more. Balan was right, they had been walking through the frozen snow landscape all this time. She finds herself standing in a snowstorm in front of a yawning cave mouth. Inside is black and gloomy, there are deer hides hanging from the rocks and deer filth on either side of the opening, piles of it. Flies are everywhere. The stench of rot and decay is unbearable. The snow is a flurry, densely packed, and the wind howls still treacherously around them. The cold is biting at any exposed flesh.

Chris's eyes flutter open, startled awake from the enchantment. He begins hugging himself in his jacket like a person being brought out of a trance. He falls to his knees in shock and face first into the entrance of the gaping opening of the cave. He is alive but slumped and unconscious. Polly and Balan rush over to check for a pulse and make a point of noting his breath drawing in and out into the frozen air.

Acting quickly, Balan shouts against the screeching wind, while the icy snow is whipping at his face "what now?", he screams in that desolate place. Unsheathing his sword in the blizzard, his eyes fixed on the yawning chasm of the cave entrance before them. Death is the smell on the wind and it calls to them. Polly shouts back "We go in to meet our guests in person, wouldn't you say?"

Balan pats her left shoulder, playfully "it sounds good to me" with a wicked grin on his face as he yells over the winds.

They both enter the opening of the cave to scout round. There is a foul stench of old, rotting flesh. Discarded bones litter the floor and thick dusty cobwebs cover the surfaces. All that can be heard is a cackling, whispering sound, at the back of the cave, in the dark. Polly looks around, from side to side and realises this cave is not the same one from her vision this morning. There was a warmth in that cave and the amber eyes in her dream were definitely ferocious, and wise yet not evil. This cave smells full of death and feels beyond foul. It is the type of place that people must be lured to and would not walk into under their own volition. They have to be desperate in some way, willing to trade something for an evil purpose to enter here. The cave is cold, and dank and has a strange blue mould growing out of the rocks and over the moss. Water is dripping from the ceiling and the silence is being interrupted by droplets hitting the cave floor, "doink" could be heard every now and then. The mounds of bones piled up in the corners, are a range of human skeleton and that of deer carcasses, but who or what has been feeding on them?

Before they venture any further, Balan and Polly walk back towards Chris and gently lift him over to the far side of the entrance, out of the winds and where it is safer. They cover him with their coats and then place their weapons in their hands, ready for whatever they find waiting for them inside.

# Chapter four - As told by Evil.

Polly walks forward into the rancid darkness of the cave, with the Sword of Hestia drawn, ready for battle. The blade is casting a ghostly pale light before her, as her amulet. Her dagger in her right hand and throwing blades are reassuringly, neatly pinned down either side of her trouser legs. Balan is close behind, covering her back in the gloom of the cave. He moves forward, crouched low. He is but shadow and smoke, tentatively, and silently moving from one side of the cave to the other. Seeking out danger, hunting it. It is dark in here. An intense blackness drops over them the further they venture inside, like the sun's warmth has been removed from the world. A brilliant light orb is conjured to hover above them, lighting a path – extinguishing the gloom. The orb is shining very brightly and is casting a brilliant glow over the contents of the cave. Tons of bones litter the floor, accrued over centuries, cracking, and crunching underfoot. Rusted hanging cages are suspended ominously from the ceiling. They have been built to host a full-sized adult. In the corner, an ominous looking butchering block and chopping table. With a meat cleaver stuck suspended in the wood. Bright red fresh blood streaks are seeping into the table - stained heavily and swollen in lots of different places. Rats fester in this place, crawling over the floor. Climbing the walls, squeaking, and wriggling over every surface. The movement is prolific, and the colour of the rodents an exact match for the rocks of the cave. Making the cave walls look alive- shimmering, undulating, and moving in grotesque waves.

Balan taps Polly on the shoulder, he has a finger on his lips, emitting a shushing sound. Drawing her attention to something he has spotted in the distance, on the ceiling of the cave. Above their heads is a hanging cage and inside is a small boy, who could not have been more than five years old. The child is standing up asleep and leaning heavily against the bars. His face pale and drawn, like a death mask. Skeletal. His eyeballs are ceaselessly moving behind his lids. Balan leans forward and whispers "he's enchanted. We are close to the source now. I can feel it. We need to break this curse to free him and the others." Balan lifts his chin to indicate the other cages hanging from the ceiling, with more imprisoned, emaciated people inside.

Polly gasps at the human captives suspended above them. Her heart aches for the small child most. He looks thin and emaciated. He reminds her of herself at that age, somehow. Polly sees three more cages, and each holds a human hostage. The people are starved and wretched, miserable, and held against their will, alone in the dark. The lights start to flicker behind The Chosen One's eyes. Anger is tickling the back of her throat. Her muscles are aching for a fight. But she cannot afford to lose control of her emotions, not now, not here. Whatever evil this is, she will need to remain calm to fight it and with all her wits about her. She cannot allow her magic to move beyond her control. Taking in deep steadying breaths, Polly focuses her mind on the amulet around her neck - bringing herself back to a place of peace and control. "Goddess protect them and give us the strength to end this evil" she whispers under her breath.

In the dimness of the cave, she can just make out a watery green glow in the distance – it is like looking at a tiny luminous green tank in a pitch-black space. Catching each other's eye, Polly and Balan both nod and start to silently walk towards the green glow. The orb of golden light is behind them, and Polly must extinguish the light, giving them the element of surprise. She recalls the orb to her, and the glowing circle comes spinning back into her hand with a hissing sound as it cuts through the air.

Balan and Polly crouch low, practically on their stomach's and begin to clamber over the thickly rising rocks. Heading towards the inner sanctum of the cave, the jagged edges of the fossilised rocks catching at their skin. They could hear shrieking voices in the distance and some way ahead. It is a gruesome conversation between witches, dark of purpose.

"Sister, I want a leg of lamb. A tender morsel, cooked in cider, with shallots and thyme. Take off the socks and shoes of the little lamb and cleave up to the thigh. The lamb is five years old or thereabouts, and he will not give us any trouble. He has been in a dream state for a week now. His skin is looser too from not eating" says the first wretched voice with a cackle.

48

"Oh, well, of course you want to start a new one. Already have an old maid's shoulder to devour but want to taste spring flesh. You gluttonous pig" says another, preachy voice, with a sneer of loathing.

"I'm the one that goes out hunting, putting myself in danger of being burnt at the stake and you get to cook and stay inside where its forever safe. The villagers don't know you, do they?" says the Wretched One.

"I take my fair share of risks. I got the old maid and caught her by the frozen lake" says the Preachy One.

"Not exactly taxing though, capturing an old maid in her twilight years, is it? You don't deserve to eat more. Always stuffing your face, but you have started to look delightfully plump and tasty yourself. May I add" says the Wretched One, pinching the other with her gnarled fingers.

"Now, ladies" this is said by a third witch. What a different voice this is, it is very distinct. A silky, charming, velvety sound that tickles at the inner ear and makes the listener sigh out in bliss "let us put these squabbles aside and eat, drink and be merry. The snowstorm will soon pass, and the villagers will be out soon, and you can both go hunting. How does that sound?"

A full pause before "Fine m'lady" says the Preachy One, voice slightly trembling.

"Very good m'lady" says the Wretched One with a tremor and cautious tone.

"Good, good. I do hate it when you are not getting along. I don't see the point of the three of us staying together if it's going to be ...problematic" the silky voice, cleaves out at the listener, with a menacing undertone and made itself understood.

Balan struggles to scramble over a very large rock, coming closer to the three witches. His sight is obscured. On top of the rock is perched a handful of loose stones. A foot hold poorly judged, displaces the debris and rubble. It slowly falls to the ground, making a loud, clattering and crashing sound.

"Why, what is this?" the silky voice, permeates and echoes through the darkness. The evil witch has released a sound pulse spell and it is searching out the source of the noise, like rings of a sonar. The sound waves are piercing through the air, probing around the cave. Stopping when the ripples hit the solid form of Balan and sends a signal back to The Queen Witch. One of the witches holds up a lamp and its light floods the cave with a bright green tinged glow. The light bounces and kisses every nook and crevice of the rock floor.

Bathed in the eerie light, the three witches stand together. Each ridge and line highlighted by the light - a gruesome sight. Comically grotesque and twisted forms of nature. The two servile witches look like witches are imagined to be, dressed in black cloaks, with wild matted hair, hunched over forms. Lopsided beaky noses and eyeless sockets on display. One of the witches has no teeth and the other, a set of needle-sharp fangs, hanging over her thin bottom lip. The Queen witch, however. Well, she looks different altogether. Younger, slim, and tall but with pure blackness of eyes and painted, blood red lips. Her skin is a glowing ghostly pale colour, almost luminous. On her head is placed the scalp and long black dead hair of one of her fallen victims. Her victim's flesh used for sustenance and the inedible body parts to beautify and restore her youth.

The Queen Witch holds her long, bony fingers to the side of her head and closes her eyes. An ancient dialect is muttered to cast a spell. The place Balan is crouching down over, starts to tremble and shake. The ground does what it is commanded to do and moves away from under him. He is being ripped up, off the ground with the force of the spell. Like a solid fog, the particles of energy are moving over him. The dense gas like substance, encases his body and he starts to involuntarily float upwards and move towards the witches three. Polly goes to jerk up and pull her sword "Stay down" he mouths soundlessly to her. The noise of him being forcefully pulled from the rock, means Polly can silently scramble to the side unseen. Not losing any time before she starts moving forward, down the other side of the cave towards the witches. She is crouched low, moving sideways awkwardly – hungry to remain invisible.

"Well, hello, handsome male friend. Your skin is a beautiful hue. I wonder if it will suit me when I wear it" says the leader witch, with polite curiosity.

Balan places a hand against the forcefield, a charge of bright light follows and the translucent barrier starts to dissolve from the inside, "Well, well. He is one of us. Sisters, now" the leader screams, "He must not escape" she says licking her lips at Balan's magical powers. Opportunity swirling in her craving eyes.

The servile witches lifting their hands reluctantly and join the binding spell. The three witches together, hold the forcefield in place. Laughing, gloating at the sport of mayhem they are inflicting. Watching Balan wriggle under the binding curse. It is so densely packed, Balan is now gasping for air. His eyes rolling in the back of his head.

"One of our own magical folk walking freely into our cave. What can this mean?" says the Wretched One.

"What can this mean indeed, a whole lot of fun for us through the long nights of cold" says the Preaching One, rubbing her gnarled hands together.

"Don't be stupid, vile wants of the flesh. We will consume him and his powers. Yes, he is what is needed to restore ourselves to greatness once more" the leader witch softly says, eyes awash with seeing her freedom stretch out before her. The Dark Witch does not expect a response. Self-assured and most very definitely fixed on her prize alone.

The Wretched One pauses and stands up "You mean, you want to take his powers. To use them and finally overcome the spell that binds you within this cave?" she says this unsure. Hesitating and genuine worry creeps into her voice. Her mottled and twisted face lifted in concern. She nudges the other servile witch and they both peer over at the third, with a deep look of anxiety. Both are aware that one magical beings' power would not be enough to break the binding spell but absorbing the power of three. Well, now that could just about work.

51

"You are not going to make this difficult, are you?" menacingly, the leader casually zaps a stream of lightning, a hairs-width from the face of the enquiring witch.

"No, n-no, of course not m'lady" The Wretched One bows, quickly looking away and stepping back, lest she be fried alive.

Balan swiftly takes out his hand blade, while they are distracted and arguing. The blade is the Argonion, wielded by a very powerful shaman once, a long time ago. The blade had magic placed upon it and he had won the dagger in a game of chance. He places the blade at the top of the forcefield and cuts an opening, vertically. In one swift move he is free. He jumps down and holds out his sword ready to fight.

"Ahem, if you are quite finished, I think I'll be keeping my magic for myself so no need to argue on my account" he says rather smugly. Balan stands tall, his six-foot two frame looms over the three witches and his flexed muscles are taut, holding his sword aloft.

The Queen Witch turns, her face is contorted with rage and her eyes resemble the coldness of large slabs of black granite. Deranged with hatred. "Why are you here, what are you doing walking into my prison? Please do not insult me by lying as I will know." she screeches "but rest assured you will not be leaving this place."

"I'm here searching for the White Hart. Have you seen it or know of the Spring walker's whereabouts?" Balan continues, ignoring her threats, treating them with contempt. He fixes his eyes on the witches, trying not to look at Polly creeping forward in the distance. She is near.

Balan's question catches the interest of the witches. The keenness of their eye's holding questions. The white hart is a very powerful being. Legend has it that the beast can cure the sick and can regenerate whole lands with the restorative power of Spring. Moving the terrain from desolate wastelands or deserts into bountiful and lush green places. Some elephants have this power too. With their mighty tusks they create or dam rivers and ravines, tilling the earth to bring new life. The witches know that the stag had been here years ago, and the larch trees were the last remnants of the forest that had sprung up in its wake. One of the villagers captured by the witches had told them a story of The White Hart's visit here and that it had moved on to Greenland. Grown ill due to the sickness of the planet and needed restoration in its own land of origin. Balan steps forward and repeated his question "I will not kill you all if you tell me what you know about The White Hart, but I am warning you, I am leaving here today and with those humans you have imprisoned over there, in cages". The witches look at each other and begin hysterically laughing. Balan laughs with them too before he stops abruptly and points the tip of his sharp sword at the witches. Crouching low, readying himself to attack.

" The gall of the young man" they cackle "Well, what's the harm in telling him. It's not like he is getting out of here alive even if he is full of swagger and bravado. We see you, boy. We see your fearful soul. Mummy abandoned you and Daddy was a drunkard, mean, abusive and spiteful man. You are frightened of becoming him. Like him and hold everyone at a distance but there is something else about you that is less obvious. Something hidden within you, trying to get out. Now let us see" speak the three in unison, eyes piercing him. Balan stares forward, his eyes narrow and his mouth downturned, but that is the only telltale sign that he is listening and that what they say is true. He jabs the sword forward barely missing the neck of The Preaching One. The two servile witches jump back in shock at the onslaught and spit forth their bile "Boy, you are nothing. A reaction to your life, not truly brave enough to be yourself or knowing of who you are. Just made up of a confused list of multiple reactions to what has been done to you, all stitched together and waiting to fall apart in the breeze of someone else's will." The Queen Witch salivates at Balan's upset.

Balan steps forward , anger burning in his eyes and shouts "Shut up foul demons. Just shut your disgusting mouths" Balan is visibly shaking now, but his legs are steadfastly rooted to the spot. Polly is near, standing up slowly but she waits in the darkness holding her breath. Balan stands there, alone. Absolutely still, but in his eyes is an intensity so fierce, that it makes Polly drift backwards. Remaining cloaked in the shadows. Whatever this is, she can tell instinctively, Balan wants to face parts of himself alone, so she holds back in the gloom - sensing his need for this to play out. The three witches come closer, circling him and he flinches in their vicinity, as they encroach. Curling their wickedness around him.

"The White Hart is in Greenland." The two servile witches croon in terrible synchronicity "Recovering in a place not wholly of this world, a portal of restoration that is accessed in Greenland. The creature has imbibed too many pollutants from the earth. Too much poison from the human world. The White Hart needs help or otherwise the beast of legend will die and if He dies then woe betide the world". They laugh "our time will come if He dies" they cackle, gloating. Polly's heart is beating fast in her chest but still she listens.

The Queen Witch steps forward, very close now to Balan, her eyes slitted together "What do you need the creature for wizard, I wonder?" as the witch says this, her thin sinewy arm reaches towards Balan. He jumps sideways, eluding her grasp and swings round with his sword aloft, towards the Preachy One and chops her head cleanly off, then seamlessly runs her through the belly with his sword - just because he could. The other two scream and howl, while thick black blood, pulsates from the body of their sister of the Wyrd.

Balan straightens up and watches the witches rage blister before them as he places his foot on the prone body of the dead witch, yanking his sword out of her belly. He then pushes the form over with his foot and then turns to face down the others. His mouth is set in a grimace, but his eyes are renewed, satisfied that he had taken back his power from her evil words that made him doubt himself, momentarily.

The Wretched One, in a frenzied rage, arms flailing as darkness is beckoned to envelope her, hisses out a threatening warning. "How dare you touch us, how dare you even try to think you are worthy of being called a challenger against us, The Wyrd Sisters." with these words of spite and malice, she flies at Balan in a rage and disappears mid- flight in a puff of smoke and reappears behind him. Her claw-like fingers latching onto each side of his face and raking her sharp talons, backwards, through the flesh of his cheeks. He is cut, blood dripping. Without thought and in a practised way, Balan turns the hilt of his sword backwards, with an almighty heave he drives the sword behind him. The Wretched One is caught by the blade in between her ribs. He rams himself backwards once more, into the jagged cave-wall pinning the witch against it. His sword drives further into the beating black heart of the wyrd sister. With eyes that are bulging in shocked disbelief, the witch gurgles out her last rattling breath.

Balan then turns with a furnace of burning rage stoked in his eyes, towards the last witch and he stares at her with a challenge in his stance. While behind him, the other witch can be seen quietly sliding down the wall, leaving a slick of black liquid on the jagged rocks in her wake.

The Queen Witch holds his gaze with an unblinking coldness, barely registering the other witch's fate. She raises her hands and summons an evil spell without uttering a word. Balan is thrown backwards, pinned to the cave wall with a spell of sharp golden spirals, which bore into him like twirling, sharp corkscrews. Spinning and inflicting pain. He scrunches his face up and bellows, gasping, while blood drips rapidly from the open cuts on both his arms.

At this point, The Chosen One steps lightly into the circle of light from the green lamp and goes unseen for a while. She holds the sword of Hestia in front of her, the blade alights and burns brightly. With tongues of lashing flames licking at its sharp edges. The last but most deadly witch turns in horror. To her black eyes and black heart, The Chosen One appears as a magnificent shaft of naked light, the essence of the pure of spirit. This light burns the witch's eyes, she cannot sustain looking at the purity of the flame and she recoils from the space where the soul of the Chosen One burns brightest. Wailing and thrashing on the floor. The Queen Witch screeches out "Nooooo, this cannot be. You cannot be here in the darkness with me. Your light overpowers and makes the darkness no more, me no more." In the distance, Polly could see a golden arch appear. The archway is faint in the gloom of the cave, but she can just about make it out. The arch is made from the blocks of ancient spells. The symbols of which, she recognises as those of the High Priestess, Bringer of Destiny and servant of The Goddess. The runes of the light are with Polly. She had seen these before They were prominently present at the waterhole, where she took the warriors test, months ago. At that time, the High Priestess named her as The Chosen One of the Goddess.

Seeing the symbols of the Priestess in this dismal place, makes Polly heart soar and suddenly she is renewed. Turning round to face the witch, Polly says "So, the High Priestess imprisoned you in here. In this foul place. I wonder what despicable evil thing you did to warrant such a punishment." Polly stands there, gazing into the witches' black eyes.

The Queen Witch laughs "why, let me show you, sweet child" and that is when the atrocities committed by the dark witch from long ago, float across the witch's eyes. Polly can see everything that the Witch had done and what The Chosen One saw made her pull away in deep revulsion. Reeling and jerking backwards in distress and alarm, Polly bellows in anger and her voice reverberates around the cave. This brought about a trembling from the rock. The cave stones above answered her call by vibrating and falling one by one onto the cave floor and onto the black witch, pinning her to the ground.

Balan, holding his open wounds, arms trembling, watching the ceiling caving in. He jumps backwards over one of the falling rocks to move away from the witch being pinned to the floor. The whole cave is vibrating as Polly bellows and screams out her anguish. Her pain at the horror that she had seen in the eyes of the witch. Balan has to stop her before the whole cave crumbles in on them all. With one swift move, he grabs hold and hugs her, whispering calming words of comfort.

Eventually, the cave and rocks stop shaking as Polly regains control of herself, heaving is her chest. Gulping in air. The Witch is on her back, boulders covering her lower half and black blood is trickling out of the corner of her mouth.

The Chosen One shakes free of Balan and walks over to the witch pinned to the floor and says "I'm not going to kill you. You can rot in here for all eternity for the terrible things you have done." Polly is finding it hard to breathe. Images of carnage floating in front of her eyes. Shaking her head in sadness of a time long ago when hell was unleashed on the innocent at the hands of this one laid in front of her.

"You think that's the worst thing you will ever see or know? Do you Chosen One?" The witch starts to laugh and then with a clarity as clear as crystal, she adds these fateful words "They have not told you yet, have they Chosen One? They have not told you what you have to do to restore balance, have they?" her laughter is hysterical "and they call *ME* evil" she continues to laugh while she sneers at Polly.

"What haven't they told me?" Polly, looking down, unsure.

"Don't listen, Polly. It's all a lie" shouts Balan, pulling Polly away from the wickedness of the twisted words of the Witch on the floor.

"It's just too delicious. It's just so very delicious. How betrayed will you feel? Trusting your little heart to the High Priestess and The Goddess…I bet Eleanora is involved too, no doubt?" the evil witch says to herself more than anyone else in the room. "Am I right little lamb? Little lamb to the slaughter." The witch is laughing so loud now, with genuine tears of mirth in her eyes. Polly stands there, at a loss for words, bewildered and confused.

"Who will betray me?" Polly asks, with a distressed tone in her voice. Balan goes to grab her arm and Polly pulls away from his touch. Bending down to lean closer to face the Witch. A spell is quietly uttered and all the rocks holding the witch down, drift upwards. Momentarily, released from gravity and the witch is free. The queen lunges at Polly with a thin, glass needle in her hand, taken from her hair. Making to gouge out Polly's eye, with the intent of pushing the object through into her brain. Polly reacts quickly, without a moment's hesitation and runs the ancient Sword of Hestia through the Wyrd One's chest. The witch falls backwards, startled, staring down at the black blood pumping out of the hilt of the sword. Unbelieving that her centuries old shell is destroyed after all this time. She moves her head round and fixes her lingering gaze on Balan and then she closes her black eyes, as her breath changes into particles and floats into the air. And then a look of relief creeps over the face that she had borrowed. The imprisoned human in her is grateful for the release. Succumbing to the inevitable, and let's decay in. The body disintegrates to dust within mere seconds. All that is left behind is the black wig, fashioned from one of her victims.

Polly stumbles, blown back by the force of the Witch's energy being released. The ripple of the energy pulse moves beyond the confines of the cave. The Chosen One is unsteady on her feet. Her face looks troubled, and her eyebrows knitted together. She starts to weave, haphazardly forward, dazed and confused. Then suddenly, the silence in the cave is cut open with voices. She and Balan both look up and peer towards the exit. They can hear human voices in the gloom, calling for help in a Russian dialect. It is the children and the adults in the cages, awoken by the witch's spell being lifted at long last.

Polly, with a renewed sense of purpose, calls out "We are coming, the witch is destroyed, we are here to help you". She looks back round searching for Balan, with hope shining out of her face. But when her gaze finds him, he is hunched over on the floor. Holding his knees, silently crying into his own lap. Reaching out to him, placing her hand on his shoulder, Polly squeezes it and silently stands there for a while, watching over him. Wondering what the witch's bile had evoked and what he had endured in his life. He doesn't look round, he doesn't make a sound, he just lets the tears flow down from his swollen eyes and silently falls over his cheeks.

After a while, she pulls her hand away, uncertain about what she should do to comfort him. As she does so, his hand shoots out and clutches hers. They hold each other in that way until Balan's tears run dry upon his face and he has no more sadness to give. "Are you ok to stand now and go with me to help the others? Chris will be awake too." Polly says this quietly like she is talking to a person gravely ill. Balan nods. As Polly starts to walk towards the cages, Balan whispers "Thank you for holding me when I felt lost and for making me feel safe." Polly smiles and lightly touches her hand to his chest. "Balan, for some reason your heart is extra precious to me" she whispers and turns to continue walking to the others to free them from their cages, just as she had helped free Balan from his.

# Chapter five - The White Hart

Polly and Balan are exhausted by their ordeal, as they walk back through the cave. Limbs heavy and clothes damp with sweat from fighting, but they smile to one another in a giddy way now the worst of it is over. Knowing that they had done a great deed onto the world this day. The cave, that once was gloomy and thick with terror, is lighter somehow. A clean air is blowing in from the west and circulating, moving the darkness out. Nature would soon fill this place with new life. This place would no longer hold evil. It would soon be a den for a large land mammal and a shelter from the snow for small creatures. It would be connected with the circle of life once more.

The children and adults, inside the rusty metal cages, hold out their painfully thin arms between the bars. Begging and calling to their rescuers in their native tongue. Frantically crying and pleading to get out. Polly and Balan rush to clamber back over the clusters of rocks to help – taking pity on them. Slipping and slipping over the craggy rocks in their haste.

Balan and Polly find the release mechanism for the cages, but it is rusted stuck. Balan takes Polly's hand and enacts a spell, they work together to slowly lower the contraptions down. When all four of the villagers are safely on the ground, each one of them collapses, unable to support their own weight. Fearfully peering into the back of the cave. Polly shakes her head and whispers to them "Get up" waving her hands upwards in a sweeping motion. They tentatively stand on their feet, holding the cave wall and begin walking slowly towards the exit. Polly looks back and the archway of the High Priestess is glowing blue. It is getting stronger and more visible but she does not go back to look at it, so certain is she that the danger was over, finished.

After a long while walking, the group is finally at the entrance to the cave. Chris is standing there, very tall, and broad shouldered, he has his back to them. He is looking out onto the snow-covered ravine below. He hears something behind him and turns with surprise, to see the group of survivors with his friends. Polly is holding the little boy in her arms and Balan is carrying an older woman, who the boy calls grandma. The other two captives were able to walk. "Bloody hell, what happened in there?" says Chris, eyes bulging as he runs over to help Polly and he moves quickly to cover the tiny boy in one of the coats. The survivors rush to moisten their lips with the clean white snow of the hillside.

"There were a group of witches. One of them, a very powerful witch, was imprisoned in the cave unable to leave. She had been imprisoned there by the High Priestess. They were holding these people captive. I think they have been eating the villagers". Polly says, barely able to voice this notion without gagging.

"Bloody hell" Chris says, raising his eyebrows and repeating himself again, Chris did not know what else to say. Polly turns to Balan at this point and gently holds his arm, checking that he is okay after his ordeal. Chris watches the exchange intently and feels a confusion and angst settle in his heart.

The dirt-stained vagabond group make their way down the ice-covered hillside. It had stopped snowing and the Siberian winds, although still cold, were less of an icy gale-force. A chill clung to the air, but it was no longer bone shattering freezing like it had been before - there was hope in the air and this always warms the heart.

Later that day, the seven of them arrive on the outskirts of a village. A group of villagers see them first, in the middle of digging a pathway through the small ring of houses, to prevent isolation from the outside world. They let out gasps and they start to shout to one another excitedly. One of the men throwing his shovel down and running off. Coming back in a short space of time with the families of the survivors. All of them rush over to embrace their kin. Hugging their relatives and their children while crying and wailing out their relief that they were found alive. The survivors are busy explaining to all the villagers gathered about the witches and when everyone had heard the tale, all of the community gasped with disbelief. Each took their turn to hold Polly's hands, thanking and blessing her for saving their loved ones. Polly takes their thanks gracefully, but remains strangely unaffected, aloof. Knowing in her heart that they cannot leave the villagers with information about witches and of magic – this being a breach of the Magical Statute that governs the magical world.

Balan and Chris had held back and waited at the edge of the Village, observing the scene from afar. Chris was kicking at the snow, subdued. A look of pure revulsion spreads across his face.

When it is time to leave, Polly gazes towards Balan and gives a slight almost indistinguishable nod. He steps out into the clearing, grim determination on his still face. Raising his hands to the sky. A black cloud swells overhead, small lightning bolts light up the underside of the gloom. The artificial cloud drifts over to settle above the villagers. Then drops a mist onto the crowd gathered. The Villagers upturned faces watch the unnatural phenomenon silently at first and then they start to move frantically away, panicked like young deer on a prairie, sensing something on the wind announcing danger. Unable to move away, a force holds them in place against their will, under the ominous cloud. A little time passes, and the villagers could feel the tension building in the atmosphere, they begin screaming with apprehension. Wondering what is happening and then all of sudden they stop, a silence descends. They look round at each other confused, asking each other what had happened? Why were they all here? Balan watches their reaction, lowering his arms. The spell is complete.

Balan and Polly silently turn around at the same time, exhausted. Heavy legs being forced forward, walking out of the village and back up to their camp. Reluctantly, Chris tears his eyes away from the gathered group of villagers. They are painful to watch in their state of confusion. Then with hooded eyes, watches the backs of Polly and Balan for a time before turning around to leave too. A strange look on his face that resembles disappointment as he trudges the path behind Polly and Balan. Reluctant and slow are his footsteps.

The boy rescued from the cave is being scooped up by his family. They are bouncing him up and down with joy. The boy gazes upon Polly, Balan and

Chris walking away up the hill, knowing as they go, that they take something with them and a shadow shines in the little boy's eyes.

Back at the settlement, Chris's unease is following him around like a dark cloud and it is evident to Polly and Balan too. It is not one thing that gives Chris away, but many. He packs the cups away a little louder than intended and his short surly answers to innocent questions are a dead giveaway. As he packs up his tent and equipment, folding it into his rucksack, there is no discernible yelling, but his body language is folded in, more sombre and withdrawn from the other two. As they set off for the private airport, Polly watches him from beneath her eyelashes and she keeps tentatively peeking over at him from under her hood. Polly sighs and thinks to herself "Well, I'm sure that within the next fifteen hours spent travelling from here to Greenland, Chris may come out of this, or he will have an outburst so it will be done either way."

They board the flight and sit together but in different rows of seats on the plane - Chris still does not say a word. He had picked up a book at the airport, containing tourist information about Greenland and buries himself in the pages throughout the flight. Intermittently taking turns to read and sleep by himself, along the way. His brooding casts a shadow over the journey to Greenland.

When they arrive in Greenland, Inuit Nanaat, they hire a large, all-terrain vehicle and drive to the national park territory, in the northern hemisphere of the Greenland island. It is not cold here; it is the height of the Greenlandic summer, so the temperature is warm but never too hot. They head towards an Inuit village, guided there by a Danish man called Villius. He is very tall, blonde, and extremely warm and friendly in character. Sharing his love of the land through stories with as many people as he can. Chris asks him about the legends and myths of the Free people of Inuit Nanaat and if any involve a stag of greatness. Villius smiles broadly in a knowing way and explains that the Inuit's, the Free people, have a number of stories about the Great Stag, The Peryton. In their folklore, this creature can fly on jets of warm wind and is the King of the land. He tells them of the legend of the Peryton and the folklore that it has a den in the topmost

Northerly part of the island. He hesitates before adding "where the horizon meets the sun and the moon in the same sky, is where you will find him" Villius says this like he is reciting a poem to himself. Balan looks at Polly significantly, here is where they will find The White Hart.

Chris calls the Professor when he is on his own. To relay the full story about the cave and of the witches. How Polly had told him that the witches had been killed and about the spell used on the villagers. Chris never expressed outright his disappointment, but the Professor could tell from the way he was speaking, how worried he is about the use of magic on unsuspecting people. The professor reassured Chris that the fight against evil is never easy, and sometimes there is only a choice between a decision and an even worse decision – something Chris would need to accept. The professor kindly expressed that he has faith in Polly and Balan to do the right thing. After a while the conversation lightens and they start to talk about the search in Greenland, and that the group are heading for the Qinnquadalen Forest, moving downwards into the South from there. The Professor says, "If this island is the place of origin of The White Hart, then you will see magic present and can follow it to the great Stag's den."

Villius takes them to a remote part of the island to set up their equipment at the designated base camp. Chris's mood is notably lifted and Polly and Balan are somewhat relieved.

A fire is started to keep them warm, and the group gather round the flames to cook and eat together. It is late evening, and the land is open, and rugged and majestic. The night sky is filled with the stars of the galaxy and casts a beautiful starshine across the land. Stories are shared and the raw natural beauty of the landscape helps to bring them to life. Nanook, a local Inuit leader is invited to join the group around the fire along with his young family. He brings with him fermented caribou to share with his hosts and Balan ensures there is plenty to eat and drink. Bringing out a feast and ending on a dessert, brought over from the mainland. A kind gesture that is noticed warmly by his guests. "My friends, what are you here for? You have the type of supplies for scouting out the land far and wide" says

Nanook, curiously. Villius responds to his inquisitive friend by shouting over the roaring fire playfully "They are being secretive, Nanook, but I think they are looking for something. A creature of myth, I would say. I have spotted relics in their backpacks" Villius says with a playful grin - referring to their swords and weaponry they carry. Nanook's partner, Uki, stirs from gazing at the fire and then continues watching the embers float up towards the starry night sky and turn to black ash in the cold air beyond the heat of the fire.

"What are you looking for, piqannarijat? What *creatures* are on your mind?" Uki asks the question openly to the group, stroking the coat of a wild dog seated on her lap. Without moving her gaze from the flaming fire. There is an edge of defensiveness to her words, jagged like blades. The land around holds its breath for a reply.

Balan, Chris and Polly look at one another and before they can make to reply a howl erupts in the wilderness beyond the edges of the shadows of the moon and then the pack, twenty strong, answers the call of the wild.

In the light of the moon, Polly's eyes glow like reflective amber disks, gazing out over the wild, untamed land – the wilderness calls to her, and her bones and muscles are aching to run with the pack – to be in her true essence. Free.

Uki catches a glimpse of the wolf on Polly's face, as The Chosen One wistfully looks longingly, out onto the great unknown. Uki nods to herself, a decision has been made. "I will take you out tomorrow and stay with you throughout your journey. We will find what you are looking for." Polly tears her eyes away from the dark shadows where the wolf pack are prowling beyond the light of the moon. Polly glances back into the circle around the campfire and all she can see is the shadow of the wolf on Uki. Polly smiles at the kindred of spirit and says, "We would be honoured Uki, She-wolf, to have you as our guide".

Nanook, looks between the women and sees the bond of sisterhood growing. He has never actually asked Uki about her strange connection to the wolf pack. He does not question any further as he can spot kindred spirits and knows best to leave this story to unfold by itself, as it is clearly fated to be.

The rest of the night is spent talking, and laughing, and Polly holds Nanook and Uki's newborn baby closely to her while she whispers stories of the Goddess, Mother of all things and tells the baby the story of her warrior test and of meeting the High Priestess. Uki listens in with wide eyed wonderment and the baby, snuggled up between the two women, has the great expanse of the universe reflected and illuminated in his eyes.

In the morning, Nanook had gone. He had returned to his home with the couple's baby. Uki could be seen driving her hardy vehicle into camp, with three husky dogs barking out into the crisp morning air, and her truck packed with gear for their journey, to Greenland's highest point.

"Good morning to you all, meet my best friends, Kaskae, Nook and Amka". There is a loud barking from the dogs at the back of the truck, as Uki mentions their names. Uki opens up the vehicle. First, Amka the slim and tall female husky, springs from the back of the truck and greets each guest excitedly with a wag of her tail and a friendly nudge with her pale nose. Then comes Nook, a very large muscular male husky and he rushes over to the group with his ears pricked up, surveying all about and jumps up at them to see if they have any treats - knocking them to the ground with the heaviness of his weight and each one of them has no choice but to belly laugh in his excitement. Lastly, the mighty and noble, Kaskae alights from the vehicle, he stands proud and tall, looking all around him and waits for the groups' leader to come to him to introduce themselves. Polly ventures forward and bends down on one knee and says "Hello Kaskae, I am Polly. I am pleased to meet you, m'lord." Polly bows. Kaskae blows through his nose and gives a friendly nudge to her but that is all. He is a chieftain husky of a noble line and does not hold store with fawning over humans. Well, apart from Uki, who he regards as an equal and his sister. After the greetings are over, and the vehicles loaded, a small dog sledge is attached to the roof of the truck and two of the dogs get excited (not Kaskae). The plan is to cover as much ground each day by vehicle then walk the rest when the vehicles can go no further. It usually takes thirty days to cover the ice sheet, the inner terrain of the Island. They are hoping it will take a week if they travel by night and day taking turns to sleep and drive. They were finally on their way.

As they travel the land, they take in its wonder. The terrain is notably flat, white and snowy with little changes in scenery and the group; Polly, Balan, Chris, Villius and Uki, at first are jovial and excited, as it is a relatively easy drive. After six days and nights of the monotony of the landscape, the same type of food and close quartered company, the group becomes easily irritated through enforced introspection. Fatigue sets in. The weather is becoming gradually worse the further North they go. Only the dogs appear consistently high in spirits, out in the depths of the wilderness. They run together, yapping, and playing, running alongside the vehicles, or jumping and rolling around the fireside.

***

Then one night, in the silence of the falling snow and in that ice filled landscape, Kaskae awoke from a deep sleep, feeling troubled. Raising his head from his front paws, flicking his ears forward. He hears a call on the wind. The moon is very large and full, descending close to the earth and breaching the horizon. He could see the luminated outline of the moon within the tent – it dazzled vividly. Looking across at his human and canine companions, he can see they are all fast asleep in the large tent they all share. Kaskae quietly gets up on his mighty legs, pulls at the zip fastener. Tugging it steadfastly, managing to release the mechanism holding the entranceway together. He steps outside, sniffing the air and feeling around with his nose. Hesitating to take a step forward. There is something beckoning him on the back of the wind.

A whistling sound from the tent being left open causes Balan to shudder and lift one eye. He had been awakened by a sound outside. Seeing a golden shimmer haze of dust seeping into the tent doorway left open by Kaskae. "Magic will guide the way to The White Hart" he whispers to himself in the darkness of the safety of the tent. Stretching, he gets up and braces himself for the onslaught of the cold outside but it is eerily devoid of chill and feels of nothing – a lost space in time. The fullness of the moon, the brilliance of the snow and void of the temperature, creates a strangeness on the land, like another dimension has slipped into this space.

Out in the distance he can see Kaskae standing alone on a raised glacier some way off. The dog's lonely figure against the great expanse of the ice and the sky that has no edges. Kaskae has his back to Balan, and the form of the husky can be seen intently peering beyond the pale white light from the moon and into the dark-shadowed, desolate places   beyond the light – the place of shadows. The wolf pack are howling, as if calling for Balan and it is stirring in his blood. His eyes glow as amber disks in the moonlight – the predator's prowl upon him.

Other than the sound of howling, all that can be heard is the crunching of the snow underfoot, as Balan strides over the open ghostly white terrain, to reach Kaskae. The dog does not notice his arrival, the great husky is concentrating on the horizon. Balan puts his hand out to stroke Kaskae's luxurious coat. The chieftain canine jumps at the touch and spins round, feral, snapping, with crinkled up snout and bared teeth. "Whoa, there boy, it's me, it's me, Balan. I'm sorry for not announcing that I was here." Balan crooned. The dog stares up at Balan, his face gradually softening at the recognition setting in. He butts Balan and guides him to look at a place in the distance. "What is it, boy? What can you see?" The gold shimmer of fine particles that Balan had been following, drift up towards the sky and change in frequency to illuminate the darkness in great waves. The particles of magical dust start to turn green and dance, announcing the arrival of the magic of the magnificent and vast Aurora Borealis. This is unusual for this time of year - another portent Balan thinks to himself. The dog and Balan stand still, close together and watch the green lights undulate across the seismic changes in the sky. The magic of the Aurora Borealis, one of the natural wonders of the world, is so very close. It starts to envelope and land around them.

Meanwhile in the tent, the thrumming sound of the beating heart is pounding in Polly's ears, pulsating. Waking her from a fretful sleep. The beat is loud, almost deafening. The *thrum, thrum, thrum, thrum* continues on, and she feels the air rushing in and kissing her face. Noticing that Balan and Kaskae are missing and their sleeping bags are rumpled and left open.

 Heaving herself up, she stands with one hand on her amulet and the other hand drifts to her sword, listening to the noises outside for a while. There is a long line of golden particles leading out of the tent. Polly strides into the open night, followed silently by Uki behind her. The green dancing lights cover the whole sky, it is breathtaking and Balan and Kaskae are silhouetted black against it. In single file, the wolf pack come padding down from the outskirts of the desolate planes of snow and walk into view, and as they do so, it starts to heavily snow. Thick, soundless, cotton wool type snow, which blankets the ground around them, as large and as thick as dove feathers. Uki holds out her hand to catch the strange snow and she turns it over in her hand. The snowflakes are formed in the shape of dragons - Uki looks down with amazement at the feathery snow in her hand until it is a pool of water. She catches another then another and they are all identical, the Kaida symbol. What does it mean? Then the green glimmering sky, moves strangely. Striking out to layer itself around Polly, The Chosen One and Balan is standing close by.

The wolf pack circle round, following each other in a line and kneel before Polly. A chorus of howls fill the air and then the pack retreat. Stamping their paws and growling at Polly, straining to move out to the shadows. Uki cries "We must follow, they are asking you to follow them, and it is urgent. There is no time to waste." Uki warns, rushing to catch up with the wolves, who have already started to run ahead. Kaskae barks to Balan and Polly. In the distance, a low braying can be heard faintly on the gusts of wind. Blowing, dancing in between the fluffy snow. Polly hesitates and looks back towards the tent, she shouts out to Uki "What about Chris?".

"Nook and Amka are with him. No harm will come to him this night. I don't think we are still on the Island. The smell of this place is not of my home. We must go. There is no time. Something is wrong" Uki's eyes are aglow with sudden panic, she shouts over her shoulder as she continues to dash forward and then she bends down on all fours to sprint with the pack.

Polly nods and places her sword in its scabbard and starts running at superspeed to catch up with the front of the pack and then when she does, they all plunge into the unknown darkness together. Beyond the realm of the physical. Entering the place where the moon and sun meet. The dimensional plane where magical creatures go to take their last breath - nature will mourn another loss to the history of the natural world this night.

Polly stops running in the twilight of the world between the moon and sun. A bright light is building and in the distance, she comes across a sight that she does not quite understand. Ahead, there are polar bears and large seals guarding an entrance way made of snow. The mournful braying can be heard up close now, coming from deep inside the structure guarded by the animals. Polly holds her hands up to the rest of the group as they each clamber to a halt behind her. "We must be careful and respectful to the guardians of this place. To my wolf pack, please wait outside." The wolves circle and sit down on the freshly laid snow opposite the entrance. But the noble Kaskae bears down with dignity, lifts his head defiantly and moves forward towards the opening of the ice cave and the sound of braying within. The polar bears step aside and out of the chieftain dog's way. Polly raises her eyebrows at Uki and at the haughtiness of Kaskae. Balan follows them all inside the ice cave. On the other side of the entrance, a slope gives way and leads to an underground level. Polly holds up her amulet to light the way under the tunnel, this one has been dug out by the animals. Claw marks clearly defined and frozen in time, line the tunnel walls. The cotton wool type snow has fallen very heavily, covering the top of the igloo structure and provides thick insulation to make the air warm inside. Sound is muffled in this place. The smell of animal and sweat is stringent in the air. Polly walks down ahead of the group to a lower chamber and into the den of the magnificent White Hart.

The great beast is laying on its side, huge and more than its description – it is five times the size of a male stag. Its fleece is brilliant white, and its pronounced mane is gold, interwoven with Linwood tree buds and large white daisies. Its large antlers are made of silver birch, twisted upwards and proud. What once was strong and majestic, is now ailing. Horns are flaking and the buds in the mane are shrivelled and dry. The creature is losing its breath and braying mournfully in pain. Its crystal white eyes are dull. Unseeing and its nostrils are quivering.

Polly understands almost immediately, if the beast passes then Spring will arrive no more and all will be lost to Winter, triggering the apocalypse.

The urgency of the situation is understood by the animals of this world. They wait with bated breath in their place on this earth, waiting for humans to know what the right thing is to do. Only the animals understand what is at risk tonight - to live through the horrors of a never-ending freezing winter, of famine, of cold and of death. Around the world, the animals are fearful that humans cannot be trusted to do the thing that needs to be done this night:

Wolves howl, the bear paces, the seal holds her cub to her stomach knowing the babe will turn to ice in the prolonged winter cold to come, the whale in the water cries and blasts its dismay through its blowhole. The big cats prowl and roar on the planes of the Serengeti. The snow settles in restless wait, knowing it will not transform to rain in Spring or dew on the grass of Summer mornings; without The White Hart walking this earth, as sure as the mountains are eternal.

Uki falls to her knees and cries out her anguish at seeing the magnificent beast in its final death throes. Bowing her head before the majestic beast. "I am ashamed to look at him. I am the face of humankind to him, look what we have done, Mother Earth forgive us."

The celestial Guardian of Spring brays and places his huge snout under her chin and butts it up. Looking at her closely with one of his large eyes. Uki looks at herself in the reflection of his great eyes and she sees herself covered in the spring of her childhood, carefree and loved. He shows her that he is forgiving, and he sees all, and that to him, her heart is true.

Polly watches the exchange, while a tear trickles down her cheek. She looks down at the amulet, confusion settles upon her. She needs the stag skull for the ancient prophecy to save all life. Her anguish in her chest is frozen and heavy. She thought she knew what this meant, what had to be done but now, in this moment. She is not so sure. What would life be without the changeable seasons? What would we be without the turning of time? Where would we find the balance that all life is made of?

Polly stands in the stillness of the decision, alone.

And awakens from her reverie, her eyes fixed forward and true. She knows what she must do.

There is no choice but to save the White Hart, to cure him of his illness so the seasons can continue on, so the world can remain whole - children can experience the gifts of living through the darkness of Winter and of the precious, life affirming feeling of emerging from the darkness and of the first flickers of hope of the newness of the Spring sun.

"There is only one way. There is only one thing that I can do, and it is to remain true" she utters to herself, holding her hand to the centre of her chest. "I will find another way to make the potion to stop Armageddon".

Balan holds out his hand and stops her, going on to question her imploringly "Don't we need its skull? Shouldn't we let it die? What if you are wrong?"

Polly is taken aback by Balan's questions, but she tries not to show it. She glances down at the White Hart; she can hear the thrumming of the Ancient Drum of Destiny beating in her ears and against her chest. The thrumming is some kind of code that she hasn't yet cracked but she knows it is some kind of a guiding presence. The possibility of another option rears into view; of ending the creature. The thought terrifies her. It slivers down her throat and chokes at her spleen. Harming the creature in any way is strange and alien to her. Polly replies, "I can only do what I feel is right, in this time given to me and maybe I'm not supposed to save everything, and maybe I am here just for this short time on earth to save him." She is consumed by the weight of her decision, turning her back on Balan and also, on what she has been told.

Polly readies herself. Holding her amulet in one hand, she places her other on the great stag's brow. Recalling the Willow Tree in her mind's eye. She closes her lids to concentrate wholly on the task at hand, and that is when a pure, healing, pulsating light of immense energy emits from her hand, cresting the magical creatures' horns - he bows his great head to take it all in.

All the while, the green light of the Aurora Borealis shimmers across the night sky above the chamber and joins Polly's purpose, to save the greatest magic of this world. The lights combine and consume that tiny speck of a den with the energy of life. Wrapping around the White Stag and it draws the pollution up, out of the majestic animal. Dispersing the blackness into the endless night sky above. To the never-ending universe, the pollution is but quarks and bosons - the parts that atoms are made of. Specks of dust compared to the great expanse. The pollution will be consumed by dark matter to be assimilated back into energy once more.

The planet takes a deep intake of breath and a vibration swells around the earth. The animals of this world feel its echoing power, its all-consuming vibration.

The wolves chorus, the bears growl, the seals bark, the whales jump, the eagle screeches, the dolphins chase at the never-ending waves, the big cats roar, the chimps chatter. On and on, the creatures of this world call out in unison, in their harmonious voices. Altogether in the oneness of the universe to save something that if lost can never be again.

Shards of light, of gold and green explode outwards and the brightness is all consuming. There is nothing left but a white blankness of space, of beginning. Polly pries open her eyes against the blinding brightness, to look at the stag, to see if he is healing. He stands up, strong and tall. He shakes out his antlers and they are covered in the growth of spring; buttercups, snowdrops, daisies and green cloves are growing once more in his mane. His diamond eyes glow brightly like the forming of a star, and he snorts and stamps ready to return. Polly's eyes cannot contain the swell of her tears, joy feels her being and a warm light lifts her. The great White Hart is temporally shifting in and out of focus. Leaving this deathly plane and returning once more into the world to aid the turning of the seasons, until the planet needs him no more.

＊

A gift is shared by The Great Stag before he vanishes. A vision is given to Polly before blackness takes her for its own.

## Chapter six - The Hidden

Polly sits alone, gazing out of the tiny window of the cargo plane, they have caught to return to the United Kingdom. Mournfully, watching the fluffy white clouds, blanketing underneath them as the plane glides overhead. The plane is very old, and it creaks and rattles in the high altitude, like an old whale bone carcass. Polly is thinking of the White Hart and panic raises in her throat, whenever she thinks about the decision she had made back in the den. She is returning without the bone piece and this was the mission.

Holding her amulet close to her, she squeezes her eyes shut tight and takes in big steadying gulps of air. The ancient thrumming of the beating heart is in her ears. The thrumming sound has not stopped since the den. It is growing stronger every day, something is seeking her out, she can feel it.

As her heartbeat and the thrumming synchronise, behind her eyes the vision gifted to her by the White Hart comes forth:

She can see the White Hart and he is bowing to Vusulia the High Priestess and Bringer of Destiny and then, and then, "Ugh" she yells out and stamps her foot on the aisle of the plane. The vision slips away from her. She knows how important it is to remember this vision, it is a gift of foresight, so she closes her eyes to try once again to recall it. That's when she gets a prickly, pressing sensation on her face. Feeling the sensation of someone watching her. Snapping her eyes open to look, Balan is sitting there quietly staring at her. His eyes seem oddly dark, and he has a sneer on his face - most unlike him.

"What is it?" she says bluntly, not mincing her words. Knowing his face is etched with disappointment, like Chris's had been when Balan had put a memory spell on the group of villagers after the incident in the cave.

"Well, I wanted to say that I think you were reckless in the den. You don't have to make decisions on your own. I get it, you are this Chosen One, that no one else can understand, but your decisions effect all humankind, so I think, at least we should get a say" Balan offers carefully, very sure of himself.

Chris is holding a book up to his face. He is sitting in the row of seats behind where Polly and Balan are sat. Not reading, but pretending to as he listens intently to their conversation. He weighs Balan's words, noting the questioning tone and the mistrust aimed at Polly in Balan's voice.

Polly peers at Balan for a long time but before she can reply, the words of The High Priestess, Bringer of Destiny from last year float into her mind *"you need a bit more training and a lot more self-belief to lead the planet through the storm that is coming"*. The clear voice rings out in her ears.

At last, she replies "My powers are my own Balan, they were given to me. I was tested and given the mantle of The Chosen One. The High Priestess didn't mention anything about the powers being governed by a committee and she definitely did tell me to trust myself, which I am learning to do."

"Yeah, okay. Well, you were born with the powers so not tested at all but gifted your circumstances. I still think your choices effect so many so what happens to us if you get it wrong?" this is more of a rhetorical question, but it probes into Polly's mind and stops her from replying. The first thought she has is, how does Balan know so much about the Chosen One's powers? He had never mentioned anything before now.

In her bewilderment at the verbal attack, Polly shuffles in her seat and wishes that Toni was here. Her best friend always had her back. It hurt her feelings that Balan was questioning her judgement. Her choices, but all she could do was remain true to herself. She did not owe an explanation to anyone and come to think of it, who did Balan think he is. A Chosen One? Polly fumed in her seat getting angrier.

Balan awkwardly turns around in his own seat to face the window in the deafening silence that clings heavily in the air of the plane, following the tense exchange.

Chris puts down his book in his lap, quite-over pretending to be reading and glimpses through the gap in between the row of seats. Polly's eyes are puffy and red-rimmed, her face is impassive, and she is slumped forward - crestfallen and defeated. Chris feels a burning anger bubble up in him. He hastily moves from the window seat, sliding over to the seat nearest the aisle and leans in towards Polly and Balan.

"Okay, Balan, so you want to discuss things before people make choices in the future? Are you saying that everyone's decisions are subject to scrutiny or just Polly's, I couldn't quite tell?" Balan looks round, confused by Chris's sudden outburst.

Balan replies "that's not what I'm saying, it's just her decisions impact a lot of ..."

"It's *just* what? You see the thing is. I didn't agree with what you did to those villagers. You acted like you have the right to take away their memories just because you can, but I reasoned that you're a decent guy and so I didn't feel the need to question your motives and you didn't seem to question yourself at the time either. My question would be, why the hell do you think you have the right to question Polly? She's too polite to say this to you but I will". Chris was red-faced and practically bellowing his last words out towards the end. Balan sat there in shock at the exchange. He goes to get up to confront Chris's rudeness, but then thought better of it and sat back down, quietly turning towards the window, staring out into the darkness of the night sky. His reflection bounced back at him in the thickly glazed windowpane of the plane and all he could see was a scowl on his own face - he did not recognise himself at all.

Chris gave a "harrumph" and then slowly moved back to his window seat, barely looking up at Polly. She sat there quietly with her hands folded in her lap, but she was sitting up a little taller. Chris's belief in her restored her somehow and she felt a gratitude towards him that lightened her whole disposition. Chris and Polly were linked in an invisible bond. Chris's body language was lightened too, as they mirrored each other through the seats of the plane. Polly also felt a familiar connection to Balan usually, but he felt distant and different to her in this moment in time.

They arrive at London, Heathrow airport some hours later, after catching a transfer flight from Iceland. The airport is heaving, uncomfortable and overly lit up. Polly feels disconnected from her environment as its artificial and overwhelming, especially when compared to the isolation and raw natural beauty of Greenland - everything looked harsh, concrete, and soulless somehow.

Eleanora is waiting for the three of them in the main part of the airport building, and she is getting a lot of strange looks from the average passerby. The pagan witch stands out from the crowd, with her long flowing silver hair. Her vibrant and piercing blue eyes and her powerful stance. She has a sunny disposition, with a ready smile, which plays on her lips at all times. Her passion for wearing a woollen cape in the sunny weather had not diminished any, either. This, along with other small slightly strange details about her person, made her look odd, so she is very easy to spot in any crowd.

Upon seeing Eleanora, Polly's smile spreads broadly across her face. Flying into the older witches arms nearly knocking her over, hugging her tightly. Eleanora hugs the girl back with a look of concern. The older witch places her own hands on either side of Polly's arms, pulls her forward to closely inspect Polly's face. There is a fear there and the Chosen One can barely look into Eleanora's eyes. "What is it? What happened?" Eleanora enquires gently. Balan appears and slings his bag over his shoulder, casually walking past the group without a greeting or gesture of hello. Eleanora is most displeased with the display "Balan, where in the seven hells of Indris are you going?" Eleanora says with alarm. Balan gives a shrug and carries on walking past the group, towards the exit of the building. "Balan, come back this instant." Eleanora shouts after him. Trying to drag Polly with her to follow Balan but the Chosen One digs her heels in and is immovable – like the Himalayas.

That is when Chris appears out of the thronging crowd, delayed slightly, at the baggage claim. "Chris, Polly, what happened? Why is Balan walking off like that without a word and why are you two reluctant to follow?"

Polly tears up slightly and says "It's a long story, but I saved the White Hart and didn't take its bones. I didn't feel like it was the right thing to do, I can't explain my choice, but I know I was meant to save him, Eleanora. I know that sounds crazy. Don't ask me how, but I just know. Our research was wrong. The professor was wrong. Balan is angry. He thinks I've jeopardised everything based upon a hunch. There were strong words exchanged…"

Polly looks down, quite scared about the prospect of a failed decision. While Eleanora looks at Polly with surprise, in her smiling face.

"Oh, is that all? I wouldn't worry about it, my girl."    Polly's mouth drops open, flabbergasted at Eleanora's nonchalance and ease. Wanting to double check Eleanora heard right the first time.

"But I SAVED the White Hart. I don't have its bone for the spell. What if I have made a wrong decision? It could be catastrophic, no?" ventures Polly.

"Yes and no, all things happen for a reason, Polly. You will come to learn this in time. We can only do our best with the time given to us. No one is perfect and no one can see into the future." Eleanora pauses and squints one eye in thought and starts walking the group towards the exit "Oh, apart from gifted Seers that is. Oh, yes and The Goddess but that's about it, I think. Ahhhh, oh yes and also those monks that wrote the prophecy in the Tome of Herne. They of course can see into the future but that's about it."

Polly and Chris look at each other with bemused looks on their faces, quite lost now in the point that Eleanora had been trying to make. They were trying not to laugh and the very act, made them burst out laughing together. Eleanora sternly looks round quite at a loss as to why they were laughing so much. She shrugs, quite happy that the glumness has lifted from their young shoulders.

Polly, Chris, and Eleanora walk towards the exit together and Eleanora does a final sweep of the vicinity to see if Balan is still skulking around the front of the airport. He is nowhere to be found. The Pagan witch tuts and mutters "hot headed". They walk a little further on to a more remote part of the car park covered by tall, looming hedgerows. There she summons a portal in the airport car park. A large swirling iridescent tunnel appears with twinkling lights shooting out of it and a roaring sound of a vortex pulling air in. They each take a step inside and vanish from view, just before a car pulls into the bay where they had been standing      .

***

They arrive at the bottom of the valley,  that hosts the great golden Castle Polly and Eleanora call home – sun beams alight it and wisps of cloud drift over the tops of the battlements. The castle is lovingly referred to as The Temple amongst the magical community – it is a place of acceptance. The structure of sandstone rises up out of the hilltop it is mounted on. Stretching towards the blue sky above, flags rippling in the breeze. With twelve turrets split across multiple levels, towering against the backdrop of the North Sea – perilous and of referred to as Poseidon' ruin. The structure is humungous, breathtakingly so, and is covered by an enchantment so that only the magical community can observe it. It shines gold in the glittering afternoon sunlight.

Polly sighs upon seeing the first glimpse of the castle and breathes in the cool air from the fresh Northernly wind. Salt dusted nostrils flaring. Feeling the familiar ache in her bones for the place she now calls home. Closing her eyes, she walks forward. Using her knowledge of the interior of these lands to guide her. She climbs up the familiar grass banked hill and holds on to the feeling for as long as she can, like a grasping toddler clutching a favoured toy. The sky above is a vibrant blue, with wisps of cotton wool clouds stretched out over the open expanse. The turrets of the castle pinned against the clear sky. A deer prances over to Eleanora and nudges at her hands, looking for pellets and treats the older woman carries on her for the wild woodland animals that live on her land.

Chris stretches and yawns loudly, he towers over Polly. His sun-drenched curls sweeping across the light caramel skin of his open and friendly face. His green eyes glow in the sunlight – in the joy. Polly gives out a contented sigh looking at Chris and then disappears from view. Stumbling over a large rock that she had not noticed in her path - her concentration had

80

been elsewhere. Falling, Chris holds out his strong arms and catches her before she hits the ground. Holding onto each other a little longer than intended. Polly flushes, her cheeks turn pink against her creamy pale skin. She pushes her long chestnut hair behind her ear and bites down on her rosy, pink lip awkwardly and self-consciously. She pulls her arms away, brushing her fingertips against Chris's broad chest as she does so.

"Steady, I thought I lost you there for a second." Chris says, looking down into her almond shaped eyes and holding her hand in his own.

"You can't get rid of me that easily" Polly blushes, unsteady and unsure - heart pounding wildly.

Eleanora watches the two of them play out the oldest dance of all time and she stops in her sadness, at what this means for Polly, as The Chosen One. Eleanora forces herself to thrust this thought from her mind and tears her eyes away from the two young adults. Turning away, to give them some privacy to explore this together. When all of sudden, a sonic "BOOM" blasts out across the land, the aftershock comes on in waves of sound, undulating down the hill and the three of them are knocked to the ground by the blast of the explosion. Polly is the first to jump back up onto her feet, barrelling up the hill towards the castle. Her legs as quick as lightning, gripping the ground to cover the three mile walk in a matter of seconds. As she reaches the castle doors, she turns round to look back down the hill and searchingly, she finds Chris is up on his feet in the valley below. Helping Eleanora to get unsteadily back up too. They both begin walking up towards the castle, at a brisk pace.

Polly walks over to the entrance of the castle. Placing both of her hands on the immense doors of the wooden gated structure. Only Eleanora can unlock these gates. With a heave and thrust, Polly slowly pushes the doors open with her strength. They are on two pulleys and opened usually by a handful of people or by magic performed by Eleanora. As she enters the keep, she draws to her, her sword. Keeping it close to her chest, erect and upright, and she tentatively moves into the courtyard not knowing what she is going to find inside.

Professor Rothschild is an elderly gentleman with short and neat silver hair and a bemused smile plastered on his amiable face on most occasions. He wears the requisite circular brass rimmed glasses that all professors adorn, and he is rather portly in stature and very kind in nature. He is a wizard and the head teacher at the Herne Hall School of Magic. The school is currently closed due to the summer holidays and the incidents of last year when Polly received her powers and became the Chosen One. The Professor knows he will need to reopen the school soon, for the sake of the students but he knows now he will not be returning as the head teacher - now is not the right time. Polly needs all of his focus if they are to stop evil from taking hold of the universe. He is a very old friend of Eleanora's and The Lady's. The Lady Esme had been kidnapped over a year ago or more by the Inner circle and was being held somewhere unknown.

Until now that is. At this moment in time, the Professor is running towards Polly covered in scorch marks from a spell that had gone slightly (very) wrong, and his hair is sizzling, and he looks rather confusingly, completely delighted. "Polly? Polly, how are you dear girl? Can't stop now. Where is Eleanora? Where is she? I've some exciting news to share. We have found where they are holding her sister, The Lady Esme Cadmun-Herne at long last. Praise the Goddess." Polly freezes. She could not believe what she was hearing. Could it really be true? She pointed back down the hill, back to where Eleanora was walking up it with Chris - she would want to know about her sister's whereabouts immediately.

"We opened a portal as part of Annika's lessons. Annika says she felt drawn to its purity of energy and we could hear the Lady Esme's voice but could not open the doorway. There is a spell blocking it. We traced it back and we have the address. It's in Soho, London. Good grief, where is Eleanora? She will want to go to her sister straight away" The Professor shouts with glee, as he passes Polly by all in a fluster.

"And the loud boom? Anything to worry about?" Polly shouts out after him, but he continues running down the hill towards Eleanora - all Polly heard was "Not really" in the distance.

Her face is set in confusion, but then it gives way to a huge broad smile. The lady Esme had been found at long last. She had been missing for a couple of years. They do not exactly know for how long as a shape shifting witch called Nuala Glamdring had disguised herself as The Lady to try to steal Polly's powers. And as for the sonic boom? Well, as she can't see lots of people rushing to get out of the castle and there is no obvious signs of smoke and fire, then it is probably safe to assume there is no immediate danger. Resigning herself to finding out what had caused the sudden explosion when someone cared enough to tell her.

There is a humming of steel, as the sword of Hestia is sheathed back in its scabbard while Polly shakes the tension out of her arms. Strolling through the cobbled courtyard and into the main living chamber of the Castle. There is no one around. A faint sloshing sound of mops cleaning the hallways and stonework of the castle, could be heard in the background. The cleaning apparatus and tools have been enchanted to systematically keep the castle clean, tidy and in a good state of repair. As Polly walks through the empty hallways, she reflects on the first time she saw a broom twirling and whirling by itself through the expansive library. Alarmed at the time, she had jumped up on a reading desk and had hacked at the offending object with her sword, believing that the castle was under attack. Eleanora had walked in the room at the time and tutted and exclaimed "What a waste of a good broom".

Polly shakes her head at the memory, titters to herself and cringes at the thought of being so very naive about the ways of the magical world back then.

Later, walking through the front door of her own wing of the castle, she searches through the post piled high in the entrance hall. Then smiles and touches some of the familiar ornaments, and plants in the hallway. This is her sanctuary, and she kicks off her shoes and immediately sighs in bliss of being home. This is when Indiana the cat comes sauntering into view. His tail instantly pricks up when he sees her, but other than that he pretends to not be excited to see her at all and blinks up at her face blankly, casually watching a fly buzz by. "Hey, Indy, what have you been up to?" she talks to him in her baby voice, reserved only for him. Her furry friend butts at her hands and her forehead, as she lifts him up and cradles him in her arms. Indiana starts to purr loudly.

On the table in the lounge is the Scroll that holds part of the Prophecy of Restoration, she had left the sacred document carelessly out and on the coffee table. Reprimanding herself, she picks up the light parchment, refurls it up and reseals the forbidden text. Then she places the scroll in a hidden safe behind one of the large gilded-framed oil paintings, hanging up in her corner of the building - the painting being part of the steep history of the castle.

Polly picks Indy back up, on her way over to the window. Looking out tenderly over the great swell and expanse of the North Sea. Staring out onto the coastland, in its rugged and untamed state. The coastline has patches of smooth golden white sand, intermingled with rising rocks and volcanic residue from a time long ago. Dried out seaweed litters the beaches and adds another dimension to the rugged landscape. The seagulls can be heard squawking as they hover on the cool gusts of wind near to Polly's windowsill. The horizon in the distance is looking grey and heavy, with drek rain pelting the skyline.

Polly's eyes droop, beginning to drift sleepily with the rhythm of the swelling waves. Her eyes open but unseeing and the heartbeat is thrumming once again in her ears. In the quiet, she stands, and begins breathing steadily slower and slower, synchronising her own heart rhythm with the sound of the thrumming in the distance. There, in that still place between wake and sleep, she starts to see the vision gifted by The White Hart once more. Snaking towards her and meeting her with more vivid colour, more definition and greater clarity this time. The vision swims into view.

The vision, twirls, and whirls like smoke; the Stag bows, The High Priestess leans forward, and both of their brows touch each other and when, Vusulia arises, she does so with a crown made of stag skull and bones on her head. White flowers are weaved around the skull. A star hovers above her. Then, Vusulia sees Polly, and The Priestesses' eyes burn brightly with an intensity.

There is something behind The Priestess, growing steadily larger in the distance. It is a ferocious, scaly red dragon. The creature claws forward hissing out a roar and opens both its amber eyes, searching out, reaching, turning imploringly to Polly.

Polly opens her own eyes with a start. A glow of amber is held in the Chosen One's iris's for a few seconds and vapour flows out through her nose unbeknown to her. What did the riddle of the vision mean? Something felt familiar to her but not obvious as of yet. She resolves herself to discussing this with the Professor, to see if he has any ideas. Suddenly, Indiana stands erect in her arms and stares into her eyes. Frightened, he jumps down in a panic and scrambles hastily to get to the door. Eager to leave, to get away from her and he darts out through the cat flap. Polly calls to him and walks after him, wondering what had gripped him with fright. Concern darkens her features, and she smacks her lips. There is a strange taste in her mouth. Like acid and her nostrils are tinged with the smell of sulphur, making her feel quite ill. She rubs at her eyes and assures herself that she is just overly tired from all the travelling she has done recently.

Polly shrugs off the strange feeling, grasping for normalcy to return. She decides her next step is to draw herself a long and well-deserved bath then she plans to get dressed, to rejoin the group for dinner.

A while has passed by, Polly has luxuriated in a bubble bath and taken a long sleep in her queen-sized bed. Next, she selects an outfit from her wardrobe and in the dressing mirror, starts to put on some make up. Dressing herself carefully in a figure hugging one shoulder, ruched dress of coral and then slips on some golden bangles and matching kitten heels. Peering at her own reflection in the mirror, other people would know there is no mistaking how beautiful she looks but Polly only sees the dress and the accessories. Sure, she feels her power standing there, intoxicating as it is, but Polly doesn't feel attractive. Then, when she has decided she is ready, she rustles out of the room swathed in the rich fabric of her dress - legs somewhat restricted by how funnelled it is. As she closes the door, a tiny speck of a drone whirs faintly into motion. The drone had been sitting quite still on the sandstone windowsill, waiting for Polly to leave. The tiny intruder casts a laser light over the room, clicking faintly as it flies around, taking photos of the apartment. The drone stops at the oil painting and then hangs in the air, following the frame and taking surveillance details and downloading the information to a central database owned by The Company. A secret organisation that carries out the illicit plans of a group of Billionaires known only as The Inner Circle.

Downstairs in the vast drawing room, The Professor, Annika, and Chris are waiting for the group to assemble before walking into the dining hall to take supper together. The smell of roasted and buttery dishes wafts through the air. The Professor and Chris are indulging themselves in a pre-dinner aperitif, it is after five pm after all. They have dressed in formal dinner attire for the evening ahead, which will end with a game or two of cards and roulette. Annika stands tall, dressed in a turquoise and silver saree, with matching intricate and delicate, silver jewellery. Looking exquisite from head to toe. On her feet are traditional silk slippers. Polly appears and Chris gulps in surprise. Taken aback, seeing his friend for the first time in the beauty of her womanhood. He blurts out across the room "You look beautiful, Polly" she stands by the cocktail bar, just at the edge by the large window that looks out over the sea. Her form is silhouetted against the pink and golden hues of the final reminisce of the setting sun. Polly's eyes glitter from his attention and not one other person in the room could be seen or heard by the pair of them, as they gaze at each other in the height of that summer evening. The smell of flowers from the rose garden lingers in the air and mingles in with the heady scent of Polly's perfume. Chris walks into the plumes of her perfume and relishes the hints of lily of the valley, a favourite scent of his from that moment on. Desperately searching his mind for the right words to say to her. Wanting her to know he feels differently now they are both no longer children but he just feels awkward, self-conscious, and frustrated with himself. He moves over to be by her side. Maybe this would be enough - to show her how he feels.

Polly's gaze lingers on him a bit too long. His tallness and broadness of shoulder show off the lines of his tailored tuxedo to full effect. She catches his anguished expression and reads him like the open book he is. Reaching out to hold his hand in hers, he relaxes into the gesture, and they stand there together completely comfortable with each other and staring out into the garden. Seeing the future of endless possibilities that this one touch has meant to both of them.

And then. Well, that is when Eleanora comes barging into the room, dressed all in black like a wayward ninja. Her silver wrought axe in one hand and her large mechanical crossbow in the other, and the Tome of Herne bulging in the confines of her cape pocket. Her usually cool and calm exterior is altered. Frenzied, agitated is the look in her brilliant, startling blue eyes.

"WHAT in the blazes is going on HERE! You all look dressed up like we are in a bloody Agatha Christie murder reveal event, hosted at a cocktail party in the 1910s. Good grief, the decadence! While my sister is being held hostage and needs us. Probably being starved! Timothy, Polly come along and now. We need a plan to rescue The Lady. She has been held prisoner long enough." Eleanora yells out adding a good deal of huffs and tuts for good measure.

Polly looks at Chris sadly, shrugs and moves her fingers to his face. "It's okay I'll be here when you get back." he whispers, reassuringly to Polly.

"You bloody well will not my lad. Chris, get out of that preening peacock of a tuxedo and come with us. We'll need your planning and tech skills please and Annika, your powers will be needed too." Chris gulps and nods at Eleanora, like a gun is being pointed at his head.

The group take a minute to go through a collective type of emotional rollercoaster. They first of all, look alarmed and then resentful at the reality that they could not just have one night where everything is normal, peaceful even, and then came the feeling of being resolute and intent on purpose, they were going to save The Lady from a fate worse than death. The Chosen One does not waste another moment more, she kicks off her heels and they skid across the glossy wooden floor and land with a "thump" against the copper cocktail bar. Next, Polly releases her carefully styled hair from its high ponytail. Shakes it out, roughly plaiting it back into a functional style to keep it out of her way. Then leads the group out of the dining room ante chamber, and into the space where the battle rhythm would be planned. The war strategy discussed - leading them to The Library.

## Chapter seven - Battle Rhythm


The main library is located in one of the wings of the Castle, situated on the other side to that of the dining hall. This provided ample opportunity for each of the group to rush off to their own respective rooms; to get changed into more practical combat gear. Chris hadn't wanted to turn up in the strategy room in his 'preening peacock' attire, which had seemed to annoy Eleanora somewhat. Each of them brought back down to The Library their respective preferred weapons of choice. Annika is standing in the Library wearing a ringlet of gold on her head, crafted by Eleanora and a magical spell has been cast over the simple object. The precious metal helps Annika to feel protected and safe when opening or venturing too close to the evil red portals, and the demon creatures within that scare her so.

Chris is carrying his glass wand, without telling the others about his new secret. He has been diligently learning how to use magic. The Professor had been privately teaching him some basic magical spells for protection. At first, Chris had not shown any signs of possessing magical powers at all, but the more he had studied and practised, the more evident it became, that he does have magical abilities. Becoming more accomplished, Chris could do some rather complex magic, but he tended to use his abilities for more practical and mundane tasks like floating books down from the high shelves of the library. His primary power is the ability to draw on fire from the sun and his secondary power, its counterbalance, extracting vast quantities of water from the moisture in the air. Last winter on the grounds of the castle, Chris had helped Balan to corral a herd of water buffalo and some sheep that had broken into the harvest storage barns, by shooting fire bolts into the air and making them explode. His magical abilities were coming along and developing remarkedly rapidly , requiring consistency and practise on his part. He did not feel quite ready yet to reveal this to his closet friends, Polly, and Toni, who were both accomplished at wielding their own powers. Part of his issue was he still felt uneasy and awkward about magic and the limitless power of it. He felt out of control when using it, which he had not quite reconciled within himself.

While the group were getting ready, Polly had quickly changed into her battle fatigues. Along with Eleanora, she had started searching the building plans of the nightclub in Soho, where The Lady Esme is being held prisoner. The Lady was being held against her will by Miles Luxemburg, a tech and social media giant and his billionaire club, known in the underworld as the Inner Circle. Polly and Miles are locked in a race against time to find the seven magical objects that can be used to start or prevent the apocalypse. The objects, when brought together and binded in a spell, can also be used to heal a planet in climatic decline. Miles planned to use the objects to start the Prophecy and wipe out the rest of the inhabitants of earth, while living underground in the city of bunkers he and his cronies had built to survive and live long enough to reshape the new world. Miles needed one of the relics called the Vessel of Life to cast a spell to give them unnatural long life. Polly had barely managed to get to the Vessel of Life before Miles last year and now she was hunting down the rest of the seven magical objects before the Inner Circle manage to get their clutching hands on them.

Polly, standing beside Eleanora, is staring at the plans not being able to make much sense of them. The building is very complex and intricately designed, it had more rooms than was possible, which implied magic was used as the foundations for the structure. There are many levels but from the outside it looked like a normal three storey structure. The two women are finding plotting the quickest route to where The Lady Esme is being held, quite impossible. Eleanora stands back to assess the situation and then clicks her fingers together, "Thats it!" she exclaims in a eureka moment and waves her hands across the plans. Turning them into to a 3-D solid image of the building. Eleanora places a few oats, that she had conjured, into the room on the plans where they know The lady is being held and then places a slim mould on the entrance to the building. Polly says "Right, ok, we don't really have time for science experiments right now if we are to..."

Eleanora makes a shushing sound and places her finger on her lips. Chris walks into the room. Immediately curious and comes over to the table to watch. Eleanora then sends a spell over the mould, and it bursts into life. The curious life form sprouts forward in little rows of crystal-like webbing, rushing through the maze of the 3D structure, navigating its way to the small replica of the room where the lady is known to be held.

Eleanora looks up at Polly with a steely look in her eyes "Thats it my girl, that's the quickest way to get from the entrance to the room" she says, as surety takes hold of her.

Polly looks at the mould and arches an eyebrow pointedly "We are going to trust fungus to plot our route then?" she says with incredulity.

Eleanora sniffs in a defensive way, chin raised and tersely replies "My girl, single cell mould is ancient and wise. I trust it more than you will ever know, and it has been navigating tree and root underground since time began. It looks after the planet and will outlive us all; you mark my words, Pollux" Polly subtly rolls her eyes and continues to look doubtful but knows not to argue with Eleanora. The older witch has been tense, and very stressed since learning of her sister's whereabouts. Determined to rescue her and she had this aura about her that nothing or no one was going to stand in her way.

"Well, you see, Japanese scientists have been using single cell mould growth for some time to chart the fastest and most efficient paths to a number of places. The mould has a sense of how to navigate the quickest way to a food source without expending much energy. Japanese scientists have been using it to rechart their entire underground tube network to..." says Chris, before Eleanora rudely interrupts him with a "Not now boy, we've got to finish planning the attack. There'll be plenty of guards and demons and probably a witch or two to overcome on our way to my sister". The Professor then walks into the room with Annika, and they come over to the table. The mould is still spreading through the structure and had become engorged and fuzzy over the place the oats had been left out.

"Slime mould navigation?" the Professor says, with a chortle. "Well now that takes me back to when I was a student in…"

"Ahem, Professor, you were going to tell us about the Company's protection detail posted around the building" Eleanora says, interrupting what would have surely been an entertaining but very long story that they really didn't have time for.

The Professor looks at their upturned and expectant faces and then sets about explaining his research "The club is really a front for a money laundering operation and The Company agents use the club as a place to store cash, and weapons, and other illicit items, in London. The nightclub is run by three vampire siblings: two twin brothers and their sister. The family name is La Magra, part of the line of Dracula. The vampire siblings are very powerful. Not to be underestimated in any circumstances. They are ancient and have managed to survive even though they have been hunted for many a millennia. Trying to be brought to justice for the many atrocities they have committed. The siblings have managed to escape justice time and time again, stretching over thousands of years. Currently, there are a troop of six company agents and also a dark witch, Esmerall known as Blood Moon, guarding the place. The club is well established, and part of the Goth music scene and partygoers regularly go missing after a night out there, but the police never seem to investigate so I think they are using protection and concealment magic there."

Polly's face is ashen "Okay, so we will need a protection spell against vampires, I assume?" Polly says, uncomfortable at the prospect of facing down vampire demons, "Eleanora, can you take care of that? Chris, we are going to need cross bows and silver swords I would guess, Professor?" The Professor nods emphatically to Polly's question.

The Professor gravely says to all gathered before him "These are ancient demons and very powerful. The only way to be sure to stop them is to cut the head completely off. It is the only way to be certain." Polly, Chris, and Annika glance at each other with concern. The Professor had made a point of telling them to not hesitate to cut the head off. He had emphasised this so they understood how serious the situation is, it is a key fact that the

92

group will need to deal with. They are no longer children and the fight against evil all too real.

They each move to leave the room to prepare for the rescue, when the Professor takes Polly to the side and says "Be careful, Polly. This is something that you have not battled with before so keep your wits about you. The vampires are terribly powerful and use illusions and enchantments and can shape shift. Also, I'd like to talk about The White Hart incident when you return, please. I would like to hear about the witch and the cave too. I am a bit concerned about the circumstances of how she died. A powerful witch like that does not usually die so easily".

Polly nods and morosely thinks out loud "IF I return by the sounds of it", her eyes are wide with terror. She does not feel safe knowingly entering into the liar of vampires - fabled creatures of myth and horror. The stories had always frightened her as a small child and made the hair on her arms stand up, like it is even now. The Professor offers a short smile and whisks off to prepare some potions.

Polly watches his back as he departs. Gradually, lifting the comforting handle of the Sword of Hestia. Holding out the sword, with Celtic runes scribed along the blade, in front of her chest. Polly runs her index finger along the sharp blade and swings it in a cutting motion. Hearing the silver ore sing reminds her, she is no longer a child. Vampires can be killed even if it means doing the unthinkable and cutting their heads off. No longer a daunting prospect for her, she would do what was needed to be done.

Two of The Company's Agents are dressed in white shirts and black suits with matching ties. The two Agents both have on mirrored sunglasses and are standing with their hands folded over their muscular chests, biceps straining the material on the upper arms. Clear plastic mouth pieces are attached to the side of their heads in order to relay messages, keeping the surveillance loop complete. They are there to guard the entrance to the nightclub in Soho with military precision and the nightclub has a 'no nonsense' reputation. A young woman, stumbling along on very high heels ambles by and she is teetering on the brink of falling on the pronounced cobbles. Neither agent even blinks in her direction or offers help - this would break with protocol, in leaving their post. This is markedly different behaviour to that of an everyday bouncer. Flirting and cavorting with partygoers is a perk of the job. The young woman slips and falls, then gets back up, by drunkenly holding the wall. She swears at the agents under her breath for not trying to help her. They do not even look round or respond, carrying on guarding the front entranceway, as if she had not even been there at all. It is a Friday afternoon in Soho in July, in London. The teeming, hot baking streets are packed full of people making the most of the sunshine. Searching for somewhere to eat lunch over a glass or two of chilled wine. The tourists are out in force and looking for excitement between their booked attractions.


A little later back at the castle, Annika has opened a portal that leads to the club in Soho. She is peering through to the other side, trying to look past the shining effervescent lights of the gateway tunnel. Annika can just about make out the London soho building on the other side. She waves goodbye and watches as Eleanora, Polly, Chris, and the Professor walk in single file and then drop down out of sight into the hallway of the club, beyond the hawkish eyes of the two agents posted at the front door of the club. Annika has a bad feeling when she closes the portal, but she shrugs it off and touches the protective gold ringlet on her head but there is no denying, she is scared for the safety of her friends.

Polly drops out of the other side of the gateway and crouches low in the black painted hallway of the Georgian building. Silently, she peers up the dimly lit stairs to check if there are any guards nearby, before doubling back to help the Professor Rothschild down from the portal gateway. His old gunshot wound courtesy of an agent called Kane, from last year still played him up, leaving him cautious about jumping or stretching, so Polly holds out her arm in the gloomy, windowless stairway and supports him to step down.

Eleanora and Chris jump down lightly behind. The portal closes with a whomping sound and Chris grimaces – there is no way out but through now. The four of them quietly creep up the stairwell and onto the landing of the first floor. The Lady Esme is being kept in a locked room on the second floor, in one of the corners of the house. The room she is in, overlooks the backyard, onto a fire escape. They plan to use this as an exit route. The battle plan is for the Professor and Chris to cover the rear of the building and for Polly and Eleanora to move forward, scouting ahead. Polly keeps her sword drawn and the crossbow loaded – keeping tension on the release. Her concealed line of small silver throwing daggers down each trouser leg, are reassuringly heavy against her thigh. Polly holds up her gloved hand and the group come to a stop behind her. She alone walks forward, casing the hallway, before calling to the others that it is clear ahead. Eleanora enters the area behind Polly with her glass wand ready and her eyes bright and alert. Alive like sizzling lightning bolts, and as hard as steel - her eyes are telling the story that she is not leaving without her beloved sister.

Polly cautiously runs further on and turns to look up the next stairwell. When a door that had been left slightly open, suddenly creaks wide - Polly is ready, dipping out of sight. Two agents dressed in pale grey combat gear come flying out of the door. The two men vault towards her - mid-roundhouse kick. She ducks and twirls and does the same again. She jumps in the air above them and brings down both fists hitting the two agents with such force on the tops of their heads, they are knocked to the ground. A loud "CRACK" sizzles through the air behind Polly. A lightning bolt is sent forth, zigzagging through the air, past her. The crackling sheer power of raw electricity, hits its target and burns a hole straight through both the agents' chests on impact - leaving a smoking gaping hole behind in their chest cavities. Eleanora stands, with smoke coming from her wand in plumes. Polly is motionless, stunned by the ferocity of the pagan witch's attack. Tilting her head, silently listening in the dark and gloom of the black hallway, straining intently for a sound, which would indicate someone had heard the scuffle. A few minutes pass and there is no sign of life. Satisfied no agents are coming, Polly moves the group on. They are all on high alert. Polly signals that all is clear ahead, and they all cautiously take the second flight of stairs, up into the denser parts of the building. But all was not clear . . .

Suspended above their heads in the gloom and shadows of the hallway ceiling, a cold whispering begins. A sentient form, pearly white and human-shaped, unfolds itself from the corner - where it had been clinging to its latest victim. The creature pulls his long teeth out of the neck of the girl - a queasy, puckering sound. His victim is covered in a sticky, organic liquid, which had been spat from his fanged mouth – the smell was acrid and organic. Holding her in place, to render her unconscious to feed on. His victim is now groggily waking up from her sleeping nightmare into a waking one. Staring at him with eyes filled with a horror-struck quiet terror. Opening her mouth to call for help, but she is too late. He bores his hypnotic eyes into her to hold her still, as he slits the young girl's throat with a single bleak and razor-sharp talon. Like a predator, his gaze moves, dropping to the four people silently creeping up the stairs below him. When they have moved out of view, the creature then begins crawling along the hallway wall. Following the group silently up, up, up the stairs. Disks of gleaming red light in the shadows, follow the group silently watching the back of their heads. His mouth fully extended, sifting and tasting the air, the sound like a suction pad. Dried human blood cakes his prominent chin. He licks lecherously at the sides of his mouth. Enjoying the last morsels of flesh, as the cold-blooded monster follows his new prey.

A cold prickling sensation tickles at Eleanora's spine and she shivers in the darkness. There is a need to keep looking back, peering into the blackness at her back. She is quite certain they are being followed. "Professor?" Eleanora whispers.

The Professor holds his hand to his right temple and sends out a sonar wave outward, permeating  through the structure of the building to see if he can pick up any sign of movement in the house. The sonar ripples and the creature stops while the waves move over and through him - he is undetected. The only warm bloodied beings the professor could sense are the two guards posted outside the entrance. Their thermal signatures indicate they are relaxed, and the professor has detected a figure in the room above with The Lady. The dark power emanating from the being implies it is the Witch, Esmerall, in the room with the prisoner. The Professor conveyed this psychically to Eleanora. Scrunching his forehead, he is rather confounded, the La Magra's are not onsite it would seem, but why?

Eleanora leans forward to whisper in Polly's ear "Change of plan. The Professor and I will go upstairs. We can take out the Witch Esmerall unawares, by stunning her from the outside. You and Chris wait here. Keep alert and your sword drawn at all times. I feel something evil is lurking in this place. I don't care what the Professor says. There is something here. Something that the Professor can't see. " Polly nods in agreement. Eleanora and the Professor ascend the staircase and move off out of view.

A chill slides over the Chosen One, her senses are spiralling. Something is out there in the darkness – she can feel it. Polly starts to pace the step – backwards and forward she goes.

Chris watches Polly, wanting to say something to her. To let her know how he feels about her. If anything should happen to her and he was too gutless to tell her, then the consequences are just too awful to think about. It is driving him mad; the urgency is pressing in on him, but he comes to the conclusion that now is the wrong time and swallows down the dryness in his throat.

All the while, Polly continues her aimless pacing, distracted, she is listening intently above. Attuned to each noise and creak. A couple of minutes pass in this heightened state and then all of a sudden, a door explodes inwards above. Eleanora and the Professor can be heard shouting out an incantation in unison at the tops of their voices. A crashing thunderous sound shakes the building and The Witch, Esmerall can be heard, hurling backwards and out through a broken window. The tinkling sound of glass splinters, crashing onto the pavement below. A loud "POP" announces that the witch Esmerall has chosen to vanish through a portal before hitting the pavement. Fleeing the scene.

Polly squints her eyes to peer up the stairs, the realisation that the agents guarding the front will be coming soon, immediately springs to her mind. Polly lifts her sword as she turns around to face downwards, towards the exit. She looks up listening to the sounds of Eleanora and the Professor above, they are running towards her, dragging, and carrying the unconscious form of The Lady. She is being lifted between them. Her legs can be heard clanking, as she is dragged over the stairs.

Polly looks back down the stairs and stops dead. The energy has shifted, changed to a chilling cold, by the sight that greets her.

Chris is standing there with a look of sheer terror on his face, eyes wide with fear. His hands are at an awkward angle behind his back and his face raised to the ceiling, unnaturally. He has blood dripping steadily from his neck.

"Chris?" Polly calls out, her voice is tremulous, and her eyebrows knitted together in confusion and concern. A bead of sweat is silently trickling down Chris's forehead and then the most horrifying sight can be seen. A long black taloned finger undulates over Chris's shoulder like a caterpillar. Moving slowly around the skin of his neck to pinch the flesh near the artery – the vein begins to throb. Chris takes a gulp of breath, wincing in pain as he is nicked to give a demonstration to the people watching, as the situation slowly starts to unravel before Polly's very eyes.

A shadowed face appears at Chris's shoulder. It has two large blood red staring eyes, piercing the soul, as it slowly rises from behind Chris. With more taloned fingers grasping, clawing to keep hold of his neck. The creature moves like a shadow, slithering to the side of Chris like vapour, as it takes shape. Rising, tall and steps out of the blackness, dragging the blackness in on itself. Confidently, it covers Chris and claim's him as it's prize – sucking the blood from Chris's neck.

At that point, the two agents come running up the stairs and halt to a stop, as soon as they lay eyes on the creature. They visibly recoil from it and jump back onto the steps below - a safer distance to be.

A wind rushes forth and a sound like tuneless violins screeching out, mixed in with words can be heard "My sssister and bbbrother will be pleased when they get back. Devouring the flesh of the magical amplifies ooouuuurrrr powers." he speaks like word formation is unnatural to his biology and he is making sounds rather than using a voice box to communicate. The words have a hypnotic, rasping quality and don't synchronise. His eyes are salaciously seizing onto Polly. He could smell the power coming from her and he could be heard sniffing, inhaling her scent.

"Pollux, be on your guard. This is a slithering creature of hell", Eleanora spat out behind Polly.

Polly closes her eyes, meditatively searching. She steadies herself, her eyes open to challenge the creature. Not blinking or lowering, meeting the demons full glare with a ferocity of her own. On her delicate face, a scowl forms and her grimace sends out an unspoken warning to the creature of evil before her. She twists the handle of her sword in her grip, raising the blade sideways to her eyeline. Crouching down low on her left leg, while sliding her right foot out straight, with the heel of her foot flexed. Ready like a coiled rattle snake to spring into action. Polly blows on the gleaming sword. The pagan runes etched into the silver, glow blue and the blade sets aflame. Polly is twisting the sword in her hands, and it is dazzling before all.

The creature screams in the glare of the light and Polly shouts to Chris "Ttwieo-chagi." Chris takes a split second to smile at the instruction, a team combat drill awakens in his mind. Immediately, he pivots and leaps forward, kicking out. Landing on one foot then volleys back round. He kicks out to the side with his other leg, catches the vampire in the throat. Polly springs forward, joining Chris to kick the twisted creature in the chest. The force of the two together is potent and the vampire flies backwards down the stairs, careening into the two agents. Gunshots ring out randomly into the air as the two agents lose their footing. Polly did not miss a beat. She used the opportunity to cannonball into the two agents and knocks them down like skittles, with two carefully placed punches – they are knocked out.

The creature is rising like shadow and mist. Polly is nearby, holding her sword high. Her reflexes take over, she arcs the blade round and slices through the air. In one fell swoop, decapitates one of the oldest living Vampires the world has ever known. Its head rolls off its neck and onto the stairs below. His tongue frozen in a protruding position as the vile creature had screamed out its last breath. Looking grotesque. Polly stood there panting, splattered with the monster's black blood.

Chris rushes forward, pulling off his shirt over his head and hands it to Polly to wipe her face. Without so much of another word, the Professor and Eleanora carrying the unconscious form of The Lady between them, walk past and down another flight of stairs out into the hallway where the portal was opened earlier - there is no time to discuss what happened, they all needed to get out of the building and fast. "Now Pollux. Come now" Eleanora shouts up the stairs, desperation in her voice to get her sister to safety.

Chris is holding a piece of his shirt to his neck to stem the flow of blood. He is pale and trembling. Chris touches the sweat dripping from his forehead, and it feels greasy thick and icy cold to touch. Wiping the strange sweat on the back of his jeans, and it leaves behind a glistening oil like smear.

"I'm - I'm going to help them carry The lady" Chris says to Polly, eyes dazed, and he looked confused - distant.

"Are you ok?" Polly asks him, as she rubbed at her own face to remove the blood splatter.

"I'll be better when we get out of here." he is swaying slightly "Eleanora is opening the portal so hurry up, ok?" Chris says, while holding the banister as he jerkily walks down the stairs.

Polly could hear the rushing and swooshing sound of the portal being reopened on the floor below, followed by a tinkling sound, like little silver sleigh bells, due to its being held open with powerful magic. Polly prepares to go downstairs and stops suddenly. In the distance she can hear the heart beating again. A thrumming in her ears, but it is much louder than it has ever been before. There is something else, a tugging and pulling on her, like being led by an invisible force somewhere that she cannot quite describe - the words are elusive to her. Walking down the staircase, the thrumming continues to get louder on the ground floor landing. Allowing herself to be pulled forward, Polly walks passed the glowing light of the entrance to the portal. The thrumming beat of the heart gets louder still, she has no choice but to continue to follow, and walks out into the melee of Greek Street, Soho - deep in the heart of London.

The London scene outside is chaotic. Full of busy people going about their daily lives. Each person in their own little worlds. Consumed by their own tasks. But to Polly's eyes the bustle of the city is all too familiar but there is something odd and eerie about this landscape. The Londoners are like grey washed-out shadows, untouchable, not of solid form but ghost shapes that she can walk straight through. All is fog and diluted. All is shadow and blankness. There is no sound, everything is muted apart from the sound of Polly's own heartbeat and the thrumming of the separate heart in her ears. People are walking past her not able to see her. Like ghosts, reflected in prisms casting grey shapes of light. Unaware, that they are wisps of impressions of people made from memory. The city landscape is of shadows too – flicking in and out of focus. The sun is watery and pale, casting a silver light overall, people and buildings alike. The smell of the city is gone. There is nothing but a blankness confusing her senses.

 Polly is of solid form walking through the streets of London, that much she can tell but she feels this pull, this dull ache that she is struggling to describe.

The sadness behind her eyes intensifies. The realisation hits her, she has no real connection to this earth. No family of origin, no siblings or blood relatives of her own. She is the only person really here, walking alone through the historical streets of London. Her footsteps are shatteringly loud in her ears. Beating on the pavements – tapping out a tune that reminds her she is alone. A silent sob catches her throat. When out of nowhere, a vibrant pink cherry blossom petal flutters towards her and lands on her mouth. Putting her hand up, her fingertips grasp to remove the petal, its stuck in the moisture of her lips. Then a heavy stream of thousands of cherry blossom petals blow into her, as she walks down the colourless dreary blank streets. The thrumming is reverberating loudly, echoing all around her, reflecting back her sorrow. Is she going mad? Is the

101

thrumming real or is she just too lonely and stressed to discern reality anymore?

The petals look illuminous and vibrant in contrast to the colourless backdrop of the grey, other-worldly city landscape. The heartbeat is becoming louder, deafening, and slowly synchronises with her own. She closes her eyes to listen - *thrum, thrum, thrum, thrum*. The liquid sound of life thrumming through the heart centre, pulsating in her ears.

She stands still on the pavement turning to look at the building where the heartbeat is at its loudest. She recognises this place. Looking in at the black and white tiled front entrance of Claridge's hotel and there's something else. She could not later explain it, but she was guided here for a purpose to this place, and she exhales. Face planted between the bars of the iron gates that stand as thin sentinels outside the hotel. Inside her is a longing to reach out, to touch the doorway and be connected with the other heart she hears in her own ears. The promise of connection leaves an impression in this space, and she is mesmerised, spell bound by it. Waiting for the next step in the telling of her own story - *thrum, thrum, thrum* - is all she can hear and it's all she wants to hear. She leans her head forward, closing her eyes and exhaustion sets in.

**Chapter eight - what is discovered.**

Opening her eyes, the colours and sounds of the city streets come crashing back in, in glorious technicolour and sound. City life floods Polly's senses - she reels, disorientated at first, like emerging from the isolation of scuba diving into the crashing waves above the silent ocean floor. Gone is the strange washed out grey landscape. Colours return in full, and the buildings and pavements are filled with people once more. The sound of the city returns, rushing in, alarming in its decibels. This, alongside the sounds of chattering and yelling from the people of the great city of London.

Polly is staring into the Grand Hotel entrance of Claridges – the British institution frequented by the great and the good of the united kingdom. There is an impatience to know why she has been drawn here, to this place. There is something here to discover. She can feel an energy vibrating from inside the building – it is calling to her.

Polly walks up to the grand entrance where the Claridge's door-porter smiles at her, clothed in all of his finery. He nods and holds out his hand in a welcoming gesture. She hungrily peers in, ignoring his hand. "Are you okay? You're covered in a black liquid" says the doorman. "I don't mean to offend m'lady, just wondering if you need help, is all?". Polly had become accustomed to not being seen, hidden inside the ghost world that had melted away, and she flinches away. Stepping back. He continues on, enquiring and looking at everything about her person. It could be her imagination, but he seems to be searching for something.

 "What is this place?" Polly asked, knowing full well it is a hotel but wants to know more about its origins, its history and why she had been drawn here at this moment in time. The Porter does a double take and looks at Polly, then says very seriously "You need to come inside". His face is changing, getting longer and he himself is getting taller, stretching.

Footsteps can be heard approaching on the pavement outside "Pollux, you cannot enter here", it is Eleanora, looming into view from behind her. "Come child, come away from this place and I will explain."

Polly stood there feeling very tired and suddenly confused, looking between the place and Eleanora. The Grand Hotel held the answers to her longing, the essence of this place spoke to her, albeit a lamenting tune. Calling her like a sorrowful violin acoustic that is bringing her home, at long last. She then turned her gaze to the woman who had placed her on the path of her current journey, into the unknown.

Polly moves backward and forward in her desire, in her indecision and weeps with the confusion of it - scared of making the wrong choice. The past and the future are both important to her, both full of promises. Deep down she already knows that she will seek safety above all else. Since a small child she had tended to reach for comfort automatically, something she is ashamed of. But still, she turns to Eleanora and quietly says "Please take me somewhere to explain. I will serve, I will be of service, I will be there to win each battle for Her, but I need to know where I began, my anchor, my sacred self. At the very beginning if you will please.

Eleanora looks at Polly with incredulity and in anger "You are not ready, Pollux. You talk of service? If anyone requests servitude without question than they are doing so for their own gain, that is not something asked for by the Goddess. She is giver of life and understands, honours its unpredictability" Eleanora says sternly and with disappointment, looking at Polly with eyes full of concern.

Polly bites back a retort. Turning away from the building, to face Eleanora but she manages to suppress her rage and with that very action, her eyes glow amber with anger and a sulphurous vapour involuntarily escapes from her nose. Eleanora recoils from her, she is startled. " This is. . .new?" ventures the elder witch, looking into Polly's eyes for a long while.

"What is new?" Polly asks, quizzically, not understanding.

"Your eye colour changed. You had the look of the, of the..." Eleanora stops, turns and without saying another word, puts a stunning spell on Polly, who crumples to the ground.

The visage of the porter starts to disintegrate and the particles in the air swirl like a clock and reform into a tall priest with a shaven head. A Celtic symbol in vivid blue, pronounced on his forehead. His eyes are pale silver.

"She is not ready, and it is not time" Eleanora says rather curtly to the Being that once was the visage of a Hotel Porter.

He nods back and says, "When will she have all the sacred objects? We need to know".

"When she does" Eleanora says with an indignant sniff and picks up Polly, turns on her heel and leaves without so much as a backward glance.

"That's very helpful, Eleanora. Really detailed answers as usual!" the Priest shouts behind her, with a wide false smile and rolling his eyes. He tuts and walks back into Claridge's, and with each step, gradually allows the human porter to come back into being.

Eleanora carries Polly in her arms. Walking back towards Soho, under the cover of a glimmer spell. People are walking by. They do not see the witch in her glimmer state that reflects light and makes her look invisible, nor do they understand how important the person she has cradled in her arms is to all of humankind.

Eleanora's feet are beating a rhythm into the pavements, as she walks along the London streets, her eyes rest on the girls open and unconscious face. Reminding her of her own sister. This connection made Eleanora uneasy and fearful – she shifts Polly slightly, so her face falls the other way. How could she carry out the mission when she has these inconvenient feelings for the girl? Each step she takes starts to feel heavier and heavier, this matches the feeling in her aching heart.

Eventually, she arrives back at the building in the heart of Soho.

Earlier today, Eleanora had noticed Polly was missing when she had been conjuring the portal to get her sister home. She had not noticed Polly was gone in the physical sense, but she could sense the Chosen One was missing spiritually, which was a lot worse. There was something else, The pagan witch had sensed the presence of a creature as old as time itself, not good or evil just a being of great power. The essence was following the girl, so Eleanora had waited to close the portal behind the others before she pursued Polly through the streets.

Eleanora needed to think fast. She was on her way back through the portal to the Castle and her priority was to check on her sister following her ordeal, but how would she explain Polly's state of unconsciousness to the others without revealing too much? There was nothing else for it but to put a memory charm on Polly.

The portal opens with a blinding swirling iridescence, lighting up the gloom of the library of the Castle, on the other side. When Eleanora jumps down with the limp form of Polly in her arms, the Professor rushes forward. Chris and The Lady Esme had been helped to the healers' quarters immediately upon arrival but the Professor had waited behind for news of the Chosen One. "Good Goddess, what happened Eleanora? Is Polly, ok?" says the Professor in quite the fluster. Eleanora looks at the Professor and shifts her weight from one foot to the other, nodding before saying "stop making a fuss Timothy, she's the Chosen One for Goddesses sake, of course she's going to be ok. I think the encounter with the vamp may have drained her some. Nothing that a good rest won't cure." Eleanora says all this a little too defensively. The Professor weighs her words carefully and gives her a penetrating look over the rim of his glasses, before replying "Well, if you are quite...sure." He goes to touch Polly's forehead with his outstretched hand and Eleanora lurches away, out of his reach. The Professor glares solemnly at Eleanora.

Without another word, Eleanora departs from the room with the limp form of Polly still in her arms and she heads to Polly's wing of the castle. Eleanora is tiring now, and her arms are aching under the weight of what she carries, but not necessarily related to cradling Polly. Eventually they arrive in Polly's warm and cosy apartment, and her sleeping form is placed on her soft and comfortable bed – she sinks into it. Indiana the cat rubs and winds against Eleanora's legs before he gently hops up on the bed. Sniffing at Polly, the cat jumps back and stares wide eyed at Eleanora in an accusatory way and lets out a mournful meow.

"Don't look at me like that, I had no choice. She found The Sect of the Oneness too early so this was the only option. She'll be fine." the cat meows again, huffs out air through his nose then curls up next to Polly in his usual spot, next to her ribs. With the intention of keeping her warm until she rises. Eleanora strokes his head, and he begins purring. Polly and Indy remain that way, as Eleanora leaves and closes the door behind her, while whispering "sorry".

The pagan witch is rushing, clambering down the stairs two at a time. She is in the healers' quarters in no time at all. It is there that she finds her sister laid out on top of one of the beds. Eleanora can just make out that Chris is in a room next to The Lady Esme, being tended to with a bandage around his neck and a pot that is curling with smoke before him.

The Lady Esme laid flat on the bed, looks small, grey, drawn, and skeletal. Her once piercing blue eyes are dull and deep-set in her eye sockets, black circles underneath. "I must say, I thought your choice of holiday destination quite abysmal, Esme" says Eleanora, to her sister and choosing to use her real name instead of the moniker of The Lady. There is a casual hint at a shared joke, which belied the desperate tone in her heavy voice.

Esme croaked out a reply "The brochure was quite misleading. The young man was insistent on games every night and he was such a terrible bore, my good sister, Eleanora" The Lady whispers hoarsely and weakly, the beginnings of a smile playing on her dry and cracked lips. Eleanora's eyes become glassy, her shoulders unclench, and a bone weary, terrible exhaustion runs through her body. She slides her hand into her sister's and silently cries tears of relief. The Lady closes her eyes and sighs, this heartwarming gesture is the first bit of kindness she had experienced in the last couple of years and the contrast is like wandering into a lush oasis after being lost in a vast, lonely desert for centuries.

"I know that you want answers, but I am too weak right now. What I will tell you is the prophecy is most definitely in motion. Miles Luxembourg is but a conduit. There is something else at play and I cannot see who it is behind Miles yet. Don't get me wrong, Miles knows things that he should not, but I think he is but a pawn, he is foolish and egotistical. A mere babe himself, but he does need to be stopped. He is dangerous but he is not the Dark Lord. To add insult to injury, Miles made me play chess with him and he is not very good at the game" with that, Esme falls into a deep, restorative sleep, barely conscious.

Eleanora sits up a little straighter, more alert. Weighing every word carefully. What her sister had said made more sense, that Miles a mere mortal is a puppet and something else was trying to start Armageddon. That would explain why Polly was being called to the place of The Oneness, but who could be behind it? It would need to be someone or something very powerful indeed to remain unseen with all the eyes of the magical community watching. The Chosen One was being called earlier, which could only mean one thing, that it was a being powerful and so evil that The Chosen One would need more power than first thought to stop the prophecy. The Pagan Witch gets out her small clay pipe and sucks on it without lighting the end, out of habit more than anything else. She is in a healer's quarters after all, but she did this to help her concentrate, to expand her mind to look for the hidden clues.

### Chapter nine - the choices of the Father

### Miles

Miles Luxemburg's company boardroom is impressive. This is where his Board of executives convene to make corporate business decisions over his global tech empire. There isn't a social media or AI system on the planet that was not designed and agreed in this very room. The room is large, painted in a brilliant reflective white and has an oval shaped table that could accommodate fifty people or magical beings. The term 'Magical Beings' is important here - Miles liked to be seen to be magically inclusive. The room gives the illusion of having no ceiling, just open sky above. Glass encloses the room, like a large, cube bolted onto the New York city skyline. The panoramic view is spectacular, looking out over the Atlantic ocean. It is a very warm day in July, yet the ocean swells and crests turbulently, like a million humpback whales breaching the surface at the same time.

Miles is standing on the impressively, expansive deck that runs all the way round the glass cube architecture. The sea breeze flicking at his pale blonde hair, and absentmindedly, sipping espresso from his Buddhist cup, recalling a memory from his distant past. Rubbing the delicate handle of the porcelain cup between his index finger and thumb, recalling his time in a Buddhist monastery long ago...

Years ago, he had travelled to Tibet as a teenager, seeking enlightenment following the cold rejection of his German father, who is a descendent from the Germanic royal family pre-1919. Miles was not acknowledged by his father, being born out of a sordid one-night stand with a Las Vegas dancer. His father had deeply regretted this indiscretion. This moment of weakness and the result of it. Miles' biological father had maintained that his mother had taken advantage of him in a drunken state and the rest is a nasty history of his Father's constant bitter overtures towards the young Miles and his mother.

The first few times that Miles had contacted the austere man resulted in lump sum payments being credited to his mother over and above her monthly allowance, with a message that advised her to keep the boy away.

Miles took this as a challenge, that his father saw him as less- than-nothing due to him having to financially support them both.

Miles set about building a business plan to commercialise social media and within the year was a multi-millionaire. He sent a message to his father's legal team advising that they both no longer needed his father's money and was reaching out as an equal. Claude, his father, was outraged at his son's perceived impotence. Sending back a message to his illegitimate son, which made it very clear that he considered him common and not fit to breathe the same air, ending the note by explaining that no amount of money would make him part of the noble line of Luxemburg. Miles was devastated at first, feeling inadequate in anyway left him with rage in his heart. He could not understand why his father would not give him what he wanted - to be recognised as exceptional and part of the royal line.

Miles's rage had simmered on and eventually he had sought out a reclusive and isolated set of Tibetan monks, who he hoped would teach him how to conquer this feeling - stopping any feelings from being experienced at all. He spent nine months with them. Learning scripture, the discipline of martial arts, prayer, and silent meditation – honing his mind to remove the pain of suffering. The rage did not subside, he just became more adept at placing an ice-cold exterior over it while he waited in agitation, every second of the day for that one lesson that would remove the rageful feelings altogether.

One day he was sitting cross-legged at the temple with his brother monks, when an older and lifeless man was brought in on a stretcher covered in flowers. He was being laid to rest in that sacred place. As the ceremony went on, Miles learnt that the recently deceased man was to be buried nameless, one of the disgraced and excommunicated monks, who had taken up arms to defend villagers. The monk priest had given up his vows after seeing the atrocities inflicted on his people. He had however, later rejected the path of violence he had chosen, and tried to atone and repent for his choice but it was too late, he had taken a life. There was a great turmoil in the temple that day as compassion was mixed in with a heightened desire to ensure that all life is considered sacred, even the fallen monk and equally, the ex-monks' victims.

Miles sat there and watched the monks furiously debate scripture as to what would be the right thing to do - the ex-monk's dying wish was to be buried in the temple along with a written account of his acts of kindness. The ex-monk had meticulously documented these as acts of redemption and was seeking forgiveness. During the furious and heated discussions that had followed, Miles' had heard a simple phrase used, that set out the three important truths that can measure your life, which are "how much you loved, how gently you lived, and how gracefully you let go of things not meant for you". This verse struck a chord with the then young Miles and awakened with him a sense of stillness - well, a cold and controlled calm would be a better way to describe it. Later that same day, he had advised all his brother monks that he had achieved enlightenment on the subject of rage. Personally, thanking each and every monk in the temple and advised he would be returning home that very day. The rage had lifted, he told them, and the monks rejoiced at his awakening and the obvious ease within himself.

One monk helped him collect his old clothes from his room and chattered incessantly as he followed Miles out of the doors, and beyond the gates, on one long night in the middle of winter. The monk priest was a keen academic and scholar, so asked Miles for his insight into his personal interpretation of the phrase and why it had such a profound effect on him.

Miles was busily getting on a donkey that was being guided by a sherpa back down the mountain range at the time and his response left the monk speechless and afraid. Miles said this "I have loved my father, I have tried to live gently and peacefully, building media for people to share ideas and receive information. I did this to share my gifts with my father and now I must peacefully let him go and the hold he has on me will be diminished." The monk had hesitated initially, a curious look passed over his face, his smile slipped a little at the burning and intense look on Miles's face. "Oh, good, you mean you are letting IT go, right?"

Miles had said impassively "No, that's not what I said. I am letting him go and I will need to be holding him at the time though".

Miles eyes stared, unblinkingly at the monk as the donkey kick-started its rocky descent down the mountain, leaving the monk to stand alone in the silence of the shadow of the remote mountain – the monk felt as lost as the scenery that Miles and the sherpa were leaving behind.

This incident had troubled the monk greatly, he kept waking up in the middle of the night in a cold sweat and he was finding silent meditation challenging for the first time in his life. Miles's eyes continued to haunt him. He was beginning to see them everywhere he went - they represented his complacency.

He appealed to one of the senior monks and he was offered reassurance and absolution, but he still felt uneasy. What was he supposed to do? Miles had not actually said anything wrong, but it was the look in his eyes. The monk just knew.

A couple of weeks passed by the monk remained unsettled. A chance came along. He was offered a posting to teach scripture in a temple in India, so he accepted the offer with wholehearted gratitude. Upon his arrival in the country, he was kept busy seeing all that he could of the great cultural experience that is the vibrancy of India. At night, above the noise of the city, he kept thinking about Miles and his Father. He needed to know what had happened.

Eventually, he took the time to look up the name Luxemburg on his laptop. It was as he had feared, news items revealed to him that Miles's Father had died in a tragic accident. Where he had fallen from his apartment balcony. The monk had used Miles's search engine to look up these details and it was Miles's news network that had reported the story as a tragic accident. The monk closed the laptop and refused to engage with technology ever again. Fearing the power of its potential for manipulation. Immediately, he returned to the temple in the mountain and restored his vow of silence and isolation - he prayed for Miles' soul.

That was a long time ago now and Miles had learnt a lot since then. Miles never got tired of looking out over this view of the ocean from the decking of his Boardroom. At the great expanse of water that covers the mysterious ocean bed. The water covered the unknown and this appealed to him, imagining there to be a lot of unmined potential within the watery kingdom below the waves. He heard a click of a door handle and then light stilettoed footsteps on the decking behind him. He slowly turns as he takes the last sip of espresso from his cup. The grains in the bottom leave a bitter film over his tongue, rubbing his tongue vigorously on the roof of his mouth to dispel them. As he does so, he chucks the little porcelain cup over the side, looking round to see who is there. The hooded shadow creature snakes forward, he can see it out of the peripheral view of his vision, but when he faces it head on, the shadows change shape and turn into the beautiful feminine form of Nuala Glamdring, the dark witch. His co-conspirator and confidante about all things magical. She projects the image of having raven black glossy hair, translucent skin, tall slim limbs, and violet eyes, with barely their pupils. She is dressed in a peppermint green tunic dress and had a simple gold necklace clasped around her slender neck. Miles is dressed in his trademark black t-shirt, pale blue jeans, and trainers. Both of them look dynamic and dressed down in what the locals call New York chic.

Nuala smiles languidly, like a fox cornering a rabbit and then she disappears in a cloud of thick lilac-grey smoke and reappears next to Miles with her wand pointed upwards, under his chin. He laughs, he did enjoy her parlour tricks. A strange look passes over Nuala's face, and she pushes her wand deeper into his neck. For a microsecond, he is unsure of her next move. Nuala's eyes are blank, turning cold, staring at him. Like as if she is weighing up how she feels about him and then the tension is broken as she breaks into a smile. As she walks away, Miles blows out the breath he had been holding in and releases the stress built up in his shoulders. For a second their Miles was not sure of the witch, he had not known in that instance if she was going to let him go but he shrugs it off, promising himself to be more cautious around Nuala.

"I have the new compound that has been extracted from the skeleton of the two-thousand-year-old woman. Do you want to test it? Maybe do a little together and see what powers we get?" she is holding a vial and tantalisingly shaking it at him, biting her lip suggestively. Miles hesitates, he does not want Nuala to take any as she is too unstable and untrustworthy enough as it is.

"I'll take the potion myself to see what it's like. I don't want to put you at risk. You are too important" he heard himself say.

Nuala throws her head back and laughs loudly "sure Miles. Whatever you say. You just want to take the compound by yourself and have superhuman strength" she says with a knowing smirk across her mesmerising face.

With a flick of her manicured hand, the vial is thrown up in the air at him. Miles is not expecting this and scrambles, managing to catch it just in time before it plunges over the side of the decking and into the icy sea below. "Hey, quit messing around and be careful Nuala", Miles says as he stands there looking at the mixture within the glass tube for a long while, to see if any of the precious content had been lost. The sea breeze is lifting at the ends of his tousled golden hair and the sun glitters across his face. His blue eyes shine brightly. "and so, is this the purest form of the compound and has it been amplified with your powers? Will I have the same level of powers as the girl, Polly?" he asks excitedly.

"No, not quite. This batch of serum is not as pure as it should be. You will have powers but only for a day or so. At least you won't change into one of those vile creatures that were part of the first lot of experiments. The demons known as the Horde. They've escaped from The Company's control, you know? A small group is out there somewhere without supervision" Nuala carefully explained, eyeing him before adding "but Miles, there is something you need to know about magic, the universe gives it at a price. The more powerful, the bigger the payment. Does that make sense to you? Everything is about balance" Nuala cautioned "my people have a saying that the universe restores all, it will always turn out how it is meant to be. The rest is distraction along the way." Miles is watching Nuala, her mouth opening and closing but he has not heard a word. Her voice is faded into the distance. His eyes are on the potion. He sees nothing else. He licks his bottom lip. To be exceptional. To be so very powerful, is all that matters, as he always knew things would be for him one day. But then….his eyes flick up and he is paying closer attention to Nuala. Catching a word from her on the breeze and it floats into his mind directly.

"…The horned God, the embodiment of the hunt, of the primal urges to kill, to devour the flesh. He is awake and if you want powers permanently to destroy the Chosen One and take the planet for your own then you will need to seek him out" Nuala pauses and looks expectantly at Miles, she had planted a seed and now it must be allowed to grow and grow abundantly wild.

"Hold on, what do you mean? There's a way to obtain powers and keep them indefinitely?" Miles asks and Nuala nods.

"If I heard you right, I need to seek out this Horned God and ask him for them and tell him our plans are aligned? He wants the end of the world too?" Miles had so many questions.

"Miles, were you actually listening to me? Of course, you don't just go and find *him*! Why do I even bother with *you!*" She spins round angrily and makes to walk away, but Miles holds her arm.

"Hey, wait. Sorry. I'm listening now. Please don't go. Continue. I'm all ears".

Nuala gives a tight smile, crisp and slightly ruffled. Wrenching his hand away from her upper arm, through slitted eyes of contempt. Her voice takes on a menacing tone, as her black hair whips wildly around her face and her eyes blot over into black pools. "He is the God of the hunt. He is destruction and chaos. He is war. He is death. He is carnage and bloodlust. Battle rage fizzing in form. He is annihilation and there is no seeking him out. He is only kept in balance by the Goddess who is His opposite. She is the living energy of life. Giver of breath and of heartbeats. Caring of all and defender of her blood lines, which is to say all living things. To hurt living things is to offend Her. Polly is the Chosen One of the Goddess and The

Horned God is about to select his champion, to bestow His gift" Nuala ends her torrent of foretelling and her eyes are wide and growing blacker - Miles does not heed this warning.

The sea is swelling and chaotic. Slamming into the rocks beneath the decking. Shouting now, Miles demands "How do I find him and convince him?". Barely audible above the coming of the sea.

Nuala laughs mirthlessly, the sound makes the shadows around them both, bend forward to consume her next words, "He is drawn to carnage and destruction" Nuala slows down her words playing with Miles, who is at the brink of desperation to hear how he appeases The Horned One – his knuckles white on the handrails of the deck. She inhales his energy and feeds on the turmoil, and then continues "Everything you have done so far, the hurt you have inflicted on humanity through your companies. Well, I would say you are on his radar already, but he is drawn to violence physically. The act of violence is an offering to Him. If it is substantial enough to attract his attention then he will find you" Nuala waits now, assessing Miles and his reaction - has Miles taken the bait? No reaction yet, but her words were being weighed and thought through. He is being provoked behind his blue eyes; she could tell that much.

Nuala slowly walks quietly out of the room and slides shut the glass door on the large runner until it gave out a heavy clunking sound. She had played her part well.


Miles heard the door click shut. Holding the vial tenderly in his trembling hand for a while, caressing the tube. Biting his lip and dwelling on how much he wants the powers permanently. He raises the vial to his lips and flings the liquid content back in one gulp. At first, he felt nothing and stands there observing every breath and twitch of his muscles, waiting for a signal from his body that he had changed in some way. Nothing. Ten minutes passes and then another, still nothing happens. A dryness creeps into the back of his throat, very thirsty and dizziness setting in. He walks into the room where the water cooler is stored. Reaching for a paper cup, his fingers brush against the metal cylinder stand of the machine and they leave long indents streaking down the sides. Pulling back his hand, he inspected the damage closely. He then run his hand across the plastic of the upturned bottle, and it instantaneously folds in, and water comes pumping out of the top - gushing over the floor. He starts laughing to himself. A cold, terrible sound. Then he heads over to the oval boardroom table and places his hands underneath. Lifting it up on one side -with ease - standing up straight with the table above him. Balancing it on one hand, he takes a step back and throws the monstrously proportioned furniture through the sheer glass window. The table smashes through, splintering the glass and flies out into the distance. Growing miniscule as it heads over the sea towards the horizon and landing far away into the ocean with a small, faraway 'plop'. Miles starts laughing uproariously to himself. His eyes are wild, unblinking, and roaming. He is unaware that he has lost focus, overwhelmed, and consumed by his abilities. Running forward, he takes one bounding leap and jumps off the deck, over the safety rails and dives headfirst into the ocean.

Emerging several hours later from the water, Miles' eyes are as black as flint and his pale blonde hair, plastered to his head. Cold rivets of water cascade down his chiselled body. He pushes his muscular legs through the riptides of the sea, his feet taking anchor in the stone bed below, dragging a large humpback whale by the tail behind him onto the rocky shore. The Horned God demands carnage, violence and sacrifice of his champion and Miles planned to put on a show that the Horned One would not easily forget.

## Chapter ten - The Wheels of Industry come off.

Over the last couple of weeks Miles has been working with his executive assistants to plan and host an extravagant party on one of his many private islands. The event was being arranged to launch one of his new projects. The new Artificial Intelligence (AI) product had been designed with the capability to act as a personal assistant. The technology can make calls in its owner's voice, arrange appointments through website bookings, schedule repairs around the house, interview staff and a whole lot more - all the things that humans were too busy to do nowadays. The most important part of the product is that it includes the capability to download training material, reprogramming the human brain directly to learn new skills. The software has been condensed into a three-millimetre pod that is proposed to be injected into the base of the neck - the first fully transhuman product that would interact with the subconscious and the conscious part of the brain. Miles required global leaders' approval to go ahead with launching and marketing the tiny device that is expected to have an immense impact. He was arranging to fly out dozens of world leaders and mass- market influencers to his dinner party tonight. To provide a demonstration of the new human hybrid techware and to confirm hefty donations to each leaders chosen cause or to themselves - they got to choose.

He is currently on his private jet flying out to his private island, off the coast of Malibu. When Miles touched down, he intended to go for a swim in his freshwater swimming pool then get ready to host the large-scale event tonight.

The activity of yesterday was on his mind, he had enjoyed the power and felt free of the need for validation that he constantly craved – to be exceptional. The compound had given him his heart's desire but it simply wasn't enough. When he had woken up this morning, he felt empty without it, small and vulnerable, and less somehow - all he knew for sure was that he wanted that feeling permanently. Looking over at the locked briefcase containing the compound, he caresses the smooth black outer casing lovingly. Nuala had given him fourteen vials of the powerful liquid and told him that she needed to make some more. She had promised to meet him in a couple of weeks' time. That is when he had felt an ice-cold feeling in the pit of his stomach. What if she refused to make more? What if the compound run out? What if something happened to her or should he refer to her as it? As she/ it is a shape shifting shadow creature? He shakes his head. He's brain felt muddled and he was getting sidetracked and bogged down in the detail again. All he knew for sure was that he is way too dependent on Nuala. He needs to figure this out, to gain these powers permanently and the only way to do that was to reach out to this Horned God and become His champion.

Miles was on his private jet, looking out of the window. Opening up his laptop and typing in the search engine details of the Horned God, a large number of information excerpts popped up. Hastily, he starts systematically clicking through them. There is a pattern. Repeatedly, the same key words appear over and over again with paganistic symbols follow the letters - *the union of the divine and the animal, which humanity is included in the latter - the consort of the feminine triple goddess - the male triune god of the life stages of the masculine energy; of the warrior, the father and the sage - the oak king - the god of the wild hunt - the god of the witches and witch craft.*

Miles is drawn to a photo and clicks on the icon to expand. An image appears of a large muscular man with a beast like face, broad features and glowing amber eyes with antlers on either side of his proudly held head. The depiction of the God is masculine, broad shoulders and a thick neck held up his head. He had a defined chin, and a virility was pronounced in his taut physique, of the rutting energy of Spring. Underneath the image, there are words that describe the divine balance of feminine and masculine energy, which when in synchronicity, creates harmony, the ability to develop contentment, devotion and love. When one of the energies is out of balance, then the deities become a wildly over exaggerated form of their own power. A dark turmoil unfolds, of struggle and chaotic energy descends upon the universe.

119

The universe can only be fused back into balance by a ritual that is explained in an ancient prophecy in The Tome of Herne. The sect of monks that wrote the Tome were slaves of The Horned God. In defiance, they had recorded the prophecy and hid the ritual inside its pages to restore balance to the universe.

Miles closed his laptop, his eyebrows knitted together, displaying several creases etched into his forehead. Leaning back, he shakes his head again. What he had read does not make sense to him. He cannot understand at all. Why would The Horned God accept balance with the Goddess when he can have power and control over Her and by Himself? It did not make sense to him on any level. What was the value of such balance? He could not comprehend; the explanation was like a lot of gibberish to him. He would help the Horned One by becoming His champion and help Him maintain control to ensure that He reigned supreme and subjugated the Goddess. While Miles was musing, a flight attendant quietly brought over a drink and some fresh exotic fruit salad. In her eyes Miles looks tired and dishevelled, manic even. She hopes that the food and drink would help him relax, as it was his favourite. Her smile was warm, compassionate and kind. He looks through her, anger clouding his vision, and the rage grew within him after reading through the information on his laptop.

After landing on the tropical private island of abundance and scenic beauty, Miles steps off the plane and gets into one of the fleets of electric golf buggies, stationed on the runway. Used to get around the vast island by his guests. The whirring of the buggy echoes as it wends its way into the hills, spiralling along the palm tree-lined roads and up to the main estate of the island.

The island is a tropical paradise, untouched mostly, but kept well equipped, for any and all eventualities. There are ten different saltwater swimming pools, a tennis court, golf course and separate guest and staff accommodation. Underground a bunker and a hydroponic food growing area as well as small patches of farmland above ground. Miles had put in solar panels and a backup hydro-powered generator that run on sea water -

the whole island was run off sustainable energy. Chickens, pigs and goats had been let free to roam in the wild and hunting parties were organised whenever Miles was staying here. Preferring to only eat his own food that he had hunted and harvested himself. Staff were busy decorating the communal eating areas for tonight's celebration. The theme was Black and white. The guests had beautifully and intricately crafted burlesque style masks to wear for entertainment, and also to protect the guests' identities from one another. The entertainment was a mixture of dancers, fire eaters and a global singing sensation was being flown in for a thirty-minute melody performance of all of her most popular soul and R&B hits. The night was planned to be extravagant with no detail and expense spared.

Miles was restless and he kept pacing up and down, he hated these types of events where he needed to be polite and available to all, for long hours that stretched into the night. His six assistants were on edge, knowing that the strain of the party would inevitably mean that he would explode at small details, not being to his liking. Checking and rechecking everything compulsively. He is walking around the marquee reviewing all the finishing touches on the tables with his eagle eyes. He hovers over one particular table for a microsecond longer than the rest. There is a sharp intake of breath from the assembled crowd of staff and then as he nods, and moves on, they all exhale. To the stage he moves and stands in the centre looking up at the lights overhead. Dazzling as they may be, he spots a dullness in the corner and bellows "A bulb is out, get to it now" Off everyone scuttles in different directions, not wanting to look Miles in the eye, least he find something else to shout about.

Eventually, the afternoon fades into evening. The light blue sky gradually turns to dusky orange and pink hues, before settling into darkness. The setting sun is creating a ripple of haze across the deep turquoise water of the ocean and the horizon shimmers. Planes start landing in relays. A few helicopters too. Unloading large numbers of guests. The crowds are of the rich and the powerful. Instantly recognisable from the entertainment and finance industry. Celebrities, politicians, royalty and leaders of corporate industry sectors are walking off of the planes. Dressed in their finest outfits and jewellery, ready for the best of everything to be served and chatting excitedly about the night ahead. The attention to detail is impressive. The groups landing are greeted by swarms of staff, each of the guests have their coats discreetly whisked away. Other staff then step forward to hand out Cristal champagne, served chilled in precious silver flutes. Porters then take their turn to step forward, to escort the guests into electric buggies, and drive them to the large marquees in the grounds. Then, as the vehicles leave the port, there is a flurry of activity as the workforce act like hurried worker bees to start the whole process over again, ready for the next plane to land.

The large marquees gradually fill up with guests dressed in black, white and wearing their elaborate masks and headdresses, of all colours and textiles. There is an excitement in the air, as the food is served, and more champagne is poured. The place abuzz with heightened expectation and speculation of what new advancement in technology is going to be announced tonight. Guests are giddily discussing the topic and making guesses as to what the announcement would be. Some guessed that it would be a robot pet - one like Miles had designed to land on Mars during the Challenger expedition to take samples of the crust to start studying if life could indeed be sustained on the planet. Others speculate that a new virtual reality game-world would be launched, where players are fully integrated and immersed into the platforms that they enjoy playing. The crowd are hungry to get insider views so that they could invest at the start-up point, making millions for the already wealthy crowd.

Suddenly, the tent goes black, as the lights are cut and carefully orchestrated seconds tick by. The blackness is full of expectation, the tension is building, and an excited hysteria breaks out over the crowds. People start chanting *"Miles, Miles, Miles"* and others started hollering and whistling. All are straining to look forward, toward the stage, even though they could only see blackness at this point. Then a small light flickers in the centre of the stage, it grows in size and ferocity then explodes into life, with the announcement of a banging, indoor firework display. Heavy duty lighting springs forth projecting onto the stage. The crowd are on their feet braying and screaming at the high energy activity on centre stage. Miles appears at the top of the tent, under a spotlight. Standing on a glass square that begins moving, downwards in a spiral, circling the inside of the marquee above the crowds and at the halfway point, he jumps down into the flames. Obscured from view. A few seconds past, the crowd are left stunned, turning into horrified silence and then someone starts screaming hysterically and others begin shouting "help him, help him he has fallen" then a tiger's roar could be heard through the speakers. Miles jumps through the fire onto the front platform, then Nuala appears under a spotlight and conjures water streams from her hands and douses out the naked flames. The crowd move from fear to elation then adulation very quickly, realising that this had been part of the show. People get up and clapping their approval at the beginning of the opening of the show. Miles stands in the centre of the stage, and he talks into a microphone that echoes and amplifies his voice around the arena.

"Welcome, welcome all, to the beginning of the next phase of AI and human evolution" and with that announcement, drones appear. Assembling themselves into a moving image of a human brain. Imitating the human brains neuron pulse signals, by rippling like waves. An image of a microchip could be seen being inserted inside the stem of the brain via holographic imagery within the exhibition. Miles was talking the crowd through this new evolutionary technology, that his company had created and owned. He tells the assembled crowd about this new advancement. Humans would be able to interact with the internet with their own thoughts via an AI executive assistant or concierge type programming system and that sensations and imagery would be processed directly into the human brain, reprogramming the brain itself. Humans would believe that they were exploring the rainforest or walking on Mars and physically feel these sensations and experience these things without leaving their homes. AI would access and reprogramme the human consciousness and unconsciousness. The crowds gasp. A new dawn of immersive experiences is here, and the cost would be as little as three hundred pounds sterling, to purchase the tech with an ongoing monthly subscription fee, and every inhabitant of the planet would want one.

"Who's with me in profiteering from the greatest interactive and immersive experience on the planet. We will open the door to transhumanism advancements, which has the capability to download directly into and reprogramme the human brain?" Miles raises his hands over his head, with his fingers splayed open. Calling to his disciples to praise him - the tech Messiah. The crowds leap to their feet and an applause erupts, screaming and shouting out their excitement at the billions of sterling pounds that this new product would generate.

"Tonight, you will all be the first to have the microchips implanted so you can connect with the programming system and explore this brave, new world just waiting to be discovered by every single person on this planet, for a price that is!" thunderous applause reigned in the tent. "You are in a brave new world. The chosen ones to come with me on this journey as we explore humanity's greatest invention" the crowd were going wild and hanging on to each word. "these devices trick the human brain into creating the illusion of being anywhere, doing anything, being anyone you can imagine" screams, yelling and a mass hysteria was rippling through the crowd.

Miles pauses, looks out under the floodlight, over the crowd at all the people excitedly celebrating. He sighs. Throwing down the microphone and whips off his dinner jacket, leaving it in a crumpled heap. Hand on the makeshift stage, he hurriedly jumps down into the audience arena and as planned; a global mega popstar appears on stage behind him. Starting to sing and gyrate to one of her pop classics. A real crowd pleaser. Wearing a crystal covered catsuit and the spotlights shining on her, make her body glitter and sparkle. The crowd jump to their feet, ready to party.

Miles walks through the main part of the tent, lots of people run to him, slapping him on the back and congratulating him on this new product. Miles smiles, he hugs them back and accepts their thanks. Encouraging the party goers to go back to their tables and enjoy themselves. To celebrate and all the while, he is slowly and quietly making his way towards the back doors - towards the exit. He happily leaves the party behind to heat up in the background. Entering the main building, walking through the doors he pulls off his tie and runs upstairs along a parred down stone stairwell and into a large, whitewashed room. There are six black leather two-seater chairs formed in a circle. A sizeable chandelier drips from the ceiling in the middle, casting cascades of prisms of light into the circle that is formed from the positioned chairs. The brilliance of the light leaves an eerie dimness in the outer edges of the room. Down one side of the room, decadent floor to ceiling glazing, opening out onto the marquee below. Five shadowy figures are sat on the chairs and Miles joins them, by sliding into the last remaining chair in the circle.

"Well?" says a thirty-year-old tall, lean Chinese man, who is dressed in a plain grey-blue tunic and tight trousers. He has a penchant for fasting for seventy-two hours a week and eating one meal per day for the remainder of the time, which gives him a very thin physique and keen, warm brown eyes. Trained as a meditation expert and has extensively developed his understanding of brain function to enhance his intelligence.

"Yes, come on we want to hear about their reaction to our new product?" says a Russian woman in her mid-thirties with bleached blonde hair, bright red lipstick and is wearing a black Alexander McQueen couture leather dress. She too is exceptionally thin and tall. Like a spindly black widow spider.

Miles looks around at the other three shadowy figures and each of them lean forward in turn to indicate that they too want to hear what he has to say. The inner circle are assembled in this room, all together. A much older, tall and slim man born in Jerusalem, leans one hand on his thigh and with the other, flourishes his hand in a twirling fashion "Did the monkeys dance out their excitement?" a smile is on his lips, but this did not reach his eyes, remaining cold and cruel, and unflinching. Miles feels uncomfortable in the man's presence. Sensing something hidden within, behind the eyes. Something indescribably cold, but he overlooks this because he admires the man's brain. His strategy and does not look any deeper - for now that is. The other two remain silent, contemplating the words spoken. A gentleman from Africa and a woman from Australia.

"Yes, the product was launched to an overwhelmingly compliant crowd of global influencers and leaders. They are all being injected with the software now. Unsuspecting. They will all promote it via their communication and media platforms, creating a frenzied anticipation and then we will open up for sale in six weeks times, bang on schedule. When the time is right, the implants will deactivate the brain of people selected." Miles explains quite bored with it all.

"Painfully?" says the woman.

Miles shakes his head. "Who knows? We can't exactly bring people back and reactivate someone's brain and ask them about their experience, can we?"

The woman shrugs, and takes a sip of her sparkling water, like it is of no consequence really and doesn't matter either way.

"There is something else?" The Man born in Jerusalem  says with an accusing tone.

Miles is looking at a speck of dust on his black t-shirt and is obsessively trying to remove it. "Miles, is there something else you wish to share with us?" The Man born in Jerusalem  says impatiently.

"Uh, like what?" Miles looks up not really paying attention to the conversation in the room.

"Krones, would you come in here please?" The Man born in Jerusalem shouts out, quite suddenly. What looks like a very tall man,  walks into the room, but he is extraordinarily large and muscular. Intimidating to look at and his jaw is set in a grimace of contempt. He is well built, and a faint glow around him. A ringlet of pure gold on his head.  Behind him Nuala strolls into the room. "Miles, in your own time do give us an update on the seven sacred objects to start the prophecy and your hunt for The Chosen One".

Miles is horrified to see Nuala aligned with The Man born in Jerusalem and he is now concerned about this being called Krones, he looks god-like and terrifyingly strong. He wonders what Nuala had been saying and to whom. Miles peers around the room and decides to remain calm.

"Well, you already know that there is a prophecy and about the ancient ritual and spell that has the power to invoke Armageddon. Three-hundred years of natural disasters that will wipe humanity and all living beings from the face of the earth. To start it, there are seven sacred objects that can give the bearer and their allies unnaturally long life. The seven sacred objects are referred to as; the two feathers given to the chosen, the coin of Malvern, Vessel of Life, the ring of Vusalia, the bone of the elder and the crown of the White Hart and to bind them, something called the tears of the earth is needed.  I have found one of the seven sacred objects, the Vessel of Life but the Chosen One, Polly got to it first and then used it to escape. My spies indicate that the Vessel of Life is stored in a castle in Scotland, in a cave system underground. I and my team are preparing to drop into the place under cover, but we have put the area under surveillance  by a set of miniscule drones first, to understand their defences. We don't want any mistakes……" explains Miles.

"We don't want any mistakes THIS time" says the Man born in Jerusalem, antagonistically. Miles glares at him. Krones roars with laughter at this point.

"Well, I suggest you take Nuala with you THIS time to take the Castle. She can call me if needed" Krones says in his deep, masculine voice and the golden haze emanating from him grew thick and dense, and menacing.

Miles is starting to feel outnumbered and outmatched; he would need to bring forward his plans to catch the attention of The Horned One, he needs the powers gifted and to become His champion.

## Chapter eleven - The Lady's Discovery

Polly is on the lower floors of the castle, working out in the gymnasium. Her lessons today, include continuing to practise fighting with an axe and a sword, as a combination weapon. She had been working on honing this technique, developing the style over months. The Chosen One is now an accomplished weapons expert. Her favourite is her axe-wielding combat drills, much to Eleanora's disdain - this skill took the pagan witch years to perfect.

Eleanora is watching with a critical eye as Polly starts twirling the axe overhead and then jumping up and kicking out sideways at imaginary assailants, before gently landing and catching the handle, as the axe comes down with the force of an almighty blow - this is a sequence move that she has honed to utter perfection.

Eleanora tuts and shouts "Showing off like you are the lord of thunder won't save you in a battle, youngling."

The Lady, Esme laughs at her sister's gruffness towards her student. Polly looks round at Eleanora, wide eyed, with a smirk on her face, while she commences juggling the axe, the Sword of Hestia and her throwing knives in the air with one hand.

"Neither will acting like a buffoon clown" Eleanora continues with a disapproving sniff, arms folded. Polly clucks her tongue, crosses her eyes, all the while continuing to smile broadly to herself. Ignoring Eleanora's moods with joviality, had become a particularly happy pastime for Polly these days, it really seems to irritate the pagan witch.

Crossing the arena with long strides, Polly takes down from the wall brackets, a long bow and arrow set. Expertly lining up the arrow to her eye and then proceeds to hit three bullseyes in a row, in short succession and then mischievously turns to aim the arrow at Eleanora. She let's go and the arrow glides, with a dead shot through the air, on target to hit Eleanora between the eyes. Before it lands, the weapon turns into a beautiful, full headed rose and plonks Eleanora gently on the nose. "A gift for you my mentor" Polly shouts out with a laugh.

Eleanora had not even flinched, so certain was she that The Chosen One would never hurt her but she did bellow. Going red in the face, she shouts "No time for pranks when we are trying to stop the planet from being destroyed by the coming of an ancient prophecy.". Polly raises her delicate eyebrows and giggles once more, at the vexatious witch.

Esme is intently watching the exchange "Sister, must you be so hard on the chosen one? She pretends that she is not, but she is quite sensitive of spirit. She adores you and wants your approval. Go a bit easier on her please" The Lady Esme says quietly, not letting Polly overhear the conversation.

"She can't be the Chosen One and soft like a soggy piece of bread, Esme. You know what she must face" Eleanora huffs.

"Well, she is sensitive, and everything will all come together in her own time, Eleanora. The girl needs to feel love and goodness, to know the value of what she fights for and is trying to save. It may matter in the end a great deal" The Lady Esme, says this with care and then looks over at Polly in the centre of the gym, standing on her own. With a sudden insight and realisation, understanding dawned on Esme's face. "Are you behaving this way more for your own sake than for Polly? so that you don't grow too attached to the girl, Eleanora?"

Eleanora spins around and looks startled at her sister. With haste, she turns away and picks up an axe mounted on the wall and shouts to Polly "Okay, you've had enough fun, Pollux. Let's see your defensive stance, now fight." With that Eleanora jumps in the air and without any further warning, brought her axe down in a wide sweeping motion on Polly. Polly grins and rises to the challenge. Jumping up in the air and spins around as fast as a tornado. Sword held aloft, to meet Eleanora head on. The clash of metal against metal rings out in the stillness of the combat arena. Sparks glint off the weapons, as Eleanora bore the brunt of the full force of the Chosen One's mighty strength. The older woman falls backwards, staggering directly into a large barrel of water, bottom first. The water sploshes up, covering the floor and Eleanora is drenched. Polly laughs a little too hard and The Lady does to. Holding her ribs in pain as the bones are still healing. Eleanora grumbles and then leaps forward, out of the wooden barrel and starts drying herself off with warm air from her glass wand. Eleanora looks round and can't help but notice her sister laughter for the first time in ages. Suddenly, feeling elated that her sister had found her joy, and Eleanora could not help but to laugh too. The three women held on to each other and enjoyed the joke together. Polly leans forward and touches Eleanora's hair to see if it is drying. Eleanora in turn, takes Polly's hand along with her sister's, Esme's. Holding them both to her heart. There they stand silently together.

The Professor bolts into the gymnasium without ceremony or announcement. He is holding up a very old and worn, leather bound book in front of his face. It's called The History of Witches. Reading from the tome rather loudly and excitedly, when he first bursts into the room. He finally looks up at the three women standing there and realises that he has interrupted a very special moment. A moment in time that stretches into forever, as it cements the bond between the three women.

"Oh, I'm sorry. I'll come back in bit" offers the Professor in a quiet, softer voice, as he turns to make his way back out of the room.

"No, no, please do come in, the lesson is over, and your lessons are just as important as the one I have just been taught, about humility" Eleanora says this with a smile at Polly, who responds with letting go of Eleanora's hand and squeezing her arm. Esme gives a nod and knowing smile and wipes a tear away discreetly, from her eyes too.

The Professor looks confused, and his bushy white eyebrows knit into a line, but he did not ask any more of the three women. He could feel the energy in the air and there were pink plumes of oxytocin surrounding the three women, so he knew the love-bound was strong in the air – the bonding chemical.

"Ahhh, I see. Well, where was I? Yes, I was just looking through this book, The History of Witches and I suspect I may have happened upon the witch that Polly and Balan destroyed in the cave in Russia. It is a most disturbing entry about this witch, and I wanted to share it with you all immediately."

Polly stirs, something in the way that the Professor had said this made her think about Balan and his unusual rudeness on the plane coming back to the United Kingdom. "Professor, what is it?" Polly says with an urgency that she didn't quite understand herself.

"Well, the book is about famous witches that had a significant impact on world history" the professor says, very gravely "and there is an entry that I wish to share. Centuries ago, a girl was born called Cordelia Herron, the daughter of a farmhand. Her family were very poor. Legend has it that she traded with a demon for some food for her family and in exchange, the demon would own her soul when she passed over. As we know this would stop the poor girl's energy from rejoining the universe. Well, what the demon didn't know was the poor girl had magical powers to extract essence from living things and move energy around, to channel that energy to make things grow very fast, things like seeds springing into an abundance of fully grown plants. That sort of thing. Well, as she got older, she regretted the measly trade that she had made at a very young age. She had been angry at herself for being foolish and started to learn black magic. At first, this was to understand how she could defeat the demon but then her ambitions grew along with her lust for the dark arts and power. She started to enjoy the blackness she wielded. To prolong her life, she would feed from the energy of young children to absorb their essence and avoid death. She had the ability to possess humans too, and consume the powers of magical folk, and was feared by magics and non-magics alike. Anyway, she did kill the demon that she had made a pact with. Then there are records about her raising an army of humans with dark souls and magical folks and demons too. She would lead the armies to exterminate whole villages to feed on their life force and plunder their wealth. Eventually, this level of carnage and imbalance drew to her the attention of the Goddess. The Goddess sent her High Priestess and the armies of the light to contain the issue. The High Priestess found Cordelia who was then known as the Black Dahlia, and she was found in Russia. The text goes on to tell of a great battle between good against evil and The High Priestess imprisoned the evil witch in a cave as she was too powerful to be killed. I assume, this was in Oymyakon as the description in the book depicts a freezing cold land. The witch that you came across in the cave, please tell me some more about her and the circumstances of her death."

Polly drew a breath, slightly mesmerised by the Professor's words, and she closes her eyes, strangely, she is unable to recall an image of the witch.

"I can't seem to see her, something is blocking my view", says Polly, straining to concentrate and see the witch in her mind's eye, holding her fingers up to her temples.

Eleanora steps forward, "That is odd, who would be blocking the Chosen One's view?" she says.

"Let's not worry too much about this for now. Polly, tell us what happened please?" says the professor "I fear this is most important."

"Well, Balan, Chris and I walked into an enchantment. We were in a snow blizzard up a mountain and all of a sudden, we strayed into a summers dream. Chris was enchanted but Balan and I were not. Chris led us to the witch's lair, and I smashed the source of the enchantment, which was a mirror" Polly hesitated, her eyes were closed as she started to recall the grizzlier details. She took a deep steadying breath "and then, well, and then, Balan and I went into the cave. It was horrific. Bones of children littered the floor" Polly's voice grew unsteady, she held a sob in her throat "Balan was seen, and I crept forward hidden. Balan fought with the witches. There were three of them and then I stepped out and the witch showed me what she had done all those years ago. She had killed thousands upon thousands of innocents to save herself and I cut her down, the leader. I think the other two were frightened of her. I saw the High Priestesses spell and it appeared as an archway, glowing in the dark so I knew the lead witch had been imprisoned in that cave." Polly closes her eyes, seeing the faces of the victims, once more.

"Anything else? The details are very important. Please think. Did anyone lose control at all?" enquires the Professor, "The Witch known as the Black Dahlia exploited the vulnerable, at points of particular weakness. She needed to lure them into a certain point of vulnerability and then she could inhabit them. What happened when she died?"

Polly hesitates, it's a small detail, but she recalls Balan's tears that day, but feels she would betray him to the others, sharing his secret. "No, I don't know, I'm not sure." Polly says, looking away from their concerned faces. The Professor peers at Polly, with an assessing look in his eyes. She knows he can tell she is withholding something.

"Let us be sure this is the same witch. Polly please try to recall the image of her. Did she look like this?" The Professor holds up a hand drawn picture of the witch, the Black Dahlia. Polly recoils from the image, in alarm from the familiarity of the darkness of the eyes.

Polly closes her eyes and shakes her head again "I cannot see her. Please don't make me think of those horrors again."

"Let me try to help" The Lady Esme slowly walks forward, holding her ribs tenderly as she does. Places her hand on Polly's forehead. Releasing a spell to support clarity. Immediately, upon the touch, the thrumming starts building in Polly's ears. Her own heart is drumming against her chest, she cannot breathe, and she is struggling against the hand of the Lady. A discomfort arises and then all of a sudden, a surge of power, in the form of red and orange lights, exploding out of Polly. Knocking The Lady and Eleanora and The Professor to the ground. They are pinned there underneath a raging wind. As Eleanora forces her head up against the powerful stream of energy, she looks at the Chosen One. Polly is engulfed in flames of golden mist that are the shape of a winged dragon of mythical proportions. It grows large in the light pulsating out of Polly. Sulphurous smoke, undulates and curls its way around the gymnasium, covering everyone and everything in its wake. The Chosen One stands proud and tall before the image of the dragon. It dwarfs her by its size. Polly's eyes are but amber slits, like a lizard and from her nostrils, fire streams forth around the room, and the castle trembles.

Balan had not returned to the castle after the plane journey home. He was wandering in the fields of Glossop, near Herne Hall. On his back is a large rucksack, bumping up and down vigorously, while he is walking the rugged, wild paths. His tent and sleeping bag tightly packed within, along with portable cooking equipment. Wild camping and living off the land, was a favourite pastime of his at present. He found himself craving isolation. Still brooding over the incident on the plane. Left feeling very misunderstood by Chris and Polly, and slightly confused with himself, if he were to be completely honest. *Why had he said those things to Polly?* He was rubbing at a strange tightness in his chest while he was thinking about this. What he did not want to admit to himself, was that he felt embarrassed at his behaviour in the cave, being reduced to tears by words. Words from evil mouths, but he had crumbled nonetheless at hearing his childhood played back to him and his fears presented to him by the witches, three.

Balan shook his head, to shake the memories of that fateful day in the cave, from his mind. He stumbled on, unseeing in a fog of regret. His feet were carrying him forward, to a destination not entirely of his own choosing, but he was not paying enough attention - still smarting from the way his friends had behaved towards him. The deep ache in his stomach, was of feelings of being let down, yet he preferred to say to himself that he was feeling hungry. More than admit that he really was aching for his friends to say sorry to him, so he could return home.

A stile appeared in the distance, and he clambered over it. Noticing, he was in the field at the edge of the Herne Hall estate – The Lady's lands and where the academy of magic is. With each step forward, the Manor house was coming into clearer view. The banners and ancient Coat of Arms of the Herne Family, detailing a huge stag surrounded by roses on one side and a majestic sword in the other, on display. As he got closer, the ground changed to a crunching underfoot, as the grass gave way to neat, sand coloured gravel pathways, that led up to the stately house. The smell of wet grass hangs in the air, mixed in with forest fauna. Stags, and deer and other

136

small woodland animals, could be seen, outlined in the thickly dense forest. Ospreys, and kites and other birds of prey were twirling and flying overhead. A huge stag loomed out from between the trees and tentatively smelt the air, blowing out his nostrils in an agitated fashion. Balan prided himself on the instant bond he was able to form with animals and creatures, due to his caring disposition. On this day, however, he looked at the stag's eyes, which were wide and bleak, and he stopped in his tracks. The stag brayed out a warning to Balan, but he did not heed the animals bellowing call. Slowly, he continued walking forward. Inconceivable to him, that the animal would feel threatened by his approach. He still did not stop when the animal lowered its head and began pounding its large hooves on the ground aggressively. Then, reared and charged at Balan. The stag struck out with its antlers, digging into Balan's arm and puncturing his skin. Again, the animal reared and again, he was punctured but this time the great stag impaled him by the belly. Picking him up on his great antlers and flung him into the long grass, covered overgrowth. Where he lay, slowly bleeding out, and assumed dead by the animals and insects, scurrying around him.

Later on, that same day, a girl from the academy, was walking through the woods. Picking bluebells and forget me knots. Admiring nature in full bloom, in the forest glade. As she was walking a patch of long grass, she came across Balan's long, stretched out form. The girl was a healer, so started to tend to his bruises and wounds, while he remained unconscious. The punctures took a while to clean, rebind and heal, as they were very deep, but eventually, she was satisfied that he could be moved. Placing her hands on Balan's head, floating him upwards, ready to move him towards Herne Hall.

In Balan's dream state, he was surrounded by wind, which was whipping around him like ice blades. Tearing at his goose bumped flesh. The high-pitched screeching from the gales was deafening. Piercing his eardrums. He was surrounded by blackness, whichever way he looked, and he felt ice cold and alone. A small shadow kept reaching forward, toward him, through the winds and with its small arm, trying to grab at him. He took out a dagger and slashed at it once, twice and then stabbed forward and it left, but the wind continued screaming in his ears.

Deliriously, Balan battled the darkness and the wind in that dark place. He was lost, in an eerie landscape. Locked in his own body and in a state of confusion. A black figure was stalking him, coercing him, and corroding his sense of self, with its blackness of speech.

A couple of days passed in that place, while his body lay still in the wood. Balan in his delirium with a burning temperature, remained on the floor while the sun and the moon took turns to move across the sky, but he, in his isolation of sickness, did not notice them. By the third day, he could hear the bird calls and squirrels scurrying in the woods and all around. The sounds of life were in the distance, like an echo in his mind but were reassuringly there. When he surfaced from unconsciousness, he immediately retched out yellow bile from the bottom of his stomach onto the grass, as he had not eaten or taken in any fluids for days. His eyes were puffy, and his face was bloated, with the inflammation left over from his body fighting off the infection. Blurry vision and crusted eyelashes, made orientating himself difficult and near impossible. He croaked out a spell to conjure water and gulped down urgently the nectar of life, until his dehydration was less severe. His head was spinning, he had flashing lights behind his eyelids. Washing his eyes sparingly with a few drops of the water, all he could hear was the buzzing of thousands upon thousands of blow flies. Swarming next to him. They were butting and lazily flying into his face and arms. He, at first, thought it was rain, due to the multitude of the contacts. As he opened his eyes and the crust had dissolved, he was presented with a sight that made him wish for eternal blindness. A young girl laid there besides him, cold as ice, soulless. Her flesh was dehydrated like it had been drained of all moisture and energy and her eyes were glassy, staring, dead ahead. A look of fear was on her face and his dagger was protruding from her ribs where her heart used to beat and thrum.

Balan stood there, quite still. Confusion spiralled in his mind and the realisation crept slowly up his neck and trickled over his brain, and thoughts of murder tickled at his mind. "No, this cannot be" he says to himself horror struck.

"Yes, yes. It is before your eyes" whispered the dark stalking shadow in his ear.

Balan put his hands over his ears and crouched low, a sickness slid into the back of his throat. "No, No, No, No,No……" he cried to himself, rocking on his heels. A laughter careened on the wind around him. The dark shadow took the form of Polly, but it was grey and blank, a peculiar replica of the human form. The shadow placed its hand on his shoulder, imitating her touch, her safety. He was confused.

"Come, there is something that will make you feel better in the basement of the manor house. The ancient magic will help you forget yourself" The shadow creature gently crooned.

"Polly, shouldn't we bury her?" Balan says, eyes wild and red rimmed, looking quite insane. All traces of the laid back, likeable and confident young Black man were gone.

"The flies will dispose of her for us. Her energy has been devoured to restore us. She will rapidly decay. Now, come now beloved vessel. Come, let us go to the Manor House and then on to the School."

## Chapter twelve - Webs of deceit

Rigidly walking towards the Manor, Balan was able to see out of his own eyes, but he did not have control over his limbs. He could see that small creatures and birds were fleeing before him as he walked beside the shadow-Polly. Trapped inside his body, he does not hear any bird calls or gentle tapping of woodpeckers in the woodland. He is cut off from the natural world, imprisoned in a dark shadowy place that evokes a sense of cold dread. Walking the gravel path up to the manor house, he can no longer hear the crunching of the gravel underfoot. He is in a tunnel underground imprisoned in his own body and the echoes of the outside world are being fed to him in this small place he inhabits inside. He is screaming to connect to his own body, to feel sensation in present time but it does not come. The shadow is all around and it consumes him. His own fear is numbing him, so he does not feel the full brunt of the pain he is in - the isolation. The gentle plodding of his feet moving up and down on the path, remind him of the days where the joy of life was with him with every breath he took. The grief settles in, and he laments those times he took for granted. Of the life not fully experienced, always waiting for something else, to be someone else.

They arrive at last at the door to the manor house, the opening is large and made of wood and of iron. **I R O N**. The word held meaning. In fables, darkness and shadows are frightened of iron. It is a long-held fear for evil.

He strains to hold his body back to observe. The shadow recoils the closer it gets to the metal. The particles of the creature of shadow start to seep back into his body, joining him and to bind itself within his chest - like a snake slipping and coiling itself into a wicker basket. A tall, thin woman dressed in tweed and sensible boots comes out of the door and she greets him warmly. He can hear her say "Hello Balan. We weren't expecting you. Is the professor here with you?".

As he walks closer, she gets a good look at him. "Balan, are you ok? You look dreadful. Come in, come in. What happened?"

The housekeeper takes my hand to guide me, but I feel nothing but this blankness, not even of my hand being touched and elevated by hers. I can't even really hear her words. They are muffled to my ears. I am being walked into the vast hallway, clean and decadent, familiar but to my eyes, grotesquely ordinary and far away. How dare it be ordinary when I am walking in this place of pain. I scream from inside of my own body "I am in here. Please help me" but I am unheard as the lips of my body have not uttered a sound to her. The housekeeper is shouting to get the attention of the other staff now with some urgency. My eyes are shaking, my head is butting against my chest. The housekeeper is no longer calm. She is screaming for help. The hallway is spinning and the black and white marbled tiles are coming closer and closer, until my head rebounds off of them and my eyes flicker open and shut until the blankness takes hold.

My body is laid down in a soft bed. I know this much because when my eyes flicker open, like shutters on an automatic timing mechanism, I am facing the ceiling, looking upwards. Moving my head requires energy and I can only take hold of my body when the shadow creature is otherwise engaged or distracted. Gradually turning my head, my eyes are on the large wardrobe and chest of drawers. "Great, I am dying. Possessed by a demon and I can't even see out of the bloody window and onto the huge expanse of blue sky" I say to myself inside of my prison that is my body. I silently mourn the small things that I have taken for granted all of my short life. But in my despair, I keep looking closer. I can begin to see the creativity in the wardrobe and chest of drawers. The ingenuity of the human spirit. It is there in the design of the wood. The loving way it has been handcrafted in shape, the handles that have been carefully selected, in the sanding down and varnishing, I can see the carpenter working on the wood, every break taken during the process while they sat and stared out of the window daydreaming - they are here with me. I see every human that has ever been creative, and they are with me, here in this space and for all of time. I sob, I cry for my lost connections.

The door opens of the room my body is laid in. It is the Professor, my heart soars and a prickling feeling of hope tingles in my stomach. He is accompanied by Toni. Dear sweet Toni, Polly's best friend, the healer witch with such immense power that she became addicted to it last year so she mustn't use the power for a while. They look pale and frightened looking down at me. The Professor is talking to me in a soft voice like the ones used in a Chapel of Rest.

Yes, I've seen a few dead bodies in those places, mostly family members but one of them was my best friend when I was eight years old. He died, choked on his own vomit from an illness that doctors were baffled by. "Unlucky" he was labelled but I was the unfortunate one, I was left behind.

I was taken to the Chapel. All of the adults from social services decided that I would need some time to say goodbye to him before the funeral, so I was not overwhelmed. Lots of psychobabble that indicated they didn't really have a clue. The adults walked me into the Chapel that day and watched me, waiting for me to scream and cry and howl out my pain, but all I could feel was a blanket of numbness. There was a dead body in the room with me, with make-up plastered on its face, to look like a living face, which made it a terrible and grotesque joke.

I remember the reek of death lingering in the air and for weeks afterwards as I tried to wash it out of my nostrils. I could smell the reek wherever I went - it followed me as a child. I was scared that others could smell it on me too. The face in the Chapel, was the face of my best friend but it was waxen and unfamiliar to me. There was no person inside; all the scraped knees, showing off, laughter and skateboarding, beatboxing and terrible jokes had gone up into the ether somewhere. I stood there in that Chapel of Rest confused, unsure of how to behave, or to perform so that the adults in the room would say "he has said his goodbyes" and let me leave the place that had stolen my best friend. I disconnected from myself that day and stared out of the window in the Chapel for what felt like hours and that is how I feel now. My face pressed up against a window looking out into the world around me, disconnected and alone – my body belonging to someone else.

The Professor's lips are moving and then he casually mentions Polly. POLLY. He is saying that she told him about the Black Dahlia. I heard Polly's name loud and clear and in focus – I felt myself reclaim my body for a second. Her name must be powerful for some reason, I pocket that information and I stir. For the first time in a long while hope blooms up before me. That is when the shadow came stalking in and took over my body from me, and I am pushed into the background once more. Held inside against my will.

"Professor, I'm so glad to see you" the shadow says and sat up in the bed pretending to be me, alert with a painted smile on its shadowy face. "I was attacked by a stag. I think it may have been protecting its young and felt threatened for some reason" It smiled, and the Professor nodded but a strange look came over Toni's face, she looked curiously at the body of Balan and the shadow creature imitating me. ME. *Toni, I'm in here I shouted.* The Shadow carried on talking and says "You mentioned the Black Dahlia earlier. Was that the witch in the cave, then?" and The Professor nodded. It went on "Polly was alone with the Witch for a long while and she was crying and screaming at one point. I hope she has recovered from the ordeal. Poor sweet Polly"

The Professor looked concerned "Tell me Balan, did Polly seem ok after the encounter with the witch?" Toni looked at the figure of Balan and watched carefully as it responded "She kept getting angry and put a spell on a group of villagers, which is unusual for her. Why do you ask, is she ok?" a seed had been planted and the Professor took the bait, looking deeply concerned.

The next thing that the shadow says disgusts me and I scream out unheard "Professor, if The Chosen One was to ever turn bad, there is a way to stop her, isn't there?" The Professor looked nauseous, closing his eyes tightly to shut out the distress, but he managed to weakly nod in the affirmative and Toni's eyes grew wide with incredulity at the discussion and the scandalous, disloyal implications of the words uttered by the body of Balan. They both say their goodbyes and rushed out of the room. Their angry words at each other could be heard in the hallway. It sits there laughing and I am imprisoned, watching hopelessly at the wreckage being done to my life and the deceit that is being woven by the shadow into the fabric of truth.

143

Later that same day, something is happening. My body is being floated downstairs in the middle of the night. There is this feeling of being held up by air and floating downwards. I strain to look round and there is a young boy with his arm stretched out over me and he has in his hand a glass wand. From it he has cast a spell and we are both moving down a staircase that is made of glass and wood. It is dark down here, unnaturally black and I am getting an ill feeling of dread in the darkness opening out in front of us both. I look closely at the boy and his eyes are white. The shadow has hold of him like she has hold of me. We come to a stop at the end of the stairwell, the boy and me. We are captives to The Dark Witch Queen's will. A large door is on the other side of the hallway and a cold that chills the bones settles around us. The boy takes out a black key and within seconds, it inserts itself in the keyhole and starts turning by itself. I hover there helplessly, doomed to watch as the ghastly events unfold. The door creaks open and we both move forwards, he on his legs and I am floating under the spell on my back.

The room is cavernous and large, lit with black candles with flames of black, purple and blue. There are dark artefacts and trinkets on each shelf and in glass boxes all around the room. The shadow-Polly slips out of me on a stream of dust particles and then manifests itself into a shadow creature with a blank face. It looks round the room as if searching for something. It finds it, the smoky particles that help it move, start glittering black and wisping forward, towards an old, battered silver box with intricately carved runes on the sides. The Dark Witch calls the boy over to be close to it. I scream to try to stop him from going near the shadow. The boy cannot hear me and he flicks his wand, and I am laid gently down on the floor. He does this so very carefully, so I am unhurt. This gesture sums up the boy. He moves forward to stand in front of the silver object. His little innocent fingers lifting the lid and he takes out a vial made of glass and silver; the stopper is decorated with a coiled snake. The shadow whispers in his ear and he opens the vial, and the little boy drinks the potion within. Standing stock still he is while the shadow creature rears up behind him and merges its smoke like hands into each temple at either side of the boy's head. A dazzling blue light appears. The boy turns into a shrivelled, shrunken and devoured thing, lifeless. He falls motionless to the floor. She is in solid form now. Her hair is raven black, she is tall and is now licking her fingers to devour the last remaining essence of the boy.

That is when she turns to me, creeping forward, a wickedness glinting in her eyes, and she changes into smoke and nestles in my chest. The dark witch queen is expanding, her energy is crushing me, suffocating me. I can no longer breathe. With my last breath, I shout out "Polly."

And like grains of sand blowing away over time, she removes me from myself, I drift away particle by particle, up into the ether. Released from this earth and I am gradually…

N    o    M    o    r                    e.

Another party is being organised by Miles' team of event coordinators. This was a smaller gathering than the last. Consisting of two thousand of the guests that were invited to the last launch event and, a further thousand more people were invited. Made up of social media influencers with followers of one hundred people or less. Mile's coordinators did think this an unusual choice given the need to promote the new product but no one dared to raise it.

The guests were asked to keep the event secret until after launch night. To ensure that they did as instructed, the invitation was accompanied by a set of Non-Disclosure Agreement documents, and a box that contained cartier jewellery, bottles of Cristal champagne and a gold covered mobile phone, with the promise of more freebies at the event. Who could say no to such an extravagant offer?

The Company Agents were out in force and overseeing the event and its security detail. This was to be an outdoor party, held in the sprawling Beverly hills estate that Miles owned on the edge of Calabasas. As guests arrive, they are injected with the new software chip, as a condition of entry. This did not take that much persuasion as they all seemed thrilled to be the first to have one of these highly sort after devices. Music was blaring out of the speakers dotted around the acres of land. The paths were lit up with twinkling lights, which would lead the guests to a place that is off of the manicured residential land. Out into a canyon. A deep recessed area below the main building. All is quiet there; all is dark in this hidden valley and the guests assume this is like the other event where there was a carefully orchestrated building up of the introduction to the product - but they are very wrong.

When all the guests are assembled in the darkness and all three thousand souls are gathered on the same plot of land. A large, tall beacon is lit. Built of wood and tree branches, and it had been stacked before a shrine. A warlock starts to speak in a dialect not heard in centuries. His voice booming out over the canyon and his speech reverberates all around, not through speakers but through the power of the spell that is being recited. The night sky that was once a velvety and welcoming navy blue full of twinkling lights, is now darkened by heavy and thick black clouds. A stillness settles on the crowd of apprehensive exhilaration. Miles looks on, shrouded in a hooded cloak. He is waiting before the shrine with bated breath. Eventually, the priest comes to the end of the rite and nods to give Miles his cue. Miles deliriously happy, as he finally raises his hands to the sky and bellows "Find me worthy to serve you as your Champion oh Horned One and take this offering as a gift from me" and with this pledge to serve Him, he pushes a button and three thousand detonators bleep simultaneously and flicker red in the darkness. It is foretold that the Champion must be born from blood, after all.

Miles wakes up in bed at his Calabasas estate, the next day. Remembering nothing of the night before. With the exception, he was visited by The Horned One in a dream, and He stank of testosterone and was half crazed with animalistic wildness. The Horned One had gibbered relentlessly about the Goddess and her cold rejection of him in his current decrepit form. Paranoia and dizzying intellect stretched forth from The Horned God, like dark shadows, shocking Miles' fragile human mind. He commanded Miles to complete three tasks before he would give him the mantle of His Champion.

Miles felt disorientated and remembered that he must complete the three tasks set and these were; to injure the enemy and take the crown of a demi-God. The last task was pretty impossible, and it was to enter the realm of the underworld and bring back to the lord of the hunt, his broken horn. Miles sighed and reached for a vial and decided that there was no time like the present to get on with the task at hand.

## Chapter thirteen - To be the Seer of Truth

*There is a story of old that tells of a stone. This is no ordinary stone but one with great power, it can be used to save the natural world when it needs protecting. Well, more specifically, the stone can rebalance the energies of the universe – restore natural order. The fact is the ancient stone is the heart of the universe. Used to bond back together humankind with nature, restoring our natural symbiote relationship with the life force of the earth, with the cosmos and of the universe - with everything. The stone is known as the Heart of the World. To perform this extraordinary feat of magic , a powerful being needs to heat the stone to temperatures not of this world, to turn back to its original state of lava – the tears of the Earth. Through its tears, it can reverse the damage of a dying planet. The stone along with the seven objects of power, all symbols of nature and the universe, must be brought back together at the right time at the High Seat of the Universe. The outcome of the prophecy will depend on whether good or evil, brings them back together and whoever sits upon the High Seat, will share their energy, sealing the fate of us all.*

*Let us hope for all our sakes it is the Chosen One of legend. The alternative does not bear thinking about just now.*

*The thrumming heart beats within this stone and in us all, we are linked to it. Touch your heart and you will feel it too, you have just forgotten the power of the one. The stone is sending out a message, calling out throughout the universe to awaken humans and the ancient beasts of legend that will support the legend to come to life.*

\*\*\*

Polly has her air pods in, listening to music by herself, completing some mundane chores at home. An old 80s classic comes on her playlist, Salt N Pepa's Push It. The beat takes over. Slowly at first, she starts tapping her foot and then swinging her hair, moving in time with the beat and then she starts to fully let go. Gyrating round the hallway. Dancing and singing for her imaginary audience. Her cat Indy is watching her from the sofa, with a look of utter disinterest on his feline face. Unimpressed, laying with his stomach fully extended, legs akimbo and his paws up in the air. The song is coming to an end. The Chosen One leaps up in the air, landing lightly and slides on her knees, across the hallway floor towards the front entrance door. Nearing the end of the slide, she opens her eyes. There, towering above her is Toni, on the brink of bursting into laughter and the Professor, who at this time, is looking at her with an assessing gaze. It's as though the words he is thinking are etched like ancient runes across his face *'oh dear, she has gone quite mad. What with turning into a mystical dragon yesterday and now this, she maybe possessed after all.'*

Polly whips her Air pods out and jumps up off of her knees, onto her feet in one neat bound.

"Polly, sorry to interrupt your, erm, chores but we must discuss something with you, quite urgently" the Professor Rothschild says, with a serious tone to his voice. His eyebrows wiggling the whole time he is talking.

"Yes, sorry but we really must *Push It* along and have this conversation now." Toni says lightly, with a huge grin on her face.

"Well, I wouldn't expect you to delay. Let us *asSalt* the issue together" Polly replies with a grin on her face.

"That's… *Real Good*" says Toni in a sing song voice, and with that both young women crack up laughing and can't seem to stop themselves.

The Professor looks at Polly and then at Toni, quite bewildered and then wonders if someone has placed a spell on the pair of them so arranges his face in a sympathetic gesture, but inside he is confused "Yes, well, I think I will let Toni explain and then please do come and find me in the library when you have finished getting ready" the Professor says, excusing himself from the room. Polly was holding her stomach and Toni was wiping away tears of laughter from her feline shaped eyes.

"Seriously girl, I've got something to tell you and you might want to sit down" Toni says, quite gravely. The atmosphere changed in a second.

Polly gasps, eyes wide "has somebody died? Oh my god, please tell me someone hasn't died."

"No, but Balan might after you've heard this" Toni looks seriously at her friend and touched her shoulder tenderly "let's sit down." They both walked through the hallway into the lounge to make themselves comfortable on the sofa. Toni explained what happened and of Balan's comments, raising questions about Polly and her judgement. Insinuating that she couldn't be trusted. Polly sat there quietly listening. She did not want to overreact, so she sat there with the sickly distaste of Balan's treachery in her mouth. The upset shone from her eyes and her eyelashes were wet with the onset of tears.

"Hey, I'm telling you this, so you know. There was something a bit off about it. Balan didn't seem himself and his aura was grey nearly black. Are you okay hearing this?" Toni suddenly blurts out, worried for her friend.

"What, like he was under a spell do you mean?" enquired Polly "you couldn't show me the exchange could you?" Polly asks.

"Yes, of course. Do you have a stone basin with river water? They give the clearest vision in my opinion" responds Toni with the insight of an academic on all things magical these days.

"Sure, it's over by the window" Polly takes Toni's hand and they both walk over to the other side of the room together. "Erm, are you supposed to be using your powers yet? I don't want you to anything that effects your recovery" Polly says, concerned and referring to Toni's addiction to using magic that was made evident by the events of last year.

"It's only a little spell, Pol assault. It will barely register at all" Toni says reassuringly. Polly looked doubtful but was guided by her friend's good judgement on this.

The stone basin is stored on the windowsill, in a place that opens out onto the sea. It is a beautiful sunny day outside, with blue skies overhead and gulls calling to one another in the distance. There is a calm rhythmic motion to the huge expanse of water below and marine life of all kinds is visible in the shallower parts of the Great North Sea. A pod of dolphins can be seen skipping and playing on the surf nearby. Toni pours the fresh river water into the basin then swirls it round with the tip of her finger, all the while charging the water with a golden electric energy. The crackling energy moves down her arms, through her fingertips and into the liquid and it sizzles. Her eyes are cloudy as she is sharing the vision and placing it in the water so Polly can see.

Polly leans over the stone bowl and the image of Balan swirls into view, on the water surface. There he is, laying down on the bed motionless, staring into the distance with tears in his eyes. Then all of a sudden, when Toni and the Professor walk into the room, a dark shadow crosses over the face of Balan and then he sits up, with a strange smile on his face, not quite reaching his eyes. The body of Balan is sitting there talking to Toni and the Professor just as it had happened during the visit. The eyes start to turn black like ink, including the outer area of the eyes. Polly is watching the images in the basin, as a thick fog of blackness extends forward and undulates around the room, engulfing everything in its path. The face of Balan tilts upwards and the creature's eyes connect directly with Polly, piercing through the darkness in the room. It can see her. An arm extends forward and a bony thin finger points at Polly. The index finger curls back, and Polly feels herself lift off the ground. She is being pulled under a dark spell into the room within the basin. Polly grips on the masonry of the windowsill, but she can't hold on against the force and it starts to crumble away in her hands, she is tipping forward. Losing her grip, her head and torso are in the room and her toes are just about managing to keep a hold on the floor in her apartment.

"Toni, help me, help me please" she yells and Toni in a trance, is roused. Her eyes are jet black, but her friends' frantic calls awaken something within her. Toni unfastens her stuck hands from the basin, she holds them up, palms facing towards the sun. With an almighty crack of power, golden light meets blackness of energy, and a colossal 'BANG' emits over the basin and cracks it apart, and into two. Sending the two young women flying backwards across the room and smashing them with a ferocious force, into the wall.

Polly is up on her feet immediately, but Toni is dazed and confused, the blackness that was infecting her eyes during the vision, has turned her blind. She calls out to Polly, hands outstretched. Frantically feeling around her, she is lifted into the arms of the Chosen One. Transported down to the healers' quarters at superspeed. There is no time for politeness. Polly barges into that tranquil space, where the healing rooms are. A fountain is tinkling in the background and dreamcatchers hang in spaces near entranceways, with large earthy crystals mounted on recesses in the walls. The energy in here is gentle, grounded, but as soon as Polly walks in with Toni, the air is charged with evil, the lights flicker erratically. The fountain at the centre, starts to gush angrily, and the crystals burn with red-hot centres that glow. The healers rush forward, and Esme looks round startled. She had been tending to Chris's neck and finishing another blood transfusion, before the intrusion.

The healers try to pry Toni away from Polly's arms, but at first, The Chosen One does not let her friend go. Not until Esme steps forward and softly says "Come on Polly, you can let go now, we need to help Toni."

Polly, through tears, nods her head slightly and sniffs out a "She was trying to help me by showing me Balan and then, . . and then an evil appeared. Balan is in great danger. Toni absorbed something in that room, and she could only break it by doing this really powerful spell to sever the connection. Please help my friend." Polly says plaintively.

"We will but let us take it from here. We have a small amount of time to withdraw the blackness. Leave us to do our work" Esme says and then nods to the others, who then pick up the limp body of Toni and take her to one of the rooms in the chamber.

Chris waits for the healers to pass by before ambling over to Polly. He puts his strong arms around her and draws her in for a hug. Kissing the top of her head and Polly starts to cry, deep sobbing tears are coming out.

"Would it help to talk about it?", Chris gently asks.

Polly wipes her tears on her sleeve and explains "Balan is possessed I think by the Witch that was in the cave and Toni consumed some of the evil from the vision. It's all my fault. I shouldn't have asked her to show me."

"Polly, she would have told you if she thought it was a problem and look at it like this, if you hadn't of asked her, you wouldn't have known Balan is in trouble and needs our help either", Chris reasoned. He looked on thoughtfully then continued. "The other day in the airport, Eleanora was right about one thing, but she explained it in such a garbled way that we didn't understand her at the time. There is no right or wrong, just actions and learning from what we do. We can't personalise what happens or what others do, it isn't about us. I'm starting to realise this myself."

"Garbled, huh? My dear boy, I said it quite plainly. The lesson is in the doing, not in fretful worrying or explaining and it was very clear what I said at the airport the other day. I can't help it if you chose not to understand." Eleanora says, with a sniff, definitively, without any expectation of a response.

Chris raises his eyebrows in surprise. He wasn't expecting Eleanora to be in the room. Gulping, he is ever so slightly intimidated by the Pagan Witch. She strides past them and goes to help her sister tend to Toni.

Polly hugs Chris tightly, then leans back and looks at him and the packing on his neck "Are you ok?" she asks, indicating his injuries had not yet healed.

"Yes, I will be" is all he offers and doesn't seem to want to talk about it any further, so she stops, not wishing to pry. Biting down on her lip. Noticing Chris is colder to touch, and his green eyes have a fine red rim round them too.

"Let's go and see the Professor while we wait for news of Toni, ok?" Chris says and Polly nods.

Walking through the castle together to the library, Polly is taken aback by her surroundings. Pleased to note, the grandeur and opulence of the Castle, still gives Polly goosebumps and a kind of awe she can't quite describe – the castle is in her blood, a part of her now. The might and majesty of the longstanding magical world is evident in every detail of the sandstone walls of the castle structure, in the soil that the building stands on. The majesty of magic is evident all around them, as they both walk together, quietly through archways and along the vast hallways, hung with immense portraits of prominent witches, wizards, warlocks, elves, dragons, and mythical creatures. Their feet whisper on marble floors, as they glide by historical tapestries, mounted on the walls, depicting ancient battles and adventures of heroes and heroines of the magical community, throughout the ages. Polly takes this all in, every sight and every sound is coveted. She sometimes could not help but feel awe-inspired to know that she was a part of this history now, wondering if she would be remembered for some act of bravery – inspiring others in their darkest of moments. To plant the sapling of a mighty tree and know it is for future generations to shade under is the greatest of gifts.

An archway appears in the hallway before the library. Polly could not recollect seeing this place before. Peeking inside curiously, as her senses are tingling and drawing her forward. Reaching out to her and encouraging her to explore further. "Excuse me for one moment, I will meet you in the library. You go ahead" she goes to turn away, but Chris extends his arm and holds onto her hand in his own, lightly.

"What is it?" he asks her "what is it you can feel? I have seen this look on your face before and I trust it."

Polly blushes "it's a feeling that I get of Deja vu, like something is guiding me to do or to see something, and I get this sensation that taps me on the shoulder, asking me to pay closer attention" she explains and looks at him, nodding, hoping he understands.

"I don't understand what it is because I have no idea what it's like being The Chosen One of legend, but I know you and I trust in you so, let's go together" he says, his face open with anticipation. Hoping she would trust him and not pull an *'I am the Chosen One'* thing and insist on going it alone.

The archway is in darkness and shadow, Polly peers down the dark hallway and then up at Chris. She knows she doesn't need him to come with her, but she wants to share her world with him and for him to be a part of it. Polly nods and Chris breaks into a lopsided grin, relief flooding his face.

His eyes crinkle at the edges and he blows out the tension he was holding in with his breath.

They both enter the dark hallway hand in hand and together. Effervescent lights spark into life and light up the long length of tapestry, which is stretched all the way along the hallway and into the distance. The stitches look very ancient, crumbling and worn in many places at the beginning. Polly looks at the story woven into the fabric. The tapestry scene starts with a small primitive-looking woman holding her belly, and then moves on to the woman giving birth mortally wounded. And then the yarn and stitches show a baby being born with a sapling in its hand. The High Priestess is depicted planting the tree sapling into the ground. The story went on, the mother had died, and the High Priestess was shown holding the baby and giving the baby to a wolf. The baby was represented as growing up – baby, girl, woman - standing in front of a willow tree with a wolf beside her, throughout the years. Then the tapestry shows the young woman that the baby had become, in various battle scenes sown into the cloth. The young woman had fought shadow demons and stopped monsters. The girl had managed to stop a meteorite from colliding with the world by jumping into a volcano - sacrificing herself. Polly touches the bumpy stiches of the Willow Tree. It is depicted on numerous occasions throughout the tapestry, always near the baby and the woman the baby becomes.

Looking further down the hallway, there is an image of another baby born in front of the Willow tree. The wolf once again, stands there, tall. Polly's eyes are unblinking, wide with fear. Running further and further along the stretched fabric of the tapestry , counting baby after baby being born in front of The Willow Tree. Ten in total. The story of the birth of a little girl being repeated on the cloth again and again. Each time a young woman is stitched in as saving the planet in some way. Realisation dawns. Speeding up to the end of the story woven into the tapestry, there is plenty of space to add more scenes to the blank folds of fabric towards the end of the hallway – it carries on for miles. But the pictures end and that is when Polly draws to a complete stop. Before her, the image of her birth mother and a god-like man. Both depicted as standing in front of the willow tree with Polly as a baby – she didn't know how she knew this, but she just did.

 In that quiet and hushed hallway, where the legs of scurrying spiders are the only sound, time stood still. While Polly caresses the embossed image of her birth mother and father. The strangest feeling wraps around her, of both of her parents standing beside her in that hallway, in another version of time. The she-wolf is depicted on the fabric, staring out at her maternally from eyes that can see her. Besides the she-wolf, another bundle with an outstretched baby's hand. Tears leak from Polly's heavy heart into her eyes and drop onto her outstretched hand, running along her forearm, and sliding into the material of the thread, leaving the stitches wet and engorged. Her throat is constricted, her chest is swelling with feelings too great for her body. Choked, realising that she is looking at a different way of life that could have been, but she had blinked and missed it - slipping through her fingers. Lips trembling, regret for what could have been tightening against her chest. "Chris, please leave me here a moment" she involuntarily whispers, while staring at the images of her mother, father, the baby, the she-wolf and the bundle, on the floor of the forest - her true family.

"Don't send me away please. I will wait here quietly until you are ready" he whispers urgently , tears in his own eyes "let it out, don't hold on to it. The pain will make you sick if you do."

With these words, Polly crumples to the floor like she has been given permission to fall apart, sobbing, and cradling her hand to her strong but breaking heart. In the wretchedness of the pain, all she could think about was Balan being in the grip of the evil witch or worse. She shivers, she feels his sorrow. Balan needs her to be strong, to find him, but she knows that the pain must come out or otherwise it will drive inwards and poison her - polluting her soul. Changing her to fractions of multiple reflections of light, reflectance of the outside and not the person she is inside. Shattered and broken across too much pain. Like feet walking through miles of splintered mirrored glass. This is where the universe splits apart, when people avoid the emotions in their hearts, and imbalance first begins in us all.

The thrumming of the ancient heartbeat rings loud in Polly's ears. *Strength* it whispers, *courage* it echoes, soothing her. Calling out to The Chosen One guiding her to know it's okay to embrace her pain. It will serve her well and show her, her heart is her true strength. Destiny continues calling her. In the background like a battle drum. There with Polly even when The Chosen One is a heap of a mess on the floor, beaten temporarily by her overwhelm.

Her head is spinning. There is still something missing, something the tapestry wants to show her. *Balan. Balan. BALAN*, she repeated to herself over and over, in her mind.

Far away in Glossop, something stirs. A wind picks up and blows through the leaves in the woods. A whisper of the words *"strength"* on the clear air of the forest. Slowly but as sure as the sun rises, the particles that had been blown apart by The Evil Queen and left swirling in the air without a home to return to. Well, they heard Polly's words. The particles start to rewind and rebuild themselves. Complex structures rebound together, sinew, bone and the thrumming of life started up once again...........

y        l        o        PP        o        l y.

*"Polly"*, The word of The Chosen brought Balan back to life and with a renewed strength. Even in her moment of weakness, she was selfless and called to him, guiding him home.

Balan took a huge gulping intake of breath and his eyes flicker open in that space between life and death, in the magical realm. He would be ready and waiting for a chance to seize his body back from the Evil that had taken possession of him.


A while later, Eleanora walks through the hallways of the castle, retracing Polly, and Chris's steps on her way to the library. The sobs she could feel with her own heart, she did not need to hear the girl with her ears. Eleanora moves into the hallway, bending down over the crumpled form, and she silently motions to Chris to help her get Polly to her feet, which he willingly obliges. Eleanora's eyes take in the girl standing there, empty, shutting out the world that had hurt her so badly and that was when her sister's words came back to Eleanora *"The girl needs to feel love and goodness, to know the value of what she fights for and is trying to save. It may matter in the end"*.

"More than you will ever know" - Destiny chimes in Eleanora's mind and rebounded in that place of awakening, the subconscious mind of humans.

"Come my girl, do not wallow in this place. It is good to know your origins but not to dwell on what could have been. It is torture for the human spirit to live with regret. We have but today and each hour ahead of us. To live, is to feel. Let's go to the library and we will talk through our next steps and get you something nice to eat." Eleanora says and starts walking Polly away from the Kaidaluminere bloodline tapestry. As they walk away, the lights illuminating the history of The Chosen One, individually blink out one by one. The hallway entrance disappears from the castle once more, and the tapestry is not seen again for thousands of years, but the Kaidaluminere line is stronger than ever and lit from within, settled inside the heart of Polly.

Together, Chris and Eleanora walk Polly to the library. As the enter, the Professor looks up from his scroll and does not make a sound. They each sit down in the comfy chairs by a small fire that is flickering, alive in the hearth. Sage, chestnuts and pine bark are burning, mixed in with the wood on the flames. The scent and particles of the forest swirl into Polly's chest and fill her with a renewed sense of hope for the future, it is restorative.

"Whatever is it, Eleanora?" asks the Professor quietly, not wishing to intrude.

"The tapestry appeared to her" Eleanora mouthed.

"Oh, so soon?" The Professor looks round alarmed. Eleanora nods in response to the Professors question. "Polly, what happened to Toni?" Polly turns her head to the Professor, looking tired and drawn so Chris answers on her behalf.

"Polly and Toni were looking in the basin and were touched by the Evil witch…"

Polly interjects, withdrawn, tightly closed physique reflects her state of mind "It's got Balan. The Evil Witch has him. I saw her shadow over him. Is she indestructible? is that why she was imprisoned in the cave, and I couldn't destroy her either? I need to help Balan before, well before…" Polly looks away and at the fire.

The Professor shoots up and starts pulling down books on evil witches and piles them on his desk, opening the first book to read. Chris hurries over to the reading desk in the corner and starts up the computer to commence researching too - they all felt the need to do something, knowing full well what Polly meant with the words she could not bear to speak. "*We* let him go. *We* didn't see the dark witch had hold of him" Polly says through her tears. "We have to find a way to destroy her and get him back."

Eleanora stands, looking down at Polly for a while, with a thoughtful expression. The girl is distractedly staring into the fire, welcoming the silence. The Chosen One is shrunken down and in pain that is not just physical. The Pagan Witch is afraid.

At that moment, Toni hobbles in. Heavily bandaged; her hands had been badly burnt and the magical spells that were administered by the healers would take time to grow her skin back over the wounds she sustained. "Well, what is the plan to rescue Balan then?" Toni hurls out into the room, standing with her bandaged hands on her hips, defiant. Challenging anyone that says anything to displease her.

Polly starts to laugh, holding her stomach because of the mirth that explodes from within her. She is looking at Toni with the warmth of gratefulness. Gazing in admiration at the fierceness of her best friend.

"Well, the only person that can tell us about this witch and how to free Balan is the High Priestess, Vusulia, Bringer of Destiny." says Eleanora, with a twinkle in her deep blue eyes. "You know where the tunnel entrance is Pollux, to her hidden Kingdom." The wind from the chimney in the fireplace blows harder into the room and whips around Eleanora as she speaks of the Destiny. It careens and howls through the chimney of the fireplace or all ears could have been mistaken, and the howl was from the call of the she-wolf reminding Polly of her bloodline.

Polly stands up and unsheathes her sword - The Sword of Hestia. The steel sings and vibrates in her hand in answer to the call to arms. Polly says with strength "so, what the hell are we waiting for" with this utterance, she slides out of her seat, pats Toni on the shoulder and the two friends lock arms, in a grip of sisterhood. Chris gets up and pushes the chair out of his path.

"I'm coming with you this time and I'm not taking no for an answer" Toni studies Chris with her keen eyes and smiles. Clucking her tongue, looking him up and down. "Well, well, look at you Chris, entering the arena at long last and I'm loving the lion looking back at me, proud and strong." Toni says to him, and she playfully hits his chest with her clenched fist and notices it is like hitting a slab of marble. A look of apprehension moves across Chris's tired face. "It would seem we are all discovering new things about each other, no?" Toni says secretly to Chris.

Chris smiles at Toni, blurting out "Well, what's the worst that can happen to us?" he says raising his eyebrows expectantly.

"We can get imprisoned by an evil witch for the rest of all time in the dark fortress of her unholy soul?" Polly offers.

Toni widens her eyes in shock at the very detailed description of bleakness that Polly had managed to conjure up within seconds.

"Oooooor, and on a lighter note, eaten by a Giant for supper or gnawed at by a bloodthirsty, Dos Vampires" answered Toni jokingly, in a bad Transylvanian accent and pretending to have fangs. Casting her gaze over at Chris and winks.

Chris places his hand on his chin, thoughtfully and says "Well, we will sit in his belly together and give him the worst kind of gas then" Chris says while raising a sword, intending to inspire the others with his fearless fighting banter, but not really getting it right. Although, It was very endearing when he tries.

"Erm, okay then" says Polly, looking at Chris with a laugh playing on her lips and then she says, rather seriously "as long as we are together, even in a giant's or giantesses' belly" Polly nods at Chris "I think that's all that matters in the end" she says to her friends.

The three of them leave Eleanora and the Professor in the room while they go to pack some essentials for their journey, into the great unknown. They are starting to realise that nothing else matters, apart from their strong bond with one another. As the trio walk out of the room together, the Professor sees a golden haze surrounding the three of them. Taking off his glasses to clean them. He reflects that the trio seem to be sharing more than just their friendship once again and this is not the first time he had noticed.

## Chapter fourteen – Of Gods and Goddesses and Wicked things

The trio of friends gather at the large wooden gates of the castle in the chill of the cold morning air. Eleanora, Esme, Annika and the professor are there to see them off. Eleanora steps forward out of the crowd. Taking Polly to the side to talk quietly with her while helping her on with her backpack "Listen my girl, the entrance to the High Priestesses kingdom is a carefully guarded secret so Toni and Chris will need to be blindfolded along the way. The entrance is on my lands, but it is not at the same time. It is temporal and exists within multiple dimensions. If the High Priestess believes there to be a threat, she does tend to remove her Kingdom to a place in the universe and at a time that is safe. Make sure she trusts you and your friends or otherwise you will be transported to another dimension or timeline that we may not be able to locate you in and pull you out of, do you understand? Warn Chris and Toni not to touch or do or say anything that will offend or make her feel that it is not safe to remain on earth and here in the present day." Polly looks at Eleanora with a sudden wonder at her words "Did you hear me, Pollux?" says Eleanora more sternly this time.

Polly nods, "Eleanora, are you and Esme going to help Balan while we are gone and get him to safety?"

"No, the evil witch queen has him for now. We need to know a way of defeating her for good and hopefully the High Priestess knows how. In the meantime, Esme and I will cast a spell to bind him to this plane or otherwise the Black Dahlia could consume him. We will do this straight after you leave. You have my word."

Polly gave her a small sad smile as a way of saying thank you. Eleanora pats the Chosen One on the back "stay vigilant and trust your instincts above all else and……" cautions the pagan witch.

"Eleanora, you are making me feel nervous" Polly interjects.

"Fine, fine" says Eleanora waving her hands up in the air "It's *nothing*, you are only meeting the High Priestess of The Goddess after all" Eleanora tuts.

"For a *second time.*" Interjects Polly once again and then adds "You didn't caution me like this when I was meeting her for the first time as part of the trial" Polly reprimands the Old Witch.

"Yes, but now we know for sure you are the Chosen One, there are certain rules of magic that must be obeyed, and The High Priestess will expect as much".

"Great, so now you tell me all of this just five minutes before we are due to depart. Anything else? Am I to ride a dragon through the tunnel this time too?" Polly says with frustration dripping from each syllable, annoyed at being kept in the dark once again.

Eleanora's face whips round and cracks to attention "What do you know of dragons, Pollux and why did you raise them to me now?" Eleanora looks on with a questioning glare.

"Erm, no reason" Polly says in a concealed way, thinking back to the large scaly egg that is at this moment, nestled in a warm chamber of earth under the Willow Tree. Eleanora eyes Polly suspiciously.

"Ok, well then. Must be going. Toni and Chris let's be on our way then. Bye for now all and see you soon" Polly shouts this to the group, trying to not make eye contact with Eleanora and aiming to make a swift exit.

The three friends walk out of the castle gates and descend into the fields of the hillside below the Castle and of which the huge structure stands on.

Eleanora watches them walk single file through the gates and then turns to Esme to say, "she mentioned dragons just then before she left".

"Well, it was only a matter of time. When I look at the basin to check on Polly, I have been hearing the heartbeat for the last year too" Esme says this with a sideways glance at Eleanora.

Eleanora's face forms into a look of astonishment "I have not heard the heartbeat and Pollux has not mentioned this to me. I wonder what other secrets she is keeping?" Eleanora says this with a look of deep concern across her usually smiling and open face.

*** 

The three friends had been walking for over an hour, down the rolling grasslands of the large hill. Reaching the bottom, they tread the wild paths out into the valleys below the shadow of the castle. At the ridge, where the land flattens out and the first smattering of trees-lines indicate that they are entering into woodland area, Polly stops. Placing a hand on Toni and Chris, she is fumbling to find something in her backpack. "The entrance to the High Priestess' kingdom is carefully guarded by the magical community and is a secret location. You will need to put blindfolds on, and I will hold your hands to guide you the rest of the way. Is that ok?" Polly asks.

"Yes, of course" says Chris without hesitation.

"What?" Toni questions angrily, at the same time, as Chris is agreeable, the contrast is startling "Polly, we are a part of the magical community too" She says, indignation flashing across her proud face.

"Thank you, Chris, for your understanding. Toni, these are the rules, and I don't make them. I am being asked to follow them just like you." Polly explains carefully, with reason.

"Fine, I will wait here. I am not going to be blind folded, like I am untrustworthy" Toni says, with a prideful voice and her chin held up high.

"Right, ok then. Chris are you still coming?" Polly says with an air of impatience that she had not shown to Toni before.

"Wait, what. You're just going to leave me here?" Toni adds, uncertainty creeping into her usually confident voice.

"Yes, I have to go in and get the details of how to destroy the evil witch so we can free Balan from his living nightmare. If you want to sit here brooding because you've been asked to follow a rule or two then that is up to you" Polly says, quite definitively and starts to walk again on the path towards the entrance to the tunnel. Usually, Polly would try to cajole her headstrong friend but today she was too tired and wants nothing more than to get the information as soon as possible in order to help Balan. Toni is just not used to this more confident side of Polly and getting her own way.

Chris looks uncertainly between the two lifelong best friends and does not know what the best thing is to do for the group. In the end he decides to do the right thing for the quest instead and for Balan. So starts walking after Polly, she would need him most in this task that lay ahead.

"Follow her will you, like the good little bat-boy you are" Toni bursts out, angrily and takes a shot at Chris in her upset.

Chris does not look back round. He cannot bear to look at Toni or for her to see how disappointed he is in her. After all, Balan is near death, and she is behaving like a child.

Polly walks on with her head bowed low, lost in her thoughts. Feeling miserable about the choices that she is making of late; keeping secrets from the group, asserting herself with Eleanora and standing up to Toni didn't feel good at the time but intuitively she knows it is the right thing to do. She is The Chosen One, but it's not just that, she is also doing this for her own sense of self. Polly straightens up a little, she has to be brave now. She is becoming a lone wolf, who does not need the safety of the pack anymore. Less inclined is she to compromise her values and what is important to her these days for the sake of keeping everyone happy. A sickness creeps up from her clenched stomach. It's all new and quite confusing – she finds herself wavering for a short while and wants to go back to sit in safety with her best friend, but she knows that no good will come of it.

*To lead is to be alone…*

"Hey, wait for me. I don't have superspeed like you remember" Chris shouts from behind her.

Polly sniffs, wiping away a tear before she manages to croak out "Well, if you want superpowers, all you need to do is to get a spray tan and be covered in a magic potion when you do." This was said in a very world wary way.

Chris laughs, "I don't think I need a fake tan, thanks" and then like usual he says the right thing "Hey, don't worry about all this. Toni will come round. She's just not used to not being the centre of your world, is all".

With that Polly lets out a loud sniffle. Pulling a piece of black cloth out of her pocket, she then ties it over Chris's eyes as a makeshift blindfold and they both walk on in a comfortable silence, hand in hand. Chris at ease letting Polly guide him forward. They walk this way through trees and woodland, deep into the heart of the wildness of the lands, for the next mile or so, until they come across the prominent Oak tree, which is the entrance way to the hidden kingdom. Underneath is the familiar tunnel to Polly's eyes.

Polly gently stops Chris from walking on any further by placing her hand on his chest – there it was again, that feeling of coldness, and she immediately retracts her hand, giving him a thoughtful look that he could not see.

Waiting blindfolded, Chris listens to the sounds of the birds calling in the trees, while Polly crouches down low, to look down the long dark tunnel. A strange whispering can be heard from within. Standing back up, she describes the tunnel entrance to him, taking both of their back packs off and lays them to the side of the opening. Handing Chris an axe and Polly unsheathes the Sword of Hestia, which was given to her by The High Priestess in this place last year. It shines an electric blue being near the entrance.

Entering, with Chris behind her, they both start the long crawl through the tunnel. Polly is on high alert. The dark, dankness of the tunnel is very warm the further down they descend. Up ahead, in the distance, there is a bundle of blankets unattended on the earth floor of the tunnel. Polly shouts to Chris to stop where he is while she moves forward to investigate. Sitting there  silently with the blindfold on,  leaning forwards so he could hear what was happening up ahead. Chris is startled to learn that  he can hear everything for miles around very clearly, with greater clarity and sharper focus than ever before.  Listening to the worms moving through the earth and the beetles digging tunnels miles away – he knows he is changing but into what?

Polly is moving up ahead to take a closer look at the blanket left on the ground. She discovers it is not a blanket at all but a silk tunic and the cloth is moving and  rustling from something moving inside. As Polly draws closer, she could hear a human baby gurgling. Pulling back the cloth, a baby of about four months in age is revealed. It's a boy, smiling and gurgling happily upon seeing Polly's face. He brushes her cheeks with his tiny, outstretched hand that is grasping. Clutching out and trying to find his mother. Polly picks him up. Holding him with tender care, she calls to Chris to join her and get moving once again. There is no time to explain what is happening, but she would do so when they reach the other side. A wolf's howl pricks at both of their ears. The primal call had come from somewhere up ahead, and Polly clutches the baby closer to her. Eventually, the end of the tunnel opens up and out onto a large expanse of old woodland. It is the middle of winter on the other side of the tunnel. Freezing cold and deadly. The green and pink lights of the Aurora Borealis shimmer and twinkle in the frozen sky overhead,  more pink than green. More nitrogen in the atmosphere here – wherever here is. The lights ripple and glow, lighting up the entire sky and they dance across Polly's upturned face.  Hugging the baby to her closely, she takes off her jacket to keep the infant warm and then with one strong arm, lowers herself out of the end of the tunnel. The baby is held in one hand, and she helps Chris down with the other.  He requires a lot of encouragement; losing his nerve in the strangeness of the twilight landscape that they had found themselves in.

Polly looks across the great woodland area and sees a sight that warms her heart. It is the weeping Willow Tree and sitting before it on a throne of spiky piled flint stone sat Vusulia, High Priestess and Bringer of Destiny, towering, taller than the tree of maternal life.

"Chosen One, *you* are late. I was expecting you before now" The ethereal giant female being says and her voice rings out clearly and the sound carries, reverberating like an echo through the woods. Echoing sonorously in the stillness of the place. Long honey coloured hair falls down her back and her large turquoise irises are gazing down upon the Chosen One's face. On her head is a shining silver helmet with a honey-coloured plume of hair that matches her own. The nose guard shines brightly in the moonlight, and she is clothed in bright silver armour and chainmail that is so shiny bright that it sparkles like the stars in the sky above her – The great armour is made from them. In her hand an elaborate shaped sword that is set aflame. The fluffy white snow bellows down in drifts and spins towards Polly. "Give the baby found in the bundle, to the wolf" Vusulia commands quite slowly and deliberately "know this, you are not being tested. This is part of your vision to help you understand what you already know to be true in your heart, let witnessing this act once more guide you directly to that truth."

The she-wolf pads forward, and Polly walks out to greet the she-wolf, feet crunching heavily on the snow. Bending down on one knee to give the great wolf the baby. The She-wolf pauses to gaze lovingly at Polly. Images of the tapestry and the wolf, the baby and the bundle spin in front of her eyes. While Polly is remembering, the she-wolf nuzzles her face and licks her cheek and then does the same to the baby in exactly the same way. Gently the baby is lifted and secured into the wolf's mouth, then the she-wolf turns to gallop away. Polly watched as the wolf run into the interior of the wood and out of sight. Standing up tall, The Chosen walks over and kneels before Vusulia, placing her sword at the feet of the High Priestess with her head bowed low.

"Understanding will come, but know this, he is Chosen too." Vusulia's voice float towards Polly "but I have answered a question that you have not yet asked" Polly looks up in a state of confusion "You have come to ask me something else today and I have answered a question that you will ask in a few days. Time is fragmenting. The evil witch is playing with the fabric of the universe. It is unnatural to do this, and it has consequences that she could never understand. Remember what I have told you this day.

You will understand in time. Now come, ask me the question that you came for and I will answer in your timeline" with this riddle of speech, Polly stands up. "How do I destroy her, the evil witch queen and save my friend Balan?" Polly asks.

"Your friend?" Vusulia cries out with a mirthful tone and then looks quite serious, as she studies Polly "Yes, I suppose that is what he is to you in your point in time" She seems to reflect on this carefully for a while and carries on "You must drink of the Vessel and kill her with the Sword of Hestia while it is aflame with dragon's fire. She will die only if you cut off her head. But there is something else, you need to be prepared for. The Horned One is choosing a Champion to fight against you, which means you will need the twins together. He is close now, he is watching. Destiny is approaching and you must be ready." Vusulia's eyes widen and grow gigantic in her head and swallow up Polly as she falls forward, inside one of The High Priestess' giant eyes and in there, Polly sees a battle scene with two dragons, as big as mountains flying above the lands, with their shadows casting down onto the vast acres of land. Turning the fields to black, in the wake of the great creatures of myth, fleeting across the ground, as the huge forms fly by. Polly and Balan are each mounted on a black leather saddle, riding on a dragon's back.

In an instant as quick as a blink, Polly is brought back to stand in front of Vusulia.

"H-h-how is this possible? Where are the dragons now? Who is the Horned God? I thought that…" Polly had lots of questions, too many to know which ones were most important to ask as she was aware that her time here is limited.

"You have one of the eggs, youngling and now you must go to the Temple of the Brotherhood to retrieve the other. You know the place I speak of, where the cherry blossoms fly in the wind. You will find the egg at the centre."

Chris starts walking towards the light where Polly and the High Priestess are conversing, the gentle scrunching of his lightness of foot on the freshly fallen snow gives him away to the High Priestess – Polly is not on her own.

Forward he walks out of the shadows and removes his blind fold to blink in the rippling light of the Northern lights, well that is what they are called on earth.

Vusulia sensing a stranger in her midst, moves her gigantic, helmeted head round and swoops down to look at him more closely. "A man that carries the corrosive poison of the Ancient Hunters, but their gene coding has been disallowed from fully taking shape and taking seed, by the golden touch of The Chosen One. I will be watching your timeline closely manchild. These events were not foreseen, now you have my attention" Vusulia announces, with a curious expression on her striking face.

"Now be gone from this place" She purses her lips together and blows up a strong gale and a tornado springs from her mouth. Dizzily revolving in this world, under the strange shadows of the willow tree that are moving against the moonlight and headed purposefully towards Polly and Chris. Polly dashes forward to avoid the spindly shadows "Wait, wait. What about the seven sacred objects and….and the White Hart" Polly screams over the gale-force winds whipping at her, pushing her backwards, her feet barely holding ground.

"Most of the objects you already have youngling, search your heart. You already know this to be true. The gifts given to the Chosen".

*The gifts given to the chosen The gifts given to the chosen The gifts given to the chosen The gifts given to the chosen* – rings in Polly's ears.

With all of her might, Polly pushes through the winds and breaks free to rush forward to ask the High Priestess one last question, but the grey tornado will not be denied. It is spinning wildly. Sucking up everything it touches behind her. Chris is in the vice grip of the dragging dust cloud, his feet lifting off of the ground and he grabs at Polly's hand to pull her through to the eye of the tornado. To him. "Where is my birth mother? Where is he too, my father? I feel them with me always, but I can't see

171

them. Where are they?" Polly screams out into the blankness of space, as an invisible veil drops over her and the words are taken from Polly's mouth. The Tornado is sucking them both up out of that dimension and spits them back out in the forest clearing where they had started. Toni is waiting under a yew tree, cross legged and meditating in silence, yet she does not stir at their sudden presence – she was expecting them. Polly let out a loud scream of frustration and smashes her fists into the ground – starting a minor earthquake.

Vusulia sits on her throne, troubled. Rubbing her forehead. In the silence that follows the departure of the great tornado, she weighs up the interaction. Allowing a worry to settle over her, consuming all her thoughts – deafening to her ears. She leans forward resting her head on her hand, trying to understand the events of the last few hours. A lot had been revealed to her. The witch had refused to stand before her, The boy with cold blood standing in the light and The Chosen one asking the wrong questions, holding on to an imagined fairytale ending and not having understood who she was trying to save or the symbolism of the baby when presented. The Ethereal being draws out a long sigh and lifts the helmet off of her head, it is heavy. Fear and wariness settle over her. 'He will win if this continues, and the universe will slip into absolute blackness for an age.' To The Willow Tree she speaks. Despondency takes hold. Then she watches as the snowflakes change patterns from falling silently in the shape of bold Dragons, to melting and turning back into The Goddesses tears.

'What does it all mean? Only time will tell…'

Vusulia stands and draws her sword, pointing upwards, sending an energy beam into the centre of the universe, asking the Cosmos to listen to her plea for insight. **"She does not trust herself Mother of All, she gives over her power too willingly to lesser beings"**. And she was answered:

SHE WILL FIND HERSELF AND FIND ALL THE ANSWERS WHEN SHE DOES, *REPLIED THE ANCIENT, THE GUARDIAN, BIRTHER OF THE UNIVERSE AND OF ALL, AND THEN THE VOICE OF THE COSMOS ADDED.* THE CHOSEN ONE IS GESTATING, SHE IS

WEIGHED DOWN BY DRAGGING AROUND OLD VERSIONS OF HERSELF THAT NO LONGER SERVE HER, SHE MUST LET THEM DIE TO BE AT HER OWN REBIRTH. SHE WILL COME TO REALISE THIS SOON, AND WHEN SHE DOES, SHE WILL BE POWER, SHE WILL BE CHAOS, SHE WILL BE THE BRINGER OF THE BEGINNING. ALL IN GOOD TIME, HOLD HER WITH FAITH BRINGER OF DESTINY, SHE WILL SURPRISE US ALL AT THE END OR BE THE DESTRUCTION OF US ALL. EITHER WAY IT WILL BE A BEGINNING AND THAT IS WHAT SHE IS FATED TO DO, WE CAN ASK NOTHING MORE. . .

Miles…

The air conditioning is on full blast throughout the New York city offices, the temperature hitting the minus in the building, but Miles is outright refusing to turn the temperature up, even though his staff are freezing cold and complaining.

"Tell them to go and work from home if they can't handle a little change and then tell them to not come back" Is how he phrases it to his executive assistants, when one of them had raised that there is a growing sense of unease within the workforce. This wasn't just about the temperature. The workforce are frightened of Miles.

The assistant slid the glass panelled door closed after the discussion with his boss. Miles was becoming increasingly erratic, unpredictable, and his eyes are wild these days. The Executive Assistant trying to mediate a solution, Sasha had noticed all these little details. Today, Miles was gibbering about a Horned God. Sasha was getting too scared of pushing the topic of the building temperature any further.

At that point, Nuala came walking up the corridor towards Sasha. His stomach clenched involuntarily; Nuala creeps him out. There is this other thing. Sometimes, when he is busy doing a task for Miles and she would drift into the edge of his vision, he could swear that he would see her as a hooded grey figure with black mist and vapour distorting her edges. Like something straight out of hell. On those occasions, when he looked up she would be solid again, model like even physically but he knew something was off.

Today, Nuala sashays past him bright and breezy. The Executive assistant asked "Hi Nuala. Can I get you anything to drink, maybe a coffee?"

"Hi smithers" that's what she had taken to calling him although she knew his name was Sasha "just the blood of a newborn with a side shot of caramel please" Nuala looks at him, dead pan and waits for his reaction of alarm, which she relishes.

"Hahaha" Sasha laughs out dryly and without mirth "Erm, good one?" Sasha says uncertainly. Exiting the hallway, without a backward glance and does the shape of the cross with his fingers.

Nuala walks in the room "Why is Sasha still here? I told you that the little *bitch* can see me clearly. He has the sight, I'm pretty sure of it. Means he is some kind of witch but just doesn't know it yet" Nuala says studying Sasha through the glass of the window.

Miles did not look up when Nuala entered the room, he carries on researching. Trying his best to find the secret entranceways that interface with Earth, to the underworld "Miles, did you hear me? Get rid of Sasha" She stamps her foot.

"hhhhmmmmm, yeah, I'll do that soon, but he makes a great espresso. Listen, I called you because I need to know where the entrance to the underworld is. Where is it? And did you bring more potion? I've nearly run out" Miles says this in a worried and frantic way. Nuala sits down and leans back in her chair, licking her lips at the chaotic energy coming off of Miles - she is feeding off of him.

"You seem somewhat. . . distracted." what she meant to say was psychotic, unhinged, but held back.

"Look, I haven't got time for your games. Tell me where the entrance is to the underworld or better still transport me there. I have a plan to get the Horn. I'm going to take a few vials and then go down into the underworld to get that horn with a troop of agents. While I am doing that, someone from The Company will kidnap Polly's mother and send a communication to the Chosen One to get me the crown of a demigod by the end of tomorrow or the mother dies." Miles sat back in his chair with a maniacal grin spread across his face, eye twitching. Waiting for Nuala to tell him where to start.

"Well, that sounds a rather exceptionally detailed plan, not! Where do you think the entrance to the underworld is? There is more than one entrance. Lost souls gravitate to the Gateways and demons tend to stay close to them. You can always spot them. The worst kind of human behaviours manifest themselves near them".

"Ahh, hedonistic places then where drugs and alcohol and sins of the flesh are in abundance, like clubs, stripper bars…that sort of thing? Looks like we are going to SoHo then. Any particular location?"

Nuala's luminous violet eyes flickered, and her pupils became non-existent once more "10012" is all she says.

Miles leans forward, picks up his phone and calls Able, one of his most trusted agents, who had lost his team leader Kane last year, "Get the squad up here. We are doing a hellava lot of the compound then heading out to 10012" he clicks the line dead.  Knowing with full confidence that his instruction would be followed, to the letter.

## Chapter fifteen - Miles to go.


The streets of SoHo are located in a busy district of New York City. The sidewalks are bustling and heaving with the afterwork crowds on a Friday evening. People are relaxing at bars in the heat of the evening, soaking up the last reminisce of sunrays. Enjoying their drinks with coworkers and friends. Craft beers, and the newest fermented cocktails and illegal recreational highs are being offered and shared round. There is a chaotic and uneasy buzz in the air but not because it's a Friday and the end of the work week or that people want to cut loose, to dance. No, this is more to do with the addicts and extreme hedonists and hungry demons that gravitate to this location and are mingling with the crowds. There is a tension in the air, and it hangs over the streets like smog. The kind that indicates that individuals have had a bit too much to drink or overindulged and the night could turn on a dime at any moment.

Miles and eight of his elite Company agents are walking the pavements and weaving their way through the crowds. They are standing out from the throng and drawing a lot of attention due to their military style of dress. Full black combat gear and heavily armed with traditional hardware but also an array of demon fighting equipment. They had on casual jackets but it did not detract from the fact that these guys were built for combat and were active mercenaries – it was in the way they all walked and moved.

A rather tall and elaborately dressed drag queen walks up to Miles to hand him a flyer. The beautiful lady squeals out into the crowd "*Ohhhh, army boys?*" as the troop walks past her. They do not react. Not looking round once, so focussed are they on getting to the club and on with the mission. They show the same disdain for the queue of clubbers waiting on the sidewalk, for their chance to go into one of the most exclusive clubs in SoHo, the 10012 club. Known for its hedonistic, non-stop, high energy club nights. There are side rooms in the nightclub where people are encouraged to hit a new high of hedonism with the aid of a designer street drug called Totem. The narrative sold to consumers is that this drug is created by The Free People, who once lived on these lands, and the drug is made of natural ingredients. Causing the taker to enter into a deep spiritual state of bliss. The reality is different, darker. What is actually happening during the takers drugged out state is an unknown exchange. People go into these side rooms and enter into unconsciousness and are fed-on by demons, dark magical beings and vampires. In exchange, when they wake, a spell inducing euphoria is put on them before they leave the cubicle - sounds like a win / win? But then why is this transaction taking place secretly and in the dark? Because with each hit, a little bit of the soul is being corroded and removed piece by piece from their bodies.

The troop walk to the front of the queue and ask to talk to Charli, the owner. The bouncers are not liking the look of the troop and start holding their hands on the agents' chests. Aggressively advising them that the place is full to breaking point. The troop square up to the bouncers and before a ruction starts, Miles steps out of the shadows and into the full beam of light that is projecting from a streetlamp onto the pavement nearby. Miles is lit up, his face instantly recognisable from his success. A flurry of activity swirls around him and the group are ushered into the cordoned off VIP area - money talks in places like this.

It's a Friday night so there are minor celebrities in the velveteen booths, accompanied by club hostesses and people rich enough to enter the small, closed off area; that purposely creates a division between the rest of the party goers, both in terms of distance and socially.

Miles takes a seat in one of the booth areas and puts his hand on the table and instantly regrets the decision - the underside of his hand is covered in stickiness. The whole club has a greasy feel about it and Miles' revulsion is manifesting into a prickly impatience. Causing him to accidentally grip the side of the table a little too tightly and the metal crumples away in his hands. The clubbers nearby are alarmed by the sound.

"Sir, sir...please refrain from public displays", says Able, looking around to see if anyone had observed the action. Able is watching Miles carefully. He's concerned. Miles had taken three vials of the compound and behaving out of control; jittery, wired like an ignition fuse ready to be propelled into detonation.

Charli the owner of the club, comes weaving his way through the dance floor. Waving and smiling with his tombstone brilliant white veneers on display. He is wretchedly slim, manic and overly stimulated like Miles. He had dyed pink hair and a deep orange tan. His sprayed-on skin tone was made more luminous by his vibrant Hawaiian shirt. He meandered over to the table where Miles and the troop were conspicuously sitting. Charli was eager to make their stay memorable, regardless of the cost. As Charli grew closer, Able noticed on closer inspection, the club owner did not look as polished as he did from a distance under the cover of the gloominess of the club. His slim frame was emaciated, he had sores that had crusted around his nostrils and his energy was low with a twitchy, anxious pull to it. He burst out a little too loudly "hey, hey, HEY, how are you guys doing" handshakes, fists bumps, and air kisses were offered but only Miles partook in the sham of being friendly and welcoming - even he begrudged the show. "Your boys not feeling it tonight or what?" a strong irritated New York twang escaped his dehydrated lips – he was offended.

"They are…focussed on what we came here to do, Charli. We are not here to party. We are here for the Gateway" Miles looked at him significantly with darkened eyes. Charli's smile slipped from his face momentarily and Mile's eyes were coldly direct - piercing. Waiting for an answer.

Charli rakes his jittery hands, nervously through his neon pink hair. Suddenly afraid. He gulps out "You know what the price is, right? Did someone explain this to youse?"

"Whatever the cost is, we will pay it. I have money…" Miles says, waving his hands like these were mere trifles, inconsequential details that he should not be bothered with.

Charli shakes his head slowly "It's not money, man. It's a different kinda currency" Charli pauses and whispers "you…you need a sacrifice" Charli could barely get the words out; his eyes are blank under his pink framed sunglasses, and he shrinks a little lower in on himself. The veneer fades and he looks out over the crowd, lost for a few heart beats.

Able looks round the club "Which one?"

179

"No, not you. It will need to be Miles. He wants to open the gate. He does the deed. That's the price. It's an exchange, y'see" Charli looks sideways at Miles wondering if he had done this before.

Miles blows out a loud breath, annoyance on his face "Fine, Fine, let's get this over with. Charli, any recommendations?" Miles looks round the club like he is choosing a bottle of champagne and asking for advice on selecting the best one. The veneer switches back into place and business is resumed "Yeah, I'll pull one of the druggie street kids from one of the booths and we will make it look like an accident. No problem at all" Charli grins, slapping Miles on the back.

Charli flourishes his hand in an elaborate show to indicate that they all should follow him, and the group file out of the VIP booth, out into the gangway and walk casually into the backrooms of the club.    Dancers in the cages, suspended from the ceiling, watch them go and look out over the crowd - wondering which poor kid it would be tonight.

Sometime later, Miles and the troop are in a deep black cavernous chamber underground - a secret level under the club kept hidden. There is a thick blackness of shadows overhead and clinging to the corners of the room – it gave it an ominous whispering feel. On the ground, there are rows upon rows of cream-coloured candles with ancient scripture written by hand down the sides. The candlelight is dim with foreboding. Miles walk out of a side door into the darkness of the shadowy space and laying on a raised platform is a human body. Hanging over the unconscious form suspended in midair, is an unfurled scroll and a large statue of a demon - grotesque and deformed. Miles' body language is light and casual as he walks past his team, bearing a silver dagger loosely in his hand. Approaching the platform, he utters the words he has memorised and performs the rite perfectly, without a single thought to the life of the young person that he took. The young person who had dreams, family, friends, a beating heart that quickened in fear and excitement and slowed when they felt at ease with the world. The young person had walked into the club that night to have a good time and create memories. They were no more, and their soul had been offered to open a gate to The Underworld - trapped inside the hell dimension for all of eternity.

As the blood drips with a slow, rhythmic 'plonk, plonk' into a gulley on the ground and seeps forward towards the silver wrought archway, the crimson liquid increases in speed as flows quickly like it is magnetised - drawn to the ancient gate. The lifeless body floats upwards and begins to hover towards the gate. A foot enters the air between the two archway pillars, and a blinding light cracks open. Illuminating the darkness of the chamber. The troop look around and into the lit-up spaces that were once covered in an inky blackness. To their horror, every inch of the chamber is in face covered in skulls positioned to look down onto the gate. Thousands of skulls lined up in rows, with the eyeholes now lit up in response to the strange light emanating from the gate.

Miles let out a slow whistle, looking around "This must have taken years to decorate. Impressive" The Agents look at each other in embarrassed silence not knowing how to respond to a statement like that. Able shakes his head at his crew and indicates to them that no one should say a word or react. The lead agent knows that Miles is too jacked up with the potion to be confronted and is behaving erratically enough already.

Charli averts his eyes from The Gate, and he is stood facing towards the door. Tapping his foot nervously. Wanting to run.

"Ok guys, you can walk through and here is the talisman to get you back out. Have a safe trip" he dangles a dull green jade necklace held by a dark leather twine. The agent with the code name Able takes it from Charli and puts it around his neck, an eerie light is at its centre. They all watch as Charli bolts for the door leaving them all behind. A couple of the agents are straining forward like they want to follow.

Miles, who visibly is shaking with excitement, couldn't wait any longer, and takes a few great strides into the Gate. Disappearing from view in a thick mist. The Agents, in a single line fall-in behind Able and they follow the lead agent into the gateway, demon guns drawn, and the safety triggers removed.

The world on the other side of the gate is like nothing that the agents had ever witnessed before in their entire lives.

The atmosphere is heavier, thicker in here, and ripples outwards visibly as the agents move through it. They could all breathe in the oxygen, but it is like sucking in thin soup – they feel a constant stream of liquid leaking out of their nostrils. It bubbles and floats up into the air in front of their faces. It's an uncomfortable feeling, like being on the edge of suffocation. In this dense atmosphere, rocks and stones hover above them, held up by an autonomous force and regular bounce off one another, with a low cracking sound each time – resembling the first cracks of thunder. The ground is covered in a dense pink gas-like substance and the smoke drifts along with them as they walk through it. They are outside in the open air, but the sky is dark red and marbled with a black substance that on closer inspection resembles three-dimensional ink blots hanging in the sky. The stars, and moons and planets, are unfamiliar to their eyes. All very close to this world or dimension or whatever the hell this place is. The planets and moons here crowd into view and look like they are on the verge of colliding with this planet and into each other. The laws of physics clearly do not apply here.

The agents have a look of horror frozen in their wide eyes. The alien terrain is freaking them out and Able needs to keep the troop focused on the task at hand "Right, troop listen up, we need to head northwest until we hit the Andrones shrine and three clicks from there is the Pinnacle of Shadows and that's where the horn is stored. What are we expecting Limey?" Able calls out to one of the troops and a smaller bespeckled and clammy looking agent stepped forward in response. He had been with the Company for over two years now as a research and intelligence officer.

"Oh, well Sir, the Horn is guarded by a curse that turns anyone who touches it into a living skeleton, so we have gloves with us with spells on them" as he says this, he holds up his own gloved hands and wiggles his fingers "but the risk here is the Guardian. Ancient texts tell us of a mighty warrior that is chosen to protect and keep the Horn in the underworld. There are no more details than that, I'm afraid, sir" says the scrawny agent, code name Limey, in his plummy British accent and pushing his glasses back up on to his nose.

"Right. Okay, lets cover each other's back and get everyone home safe" Able claps his hands together, assertively "Let's stay alert and keep our wits about us and the spell guns unclipped ready for anything. All eyes on the prize. Now go, go, go" all the Agents nod in agreement and start to prepare to leave when Miles steps into the circle. His eyes wide and glassy, blood vessels protruding. A tick under his left eye. "We need Nuala, and we need her now. Call her" Miles says while chewing the inside of his mouth. The agents step back.

"Not sure the satellite phones will work in here, Sir. We are in another dimension" says Limey with a finicky look as he glanced around the landscape.

"Nuala. NOW" bellows Miles.

"*Shush*, we don't want to draw attention to ourselves...." Able cautions Miles like a two-year-old, throwing a tantrum.

Suddenly, each agent is crouching low and holding their hands to their ears, pain frozen on their respective faces- collectively, they go down at the same time. A dot appears on the horizon, in the distance and Nuala, the dark witch, could be seen sashaying towards them, with her glass wand tip held to her temple. Transmitting high frequency screams directly into their brains, causing considerable distress. As she gets closer, she stops the sound and one of the Agents charges at her, grabbing her by her throat. She turns into shadow and smoke, disappearing then reappearing behind him and with a spell, cut him cleanly in two - straight down the middle. Able stares at his fallen team member and back up at Nuala. Making a mental note to kill the witch as soon as they were back on earth. He'd find a way to do it so help him god. " Did you miss me boys" Nuala says while blowing out a kiss to Miles.

A little while later, Miles starts walking ahead with Nuala, they are whispering to each other, and the troop follow begrudgingly in a line behind them. The agents are getting twitchy, and paranoia is setting in.

Shots had been fired at random creatures and monsters without the agents conferring. Little slug like creatures start moving towards the fallen agent left on the ground behind them and much bigger tube-like creatures, the size of a human, were popping up through the smoke and pulling themselves along too. The creatures descended and devoured the flesh and bones of their fallen comrade until there was nothing recognisable left.

The landscape is changing as the troop move through it. It is becoming more solid, and barren and desolate - the environment is ominously quiet and charged with something like discontent. Able feels a watchfulness upon him, like as if there are thousands of eyes out there somewhere staring at the group. Soundlessly, apart from the pounding of their footsteps on the molten rock that slants up, they move forward, towards their destination. The deep silence is occasionally broken by a collision of heavy boulders floating in the air and careening into one another. At the end of the black molten rock is a huge canyon. They step forward towards it, the top of a tall spire appears in the view and beneath the spire is a large structure, like a tower over a hundred metres tall. The foundations are constructed deep within the canyon. Getting closer than they want to be, they could see the tower is made out of flesh and bones of all different types of creatures. The monument stands out peculiarly against the austere landscape. "What the hell…" says Able "who made it and why?" he looks round at the troops, whose faces are drawn and lined with concern. One of them leans over and retches.

"Relax, it's the souls of the offered. You know, the people who were sacrificed to open The Gate or for some dark purpose or another" Nuala says this quite casually, like it was obvious.

"Help" a weak voice could be heard in the air "help me please".

"They are left alive and pinned together like that?" Able utters, a revulsed sickness drenches every syllable.

"Noooo, not quite alive just damned for all eternity, imprisoned here for their energy to be consumed when needed. Come on let's get moving. After a while this place can be a bit of a downer" Nuala casually flicks her poker straight black hair as she says this, and Miles nods his head in agreement.

The troop fall in behind her, trying to avoid looking at the monstrous structure, while also blocking out the pitiful cries for help from the fallen and betrayed souls – the innocent.

"So, that was the Androne Shrine" Nuala waves her hand like she is giving them a tour, sight-seeing in this strange and grotesque land "So, now we need to walk on a bit further until we come to the Pinnacle of Shadows".

The troop walk through a foetid swamp like liquid. Their heavy boots kicking up the bright red sludge. The smell is worse than compost, like putrid meat and has a greasy texture. The troop are looking all around, keeping their guns raised. Out of the liquid jumps a demon that looks like a green lizard, with sharp claws and long canine teeth. It is huge, over eight feet tall. Before Able could react, Miles jumps forward. Aching to try out his new powers on an opponent and now he had the chance. He smashes his clenched fist with the full force of his power into the face of the reptilian demon, denting its features inwards and cracking through its exoskeleton bones. The creature reels back in pain and Miles steps forward, kicking, punching. Slicing out with his dagger in his hand and brutally, without mercy, dismembering the beast where it stands. The agents watch on in a horrified kind of stupor, barely able to draw their eyes away from the savagery. Eventually, Miles finishes the task and picks up what remained of the demon, hurling the body into the distance.

Nuala asks in a bored drawl "Are you quite done, yet?" Miles wipes his brow, with a delirious smile on his face and nods emphatically and walks on.

The agents look at each other with eyebrows in their hairlines, unsettled and queasy from the cruelty and brutality they had just witnessed. Able shakes his head and points to his own eyes with two fingers and then points with the same fingers at Miles and Nuala. The group understands this signal to mean "Eyes on these two."

They could hear Mile's dissecting what he referred to as "A battle" to Nuala "So, do I need more compound when I'm fighting a much bigger opponent" he could be heard casually asking Nuala.

"No, the compound will adapt. It's a very interesting spell it's been bound to. You see…" the conversation went on with little regard to how gruesome the dialogue was to overhear.

At last, they reach the Pinnacle of Shadows, which turns out to be an ancient gothic looking temple on a mound of volcanic rock, surrounded by a lava moat that was spitting and hissing angrily.

The agents immediately raise their guns to their eye line, as one unit, they manoeuvre in a practised way, and start circling the mound. Looking for a way to cross over to the other side or any type of weakness that would enable the mound to be breached.

"The warrior is inside the temple. I will create a glass bridge to the other side" Nuala says this while she spreads her arms and begins incantating a spell. Her words form into glowing white runes and float upwards and then settled across the distance of the lava flow and make a bridge, formed between the two banks.

Miles makes a quick grab and takes hold of Limey's arm. Dragging him to go across first, to test the robustness of the clear glass bridge, before he would consider crossing. Miles was not used to his powers yet and snapped the wrist of the agent. Limey screams out in pain. Miles tuts and says "Great, now we've lost the element of surprise,"

"I think we are all going to be surprised in a moment" laughs Nuala with a knowing smile, fluttering her eyelashes peevishly. Miles raises his eyebrows questioningly and she shook her head, uttering to him "Wait and see".

Limey took a tentative step forward onto the bridge and once he realises that it is sturdy enough to hold his weight, he turns with a grin on his face and gave a thumb up with his good hand. He walks across the gangway and over to the other side, quite forgetting the danger he is in from the unknown warrior inside. He looks at the ground and notices that the mound is covered in precious stones. Distracted, he leans forward to start greedily picking them up with his one good hand, the sheer volume of gens he is holding to his chest, means that some were slipping from his grasp and rolling around noisily ad clanking on the floor.

"Well, hello Limey. Remember me, you double crossing son of bi…." With that the agent known as Kane strides out of the Temple entrance and uses the Horn he is guarding, to slice through Limey's neck. The fallen man's skin begins to immediately disintegrate under the weight of the curse of the horn. Kane picks up the rapidly decaying body of the fallen agent, casually swinging it by the foot and tosses it into the lava as if he was throwing a baseball. He turns his great bulk, towards the group and closes his eyes chanting a spell, enabling him to start floating over the steaming and hissing lava. Towards the group he levitates with hands on his hips, cloak rippling out behind him. Lifted by the heat plumes from the molten flow. Kane's armour shines brightly in the glow of the furnace of the lava. He shouts as he is moving towards the troop "I'm the warrior. Me, sworn protector of the Horn, but happy to take it with us if you get me the hell out of this stink hole.".

Nuala throws her head back and laughs, gregariously "The Horned One will be restored" she yells, her voice echoing back to – a horrifying chorus.

Able stands there and visibly relaxes his shoulders, glad to see his old commanding officer is still alive, and in one piece – even better, he has clearly got some powers. It been over a year since Kane got sucked into the Vessel of Life in the underground pagan temple. "Commando, good to see you Sir." Able salutes his senior officer.

Miles looks on furiously, concerned as Kane seems to be much more powerful than him. He narrowed his eyes "How can this be possible? You were assumed to be dead after the confrontation in the pagan temple" incredulity and jealousy, leaking from his voice.

Kane lands on the bank lightly and takes great strides up to Able slapping him on the back and grinning from ear to ear. "Come on now Miles, I was sucked into that Goddess-damned Vessel of Life and ended up here, in this hell dimension somehow. I can't explain it any more than you, but I'm here and that's all that counts" he waves his hand around "I've been here for over a thousand years waiting for the chance to escape. Nuala, good to see you" Kane nods at the Witch, and she nods back and smiled.

"But how are you the protector? How can you just give the Horn to us?" Miles says shrewdly.

"Who says I'm giving you anything? I plan on presenting it myself to The Horned One" Kane spits back, and Miles winces at the ferocity of the words and implications of Kane's challenge.

"I assume you've committed a great deal of acts of violence here and that you are putting yourself forward as a contender for the Champion yourself?" Nuala enquired, flicking her pupilless eyes at Miles momentarily before turning to settle her gaze on Kane. Waiting for his answer.

"That would be in the affirmative" Kane says with a bold laugh and an even bolder piercing look at Miles, daring him to say another word on the subject.

"Well, well, well, I do believe this is going to be a very interesting next few days." With that Nuala, pulls the group into a circle and then holds her hands out above her, towards the blood red sky and mutters an incantation. A bolt of lightning shoots out of nowhere into her hands. It sizzles as she slams the stream of light into the ground, they all jump backwards, from the swirling energy and they disappear from that plane back to earth, they were all bound.

## Chapter sixteen - The search for a life well lived.

Seventeen years ago, two witches knock at the door of a large wholesome house in North London. There are rose bushes growing in the front garden and a white picket fence borders the property. Wisteria flowers hang from the trellises that cover the house and they hang over the front door in a picturesque frame. There is lavender and rosemary blooming in the front garden and a sense of serenity hangs in the air, with a hint of house pride. A young woman in a simple cotton slip dress, with a flower pinned on her bodice, opens the front door with a large smile on her welcoming face. She does not recognise the two older women, but she unlocks the porch door, as one of them is carrying a very small baby and she wonders if they need help in anyway.

"Hello. I am afraid we have some grave news to share about your cousin Tabitha. May we come in to talk?"

"But of course. I hope it's nothing too serious. Tabitha is my favourite cousin, and I was hoping to be at the birth of her baby" says the young woman, looking concerned. Her eyes drop to the infant as she works out that the baby looks no more than a couple of days old. The young woman holds her throat in her trembling hand.

Esme and Eleanora exchange dark looks, while the woman opens the door widely and she welcomes them both into her home. It is a strange home, the woman seems relaxed, at ease and whimsical even, yet the house is domineering inside with large portraits of a man in various positions of address, in a power stance and the place was decorated to impress rather than live in – a sterile environment reminiscent of a museum. "oh please ignore the decor, not to my taste. My husband…well, he likes everything . . . a certain way." the young woman says this, a little embarrassed that the two older women had noticed that she was not visible in the house or its decorative touches.

189

Once they had settled on the sofa and the woman has planted herself on the opposite chair to the two witches, Esme gets up and hands the small newborn to the young woman, who automatically cuddles the baby to her and is mesmerised. Touching the baby's hands, her face and takin in her smell.

"I am the Lady Cudman-Herne of Herne Hall, I was a close friend of your cousin, Tabitha" says Esme, while the young woman snapped up her face to look at her when The Lady used the term "was". "I have some terrible news, I am sorry to say, your cousin died in childbirth last night" a small sniffle could be heard from the woman sat opposite.

"Did you notice anything about your cousin, did she share anything with you?" says Eleanora with a directness, which came across as being blunt at times.

With a red face and tears running down her supple cheeks "yes, do you mean my cousin having…abilities?" says the young woman, falteringly.

"Yes, exactly that. Well, this baby needs protecting from some very wicked people, evil I would say" Eleanora says as the young woman held the baby closer to her and let out a gasp. "We think she will be safest with you. You can protect her better than anyone else as you share the same bloodline, but there is something that you must do. Something that you must give up, rather" Eleanora peered at the woman solemnly.

"Anything, I will do anything" says the woman, kissing the baby's forehead.

"They will be looking for the soul identity of the bloodline. These people do not bother about names or physical form, they do not matter to these people. I'm afraid to say that while you are responsible for Polly, you will need to not have your soul imprint, do you understand? We need to remove it".

The young woman stared down at the baby, with wide open eyes and the tiny infant gurgled out a laugh. The woman stroked the baby's face and cuddled her close, nestled the infant to her heart. Nodded out a "You are saying you need to take my soul from me, so I won't be found, sorceress?

This is to protect the baby". Both the witches nod and then the woman boldly says, "I will do this for Tabitha and Polly, but will *I* be the same?" The witches shook their heads, sadly. The woman looked mortally afraid, but she whispered, "Do it anyway, but do it now, before I change my mind".

"So be it" Esme says and lifts her staff, and a gold, rippling light is sent crackling through the air and the young woman closes her eyes. The room is filled by a brilliant brightness and her body is consumed with pain. The Professor then enters, all that is heard from him is the clicking of the lounge door as it returns to its cradle. Wand raised, poised ready to perform the powerful memory charm to block out the story of the beginning of The Chosen One.

The present day somewhere in Spain…

Polly's adopted mother, who has always been referred to as Mother - intended to create a sense of distance between the two of them - is getting up to start her day. Slipping from the silk sheets of her queen-sized bed, smoothing down the lace of her figure-hugging night slip. She sensuously pouts as she looks over her shoulder. Smouldering at the man laid down in her bed. He is fast asleep, but she loves looking at him. His darkly handsome, rugged profile and muscly physique makes her tummy spiral and do-little somersaults in exquisite pleasure. Biting her lip, she pads from the bedroom and into the kitchen of their rented apartment in Barcelona.

Pushing the button on the coffee machine, she opens the large glass panelled doors that lead out onto a small balcony, overlooking the beach and ocean below. Breathing in the salty warm air, she listens to the sound of the streets below, coming to life. Market stall sellers getting ready for the day ahead. The zingy smell of fresh oranges faintly wafts up towards her. Relishing this moment and daydreaming about the hours stretching out before her, rich with the possibilities of a life well lived. She smiles softly to herself.

Her blue eyes gaze out over the ocean. She is pensive, reflecting on the life she has created for herself since leaving the castle, leaving Polly behind, over a year ago now. There she lingers on how setting out on this year long adventure around the world, had reignited her free spirit and caring nature. Long forgotten traits of hers that had bubbled to the surface during her travels. Her relationship with her ex-husband, Polly's adopted father had been a misery each waking hour of everyday. His cheating, lying and coercive nature had taken its toll on her making her bitter, spiteful, and cruel. This wasn't wholly down to him; she knows, but there was always something familiar in their relationship that she had not questioned before now. She had given her soul willingly to protect Polly when she was a baby and doesn't regret it, but the years without it had changed her into a husk. She held her stomach and caresses it lightly, glad of being reconnected with her soul. Her sacred self.

Physically she had changed too, as well as internally. She had been asking herself some very serious questions. Gone were the injections, aesthetic adjustments, severe regimen to keep her bone thin and a softer side was emerging. Growing out her natural brunette hair felt liberating. A little touch up of toner to cover some of the grey with a light tint, but her hair was glossier and long, down to her shoulders. She had put on weight from enjoying food again and it suited her. Giving her voluptuous curves and a goddess type quality. She was reconnecting with her power, and this felt exquisite. Polly's father had called her yesterday from prison, pleading once more for her not to divorce him, when he not gotten his own way, insults and abuse started. The call reaffirming her choices were right and holding the phone to her ear, she felt disconnected from him. His voice distant and alien now. Like a recording from long ago.. He was a stranger. Funny really, he just felt like somebody that she used to know, that knew her when she was a different person too. They no longer existed the two people in that entangled relationship of pursuer and avoider. The two lonely lost children that didn't fit with each other or anywhere, who tried to change each other to serve their own needs - the struggle killed them both in the end.

Whenever she thought of Polly, a deep shame bubbled up and the way she had treated the girl, she winced. Regret for the bond that could have been scratched at her throat. All those years wasted, spent looking for love from him when it was right in front of her and present in the child's outstretched arms all along.

There were lots of crumpled papers on the floor of the apartment from her various attempts at trying to say sorry to her only daughter, but none of the letters felt enough. They had started with sorry….

*for all the ways I let you down, for chasing the father figure I never had instead of being a warrior and using all of my energies to protect and have a good life with you. I'm sorry I hurt you when it was me that was hurting. You are me and I am you. I'm sorry that I did not break the patterns and left it to you to bear the pain and to take the responsibility to learn to break the cycle……*

There was so much she wanted to say but the words didn't quite come out right on paper. They looked too simple, too confined when all she wanted to do was shout out her admiration and her love for her cherished daughter. Would it matter to Polly to hear this now? She would not blame the girl if it was too late, she hoped it wasn't but would learn to love her from a distance if it was.

She heard his mobile phone ring in the bedroom, the call was urgent - it had been answered on the first ring. Her eyes are caught by the crumpled pieces of paper, strewn on the floor. Twenty attempts, not one posted. Words without action mean nothing, her therapist had said. Maybe she just needed to send one. To get started, to take the first step forward towards building a relationship with her child. She uncrumpled the best one and put it into the envelop that had been waiting for weeks to be filled with these notes and addressed it to the castle where Polly was staying.

In the communal hallway, she could hear her neighbour was closing his door in the next apartment. She run outside and speaking to him in fluent Spanish. Promises of a bottle of red wine on her balcony tonight were made in exchange for him posting this letter. He readily agreed and kisses her hand and tells her fleetingly of the man he had met last night who made him feel alive. They both giggle and he dashes off to work, already late so he shouts "adios, adios, hermosa" behind him. Her fingers touch her lips, and she blows him kisses and jumps up and down like a child. Happy for her friend. Bare foot, she pads back into her apartment. Back to her dark mysterious stranger, who had found her at her weakest point. He was perfect from the start. Presently, he was standing there in the hallway of their home. Staring out from unfamiliar eyes, distant, cold and harsh.

"Whatever is it, Angelo?" she asks him with concern. He drops his gaze, nodding towards his own hands and in them he holds a black hood, rope and a syringe that is spotting liquid onto the floor. She sighs, she is in trouble and for an instant, knows this is well deserved and succumbs to it. The ultimate punishment for the actions in her life. She was trying to make amends but secretly she had known that punishment would find her in the end, and she had been running from it for far too long. The relief that it is finally here was instant. Why did she have such bad taste in men.


Angelo was fully dressed in his black ops combat gear. He was placing his communication device on the inside of his bullet proof vest and inching his fingers into his tight black gloves, when the portal appears. He picked up the hooded and bound form of Mother and walked through the glistening light of the portal. He was carrying her limp hooded body through the swirling tunnel, trying not to glimpse back at the apartment they had both shared. He tries not to look at her either, a cold fist clenches hold of his stomach with each step he takes. Dropping down, he enters into Miles's opulent country estate that the billionaire uses as a retreat in the countryside of the Cotswolds, England. Walking into the banqueting room, he gently places mother's unconscious form on the chaise lounge, under the windows of the large country home. The agent shows a flicker of remorse for the woman that he had spent the last year with, but he shoves it aside and pulls out his glass wand and calls Nuala with it. "Got her here".

Nuala sashays into the room dressed in a liquid black shimmering latex dress. Her hair pulled back severely in a high ponytail, vampy winged eyeliner and her lips painted with a ruby red high gloss lipstick. "Well done, Angelo".

"My name is Stephan" he mutters in a quiet voice barely audible "what will you do with her?"

Miles tilts his head, questioningly and Nuala licks her lips with alarm at being questioned by one of the Company's agents. They don't usually care what happens around here, as long as they get paid "why, do you want to know, Agent?" Miles bursts out, demandingly.

Stephan hesitates, an agitation takes a grip of him "just wondered if I am needed, is all".

Miles looks at the agent with curiosity and then walks forward, leaning into his space "not developing a sudden attack of compassion, are you?" he says this with disgust and flexes his straining biceps, itching for a fight. Stephan shakes his head slowly, his long and thick eyelashes that frame his deep brown eyes are wet. He averts his gaze from Miles and walks out of the room and Miles watches him hawkishly, as he goes by.

"Right, how do we contact Polly? I want that crown by sundown."

Polly, Chris and Toni had made their way back up to the Castle following the meeting with Vusulia, that afternoon. Toni had given a strained apology to her friends, and they had accepted her words gladly, but an awkward and unspoken resentment clung to the three of them. Polly had wanted to tell Toni that she found her selfishness difficult. Toni in turn had wanted to say that she found the power shift in their dynamic hard. Chris wanted to say that he had "other-than-friendship" feelings for Polly, but he was scared because he had changed and was unsure if he would be accepted – being a shadow creature after all. He also felt a strong urge to shout at Toni for not putting Balan first. A lot of big feelings were not expressed and were left bubbling underneath and the three felt weighed down by the heaviness of their fears, which were left unshared.

Back in the grounds of the castle, they enter the library. They are greeted by the Professor with a grave look. Eleanora blankly states, "They have Mother and are demanding the crown of a demi-god in exchange for her back".

Polly hears the words and is ashamed to say she feels nothing, a blankness takes hold of her, and she looks at Eleanora and The Professor with a child's glassy-eyed stare, waiting for someone to give her direction on what the right thing is to do in these circumstances. She has withdrawn inwards; the whole situation is confusing her. Toni strokes her friend's arm knowing this news would be difficult to hear for her friend and for a number of very complex reasons. "Let's do what we can to get her back. It's the right thing to do". Toni flicks her gaze at Polly.

Polly mumbles and repeats "It's the right thing to do".

"So be it. We need to save Mother regardless of the cost" Eleanora says, surprising everyone" They have asked for the crown of Krones. We cannot take it by force. He is too strong. Stealth is the only way".

Polly nods blankly, "I'll, erm, get ready. Annika can open a portal and then pull me back through before he realises the crown's missing than that might just work". Eleanora notes the despondency in the girl's face and the general lowness of her mood. The Pagan Witch nods in agreement and watches Polly's back as she walked out of the room. Wondering if now the right time is to tell her about the sacrifice Mother had made all those years ago.


Chris was watching Polly too, deep in thought. He was worried about how much she is weighed down at present with the responsibility of everything. He clears his throat "I will go instead of Polly. I'll get the crown" he says earnestly.

"How boy? You are just a…a human?" Eleanora says unsurely, really taking the time to look at him properly for the first time in ages and realises something has changed. Esme walks into the room "another thing the Chosen One has not told me" Eleanora shouts to her sister and pointedly looked at Chris.

"Eleanora, Polly does not know" Esme says softly "there has not been a right time to tell her, yet. Chris, shall I come with you? Krones sleeps in an ice cave. If we go now, we might be able to sneak in and take it without him knowing. If he wakes, I can put him back to sleep. Well, at least try anyway."

Chris nods gratefully at Esme and they leave the room together. The Lady Esme is going to open the portal. Before she does, Esme hands Chris a set of small silver daggers. "m'dear boy, be careful. He is as wicked and cruel as he is big headed and large". Esme places her hands before her and starts moving them in a circle and before Polly even knows what is happening, Chris and Esme were on their way to the ice chamber of Krones on the World of Atmos, where the demi-god, son of the Goddess resides.

Chris steps neatly out of the portal and into the frozen cave that sparkles with an iridescent reflective light; those of the richness of glistening brilliant white and blue packed snow and ice. His breath is frozen mist that plumes out before him. The curls of his breath are made up of short bursts of air due to how nervous he feels. He had practised his new powers inside the gymnasium but had not used them outside of the castle yet. Not sure how people would react to these darker traits of magic that he had found he now possessed after the Vampire had sucked his blood and then smeared its own black blood callously across Chris's lips – infecting him.

Esme stops at the edge of the portal and Chris offers her his arm, which she gratefully accepts to get down. The Lady places her glass wand to her temple and asks for guidance as to where the sleeping chamber of Krones is located. An echo sounds back to her, and she is pleased to note, that the room is a short distance away. Stealthily, Chris moves forward without a sound but The Lady Esme's footsteps on the hard blue and green ice floor, are heavier and more pronounced.

Chris holds up his hand to signal stop and Esme reluctantly acknowledges that she was endangering them both so nods her agreement. Then Chris mounts the wall, crouching low, with his body as close to the surface as he could get it and moves silently, like a long-limbed spider across the wall, onto the ceiling and then slithers inside to enter the doorway of the chamber of Krones.

The room is empty apart from a hole in the ceiling to let in twinkling sun rays of natural light. Rising from the thick ice floor is an enclosed tube - Krones uses the ice bed to sleep in when he needs to recharge his energy stores. The tightly packed tube is made completely of ice and there is a gap in the top to get in and out of. Chris surveys the room, searchingly. By the gap in the tube, is Krones's single ringlet crown. It is made from the purest of gold from space. Relief hits Chris: a gladness steeps over him that Krones clearly did not like sleeping in it - that would have presented a multitude of problems. All around the chamber is a pink energy field that ripples and glows – an alarm system of some kind. Chris takes in a few large gulps of breath and then holds the oxygen in. Suspended from the wall, crawling forward. The tension from the effort of not breathing is making Chris's temples stand out either side of his head and a painful pressure is building behind his eyes – lung capacity was becoming an issue. Silently he crawls further up the wall and onto the ceiling. Clinging to the surface of the ice with small, miniscule barbs that extend out of his fingers, knees, and feet, enabling him to climb any type of surface. The other abilities manifesting in him are heightened senses; smell, taste, touch, sonar and hearing as well as super strength. He pauses, listening for any changes, above the tube. With some effort, he hooks his feet securely to the ceiling and lowering his chest and top half down to hover, just above the ice bed chamber. Just out of view of the hole. His developed abs and core holding him in place. His head is now spinning through lack of oxygen, but he dares not take in any breath at this key juncture. Tentatively he stretches out his fingers to grasp at the crown. His fingers brush the crown's tip, slipping slightly and a scratching sound of the metal on the ice give away the motion.

Stopping dead in motion, his veins are throbbing, and his eyes bulging, a red mist is clouding his vision, but he waits in that moment for any signs of motion from within the tank underneath him. His heart is pounding.

A few moments pass it that agonised state, he cannot wait any longer. Hoisting himself up through the strength of his core, regripping the ceiling. He places the crown in between his teeth and he silently crawls back over to the doorway, to the safety of the hall. Out corridor, he can see Esme. He body is tense and roused, wand drawn and pointed into the hallway beyond. His lungs are screaming. His breath, when he takes it in, is loud and heaving. Trying very hard to stifle a choking sound. Closing his eyes he stands, immobile from his exertions, trying to stop the swimming grey spots before his eyes. Esme takes his chin in her hand. Lifts his head to show him the urgency of the situation, shadows are moving forward in the hallway nearby. The guards would shortly be arriving. A cracking sound is coming from the room that Krones is in. He is waking.

Chris tries to lift his head, but dizziness has taken hold of him, from the lack of oxygen. There is no time. Esme must risk being heard. lifting her wand to the sky and she screams out a summoning spell to transport them back to the castle. Two golden armour-clad soldiers starts running towards the sound of the witch performing the spell and just as the guards are close enough to grab them, Esme sounds out a seismic charge spell and blows the hallway asunder and both the intruders disappear. Into an arc of sparkling light and tumble back through into the hallway of the castle - rolling and skidding along the wooden floors.


The momentum of the charge expelled by Esme, has them tumbling and rolling, finally crashing into the hallway wall, which brought them both to a complete stop. Two hands grab hold of Chris by the shoulders, and he is dragged upwards. Onto his feet. Thrusting out the crown in front of him he burbles out "I got it, I got it for Polly" he is still catching his breath and quite disorientated by the effort.

"Oh Chris, I am so glad to see you" Polly practically screams, and she crushes him under the weight of her frantic hug. "Polly" he murmurs, "you were too downcast to do this mission so…"

"Don't you *ever* do anything like this again" She bellows at him, red of face in a fit of temper "I am Chosen, and I decide that I can put my life at risk but not you. You must be safe. I've lost too much already, and I can't lose you too" she sobs into his cold chest. Chris had lights spinning in front of his eyes, unsure whether this is because of lack of oxygen or from Polly's bellowing directly in his ears – they are sensitive because of his new powers. He could not figure her out at all, but it didn't matter really.

He gently murmurs "I'm ok, I'm ok. I did it for you to keep you safe. Someone still needs to keep you safe" and with these caring words Polly's shoulders start to shake. He pulls the crown out from between them and hands it to her. "Now, go and get Mother" he says with a content smile on his face. Kissing his hands, she says "thank you" as she turns away and leaves the room.


Eleanora had sent a message to Nuala using the stone basin in the library and they had negotiated and agreed the exchange. Annika would open a portal and would send the crown through in exchange for Mother. The deal was set, and Polly paced up and down before the basin. Polly had a bad feeling about this and told Eleanora that she wanted to go through to the portal to get Mother herself but no one in the room agreed with this plan - it was too dangerous everyone had said.

A frisson of tension builds in the room. Annika conjures open the portal with one hand and in her other, holds up the crown within a pink bubble of energy – ready to move it through when they know Mother is safely coming through the portal. Annika could feel the form of Mother enter the other side of the portal. Closing her eyes, she searches for the physical shape of Mother and wraps an energy field around like a lasso - starting to wind her through. The motion abruptly stops and Mother is held firmly. In each of their heads the voice of Nuala could be heard "Start sending through the crown so I can feel it too and then I'll release the one you call Mother. Do not cross me." Eleanora nods at Annika and looks intently at the entrance. Annika floats the crown inside the portal. The crown is gripped out of her grasp with such a force , that it knocks the young girl over onto the floor. Not letting go of the cord, Annika pulls at the energy field holding Mother and it starts moving along the tunnel. Near the entrance, there is a violent jerk and then Mother is released.

 Mother appears at the edge of the gateway, while the pulsating light of the portal shimmers pink and white behind her – she is aglow like an angel. Raised above the group.    With wide shocked eyes, Mother surveys the room. Her gaze finds Polly, giving a sad warm smile. Tears quietly trickle down her soft cheeks. Her hands are holding her neck at an awkward angle and as her arms fall to her sides, blood begins seeping down, trickling onto to her chest. Mother crumples and her upper body begins listlessly falling forward, face down. Her body slides across the floor. Her beautiful glossy, brunette hair is spread out onto the library wooden slates, fallen, fanned out. A red liquid starts to slowly drip through the tendrils of her hair and out into a pool, on the floor.

A shocked vibration starts. All is quiet, all is calm until a scream bursts out into the middle of the people standing there - not knowing what to do. Polly had not realised she had opened her mouth nor that she could produce such a heart wrenching sound.

"Mother, Mum

mummy…"

Two of the Horned Gods requirements were met that day, inside that moment. The Crown was retrieved, and an enemy had been wounded…

## Chapter seventeen     Redemption

### The Letter

It was the day of Mother's funeral; she was to be buried in the grounds of the castle in one of the mausoleums near the pagan burial mounds. Polly's childhood home was being held under a joint investigation by His Majesty's Revenue and Customs and the police, to understand which of the Hanscombe's income streams had contributed towards buying the home. Polly would stand to inherit a sizeable fortune from Mother's personal estate when probate had run its course. Father had not realised this yet as Mother instructed her solicitors to place her own personal assets into a Trust for Polly. The divorce proceedings had also been finalised over the last few days before Mother's passing. He would be left penniless.

Over these days, Polly had remained in her room, with only Indy her cat for company, which soothed her sadness and wary soul. Indy had not left her side. Meals had been brought in on rotation. Plates of food were removed when she had not been inclined to eat. Staff came in and silently cleaned up around her. Chris and Toni had taken turns, at times, to sit quietly in the corner. While Polly sat in a chair, in her favourite pair of pyjamas, and stared though the window looking out over the changeable sea. She had taken to sitting there, not moving for days - she was in a type of meditative state. Present in the physical sense but not spiritually. Defeated, needing this time, undisturbed, to work something through - something was broken.

A letter arrives in a crumpled and creased envelope, with lots of Spanish postage stamps and markings, which confused everyone at first. Toni brought the envelope into the room Polly occupies and hands it to her friend. Recognising Mother's handwriting. Toni had seen various permission slips that were required during their school years together. Polly looks steadfastly ahead and the envelope flutters onto her lap, uncaught by her.

Toni quietly says, "you might want to read it, it's from Mother to you". Taking the envelope out of Polly's lap and places the wrinkled letter squarely in her friends' hands "it seems important" and then she left the room.

Polly's hand trembles slightly as she holds the envelope up to her eyes, that are red raw and like slits in her face. She curls a finger to lift up a corner of the papers edge and gradually tugs at the gum line of the envelope's lip. Opening the letter is mentally hard, she really didn't know what was going to be written inside and she couldn't bear it if it was more abuse, more hate being thrown at her, so she takes her time to pull the paper away from the envelope and begins to read the content within.

…afterwards, lifting her face to the blowing wind from the window. Her hair loose and blowing, streaming behind her, and her eyes are as turbulent as the grey sea. She immediately gets up, showers, and takes great pains to put on her battle armour. Heaving on her chainmail, the singing sound of a blade being holstered in its scabbard wringing in her ears, like the calls from the gulls outside. A warrior standing tall, she leaves the room, holding her silver battle axe on her shoulder - for courage. Her eyes glint with a renewed sense of purpose and her spirit, visibly risen.

Mothers' funeral..

The procession had started at the bottom of the hill of the castle. It is a dark and gloomy day. Esme had arranged all of the details of the funeral herself. honouring the human traditions by ordering a Hearst, a coffin, pall bearers and flowers, and the invitations asked for people to observe the tradition of wearing black - this was all very alien to the magical community. They preferred a ceremony that was linked to the returning of the self to nature, borrowed energy given back to the universe to start over again, anew. An ending and a beginning – the Rite is referred to as the rejoining.

The funeral march was to start at the bottom of the hill and wend its way up to the castle, where there was a small marquee erected. The mausoleum was of pagan design and had been built from small stones arranged without mortar - this had been built for Mother by wizards, as this the tradition. The last place she would occupy. Laid to rest.

The procession was a sorrowful sight. The Hearst, carrying Mother's body in a white coffin, snaked its way up the hillside under the cover of a thunderstorm. Chris, Toni, Esme, Eleanora, Professor Rothschild, some of the staff that knew Mother while she had stayed at the castle last year, and Father, in a black prison jumpsuit shackled to an armed police guard, walked behind the long stretched out black car at a steady pace. Polly was nowhere to be seen and Father kept muttering things about his daughter "Got her hands on the money and couldn't even turn up for her Mother's funeral, eh?".

Each time Eleanora goes to turn round on these occasions, but Esme places a steadying hand on her sister's arm and sadly shakes her head and says "What use is it, Eleanora? He does not understand the harm that he has inflicted. The wrongs that have been done are lost on the ignorant, sister. You know this."

"To wring his scrawny, measly neck would make me happy, Esme. Not every action is a teaching, well *you* know. " Eleanora replies with a sniff.

A colossal dark grey storm cloud is sweeping across the sky, it descends over the proceedings and a lightning bolt shoots down, striking the ground in front of the Hearst carrying the coffin. Followed by a cracking sound that wrung through the ears, vibrated the atoms, as the roadway tore apart – leaving a chasm in the road. A hissing and steaming from the earth, belching out black smoke. The ground rocks beneath them, and the car stops its crawl. Up above and in the sky, a figure could be seen on the horizon. It comes flying closer into view, all of the funeral group could see there is someone floating in the air with an axe held aloft. Holding a crackling, shining fire bolt, which lights up the under belly of the darkness of the rolling black clouds. Polly, it is Polly. She gently lands, dismounting. Her feet touch the ground, a slash across her cheek. Walking past the assembled group without a greeting. All are shocked, no one utters a word. A hushed silence has fallen and they stand watching her. Her axe in one hand and Krones's crown in the other. Striding forward, and without ceremony, she wrenches open the back doors of the Hearst and they fall away in her hands onto the floor. Lifting out the coffin in one heave. She flies it up with her, into the air and vanishes from sight as she enters the brooding black clouds, which are crackling with thunder and lightning above.

The funeral director had tried to intervene but just one look from Polly, quelled him back to the driving seat of the Hearst, where he pretended not to see  the coffin being stolen or a  flying human single-handedly carrying off a heavy coffin into a thunderstorm.

"What in the blazes was that and what the hell is going on? What happened? Was that…was that *her*?" Father screams out, looking unbelieving at the dot of his daughter flying off into the horizon with his ex-wife's coffin. Being flown away from view.

"For once,  will you shut the hell up, you snivelling piece of turd" and with that, Eleanora strides forward, uproariously  laughing out loud. The strain of the days before, leaving her face. Shrugging off her woollen  cloak and holding her fingers up to the dramatic and swollen sky. She steals away the memories of both the police officer and Father in an instant.

Polly lands, sopping wet and holding the coffin above her, in the Old Wood, in St Albans. Determinedly, heading straight for The Willow Tree. The day was windy and unsettled, leaves were swirling and twirling in the air and the long elongated leafy branches of the Willow tree sway in the torrents of wind and rain. Polly places the coffin on the floor and removes the lid, she gently cradles Mother's body in her arms. Defiantly, she lifts up her chin, crossing the threshold of the Willows land as she does so. Under the canopy of its branches, a calm descends. It is like entering a temple, the wind dies down and the air smells of the newness of life, of fauna, of abundance and new beginnings. Polly's nostrils flare and she soaks in the familiar smell that invokes a sense of stillness. She chokes out a wail.

They were all there. Already assembled. The She Wolf stands tall; The High Priestess is swathed in her silk tunic. The only difference on this occasion is that The High Priestess is dressed in full battle regalia; her helmet is on and her shield on her arm. This is in honour of the great sacrifice that Mother had made to save The Chosen One, to ultimately save the universe. The she wolf's amber eyes glow in the shade and the High Priestess bows in acknowledgement to Polly and the Rite she is about to perform – for the maternal, The ultimate sacrifice. The females in that clearing representing each stage of the divine life cycle of the trinity of the feminine; the Daughter, the Mother, the Warrior of Power and the essence of the Divine Femineity – The She-Wolf. Terrible in her Power as she is Maternal, the embodiment of Love and Wisdom.

Polly walks forward on trembling legs. Blood is smeared on her forehead, and in her hair but it is not her own or that of her Mother's. A hairline cut is knitting back together across her cheek. In complete silence, she bends down and places Mother in the place of the birth Rite. Pulling the Crown out from under her armour and placing it on Mother's head. She whispers in her Mother's ear, then waits with bated breath, uncertain of the worthiness. Her lip trembles when the halo appears over the lifeless head. The Rite follows on as is tradition. The body decomposes into the soil and then a wind sweeps through the clearing and smells of freshly cut grass –

206

Mother's favourite smell. The Willow sighs and The Maternal are joined. The branches swing upwards, towards The Chosen One. Reaching out to her and blowing in her direction *"Polly, Polly, Polly"* could be heard on the breeze and all around. *"I love you and I'm sorry, sorry for everything"* the Willow Tree whispers, and Polly loses her footing, the weakness in her knees, finally gives out. Bending low, doubled over, like a trunk in the howling wind. But she feels a sense of relief. There she lays still, and weeps. For the sacrifices that had been made. The Mother she will be to herself during this time of grief and when she is ready, the She- Wolf will rise in her again. The High Priestess rings out silver bells and all bow their head. Snow drops grow to meet where the Chosen One lay, the sun sets and the moon rises.

Polly had fallen asleep in that position and when she awoke, she laid still on the woodland floor with her eyes closed. Breathing in the stillness – the endless well of grief behind her eyes. She was alone. The bird's song and calls were bouncing around in the trees above her head. Sounding so very distant away to her in her mind, the grief leaking into rational thought. There was a gentle pitter patter of velvety softness falling against her face and body. When she opens her eyes, she could see the cherry blossom petals were falling from the canopy, thousands. Floating down towards her, covering her and there was an echoey sound rebounding all around – like the gentle pattering of rain. Whether she was dreaming or awake, the world looked altered and watery. Or maybe it was that she was not there, and this was a vision. Either way, she knew whatever would come next would be important. The thrumming of the heart was beating strongly, it was deafening and in quick succession.

*Thrum, Thrum, thrum, thrum, thrum.* Jumping up on her feet, ready for the awakening.

Before her, the images of Eleanora and Esme in the clearing talking to the she wolf. She could tell this was a vision from the past as the scene was watery and blurred round the edges like a film being replayed. The Eleanora in the vision turned away crying and Esme placed her staff before the she-wolf blocking the creature from taking the baby girl. The wolf ran away then a huge male entered the clearing she could hear nothing accept these words "where is my son" with understanding Polly walked forward, she was not observed, as she was not really there. This was a scene from long ago. Bending down now and looking into the bundle on the floor, where a second beautiful dark-skinned baby clutched at its own feet, hands reaching out. Searching for his mother. She watched as Eleanora and Esme took the girl baby with the necklace on - realisation dawned it was her. And when all was quiet, the wolf snuck back and started to dig at the ground and took the other baby for its own.

"Balan, Brother?" Polly stands tall with a sudden clarity of understanding and thought back to what the High Priestess had told her.

*He is Chosen too.*


Polly stands outside the Gates of Claridges, with her face between two decorative spindles of iron rods bolstered into the iron wrought gate, while the heart thrummed in her ears. Pulsating, driving her on and the cherry blossoms stream out behind her. Londoners walking the pavement look on in disbelief. The cherry blossom trees are bursting into full bloom in August and not spring, and the petals are culminating and swirling around the girl dressed in armour - like a swallow's aerial display and she is the highest point. The passersby rush to get away, so frightened are they. Quite bewildered by the strange happenings, not wanting to get involved.

Gaze fixed ahead. Looking into the entrance hall of the grand hotel hungrily, Polly wants what is waiting for her inside. Utterly convinced that what is in there is the missing piece of the puzzle that would save her new-found brother. Her real family nestled within him.

Memories swirl within her; she was always drawn to the room called The Library in this place. Polly does not remember being here due to Elenora's memory charm.

The two porters posted either side of the front entrance door of the Grand Hotel, are this moment, watching the young woman in her silver battle armour, with a clammy deep concern etched on their smiling faces "Can we help you? Do you need help?" they called to her from where they were stationed, not wanting to get too close. Looking through them, Polly is certain they are human and not embroiled in anything untoward.

Polly stands  stock still and waits, no reply is uttered from her lips. And then, and then a man with a shaven head and a symbol on his forehead, spindly and tall looms into view. With black robes, he walks out of the famous black and white mosaic tiled hallway and he looks at Polly with fearful eyes "You cannot come in. You cannot be here. You are too early. Please leave." He holds his hand up but knows this will not stop The Chosen One – all is futile.

In answer to his words, Polly boldly and quite deliberately withdraws her sword. Taken it out from where it was sheathed in a leather-bound holdall on her back. The ore sings through the air, as she slices it diagonally in a show of power and places it double handed before her. Her steely gaze upon the entrance.

"Easy now love…. what's all this about" say the porters in their thick London accents, not fully realising the precariousness of their situation, in the grand scheme of things.

"I've come to get the heart. The Dragon's egg and I will not be stopped" she forcefully pushes on her helmet. The metal gleams as if made of starlight. The nose protector, a small thin strip, covering the length of Polly's nose, gleams and glistens and casts a star beam so blinding into the eyes of the porters. "What dragon, what's this about. *You* need to calm down love and put away your sword erm, please." shrieks one of the porters in alarm.

The Chosen One is on one knee, offering thanks to the Goddess and then standing tall, calling forth a lightning bolt. It answers her call. Wrenching through the air, shooting down, sizzling through the sky and is harnessed by the living Sword of Hestia. Runing forward with her mighty weapons by her side, Polly kicks out at the spindly man's chest, knocking him backwards and throws her axe in the air and it arcs over her head and lands in her other hand, she reels back and throws a lightning bolt at the entrance of Claridges. 'BOOM', the entrance hall crumples inwards. Great chunks of the structure fall downwards in the wanton destruction of her assault. A smote cloud throws up in response to the explosion and when it clears away by the wind, Polly is standing there in full battle regalia, ablaze, in the entrance way with the smouldering amber and slitted eyes of the dragon. Unseeing but intent of purpose. Her sword and axe swinging, ready for the first onslaught.

One of the human porters that had been stationed outside, was now laid out on the floor. He then gives a little cough and waves his hat to clear the dust clouds away from his vocal cords. "Erm, welcome to Claridges" he manages to say before his head rolls sideways and he drifts off into unconsciousness.

The spindly man is splayed spread eagled on the floor, and he stays down, pinned there with her axe and Polly surveys the view inside. She confidently walks through the decadent and opulent hallway of the grand hotel. Well, it had been prior to Polly's arrival. Now, it looks quite the opposite covered in debris and rubble. Ten of the Brotherhood priests are running towards her, down the art-deco staircase. Polly raises her sword flatways, pointing the weapon toward the group and bellows.

"Give me the egg and not all of you will need to die this night" They hesitate, looking with concern at the bellowing warrior but still they come. She ran at them each in turn, pummelling, kicking, slicing and twirling, knocking their legs out from under them. She is ferocious, she is fury and chaos and they succumb to her sword, like tin cans to a handgun.

Afterwards, all of the priests are on the floor and each nursing a broken or cut ligament in some way. Polly looks to the left and into the sage and cream decorated restaurant area, where she had heard the tinkling of cutlery. To her astonishment, there are hazy shadows of human guests enjoying their meals and listening to the pianist and harpist playing in the dining area and waiting staff serving them exquisite delicacies. "So, this place is interdimensional and although, I can see the guests and staff, they cannot see me or the Brotherhood priests. Well, that makes this infinitely easier", with that, she swings her axe n her shoulder and walks over to one of the priests lying face down on the stairwell, he was the closet. Lifting his head, she questions "Where is my dragon's egg?". He burbles out a response, nonsensically about women not being strong enough to control such powerful creatures - ironically, as he and nine of his fellow priests had just been bested by one. Polly replies "I don't intend to control the dragon. The dragon is my kin. I am a Kaidaluminere."

She tuts at him, he is of no use to her in his current state, so she places his head back down. Surveying the room, she quickly realises that the other priests are pretty much in a similar condition. Sheathing her sword at her back and placing her axe in her belt, she pulls out a few small throwing daggers and places these in between her teeth, ready for anything. She closes her eyes, with her hands stretched outwards and listens intently for a sign.

*Thrum, thrum, thrum, thrum, thrum*

The heart is strumming, the beat is moving the blood of the ancient creature. Awakening from a long slumber. Polly feels the pounding and beating in tune with her own heart. "Where are you? Let me know and I will come for you?" Slowly, she starts to step forward and nearer to the sound, the vibration of the thrumming. Pulling her towards the back of the building and into one of the smaller dining areas called The Library. As she enters the room, a crackling fire explodes outwards from the hearth of the fireplace and spreads quickly. Consuming the walls, the tables, the chairs and each surface is alight with yellow, orange and amber flames of The Ancient.

Walking through the burning room and entering the fire fully. She is being drawn to the hottest point of the furnace. Where the fire is white-hot and burning brightest. In the stone fireplace is a large intricately wrought and old, silver ore box. The size of a coffee table. The thrumming is in her eyes, beating at her eyeballs. Veins throbbing and covering her sight in a redness, as she guides her hand towards the lid and reaches out to lift the battered frame up. There inside are broken pieces of eggshell and curled up laying on a straw blanket is a baby dragon. Covered in glittery scales of reddish brown. Still swamped in its own birthing fluid. The dragon slowly opens its large amber eyes. They are a strange colour, with flecks of green. Feline shaped with a bold stare. The majestic creature searches out Polly's and the two gaze at each other with the same amber and hazel eyes, instantly connected, and bonded.

Rocking backwards and forwards, to stand on its spindly legs, the newborn dragon unsteadily gets up and crawls towards Polly. Using the claw on the tip of its wings to pull itself forward.

In wonder, Polly picks up the dragon and cradles the creature in her arms, stroking its reddish golden silky scales and cooing over the wonderment of all she beholds. The Dragon hiccups and an enormous flame shoots out. Smashing through a window and igniting some detritus in the courtyard outside. "Oops" Polly says lovingly. Smiling down at the baby dragon. The dragon looks up at her face, nuzzling into her cheek, then softly snuggles into her arms and falls promptly to sleep. Completely at ease, The Dragon knows she is with her own line - her family, her mother. The flames all around the room suddenly go out and a serene calm blankets the room. The Dragon is the ancient one, the protector of the vulnerable and with her eyes she can see Polly's true heart - it is blinding to her, and she is drawn to it. The Dragon and The Chosen are One and they are the next part of the tapestry of the rich line of Kaidaluminere.

*Dearest Polly,*

*There are no words but there are so many things I want to say to you but none of it will be enough to express my deepest regret at the loss of you as a daughter. The pain I feel now for you not having or experienced a mother's love. That unconditional devotion in this life. My heart, my soul and my everything is ashamed of the way I have behaved, and I want to make it up to you and try every day, every hour, every minute to be the mother you deserve. I honestly can say that I don't understand the mess we are in, but I know that I want to do everything to put it right. I gave up my soul you see. I had to. So, the evil things could not find you.*

*I love you with all of my heart and I would like to meet you and explain all these things to you myself.*

*With lots of love*

*Your Mummy xxx*

## Chapter eighteen - Gathering

*Injure the enemy - steal the crown - obtain the horn that was broken.*

"WHATTHEHELLLLLLLLLL" Miles bellows with a cold fury and rage, which could be felt throughout his country house. A curdling angry scream shots out of the room Miles is occupying. *"SHE CAME IN AND JUST TOOK THE CROWN?"* the windows shake.

Nuala stands there, observing Miles with a casual look of bored bemusement on her perfect face. A dining table is picked up and hurled with full force against a wall. Able just about manages to jump out of the way of the trajectory, just in time. The wood of the table lay there, smashed into pieces on the floor and Able glares at Miles with a look of utter loathing in his eyes.

"Polly appeared out of nowhere. Literally nowhere. A portal opened and she jumped through. None of the agents in the room stood a chance. They attacked her and she killed them one by one. The only agent that got away with his life literally had to feign that he was dead. He told us that she was crazed with rage and screaming at them that they had killed her mother. I mean what was that all about?" Able asks looking between Miles and Nuala "You didn't kill the kids Mother, right? Right? Nuala?"

Miles turned away with his back facing the room where Able and Nuala stood. He held the bridge of his nose and closes his eyes thinking through his next steps. He cannot summon The Horned God without all three tasks being complete. Stress was building behind his eyes, making him feel confused. He needs another vial of the compound to keep him focussed. Nuala was getting ready to perform the Rite tonight to offer the objects and request that the Horned One consider Miles for his Champion. Kane had not outright objected to giving Nuala the Horn, but he had not agreed either. Now, they had the added complication of Polly having stolen the crown. At least, they now know that they had injured the enemy by her Mother being killed, so that task was complete at least.

Nuala purses her pillow like lips before saying "I am going home. We cannot perform the Rite in these…conditions. Contact me when you have everything in place."

"There's no other way then?" Miles holds out hope for another method.

The Shadow creature that is Nuala truly is shakes her head "He appeared to you and was clear with what He expected. There are no substitutes. He made His request, and we have to fulfil it. Calling Him without all three in place is dangerous, reckless. He would very well slaughter us if we don't give Him what He wants." then Nuala promptly left the room, without even a backward glance.

Miles runs to the doorway and shouts to Nuala as she walks down the corridor with her back to him "Hey, you're not going to tell Krones about any of this are you? He'll be pretty pissed off about his crown, Nuala? Nuala?", but she was already gone.

Kane enters the room, pushing his way past Miles. He gave out a low whistle "Redecorating, are we?" he says, as his eyeline is drawn to the smashed remnants of the wooden table.

Miles holds the vial to his chest and then gulps the liquid back greedily, a vein in his neck starts throbbing and his pallor is reddening, indicating that his whole body is strained under the pressure of taking too much of the compound.

"Where's the Horn, Kane? Miles asks, ready for a fight.

"Safe, somewhere very safe" says Kane, he slowly turns towards Able "So, the Chosen One was she here? Did she say where she was heading or about her plans?"

Able shakes his head and his gaze lingers on Kane for longer than he had intended. There is something different about Kane that he could not quite define. There was evidence of it in the way he had asked about the girl.

215

"Hey, Able. come with me. I need to show you something and you are not going to believe it, my friend" Kane gave Able a penetrating stare, and, in the background, music could be heard coming from Kane's room. An electric guitar was rifting on a radio in the distance. A thrumming was the most prominent sound. The tune was The House of The Rising Sun by a group called The Animals, but from afar it sounded like a beating heart.

The restoration of lost souls…


Toni looks at her reflection in the mirror of her bedroom dressing table, she is pleased with what she sees. Gone are the tension lines from last year and instead, there is a peaceful contentment. Toni uses a little magic to lengthen and thicken her eyelashes and had used a tiny bit of a spell to make her cupids bow lips more hydrated and plumper and her cheeks bones a little more prominent. She wondered what Eleanora would think about these little adjustments, considering she was not allowed to use magic at this time. Sighing heavily, but still pouting, she picks up her brush and starts running it through the long brown hair strands of her weave. Mama had all the wigs and weaves in the household professionally shampooed and cleaned last week and the smell of aromatherapy oils are delicately wafting back to her as she brushes through the hair. A tunic lay over a chair, brightly coloured and made in the form of Nigerian tradition. A matching gele headdress is placed alongside. She had asked Mama and her Aunties for help to give her the strength to use magic safely. To have more control over the power. Instead of the power having control over her - apprehension overshadowed the ceremony, which was to be performed this night. What would they do to her, and would it be as painful as the Rite they had performed on her before, she wondered?

 Lifting herself from her dressing stool, she heads over to the garment, takes it out from the dry-cleaning cellophane and shimmies into the tunic style dress and then places the gele on, affixing it tightly. She crossed the vastness of her bedroom, decorated in all white furnishings, floor to ceiling mirrors, with an ensuite and a walk-in wardrobe the size of a small bedroom. Off of one of the shoe shelves, she takes a pair of crystal Louboutin high heel shoes. "Well, hello my pretties" she caresses the material lovingly, then slips the heels on. Doing a dance to break them in, reflecting that even though the world of magic is an exciting place to be part of, she did miss the glitz and glam of the human world - the parties, the Nigerian food, the celebrations of community. The magical world is quite a serious    place and there was always a mission to complete and no time just to enjoy being alive. She sashays back over to the dressing table and sprays on Allure by Chanel. Inhaling the heady scent.   Looking in the mirror, her make-up is perfect and her outfit in place, raising her chin, with a look of determination. She zaps a small spot off of her face and walks downstairs, to the secret rooms, where rituals are performed, at the back of the sprawling house she calls home.

There is a secret set of rooms in this house that Toni and her brother, Edmund were not allowed in as small children. Unbeknown to them at the time, their Mama is a practising white witch and sacred guardian of the earth. Each generation of their family has been gifted powers to heal and remove blackness from the souls of people. This power is fiercely protected and handed down from each generation to the next. The Rite used to pass the power to Toni, did not go as planned and was left incomplete so tonight the group are gathered with the aim to complete the spell and hope it will give Toni full control over her own powers.

The scene is set. The Aunties are in full Nigerian ceremonial dress, with light linen hooded robes blanketing them. On the floor, is a great expanse of reddish terracotta-brown earth, which is powerful when used in a spell and the walls, are of stone. In the centre of the floor,  a star is drawn. Etched in with thick lines of chalk. Stationed at each point of the star is an Auntie holding a root, a rock and a candle. All but one of the Aunties are holding these objects. The other is using two of her fingers to beat a small drum made from tree and nature. Toni's father is here, sitting cross legged in the corner. Here to give his child courage to complete the Rite, this time round.

A deep guttural humming from the women, sends up a harmonised vibration into the room and the Aunties start to sway to the rhythm of the sound they are making, as a collective. The drumming can be heard, *one-two, one two, one two,* like a fluttering heart and Mama steps forward in a white linen robe, with a wooden mask, painted with natural dyes of cobalt blue and terracotta red and dots of creamy white wet chalk. The humming quickens and tribal yelling begins. Mama takes Toni's hand and leads her to stand before the first Auntie, she utters "strength of the lion" and blows a spell into Toni's face and then they move on to the next Auntie "speed of the Antelope on the planes" she gently extends her hand and blows and then they move on, "eyes of the falcon", onto the next auntie "endurance of the crocodile" and then the last Auntie "grace and heart of the elephant, oldest and wisest of us all". Mama turns to face Toni and takes hold of both of her hands in her own "daughter of mine, I give you your birthright, the power to heal others from the fullness of your own heart" with that she touches her own heart and then places her hand on Toni's "let it be with you, let it always guide you, let it be your truth", with that Toni starts to glow with an iridescent blinding white light. Her eyes turn a golden hue and the assembled crowd gasp out collectively. She is laid down at the centre of the drawn star. The ground changes beneath her, moving from earth to a view of the cosmos – Toni is floating. Tiny effervescent orbs float out of the roots and stones held by the Aunties and golden spheres from the beeswax candles positioned in the room. The orbs of light swirl around Toni, softly landing on her and melding with the luminescence of her soul. Only this time, she accepts them gladly, and with a full and open heart. The magic is bonded to her and she to the magic - they are one. Mama looks on and weeps. The eye of Destiny is upon her daughter, and she is scared of what this means for Toni and her family. The birthright and the generational power she had come to know, was being meddled with. The powers gifted this night are so much bigger than she had ever seen before. Mama's all-seeing eyes widen with fear. Whatever is going to happen to Toni, would happen to her family too - they would go with her and accompany her to the end.

When the ceremony is complete, the other aunties and Mama had left the room to give Toni some privacy. Aunty Ola had waited behind. The caring woman had wanted to check something she had seen during the ritual. Toni slips on her shoes. Aunty Ola calls out to Toni and as the girl turns her head, her eyes are covered in a thick oil-like blackness. It is as Aunty Ola had feared. Toni calls out to her "Oh, you forgot to pick up the roots. Here you go" handing them to Aunty Ola.

"We need to bury them for you to complete the Rite" says Auntie Ola and silently she turns away from her goddaughter and cries not knowing what else to do.

***

Polly had opened a portal and returned to the Castle in Scotland, carrying the baby dragon in her arms like a precious gift. Her eyes were drinking in the creature, mesmerised. Her gaze constantly drawn to her miracle one - like a moth to the flickering flame. Walking casually through the castle embracing the bundle close to her armoured chest. Not trying to be deliberately secretive, but she does want this time to herself. Walking up the stairwell, passing the history on every wall, she does not notice anything or anyone, her complete focus on the baby dragon asleep in her arms. Unlocking the apartment door, Indy strolls up to greet her and catches an unknown smell. Ambling closer, padding into the bedroom, he follows, then gracefully hops onto the bed. Indy the cat reels backwards, in alarm. He could smell the features of the creature. The scales, the teeth, the sulphur-breath. Alarmed with his eyes as wide as possible, he goes to dart out of the apartment. The creature is quicker, slippery like a serpent, it slithers up to the cat. Rearing upwards, holding the cat under the magical, hypnotic gaze of its fierce eyes. Polly puts her arm out and cuddles Indy to her "Hey, if we are going to live here together then there are a few rules that you need to know. Indy is our family, and he is my baby too, so it means he is your brother."

The cat hisses and the dragon eyes him suspiciously, but an understanding is reached – the baby Dragon understands what Polly had told her. Tentatively and silently, the Dragon moves and carefully nuzzles at the cat. Indy's shock is held in his eyes, refusing to turn his head. But he does not run and after a while, visibly relaxes - an uneasy agreement had been silently reached as Indy the cat pads over to the over side of the four-poster bed and lays down on his usual spot to fall asleep.

The dragon makes to follow, but Polly stops her "let's give him some space and I'm sure he'll come round soon to how adorable you are". The dragon nods and smoke curls the side of her snout, then she nestles down on the soft down filled duvet and falls fast to sleep.

The days passed by, and Castle life hums on in the background while Polly welcomed the dragon and made a home with her new scaly member of the family, in the apartment wing away from the others. Toni had arrived at the castle with her Mama and her five gloriously noisy and colourfully vibrant Aunties. This kept Toni exceptionally busy. Wherever Mama and the Aunties were in the castle, they seemed to spread an excited sense of wellbeing and happiness with their loud laughter, dancing and penchant for bursting into joyous song. They took over cooking the evening meals with a gusto and ushered the protesting kitchen staff out the door, giving them time off but telling them to be back for dinner, to taste all the delicious food they prepared - they would eat together. Mama was regularly out of the castle grounds, visiting the village nearest to the castle to look after the older, frailer and poorer members of the magical community, to heal the sick. She was constantly in a state of doing something for the people of the community, making potions and ointments in the mornings and then going out on her visits in the afternoon, taking her now famous Jollof rice with her and various spicy bean soups and pickles, and sweet treats.

Chris was busy too in his own world and had taken to studying in the library and then training in the gymnasium each day. His appearance had changed from a tall, gangly and awkward teenager to a more confident young man and his daily activities were changing his physique too. To muscular, filled out and chiselled. The jade green of his eyes had become more deeply luminous with a telltale ring of red around his iris. He was letting his hair grow out, both on his head and on his face.

Some of the younger castle staff had taken to making excuses to find tasks to do that were near him in the castle. When he trained shirtless in the gymnasium, some of the occupants of the castle found they had to urgently collect something or other from the vicinity. Chris was unaware of this attention; all he was focussed on was honing his new skills and brooding about how Polly would react when she eventually found out about this new darker part of himself that he did not quite understand.

Mid-week Toni tracked him down while he was practising kickboxing in the gym by himself. The gym smelt fuggy, of sweat, antiseptic, talcum powder and effort.

"My word, someone is looking mighty FINE these days. If I did not know you were a nerdy, bookie, annoying person, I'd think you were a hottie. Well, that is until you open your mouth" Toni says with a wide magnificent grin on her beautiful face. Her large hoop earrings jangling, as she whips her neck from side to side, exaggerating her wickedness.

Chris does a roundhouse kick, and the head comes off the dummy he is practising on. As he lands on his feet, he lightly rolls forward and jumps up at Toni to surprise her, deliberately making her lose her footing and fall over backwards. He stands laughing.

"CHRIS" she shouts, "what was that for?"

"For punishment" he says with a wicked glint in his eye and a lopsided grin on his handsome face. They both burst out laughing, enjoying teasing each other and being silly - the bond they share is like siblings, and strong.

"So, have you told Polly about your new abilities and what did she say?" Toni asks slyly, getting straight to the point, as usual.

"No, I haven't seen her for a few days. I decided to give her some space. y'know what with Mother and all" he replies, his large green eyes becoming quite intense and shadowed.

"Yeah, I get you, but I haven't seen her either for a few days so maybe we need to pay her a visit together. What do you think?" Toni asks, wondering if he was deliberately stalling and didn't want to talk about the situation with Polly.

Chris nods apprehensively and then stares downwards at his feet. Before another word is spoken and Chris had a chance to change his mind, Toni rolls her eyes at him and starts dragging him towards the door. Up the smooth sandstone steps, towards Polly's suite on the upper floor of the castle.

Within ten minutes, Chris and Toni arrive at Polly's door and knock lightly. They can hear movement inside. Loud banging and the dragging of furniture, and a strange roaring sound. A yell breaks out, followed by a shriek then the sound of a fire extinguisher being spurted onto the wooden floor. Next, Polly's feet could be heard pounding towards the front door - Toni and Chris looked at each other with raised eyebrows, not knowing what to expect, the sounds coming from the apartment are becoming exceedingly chaotic. Polly opens the door a crack and pokes her head outside. The smell of smoke wafts into the faces of her two friends.

"Hi there, how are you both doing? I am, erm, kind of busy at the moment, can I come and find you in a bit?" Polly says this with smoke smudged over her face and a large burning patch on her trouser leg, continues to sizzle, as she is standing there talking to her friends - Polly's is trying to pat it out surreptitiously. Toni and Chris flinch backwards as thick curls of black, smoke come out of the apartment. The sight of this alarms her two friends and they both start looking around her, trying to peer inside her home. Chris pushes open the door, with his broad hand and Polly falls back inside, she is quite baffled as to how Chris had managed to best her strength. Peering down the hallway after him, she notices his wide shoulders and muscular back, as he walks down the hallway and through to the lounge. Toni takes the opportunity to jump over Polly while she is in a heap on the floor and quickly makes a dash to follow Chris.

A few seconds pass, "WHAT IN THE WORLD" is all Polly heard Toni shriek from the living room, before she had the wits to jump up and run down the hallway after them both.

Chris and Toni are stood frozen to the spot, staring into the centre of the room at an enormous reddish brown coloured dragon, with scales the size of eggs, and as tall as a barn. The Dragon's head is bumping against the high ceilings of the apartment, as uncoordinated as a fly trying to escape through a window. The large creature is gently holding Indy the cat, in its large, clawed front paws, and nuzzling him with its large fire breathing snout. The cat is purring and gently batting the underside of the colossal creatures heavily scaled and glittering, cream coloured belly. Toni and Chris both turn to face Polly, with shocked expressions on their faces.

"Listen, I can explain, I was going to come and find you today but, erm, I can't leave Cassadian because she tends to set things alight when I'm not here, by accident of course." Polly hurriedly added, running her fingers nervously through her ponytail, and  nodding her head. Trying to encourage Chris and Toni to agree with her by placing an eager look on her hopeful face. This doesn't work. "She doesn't know her own strength" Polly says while lovingly staring up at Cassadian the lethal Dragon, with a tinkling, chuckle in her voice.

Toni stares at Polly for a while with open mouthed incredulity "Have you gone crazy? Have you actually gone MAD? Woman, you have got a DRAGON in your lounge, and it is the size of a small house. It breathes FIRE and you have called it Cassadian?" Toni shouts in shocked disbelief. Hand on her hip.

"She's not an IT, Toni and her name is Cassie, its short for Cassadian. She only breathes fire when she is upset or left alone for too long" Polly says this while straightening up. Folding her arms crossly and then says, "I am her mother".

Toni's eyes widen and she juts out her face, ready to quip back Chris quickly steps forward and stands between the two young women, in attempt to deescalate the situation. He has noticed the Dragon is scrutinising Toni and he is worried about how the Dragon will react, if Toni starts shouting at Polly.  Chris says "Polly, This is really, ah…cool, but Cassie can't stay here. She'll tear apart the castle at this size…ah, how exactly did you even get her in here?" Chris asked logically and looking around the dimensions of the apartment, quite baffled.

Polly takes in Chris, he was standing there in his black kickboxing trousers, with a loose-fitting black linen shirt casually open, revealing his hard-earned chest and abs. Polly felt a warm sensation snaking through her body. Making her feel overwhelmed. She throws herself back on the sofa and decides not to look at Chris directly for a while – he's just too distracting "Cassie wasn't this size a few days ago", she whispers "She was just a bit bigger than Indy when she hatched and she's just kept growing and growing and doubling in size each day. I don't think she has stopped yet, either" Polly has worry lines slightly etched into her forehead and she keeps biting her bottom lip.

"Keeps growing? As in, it's going to get BIGGER?" Toni shouts out in exasperation and the 'IT' snorts out a shot of fire, which barely skims past Toni's shoulder. Hitting the wall behind her, melting a small brass vase back to liquid, and it begins dripping molten metal from the shelf, ominously. Pooling onto the floor. Toni narrows her eyes and whips her neck round to look at Cassie. Holding out her hands ready to cast a spell. Cassie immediately sensing the threat, lurches forward, aggressively sniffing at her with her long snout. Teeth bared, letting out a mighty roar. Her snout is crinkled ready to breathe out fire again.

"Toni, *please* stop shouting, Cassie is sensitive and doesn't like it" Polly says this, while jumping up and standing on tiptoes to stroke the dragon's face to calm her down.

Toni went to shout something else, and Chris holds up a hand but moves quickly, to stand in front of Toni again. He says "I've got it, let's put a transmogrification spell on her. Change Cassie into something smaller. More socially acceptable. Like a, like a" then his eyes meet with Indy's friendly slow-blinking amber eyes. Indy softly meows "like a cat" Chris says. Polly picks up Indy in her arms and nuzzles his fur and then pats Cassie's cheeks, "yes, that's a great idea. They are very similar in character too. You know, playful, sleep a lot, loving and perfect" says Polly, spinning around with Indy, in her excitement.

"Crazy, psychotic, arrogant, entitled and demanding too" Toni harrumphed, and Cassie bared her teeth and Indy licked his paws, quite disinterested in the situation on the whole.

"Great, so we will transmogrify the dragon into a cat, but we will need to ensure she can change back when she needs to take dragon form. Polly, can you explain this all to Cassie do you think?" Chris asks.

Polly nods and quickly adds "Great, now we've got a plan for Cassie, I can go and get the other Dragon egg being guarded by the Willow Tree and hatch that one too." With that Polly takes Cassie's face into her hands to whisper the plan in her ear. All the while behind her, Chris looks at Toni and Toni looks back with concern in her eyes and mouths "There's another one? When was she going to tell us about all of this?" Chris shakes his head in bewilderment. Watching the Dragon. Marvelling at the beautiful creature of myth and legend, being turned into a little tabby cat before his eyes. Chris smiles to himself, revelling in the richness of his life and reflecting on the fact that no one day is ever the same.

Polly walks under the canopy of the willow tree with Chris beside her, shoulder to shoulder. He is dressed all in black armour and his curly, sun-kissed tendrils of his hair is spiralling down to his shoulders. Polly is dressed in a flowing white dress. Where her naked feet touches the ground, snow drops spring up. The trees sway in the wind and whisper to her of the Kaidaluminere line and of Destiny. "Mother tree, I have come for the egg that you have kept safe for me." The Willow Tree bows and obliges. Knowing it is time and opens her roots, the moss creeps back, exposing an opening to the chamber underground.

There inside, is the scaly eggshell, cracked open and shattered into small parts. Sitting inside blinking up at the sunlight, is a reddish-brown dragon covered in its own birthing fluid. This Dragon is different; he has a more pronounced crown of horns on his forehead and a rind of horns down his back reaching to the tip of his tail. A  male dragon, with a much bigger jawline and a larger chest. His claws are more pronounced too. Polly leans forward and picks him up to cuddle him into her arms. Gazing at his precious claws and rejoices in his rich, wise amber eyes. As she looks down on him, she whispers her love into his ears and crooning softly. His name is Casperian. Chris gazes at Polly. He sees there on her flushed face, the slitted amber eyes of the dragon. "He is going to make a wonderful ginger tom. Just look at his large amber eyes and front claws" Chris says lovingly, and Polly pushes back into Chris and puts her head on his shoulder, and they gaze adoringly at Casper the newest addition to the family. Polly feels a coldness leaning on Chris in this way. The chill of his diamond-hard skin permeates the thin material of her dress, but she does not want to ask, and he does not want to confirm and they both, through acts of omission, had silently agreed not to discuss the worrying thing that had been left unsaid. There is an unspoken fear of ruining this perfect moment in the warmth of the sunlight, holding in their arms a creature that symbolises the everlasting burning of the sun.

## Chapter nineteen - Of the coming storm

In the back of Polly's wardrobe in her apartment wing of the castle, her old and now unused, school rucksack starts to smoulder. Unattended and unseen. The two white feathers, innocently given to her by the dove in July of last year, were magically changing from soft white plumage to hardening into a type of metal material, which has never before been seen on earth. The air stirs around the rucksack. Little particles of dust fly away from the metal feathers. Propelled outwards by an invisible force. The contents of the bag are moving or a better way to describe what is happening would be to say that something or someone is coming through. From the inside of the bag, a finger digs a hole in the zipper and starts to pry the material apart, trying to push through. A man's calloused hand could be seen and that heavy hand broke through the thin cloth holding the zip in place. Two muscular arms emerge through the rucksack, clad in golden armour. Then the head, the shoulders, the torso and the lastly the legs. Crouching, the figure drops down out of the wooden wardrobe onto the floor. He standing tall. Hulking, shaking out his legs, and wipes the sweat from his face with a large hand. He picks up the metal feathers and then proceeds to stalk out of the bedroom on his long legs and into the living room of Polly's apartment.

The ginger cat silently observes the stranger walk by, he is curled in the hallway before a cool air vent. This is the ginger cat's favourite spot on a hot summer's day. Casper the dragon-cat opens one eye as the tall man walks past him and starts down the hallway. The feline casually lifts his head, stretching his large back quarters, and trots after the stranger. With each step forward taken, the cat's form starts to change. To grow in mass at an accelerated rate and the man walks before the dragon-cat, unknowing what is happening behind.

Polly is unaware that someone is currently roaming around her apartment uninvited. She is on the sofa in the lounge writing in her journal, trying to make sense of the last few days. She is completely absorbed with working through her grief at the loss of Mother. Cassie the tabby cat is laying in a lounging position between Polly's legs, in a blissed-out state.

Before the stranger could reach the doorway of the room Polly is in, the intruder feels something is not quite right. A creeping sensation is tickling at his spine and blowing on the hairs on the back of his neck for him to pay closer attention. Hesitating, he stands silently for a while to observe and then continues to stalk past the large windows of the apartment, heading towards the sound of Polly's scratching quill in her leather-bound journal. He is near to the lounge doorway now, when he notices a large shadow stretching out before him. He does not recognise it as his own. He looks around for a sign of what could be casting the shadow shape before him. When he hears the most terrifying sound. The first rumbling growl of the mighty Casperian, Dragon of the Ancient and Creature of the Sun. Changer of Worlds. Destiny awakened in form. The intruder starts to look over his shoulder . . .

Polly heard the guttural rumbling growl and large intake of breath and knew that a fire bolt would soon follow next. Cassie's ears flick back in alarm, the other dragon-cat jumps down from the sofa and runs towards the sound of the Dragon's bellowing call. Polly follows in quick succession and there in the hallway, Casper has the intruder in gold armour cornered and is opening his mouth ready to devour the trespassing foe. Casper could not stand at full height, as he was too large to fit into the hallway. Banging his head on the wall and ceiling - this was making him very angry and aggressive indeed. Just as the smell of sulphur starts to fill the air and the burning hot furnace is fully conjured at the base of Casper's throat, ready to breathe out white hot flame, Polly acts on instinct. Jumping in front of the great dragon shouting. Frantically waving her arms for him to stop. The Dragon rears backwards, before dropping onto all fours and closes his mouth hurriedly. Still glaring at the trespasser, with his teeth bared. Polly sensing the immediate danger is over, turns and shouts "Kane, what the hell are you doing here?".

229

Kane stood in shock for a while, watching the immense dragon gradually reduce in size and change back into a ginger cat. He watched the Dragon-Cat trot off to the lounge with Cassie the tabby dragon-cat not too far behind him. When they returned back in the hallway, Indy the Cat-Cat appeared with both of the Dragon-Cats. and they all padded out quite serenely into the hallway and out through their cat flap to get Chris.

Kane watched in silent amazement before he shook himself back into reality. His head full of questions. "You have three dragons? Where did they come from? Do dragons usually turn into cats?" Kane asks his eyes full of wonderment.

"No, just the two dragons that we have enchanted to hide them as cats. We call them dragon-cats, and the black and white kitty, Indy is a cat, cat…Hey, no, wait. You don't get to ask questions. Me first. What are you doing here? Why have you broken into my home" says Polly, pulling a large cross bolt from where it hung on the wall. "I'm giving you exactly one minute before I call everyone in here, and let Casper devour you, so you had better talk and fast. He hasn't had his dinner yet.".

"You're not going to believe me if I tell you so I'm going to give you something to show you that I'm not a threat" He has both of his hands with his palms facing up to Polly. "Can I get something out of my armour please?". He moves his eyes to indicate he has something under his chest plate of his armour.

Polly sternly nods once and then pulls the tension back on the bow of the crossbow, ready to use the weapon and aims the point at Kane's neck. "I'm warning you, you even blink funny and I let this arrow glide straight through your eyes."

"Understood" Kane pulls out the two metal feathers of the dove and the tigers eye ring that Mama had given to Polly on her last birthday. Over a year ago, it had a small precious stone embedded in the crystal and the ring shines brightly in Kane's hand. He held them both in his open and outstretched hand and gestured towards Polly to take them from him.

Polly raised an eyebrow "What are they? Tell me now or I'll shoot you stone cold dead where you stand. I promise.".

Kane gives a pleading look "Polly, they are some of the gifts given to the Chosen. This is the two feathers gifted to the Chosen One and the ring of Vusulia. You have the Vessel Life, right?".

Polly momentarily relaxes her grip on the cross bow, and she stares, astonished at Kane "some of the seven sacred objects, but how?"

"Touch them, you will feel their power. They will be drawn to you, you're the Chosen One, after all." Kane says this as he smiles down on Polly. Polly hesitates and starts reaching out her hand towards the objects, not taking her eyes from Kane for one second. As she drew nearer, a light wind lifts tufts of her hair from her forehead and an amber glow settles over her, gently framing her face and the glow extends out to the objects in Kane's hands. That's when the huge man does the oddest thing. He bends down on one knee and places his sword before Polly. Vowing fealty to The Chosen One. Gazing downwards, the huge man who had once tried to kill Polly, talks in a hushed, quiet voice "I am your sworn protector and I come to serve The Chosen One" and that is how Chris found them both as he walked into Polly's apartment minutes later.

Chris, Polly, Toni, are all sitting in Polly's lounge on the plump sofas, nervously sitting in silence. Drinking coffee together, the three friends are looking at Kane with suspicion in their eyes. Kane sat quite still in an armchair and waited. The tension is broken with a collective feeling of relief as the Professor enters the room and makes to sit down opposite Kane.

The all begin speaking at once to the Professor. He raises a hand to silence them all and then in a very calm voice, asks Kane to begin.

Kane looks over at Polly, beseeching her to give him the benefit of the doubt and hear what he has to say, and then he begins "Well, I was sucked into the Vessel of Life and the object transported me into another dimensional plane full of demons and evil. That's where I have spent the last thousand years. I had a lot of time to think in that place of misery and violence, I was alone. I started to see that I deserved what I got. That I had created my own hell by seeking power and living a life of violence, and greed. I asked for a way to repent. That's when I came across a little girl, wandering in the parched desert of that desolate place. She had been part of a sacrifice that hadn't quite gone to plan. I vowed that I would protect her with my life and that's when She appeared to me." Kane says this while rubbing his hands over his face and shaking his head in wonder.

"Who Kane? Who appeared to you?" the Professor, encouraged him on.

"The High Priestess, Bringer of Destiny. She told me to deliver the child to safety through the Pinnacle of Shadows Temple and then guard The Horn until I found a way to get back to serve The Chosen One. She told me that I was redeemed, that I had saved my soul and the soul of the little girl and that I was reborn, and this was my journey to the light. It had to be through the blackest of paths. She told me that those who have seen the darkest depths, can see the brightest of lights and rejoice in them the more for it. My journey, she called the thousands strokes of night. One stroke for each year I spent in one of the hell dimensions. She said to me that only through the hell of the darkness of midnight would I be able to finally rejoice in the coming of the dawn." Kane's eyes well with tears, before he ended by saying,

"I must bear the pain everyday of what I have done, I will see all of their faces and I must not be consumed by it anymore. I must serve Polly. Turning the darkness into something good" He looks at Polly "I am your sworn protector, and you are my salvation. I can't explain this, and I know it all sounds like a bunch of baloney. Even if I were blind, I would see this is my future. I just feel it in my heart" with that he thumped his armoured chest.

A slow hiss issues forth into the room. "So, we are just supposed to believe this steaming pile of bull, are we?" Toni says with eyes challenging the group. "He says he is delivered, and we are to believe it, without question?".

"Toni has got a point, Kane. How do we know we can trust you? What can you say to reassure us? Last time I saw you, you shot me in the gut, and you were trying to start Armageddon and wipe out all of humanity" questions the Professor, with a steely look in his usually kind eyes.

Kane hangs his head low "I brought with me a couple of the sacred objects and I presented them to Polly. I hope that goes someway to show you I want to atone but if it isn't then I will show you I am trustworthy every day until The Chosen One believes it, believes me. I am here for you Polly and I will do whatever you tell me to", Kane speaks directly to Polly, ignoring the rest of the group. To him it is only her opinion that matters.

Then a strange thing happens inside that moment, that made the group stop their conversation dead. Casper and Cassie trot over to Kane, lightly jumping on his legs and they both curl up on his lap together. Kane looks down at the pair of unassuming dragon-cats, with tears in his eyes he starts to stroke them both under their respective chins. Polly looks at her Dragon's behaviour and sees this as a sign.

Polly looked on with an assessing and curious look on her face. Eventually she says "Ok, well, I guess we can only play this out, so what have you come to tell me?" Polly says and a huge grin spread across Kane's large face and the tension in his eyes disappeared, as the relief set in.

"Miles is preparing to offer himself as a Champion to The Horned God. He was intending to offer three gifts named by The Horned God himself. He only has one of the gifts now. He needs the broken Horn of The Horned God" Kane pulled this out of his bag and showed it to Polly but cautioned against touching it "don't touch it, it is cursed" he hastily put it back in his bag "and Polly you have the other gift, the crown of a demi-god, so we have stopped him from becoming the champion, but he will not give up. He is crazed and taking too much of the compound. He is coming for you Polly and planning on storming this Castle with his agents. Although, he is losing agents every day and some of The Company are starting to defect and fight against him. I can call them here if you trust me enough?".

Polly faces Kane "I guess, they only way to know is to do. Let's face it, we are going to need all the help we can get" Polly says, with a steely determination. Kane slumps down in his chair with gratitude.

Toni huffs and the Professor's eyebrows are furrowed, but a quiet resolve descends on Chris, as he turns to Polly and smiles. "You always were able to see people, like, really see them and it's good to know you believe in yourself again".

Toni tuts and gets up and leaves the room in a frustrated march but not before she throws over her shoulder a few words of caution "I hope you know what you are doing, Polly is all I can say".

The others reflected on these words and in the uncomfortable silence that follows, Polly asks "How many sacred objects do we have now?" Chris counts out loud the Vessel of Life, the ring of Vusulia, the two feathers given to the Chosen One and he holds up four fingers. "Ok, the High Priestess told me I had the skull of the White Hart too, so I'll need to figure this out. That would be five when I do. That leaves the Bone of the elder and the Coin of Malvern to find".

The rest of the assembled group watch as Polly gets up and leans over to squeeze Kane's shoulder "I'm glad to have you on the team. Please don't make me regret my decision. We need strong people like you on our side" and then she left the room with the sacred objects and carried them downstairs towards to give them to Eleanora and Esme for safe keeping.


Polly charges down the stairs leaping from the top step to the bottom step in one great bound. Continuing down the levels of the castle in the same way. Within seconds she has moved from the upper floors of the castle to the ground floor. Stumbling to a halt when she reaches the west wing, the floor which Eleanora and Esme, The Lady, occupies. The Pagan Witch sisters share a large and lavish apartment together. She raps on the door a few times, dropping one of the sacred objects, the ring, in the process. Bending down to pick it up, Eleanora appears at the door. "You had better come in, Pollux. We need to show you something".

Eleanora's eyes are solemn and her posture tense and with that, Eleanora beckons The Chosen One follow her, walking Polly through the apartment.

"What is it?" Polly says with an anxious infliction in her voice. Stepping through the terracotta and cream natural plaster hallway, which is lined with a mix of curious looking plants. And out onto the balcony, where the sun is setting and the statues on the terraced balcony are casting low shadows across the tiled floor.

In the centre of the room, The Lady Esme has her eyes closed shut, and a grim determination settled on her face. Esme's face had changed since first arriving at the castle after her rescue. Gone were the hollow and shrunken cheeks, in their place were plump and fullness of face and her eyes were a glistening aquamarine blue. Esme was still healing from her time imprisoned by Miles, but her soul was lighter, and laughter came more easily to her now. So it was a shock for Polly to see her with such a sombre shadow across her brow.

"We've managed to bind Balan to this plane but as much as we try, we cannot seem to place a locator spell on him. This would help us to pull him back through to us. We are being blocked by a very powerful spell" says The Lady Esme and she takes a breath before she continues on "it's odd, it's like I open a channel and then a blackness surrounds me and there are whipping screeching winds all around and I am consumed, blinded to all. I am not strong enough for The Black Dahlia, I'm afraid."

Fearfully, Polly weighs the words and looks up into the setting sun. Holding her amulet to her mouth for comfort. She is scared but won't admit it to the pagan witch sisters. Scared of seeing the Black Witch again as she nearly managed to take control of Polly and pull her into her realm last time - a cold sweat trickles down Polly's spine. The self-doubt creeps in and she is struggling to steady her breath and calm down. What would become of the world if the Black Dahlia took hold of The Chosen One's power? Polly didn't want to even contemplate this. Polly takes a look at the Pagan Witches and knows she needs to help. "Ok, let me join you as my strength might help us find a way to pull Balan through". Polly sits down trembling with fear, crossed legged. Holding her amulet in one hand and

The Lady Esme's hand in the other, and Polly then squeezes her eyes closed.

A darkness drops suddenly like a black curtain. All Polly's senses are covered in what feels to her like an oozing tar. An alarming deafness, closing down over, like a great blanket of isolation. Polly's eyes are open but there is nothing but the fathomless blackness of the void before her and the careening winds, which screech and swirl all around in this black desolate hole. Nothing else could be heard but the silence of her loneliness bubbling up and chiming in her ears. And the screeching winds, the gales, that are goose bumping her flesh and lashing her like whips made from sticky ice. Polly calls out to Balan in that dark place, and she could hear the thrumming pulse through her veins in response. She calls his name "Balan. Balan. I have come for you. Here I am. I will take the curse and you will be free of her. You have my word. Balan. Balan" she frantically calls out into the chaos of the wind and darkness. She realises that she is alone. Searching the void for Esme but Polly cannot feel her presence at all. Panic rises up in her, she is alone and forsaken.

Beneath her feet is a yawning chasm of nothingness. It stretches into infinity, a void in time. All around her is a rushing sound, like she is falling through space. Whispering spells in dead languages are fluttering on the careening wind. Reality is bending here and bridging itself into the fabric of time and space. Her mind is being tickled, tortured, and slowly pulled apart - she could not stay in this place for too long, she was unravelling.

The Black Dahlia's gigantic black eyes appear out of nowhere. Floating above Polly's head. Lidless in the blackness all around. This was a place of dark power, of perpetual terrors of the night - this is where the predators come to devour the hunted and hold their bones until the winds diminish them into dust.

Polly is murmuring to herself, feeling demented by the pressure of the curse that had hold of Balan. She is near the evil of it and it is tormenting her. Polly could feel Balan, smell him, yet he could not be reached. From her sadness, grew an ember of selflessness, which is one of the most powerful bases for magic there is. A light grows behind The Chosen One's eyes. Her amulet glows brightly in that foul space where the curse takes hold and is all consuming. The light behind her eyes is building, brighter and brighter and brighter it glows, until the core of Polly's being begins to vibrate. It is radiating her, a seismic mass of energy wrapping around her body. Each atom in her body is holding on to an indestructible force of light. The energy charges through her and comes blasting outwards with the force of a thousand stars, the charge is emitting the white light of the universe - the energy of life. The dark matter surrounding her is pushed outwards to the fringes of the ever-expanding universe.

The dark witch, The Black Dahlia is burned by that light. She writhes around in pain, blistered and shrivelled. Her own weakness revolts her. Forcefully removed from that dimension, back into the bedroom chamber of The Manor House - back to her own reality. The dark witch crawls along and screams out her fury. Scratching at her face and arms in despair. Snarling and curling her lip like a feral beast. But then she halts, catching a whiff of something familiar and sniffs at the air. Smacking her lips and licking the roof of her mouth with her tongue, tasting the golden glow of the particles that came from Polly, The Chosen One. She has tasted this before. Sniffing at the air, turned her head slowly, catching the scent once again inside this house.

Quickly, she marches out of her bed chamber and into the next room where the prone form of Balan is laid on a cold and harsh edged table. Gliding towards him, sniffing, and sucking in the air around him. An evil smile spreads across her angular, borrowed face. The familiar taste of the golden particles of The Chosen One's power lingers in the air above Balan's muscular, but lifeless body. Laughing out loud to herself, "Oh, it is too delicious. Oh, it is too easy. What can it mean and all that power waiting to be pried open like an oyster with the sweetest golden pearl inside of him, just like his sister. Oh, we must unite the siblings, would you not say. My sweet vessel of delicious power?" she cackles and insanely laughs, stroking Balan's sleeping face. Her eyes growing into shadow and darkness, devoid of all soul.

*He is Chosen too…*

## Chapter twenty - Sacrifice and Sorrow

Polly is left floating in pitch black darkness, suspended in the void. The dead space between dimensions. Head slumped forward onto her chest, unconscious from releasing the charge of a thousand stars. Her amulet shimmers and pulsates. She jolts awake, feeling a freezing cold wrapped round her, following the discharge of such white-hot immense power. There is something else. She senses that the curse has been removed from this dimensions. There is no gravity here, so she uses her momentum to fly forward to touch the barrier that is containing Balan inside. When she finds the solid shell of the spell, she pulls back her fist to punch through the force field, but notices someone walking slowly towards her on the other side of the translucent barrier. It is the figure of Balan.

Polly screams out to him, and relief shines on her face. "Here, here. I'm over here." Polly waves with a childlike joy, tears prickling her eyes as she kicks her legs to float nearer to him.

But as Balan comes towards her, she can see in the shape of his walk and the way he is holding himself that it is not him - it is the imposter. The eyes are black, and the face contorted with rage and hate. The Black Dahlia still has him in her grip. The Chosen One's shoulders slump forward, and tears fill her hazel eyes. The Black Witch stands confidently behind the barrier in the body of Balan and she throws her head back and laughs, wickedly.

"The Chosen One giggling like a little girl, waving away and now slumped, defeated. Oh how, marvellous this is. Thank you for giving me the pleasure of showing your despair, your helplessness. The taste of it is utterly delicious to me and nourishes me even more, so please do continue" The Witch catcalls out with black eyes that glint in the blankness of the space.

"Where is he? What have you done to him?" Polly cries out with outrage, losing all semblance of control.

"He is here with me, captured and imprisoned. I am coming for you in his body. Coming to cut your pretty head open and devour your soul and you will weep knowing that it is his hand that separates your stupid head from your body". Each word is emphasised with malice and dripping with poison "Then I will take the power of the two and let's see what the universe and all its light energy does when darkness descends, little girl. When the void closes in." The Black Dahlia takes one of her fingers and scrapes a talon sharp nail down Balan's forearm. A goading glare at Polly, while she hurts Balan and Polly knows there is nothing she can do but watch hopelessly. "See you soon Chosen Wimp". The Witch then evaporates in a swirl of particles and dust, leaving her black eyes to dissipate last, and Polly's turmoil breaks free. Screaming. The echoes of the decibels of her pain bounce around the denseness of the black space. She continues to scream out in terror, as Eleanora and Esme pull her back into her own reality and guide her back to the safe confines of the Castle - well safe for now that is.

*The Witch is coming.*

Polly is screaming. Esme takes her into her arms and the older Witch listens and soothes her. "The Black Dahlia is hurting Balan, and she is on her way here now. I don't have all the sacred objects and to kill her I need to drink from the Vessel of Life and alight the Sword of Hestia with Dragon's flame to destroy her once and for all."

Eleanora and Esme gasp and look gravely at each other and a look of fear passes between the sisters. Polly rubs her eyes and blows her nose.

Eleanora looks thoughtful and steps forward "Well, crying is *not* going to help you, Pollux." Eleanora sternly says, and she takes Polly's face in her hand to look into the Chosen One's eyes "Within you is summer even when Winter is biting cold and the snow and ice brings death. You still don't understand, do you? You must understand this. You are the cosmos, my girl. The life force of everything starts with you" Eleanora points a finger at Polly's chest and the thrumming starts up in that room.

"Eleanora, no. Now is not the time" Esme says putting her arm around Polly to comfort her from Eleanora's words.

"No, Esme. Now is precisely the right time. Pollux has the power and has always had it within her. The thrumming of the Heart of the World, The stone, it has been telling her this all along. She cannot be afraid because then we are all doomed. Listen Pollux. Listen to an old women who has earned every hard-won scar and every one of them I covet because I am better for it. When you was a little girl did you not notice that when you cried it rained and the universe cried with you? and when you was happy the sun shone the brighter for it? You hold the universe in your hand and are the guardian of it and it is a part of you. So, what if a dark witch is coming. She will learn to kneel before you and be silenced by the coming of the storm within you. The Power of the stars will not be vanquished by a speck of dark dust. You are everything my girl and everything is you. Call on that power, wield it and you will be formidable". Esme smashes her clenched fist into the palm of her hand.

Polly looks up at Eleanora, her mentor and for the first time she feels she truly understands the enormity of the battle ahead. It wasn't just about getting through this battle with The Black Dahlia, as terrifying as that may be. Polly is seeing for the first time that she, as The Chosen One is pivotal in the fight for life itself. To defend the light of the universe, to ensure that darkness does not cover everything and make the light go out. "Now, Pollux find that strength and let us get on with what we must do. We do not have all the objects, but The Black Dahlia is not all powerful, so let's hope we do not need all of them" Eleanora says.

"Balan is Chosen, and she has Balan" Polly whispers, looking up through her thick eyelashes. Sullen, peaky but resigned.

Toni steps out from behind Eleanora. No one had noticed her enter the room. She had been drawn here by the magical charge of power that had been summoned by Polly "Well, then we need to find a way of separating The Black Dahlia from Balan. I can find a spell to end a possession and draw her out of him, I'm sure" Toni says, hugging Polly. "When he is free, Balan will want to fight alongside you. There is something else, Miles is coming to the castle to reclaim the Crown with his Cronies. He still thinks you have it".

". . . And I'll find a way to keep Miles and the agents busy when they arrive" says Chris, pushing himself off the wall he is leaning against and stepping forward to take his turn to hug Polly. Her heart fluttered when he held her close to him.

"And me, well, I guess I'm about the right size to give Krones a headache" says Kane, with Cassie and Casper lounging on each of his massive shoulders.

"Esme and I will keep Nuala entertained and the Professor can help prepare and fortify the castle." chimes in Eleanora.

"Mama and my aunties will want to fight too" Toni says this with a pride glistening in her eyes. "Whatever, we are going to do, we will all do together" Toni started stroking Cassie. Cassie's eyes widen in shock at being disturbed, before settling back down on Kane's shoulder, not enjoying the attention but getting used to it.

"I can't ask you to do this. This is too dangerous, and this is my fight…. I" The Professor interrupts Polly by saying "Polly, we are with you, and we want to fight with you, to protect what we know and love in this life. You are not alone."

Polly looks at the group assembled together, and an overwhelming gratitude bubbles up in her and swells in her chest. The Chosen One goes to say something but no words come out. There are no words to describe her thanks to them all. She stands there with tears in her eyes as each one of them in turn, tenderly pats her on the shoulder, as they head out of the doorway and onto the preparations for the battle ahead.

Kane stops and says, "I think Cassie and Casper will need to be a bit bigger and used to training outside and fighting in flight before they can enter the battle with you." Kane was looking down fondly at the two dragon-cats who have climbed down and were cradled asleep, in his huge arms.

Polly nods and says, "I will need to light the sword with their fire, but other than that they will need to stay hidden, until they are fully grown".

Kane agrees "I'll take them to the top bell tower, where it's just open air, stone and more stone. Completely fireproof. Come when you are ready with the Sword of Hestia".

"Come to the healers' quarters when you are ready too. Eleanora and I will get the Vessel of Life and start the spell by using the sacred objects that we have, and we will think of some other magical artefacts to balance the spell". Esme says this with an encouraging smile and holds Polly's hands in her own and gives Polly's hands a gentle squeeze, then leaves Chris and Polly alone in the room.

The silence unfolds before them and they stand apart facing each other, looking everywhere in the room avoiding each other's eyes - the situation is perilous this night and they both know it. There is so much to say, but how to begin. They both do not know. Chris's face shows the anguish that he feels inside, knowing that Polly is heading into danger. He looks at her with an intensity and she looks into his green eyes, and it stirs a nostalgic memory of long ago within her aching heart. Forgotten summers, of running in parks,

And blowing on wispy dandelion- milk witch heads.

Of play fighting with water pistols.

Of playing in wild gardens in secret.

Stealing kisses in the summer in games of chasing each other.

Of throwing skimming rocks at the swelling sea on days out.

Of balmy days and cosy winter nights drinking hot chocolate.

Of screaming at the tops of their voices in abandoned train tunnels.

And of feeling the anguish of being separated from friends for the night.

Of the care shown when she crumpled.

Of being silently there waiting when she needed him.

Of friendship that grew into longing, of being held in his arms.

If this was her last night, then she would go out knowing she had loved and been loved in return. A lump grew in her throat thinking of all the good in humans, all the potential, the love shared and the special bond of life.

At last Polly whispers, "Thank you." Chris stirs, looking intently at her. "Thank you, Christopher for giving me everything I need to fight for, I want nothing more than people to be able to continue to be, just be and rejoice in every precious moment of life, the type of which, you have given me freely. I have learnt to hold myself in wonder, especially the dark places". Repeating the words of the Professor like a question she is answering put to her so very long ago.

Chris holds out his hand and grasps for hers. Locking fingers until there are no gaps. He closes his eyes and holds her hand to his face. His cheeks are wet. Then one of them speaks but this could have been said by both of them.

"Come back to me. I don't know what I am without you. Since I first met you, I've been in love with you".

"For all this time?"

"For all this time, now and forever"

Chris leans forward and Polly does too, and when their lips meet, there in that one moment, as adults,  a million different lives with endless possibilities are created by the happiness that they give to each other. Awareness slips over them. They are the architects of their own universe; their singular energies are binding together. Chris and Polly se all those moments of joy in the future and are hungry to be a part of that future, together. They both now have a reason to keep fighting on, together and for each other, forever more.

When they break apart, Polly's knees are weak and Chris stumbles back, they look longingly at each other's mouths, each other's lips. Breathing in each other's perfect skin, aching to be touched and held by the other.

She touches her own lips. They are freezing cold. "Chris, does it hurt you, you know the cold?"

Chris hesitates and then stirs, not wanting to let go of Polly, but he could hear on the periphery of his sonic hearing the demons filling the fields in front of the castle outside. He turns back to face the centre of his world "No, not at all, Polly." he says reassuringly and then adds with his lopsided grin "The Professor thinks I've got the best of both worlds actually. The vampire transferred infected blood that mingled with my own but not enough to fully turn me, so I have the legendary powers of the nightcrawlers, the strength but I don't need to feed on blood or any of the other typical behaviours. It's really fascinating, and I've been researching a lot of the history. When we have time, I'd like to show you. I wanted to check that it can't be passed on to my own children, you see…", they both look at each, knowing what he is asking her inside that moment. He wanted everything with her and was hopeful she wanted the same too.

Polly smiles sweetly and touches the stubble on his jaw line and chin. She traces her finger along his nose and wipes a lingering tear from his eyelashes and kisses his fingers. "any child will be so very lucky to have you as a father. I hope for this for us too" then she turns away, and silently walks out of the door to go to put her battle gear on, to ready herself. To protect what is her own and it is so much more than she had ever dreamed possible.

Chris holds his own hand up to his face and touches the warm imprints she had left behind. Smiling, the relief that he is accepted floods him. He turns to look out over the balcony, to linger over the precious moment that was shared. Night is falling fast and shadows from the forest are creeping forward over the dark emerald grass of the meadow below. All he could see are the torchlights held aloft by Miles' troops on one side of the field and on the other, the demon army that The Black Dahlia is marching into view. There are a thousand flaming torches lit and the army of foes are beating their drums, riling each other, and baying out their bloodlust. Killers of worlds. The sounds of troops getting ready for battle fills the night air - death bringers and hope destroyers the lot of them. Chris's spirit is crushed, and he found it hard to breathe in the open air of that balcony. Chris blinks back cold tears, brought on by the shock of the sheer numbers of enemies before him.  All wanting Polly's death.  The end of The Chosen, so the darkness of evil could consume the world and humanity's light would be snubbed out. Leaving the ashes of their bones behind - reducing humanity to wisps of memory in the great void of time. He was not expecting to see this number of fighters walking into the field before him. It was a terrifying sight. With urgency, he stumbled backwards, he would need to get to the great hall and to the group to coordinate the defensive attack to keep Polly safe.

Polly walks into the vast hallway; her countenance altered. She had changed into a black leather outfit with a hard body of armour covering her and a small set of silver throwing knives hidden down her trouser legs. The Sword of Hestia is in a scabbard, affixed to a leather belt, worn around her waist. In one hand she holds her silver axe and in the other, a cross bow and at her back is a satchel that holds numerous arrows. Her hair pulled up in a high ponytail and she has on black running boots.

The scores of people present all stop talking, a reverent hush falls over the crowd. They collectively turn around to look at Polly as she walks self-consciously into the room. Their eyes are pitying like she is dead already. Toni catches the discomfort for her friend and bounds over first "I found a spell to pull Balan from the Dark Witch. Mama and me, we are going to perform it together", Toni holds out her hand and Mama walks into it, clasping her daughter and gently placing some of Polly's hair behind her ear, with her other hand.

"Pol Pol, there are no words. Please look after yourself this night and we will do everything we can to protect you". Polly leans forward and lightly kisses Mama's cheek.

"You've always been so kind to me. Thank you, thank you for giving me that" Polly says to Toni's Mama in a slightly disconnected voice, holding both of Tomi's mama's arms in a warm, final gesture.

Mama noticed a change, she looks around at Polly with concern and goes to say "Polly, are you okay? You don't have to do this. We will find another way…" but Polly does not hear her as Eleanora steps forward and guides Polly away and towards an area of the hall where a pentagram is drawn on the floor. The Vessel of Life is set in the middle, the silver and rubies adorning the chalice are glittering in the candlelight and the cup has a steamy smoky liquid bubbling out of the brim.

Polly stares at the Vessel with unblinking eyes. She is disconnecting from the environment, focussed on her internal infrastructure. Fortifying herself with emotional sandbags against the people around her. She cannot allow herself to get overwhelmed, worrying about everyone she loves and cares for in this castle. The prize is much bigger tonight, the prize is one step forward into saving the world and the universe from eternal darkness. Even if that means giving her last breath in order to save every living thing. Polly looks around, she tightens her grip around the handle of her axe, but she does not see the people or the castle. She looks beyond into the universe and all living things. In doing so, she recalls the tapestry of the Kaidaluminere line to her mind and the depiction of the girl throwing herself into the volcano. She was shown that for a reason, she knows this to be true now. There were promises made to Chris that she knows she might not be able to keep.

Looking down at her fingers, she flips them over and stares at them, one holding an axe and the other a crossbow. When did it all turn to violence for her? When did it come to this? The answer is simple, this started when Miles and The Inner Circle made a decision to destroy humanity and take the planet for themselves. Well, that was a decision that they were going to

247

live to regret, and she would make sure of it, personally - into the fire and at the end of everything, Miles will pay.

"Hello, I'm here to fight" says a young boy with thick black curly hair, beautiful caramel skin and he is tall for his age.

Polly looks down at him, her vision clouded in her despair. He is looking up at her and she sees the hope in his eyes reflected back in her own "what's your name?" she says, a smile forming on her lips.

"Max, well, Maximillan but everyone calls me Max. I'm here to fight. I'm good too. I've done lots of Taekwondo. I'm a black belt in karate too" The young boy called Max proudly says while he flourishes his hand in a chopping motion. Polly doesn't quite know why but he reminds her of herself and Chris, and of Toni too. He is tall and proud with a ready smile. Polly gently touches his shoulder. "I'm sure you are a great warrior, but can you do something for me? It's really important. Can you guard the healers' quarters for me? I can't be everywhere you see, and you look strong", Polly says trying to protect him from himself. Understanding that she was born to fight this fight alone.

"Aha" Max nods and runs off energetically, with a sword in his hand to the back of the castle. Polly watched him as he goes with a renewed sense of hope in her own heart. The hope of the young and the true. The hope of children like Max for the future of the planet. Polly gazes after the boy for a long time, he did not know it, but he had innocently given her a precious gift this night, a glimpse of why she had to win at all costs - for children like Max to have a wonderful childhood and a future.

Polly cannot shift her gaze from the spot where Max run off. Knowing that when she does, there is nothing left to distract her, nothing more to see. The fight would truly begin. . .

"Polly, the potion is ready" says Eleanora, as she ushers the people out of the room. The only ones left behind are Polly, Toni, Esme, and Eleanora. The spell had been started and the sacred objects were placed in the Vessel of Life while the liquid within bubbled. Esme was incanting a spell in a long-forgotten language of the celts. She beckoned to Polly to step onto the Pentagram and stand before the Vessel. "What is in the spell, we don't have all the sacred objects, yet?" Polly says this, unsure and feeling uncertain. She picks at a thread on her sleeve.

"The spell for the sacred objects has in part been used, but it will only offer protection and to fortify your powers. It will not enact the prophecy as you need all the objects to do that" says Esme, in a strange, distant voice, sun vapour swirls in her eyes, and they are tinged with a golden hue. "Now, step forward, we do not have time."

Polly closes her eyes, puts her hand on her heart and inhales a long breath and as she slowly exhales, she takes a leap of faith forward into the pentagon.

The whole world stops. Polly is alone on the inside of the pentagram; the room is gone and all around her is the night sky and the stars. Thick, icy smoke erupts from the Vessel and covering the pentagram in a dense fog. She looks either side but cannot see anything apart from the great expanse of the milky way and it is covered in a shimmering pink and yellow light of gases drifting lazily from the enormous star maker in the distance. The view of the galaxies is beautiful and breathtaking, so Polly stands still to admire the great symphony of the universe. It is revolving round her and she is at the centre of where it all began. Life. The Centre of Everything.

Her eyes remain wide open and in them, the reflection of the cosmos. Polly gets the sense that she could stay in here for the rest of all time and she would be hidden, she would be given everything she could ever wish for, whatever miracle her heart could imagine would be made available, but that is not her fate. Her gaze drifts over to the Vessel and she stands before it and thinks of her friends, of Chris, then steps forward to stand in front of the silver Chalice and she places her hands around the base, and lifting it to her lips, she begins to drink.

"Where is she? Where did she go?" Toni shouts out anxiously pacing around the chalk lined pentagram.

"Where has the Vessel gone?" yells out Eleanora "They were both here a moment ago" Eleanora was walking around the drawn star, clockwise and

Toni the opposite way to her. They were both tense and focussed on the middle of the pentagram.

Esme with the hood up on her cloak tunes out their noise, she is calm and grounded. A message is being delivered to The Chosen One in that space in between time and the seasons – the unknown of the universe's structure. She hoped the encounter would give Polly courage in the fight ahead.

. . . And then a vibrant golden line appears above the pentagram space, and the tip of a sword being cut downwards appears. It is opening up the line further, and it cracks apart and gets wider and wider. A brilliant white light covers the room, with the brightness of the first morning sun. Toni, Esme, and Eleanora squint and seek to cover their eyes against its brightness. A shuffling sound could be heard and then the bright light starts to dim gradually, until the natural light of dusk comes flooding back into the room from the windows of the castle. In the centre of the pentagram stands Polly, holding the chalice and her sword. Swathed in silver starlight, and she has a simple ringlet of silver on the crown of her head that glows offering an ethereal light. On her body, she is dressed in shining silver armour.

"I'm ready now" she says, evenly, yet the glint in her eye indicates a powerful wrath swelling behind her cool exterior.

## Chapter twenty-one - To Battle - Part One

On the battlefield a strange occurrence is taking place, between two rival factions of a single common foe. The two evil armies had not known the other was going to arrive at the castle to attack The Chosen One on the same night. Commands are being shouted and issued swiftly to collect intelligence about the other army. When the dark witch, The Black Dahlia, is told that the army of agents are being led by a human, called Miles, who has a powerful witch and a demi-god with him, The Black dahlia is intrigued. Wearing the body of Balan and still trying to harness his strength, the Black Dahlia decides to go to meet this Miles and his army, to offer him a one-time deal to join forces.

The Black Dahlia takes a personal guard of six demons. All savage and cruel, carrying with them black blades and dark magical artefacts. They stride out, tall and fierce before her, carrying her banners. The Black Dahlia glided on air behind them and as they approached Miles, she floated and gently landed with precision a few paces in front of him. Eyes opaque black and with a wicked smile on the face of her hostage, Balan.

Miles looks confused and stunned by the display "Who are you and why are you here?" he demands. Nuala comes rushing over, in a tight black lacy mini dress and slouchy, diamante covered thigh high boots. Laying her glass wand down at the feet of the body of Balan and bows low before the Black Dahlia and holds out her upturned hands.

"What are you doing Nuala? get up, who is this guy to you?" Miles says, panic stricken, and fear is starting to set in as the compound is overrunning his body, coursing through his veins. Making his heart flutter and beat in his chest.

"Shut your ignorant tongue, Miles. This is not a man. This is the Queen of Darkness. The Black Dahlia", Nuala hisses out of the side of her mouth "You are standing before a great queen of black power".

From behind the troops a large, tall man appears "There is something else about you, Black Dahlia", Krones' deep voice booms out and he eyes the black queen with doubt "You are holding on to infinite power within the shell of the man you possess" Krones muses as studies the body of Balan, with a look of contemplation on his face. "But yes. I can see. You don't know how to wield the power inside this body, do you?" Krones lets out a bellowing laugh.

The face of Balan smirks but the Black Dahlia does not move her puppets lips to respond to Krones, but looks out over the field to address directly, the assembled armies through their minds, she says this:

*"You will join my army and I will kill The Chosen for you. Are we agreed?".*

"We are NOT agreed on this in any way, shape or form" Miles states, adamantly , planting his feet wide apart. "We are not agreed at all. We will collaborate, but whoever gets to her first, will have the privilege of killing, Polly. We? I mean, I don't even know who you are",

Krones strides forward into the circle formed by the soldiers "None of you stand a chance against The Chosen One. Only I can do this task" says Krones, with a look of contempt on his large, god-like face as he surveys the amassing crowds. More demons and agents are joining the group, watching the exchange. A simmering discontentment is growing amongst the soldiers of the two armies, and it is being exaggerated by the standoff between their leaders.

"You doubt my power, Krones?" says the Dark Queen, The Black Dahlia quite innocently and pouting with disdain at the words of the demi-god. Trying to feign disinterest, not wholly succeeding.

"You were held in a cave for centuries, trapped by the mere runes of my mother's High Priestess. Of course I have my reservations about your… capabilities" Krones scoffs.

The Black Dahlia falsely smiles and then lifts the possessed hand of Balan to her mouth and blew. A black bird made of smoke and shadow appears from thin air in her palm. The bird stands up, ruffling its feathers and tweeting sweetly its birdsong. The Black Dahlia leans forward and whispers in its ear. The bird looks over at Krones standing tall, in golden armour with his red cape fluttering in the breeze. Krones is wearing another of his golden crowns on his head and his shoulders are wide, broad, and strong. He exudes a confidence too deep to describe accurately and has a magnificent sword at his hilt, which is the size of a dolphin. Requiring the strength of ten men to wield it, but Krones holds it with one arm, barely extended.

"A gift for you my lord Krones" says The Dark Witch, Black Dahlia. Her eyes hungrily looking at him with an intensity of purpose. She lifts up her arm like a puppeteer, and the shadow bird flies over to Krones. The angular tip of its wings and size, reminiscent of a swallow. Circling and tweeting it flies playfully around Krones' large head a few times. While it sings out the most melodic and enchanting tune, booming out over the battlefield with the searing sound of its song.

  Krones' large lips are set in a grin; he looks curiously at the small creature and tries to touch the bird. His finger slips straight through the shadow particles, whenever he manages to reach it. "This is a strange gift to give me, a warrior god. Why not something more aligned to fighting, more useful on this day of days?"

"My lord, you judge things too swiftly, all are not what they first seem. You will come to learn this in time" The Black Dahlia answers and her eyes holding the void, widen. Wanting a fuller view of the demi-god before she flicks her hand with a new command for her little servant. Krones begins laughing at her, amused by her riddle. Unshakingly confident in himself. His mouth widened to laugh louder.  The bird, within a heartbeat, flies inside. Not many people had seen the bird enter the demi-god's mouth. They are left in shock and surprise by Krones gags as his impressive, muscle-bound body lurches forward. Holding his thick neck with his mighty hands, slowly choking to death. His face is changing to a vivid shade of magenta and the veins in his eyes strain, popping out of his head.

The Black Dahlia watches him in his discomfort for a long time and then with a flick of her hand, she issues another instruction to the little bird. The feathers turn to large metal spikes, piercing through and out of, Krones' thick neck. Spinning on rotation from the inside, like a turn mill. Within seconds, the blades cut his head clean off. His eyes watch as his own head tumbles down before him, bouncing off his chest and lands in the long grass. His eyes unable to look away from the horror of the image of his own headless body for at least thirty seconds. Then the muscular body slumps to its knees. A collective gasp shoots up from the crowd.

The Black Dahlia softly purses her lips and whistles. The black spikes retract from inside the flesh. The little bird emerges, hopping daintily from the severed windpipe onto the ground. Where the small bird shakes out its feathers, releasing the bits of flesh embedded in its wings, before it flies back to its mistress. Sitting on her shoulder for a while, or a more accurate way of describing the scene would be to mention that the bird was sat on the shoulder of the body of Balan.

A shocked silence hangs in the air for an age. Hundreds of pairs of terrified eyes in the field are on the Black Dahlia. She took her time to pat the little bird absentmindedly on the head, as it hopped back onto her palm and disappeared from view.

She wipes her hands together "Well, my camp is over there when you are ready to join" the Black Witch Queen Dahlia announces to no one in particular, but fully expecting them all to follow her. She flies up in the air and begins moving away in the direction she had pointed to.

The agents scramble after her. Individually wondering what powers she possesses to manage to kill a demi-god with such ease, and if they were going to make it home on this night. Quite a few of The Company agents threw down their weapons and made a dash for the treeline. Disappearing from view rather hastily. Miles waited for the last stragglers to move off over the now trampled and shadow-covered, muddy field. He made sure no one was watching before he went over to the head of Krones and pulled off the crown from his large head. "Well, there is no sense in this going to waste is there?" He thought to himself. All he needs now was the Horn from Kane to complete The Horned Ones rite. Aiming for the tree line of shadows of the forest to disappear from view. Leaving his army behind to find a different way to obtain the Horn. Nuala watched him, sighed and then silently followed. Hers and Miles's fates were bound together.

Miles heard a rustling of leaves behind him and saw the figure of Nuala emerging "Nuala, how did she kill a powerful demigod like Krones? It's not possible. Is it?" Miles says this in a small voice.

"The body she is in possession of has a great power that she has not quite managed to unlock yet. I could feel the power but who knows where she got it from. It does not matter how she got it, it's that she has it and she is evil beyond anything you can imagine. We need to leave", Nuala says this in a panicked way and turns to leave through the dense trees but is stopped by the vice like hand of Miles.

"Let me go or I shall throw you aside. I am not going to wait around for The Evil queen the Black Dahlia to destroy everything " Nuala says, with an elevated malice in her tone, to avoid any doubt that she would indeed destroy him, given cause.

"Please Nuala, I need the horn for The Horned God, and you know I am meant to have it and you are meant to help me" Miles says this with an unwavering certainty. "Where is Kane now?"

Nuala holds Miles' gaze and after a while, she reluctantly nods; she knows what he says is true – their fates are intertwined. "Okay, let's do a locator spell and then we can track him down. He must be in your country home that we left but let's make sure" and Nuala holds the closet tree trunk with her hand and her wand up to her temple to perform the spell. A shimmering vapour ignites in the forest where she stands. Nuala is a powerful witch; her powers are attuned with the lifeforce and energy of the darker parts of the universe - dark matter. Her eyelids flutter and she scrunches up her forehead in confusion, a line appears between her eyebrows "This is odd. Kane appears to be in the Castle over there in the tower, with two beings of immense and immeasurable power" Nuala opens her eyes and stares off into the distance where the castle tower stands, looming out of the sky. Miles looks baffled "What's he doing here?" he peers at the tower too "does he have the horn with him?" Nuala nods but she then mutters under her breath so that Miles cannot hear "This was not foreseen, what does it mean?"

Miles stands up straight "Well, whatever this is about, I don't care, I need that horn" he points up at the tower, striding into the darkness and towards the sandstone castle. Nuala looks longingly at the interior of the woods but then with a sigh, starts to follow Miles. Their fates are bound and she must follow through with the task set by her Master, or face the consequences of His wrath. Nuala shivers and it is not due to the chill wind on this dark night.

Polly called to the inhabitants of the castle; her voice magnified. Explaining to all present what she knew of the Black Dahlia. How she and Balan had discovered her in the cave in Russia and about the possession of Balan. There were a lot of frightened people asking questions, but everyone understood that the dark witch queen had to be stopped and wanted to stay to fight.

Kane had communicated with Able, his agent friend and Able came through a portal, with about forty defected agents. They had demon fighting weaponry and casual infantry gear for the frontline assault. Polly looked around the room and felt the swell of pride at the sight of all the allied groups working together to develop a plan to overcome the dark witch.

The defected agents were positioned at the front lines of the volley, of the defence of the castle. Working out the logistics of planting rows upon rows of bombs, around the castle, that could be remotely detonated. Lines were drawn, the field was being separated into sections. Some were cordoned off, set aside as attacking areas and that of defensive zones. Ready for hand-to-hand combat, where troops could potentially be led out to skirmish with attacking forces. Light artillery was laid around the field, so that the soldiers had access to weaponry if they were driven back and overrun; defensive manoeuvres maybe needed. Smaller camps were set up around the perimeter of the defensive line. The defected agents were working alongside magical folks to cast spells of defence and shield charms in strategic places.

The Aunties, Toni and her Mama were preparing the spell to free Balan, from possession by the witch - they were planning to use the pentagram that Esme had conjured earlier and were setting up everything ready to cast the spell.

Esme and all the healers were placing protection spells on everyone and the castle, and some were brewing flammable liquids that could be thrown in small glass vials and combust upon contact. The Professor and Eleanora had called upon the magical community and more people were arriving each minute, through portals, bringing with them weapons and magical equipment.

Kane was in the topmost tower of the castle with Casper and Cassie readying the two adolescent dragons for Polly and the sword of Hestia to be set aflame.

Everyone was busy doing something, but still managed to have discussions with one another to share plans, collaborate and make sure that the overall attack and defence was strategically coordinated. Chris was nowhere to be seen. Polly kept looking for a glimpse of his tall frame in the groups assembled, around different points of the castle, but no one had seen him in hours. Toni came over to Polly and hugged her friend "how are you doing, Polly?"

"Yeah, ok. I want to get things started, to do something to free Balan but I'm scared that people are going to get hurt so I don't want it to start at all, at the same time, do you know what I mean?" Polly says looking sadly around the room.

"I know, but everyone understands the risk they are taking and are making the choice to fight the evil witch and that's the most important thing. It's not all on you. You know that, right?" Polly nodded, but did not hold eye contact with Toni, keeping her distance.

"Hey, anyway. I came over to tell you that we are going to start the spell. Y'know, to remove the queen from Balan. Hopefully, she won't know what's happening until it's too late. We are going to place her back in her true form, so she is solid and can be, well, . . .beheaded, I guess." Toni shifted uneasily, she could not imagine Polly doing something as violent as this, even though it was the only way to end it.

"How will I know it's done and Balan is free?" Polly asked.

"Well, the book of magic describes the end as a searing blue light and I guess all traces of her will be removed so his eyes will turn back to brown and won't be black anymore but that's just a guess, I'm afraid" Toni explained.

"That's good enough for me" Polly says patting Toni's hand. "Listen, I better get going to light the sword and then lead the attack out into the field. I just wanted to say, um that, well, you..." Toni flung herself at Polly and they stood there hugging each other very tightly "Tell me when it's all done and it's over. Please take care of yourself, okay?" Toni says looking at her friend, rather intensely. Stopping her from saying her final goodbye – Toni couldn't bear it.

"You too" Polly says, while putting on her silver helmet and standing up straight as she moved off and started the long climb up to the top of the tower.

The stairwell to the tower is vast, each individual sandstone brick is the size of a chest of drawers, piled on top of one another. The Fortress structure held no glass in the windows but were designed as traditional battlements so opened out directly to the open sky. The architecture looked as though it had been conjured up from the imagined castle fortresses of mediaeval times. The battlements were walkways and there were arrow slots for archers and opened mouthed lions for pouring boiling oil onto enemies of long ago. The masonry was smooth and had been hand hewn long ago, by masters of stone.

Polly stood on the top step looking out over the edge of the castle, down onto the valley below and the surrounding lands, it was covered in moving shadows. But she could see the army of the Black Queen quite clearly. Able had briefed her on Miles' decision to leave, since his army had abandoned him in favour of The Black Dahlia. Polly was lost in thought when Chris stepped out of the shadows and took her hand. "Where have you been? I was worried about you" she says brushing his cheek with her gloved hand.

"Scoping the site from the shadows but near enough to overhear the enemies plans. It's not good news, for sure. They plan to attack the castle in the early hours of the morning when people are resting, and the Black Dahlia plans to hurl fire balls at the gates to smash their way in and then storm the castle." Chris looked at Polly sadly, regretting he had to share this news. He was worried about her – her distance and the lengths she would go to keep everyone safe.

"Well, we plan a full-scale attack. Taking the fight to them first and drawing their army out into the fields, where bombs have been sown. Then there will be an agile attack of smaller groups, to circle the rear and onto hand combat for the ones that are left. I'm lighting the sword and then leading the charge. The agents should have laid the bombs by now and are in the shadows waiting to circle from behind".

"We are outnumbered, you know, by three to one?" Chris says this while running his fingers through his fringe.

"Don't tell me the odds. We *have* to win or the darkness will destroy everything. *Everything*. All we have now is hope. I will prioritise finding the Black Dahlia and killing her then the battle will be won" Polly continued to look out over the castle walls, anywhere but his face. If it came to it, she knew in her heart that she would sacrifice herself to save them all. Her grip on the masonry betrayed how anxious she felt.

"Well, I'll be right by your side" Chris murmured and drew her in, then enclosed her with his arms and kissed her lips urgently.

They broke apart, reluctantly and Polly held her eyes closed for a long while, holding on to the moment for as long as she could, then turned away. Walking alone towards the large stone fortified tower where Kane stood on the outer wall of the castle. The dragons were roosting on the top of the tower roof – crumbling under the Dragons' weight.

The Dragons had doubled in size since Polly had last seen them. Both of them, could no longer fit inside the tower or castles structures and whipped their long necks round excitedly when they saw Polly approaching. Their large claws clumsily ripping apart great chunks of the battlement in their excitement to fly to her. Polly watched as the stone chunks bounced down the outside wall of the castle and bounded on the rocks below and into the sea.

Casperian jumped to be close to his mother and as he landed, the structure shook and trembled to hold his weight. Kane had created a nest of bracken and wood, planning for Polly to place the Sword of Hestia on the surface and then the dragons could ignite the wood.

Polly was completely immersed by her Dragons. They nuzzled her lovingly. Stroking and cuddling Casperian and Cassadians' snouts and underside of their large scaly jaws, she looks down at the nest and shakes her head. Whispering to her precious two Dragons and they nod their great heads in agreement. Polly then positions herself before the majestic beasts, holding up the Sword of Legend in front of her face. A singular nod is all that she gave, as a cue to start and then both Dragons lifted their long necks to let out a roar into the night sky. Building the white-hot furnace at the backs of their throats before breathing out long streams of roaring and licking flames at the female Kaidaluminerre, as if old legend was coming to life on this night. Polly dipped her head against the river of gold translucence and the brightness of the searing flames, outshined the stars above. The Sword of Hestia was ignited and covered in a ripping blue and red flame, ancient runes running along the silver ore, ready to take down any dark foe that crossed the blade this night.

Down below on the battlefield, the enemies' army halted their activity to stand and listen to the sound of the great Dragon's roars. Some held their hands over their ears in fear, others fled, and some stood still trying to see where the noise was coming from; to catch a glimpse of the magnificent creatures was all they wanted in this life – to touch miracles. All now knew that there were monsters inside the castle waiting for them to enter and a silence gripped the soldiers of the enemy. Doubt started to creep in from that point onwards.

Polly stood up clutching the sword as it shone brightly across her face, she asked the Dragons to wait for her on the top of the tower and not to come down until the battle was over - commanding them to flee if anything happened to her.

They both paced, smashing against the sandstone brick and flicked their tails in agitation. Wiping out whole sides of walls, but both Dragons understood what she had asked of them to do, and neither had liked it. Kane said his fond farewells to the Dragons before he followed Polly and Chris down through the castle, and into the great hall.

It was time.

A great intake of breath, swelled in the silence of the hall as each person remembered their strength and thought about their loved ones, and what they were fighting for. Polly lifted the sword aflame and shouted out "So, it begins" and she was answered in the silence by hundreds upon hundreds of chorusing voices "And so, it begins" and each magical person lit their wand, and each agent that remained behind, held a lit torch in solidarity, and the dragons roared overhead, the castle shook. The strength of the mythical beasts gave them all courage.

Polly was positioned at the front of the lines, taking the lead to march the army out to the main gate of the castle. To the thrumming beat of battle rhythms on drums, to the pounding of foot and the first intake of breath, the army of the light were ready to fight to the death to defend all that they hold dear.

Toni watched her childhood friend lead rows of soldiers into a Battle that was older than time itself and she was scared for the safety of Polly. She made a vow to do whatever it takes to save her friend. Turning round in a trance like state, Toni stood in the middle of the pentagram. With her magic fully expanded, she searched through all the dimensions to find the anchor of the shadow within Balan. Sliding back all defences within herself that harness her self -control, to grip the unlimited power of the Void, without a safety net. And she did touch and grip onto that dark place connected to the Black Dahlia. Her head shot back; her eyes turned completely black as she had latched onto the essence of The Evil Queen to start the spell. The windows cracked and warped under the pressure of the powerful Rite, being performed by Toni. The glass smashed into a fine powder, which blew in all over the Aunties and Mama – scratching every surface, filing down all hope as it swept through the castle. They did not move, vigilantly guarding as they watched Toni being drenched in a thick black tar like substance. Mama was scared for her daughter and Ola silently cried, with her eyes downcast for the little girl that Toni once was.

This was a dark night indeed.

### Chapter twenty-two - To Battle - Part Two

Assembled at the gate, marching the allied army through to the outer walls of the keep, Polly is startled to see a portal gate opening up beside her. She yells to draw attention to the entranceway silently spinning into view. Witches and wizards rush forward and create a barrier round the entrance opening - nothing would be able to come out of the portal now. A head emerges and a stern looking thick set man, cloaked in black armour peers through at the assembled crowd of magical beings.

"Hold on, there please, we mean you no harm. It is I, Elmond leader of the Magical Enforcement Taskforce. We've noticed a great surge of amassing magical power in this area and a great deal of dark energy and have come to investigate. Can I and the team drop in please?" A loud cheer erupts from the crowd – it is assumed that the Cavalry is here and more soldiers are most welcome to the cause.

"Yes, if you have come prepared to fight against the Black Dahlia than you are welcome and if not, then sorry, but make sure you stay out of my way. The Black witch has my brother, and I am going to get him back" Polly exclaims, and the crowds are shocked to hear that Balan is Polly's brother. Is he another Chosen One? They could be heard asking one another.

There is a great deal of confusion. "Elmond, is that you?" The Professor shouts over the tops of the crowd and he is seen weaving his way through the packed crowds, out to the entrance of the portal and Eleanora was not too far behind.

"Good grief, Timothy. What has happened. Lots of good folk here in the Castle ready to get bloodied and no one called the Enforcement team?" The leader of the magical enforcement team says with indignation, while twitching his lavishly waxed moustache.

The Professor starts pushing down the wands of the witches and wizards that are holding a barrier to the portal and replies "Elmond, you and your team can come in and I will explain all to you, but Polly must go. The Black Dahlia is here and has an army outside going to storm this castle and we cannot wait as we will be under siege and pushed back into the sea if we don't surround them first".

"Good grief, the Black Dahlia? I can't believe it. Hang on. I'll call in reinforcements" with that Elrond leans back through the portal to shout instructions behind him and then jumps down onto the cobbled stones of the Castle Gate. A dozen troops fall in after him and more are on their way. Cheers erupt all over the castle – the cavalry is here, or at least they assume it is.

Polly starts preparing to move through the gates and Elmond shouts "Stop, hold on there. Hold on."

Polly defiantly lifts The Sword of Hestia aflame with dragons' fire, raised up in her right hand and bellows "And so, it begins" and she is answered by voices in the night air "and so it begins" hundreds of people waiting to march through the gates out onto the battlefield, ready for the charge. The battle drums had started up again. Elmond looks at The Professor with his eyebrows raised and Eleanora steps forward into view "As Pollux, *The Chosen One* says, you are either coming or we will walk over you, my good Elmond. There is no stopping us on this night. The choice is yours".

"As you were, Eleanora" Elmond cast his eyes around the castle keep and cannot deny that he would need to stop too many people from marching out of that gate under the lead of The Chosen One of Legend and this was impossible. If the Chosen One had been called forth then there was nothing else to do but to rally to her call. Elmond decided that the best use of his time would be for him and his team to join the back of the line heading into battle, under the banners of The Chosen One of legend. Which he did most gladly.

The group assembles into lines before they march out onto the dark field. Two blinks of a tiny light in the forest, lets Polly know that Kane and Able and the agents, are in position under the shadows of the surrounding woodlands. They have completed their planned tasks. Bombs have been laid and are waiting for the right time to be detonated.

The magical folk cast spells to raise barriers around the army and then they start to move as one across the field. Swishing of wet grass can be heard as they march forward but very little else. There is complete silence. The last deep swell of breath before the storm.

Polly is at the centre and leading them on, across the fields. Suddenly, yelling can be heard. There is a great deal of shouting coming from the enemy army lines stationed at the far side of the field, just before the canopy of the woodland. A great clamour can be heard as the enemy scrambles to assemble, catching sight of The Chosen One's army as it steams forth. The enemy strives to take battle formation - the enemy's soldiers were half-clothed and clearly, were not expecting a direct assault, like the one that is at the door. They had prepared to be on the attacking position, so did not have time to call out new orders or arrange a defence strike. Chaos ensued.

 The Black Dahlia looks out over the field and is gladdened that the Chosen Child is ready to do battle. The Black Witch got on her shadowy black horse and then did the unthinkable. She charged out with her personal guard of a handful of demons and agents, who were all in disarray behind her. The army that was meant to follow her, fragmented into smaller groups, unsure of what to do. Yet still the Black Dahlia charged forward in anger. Her confidence and arrogance was brimming over, doing her a disservice. She wore the face of The Chosen and burrowed from his power.

Some of the enemy rounded the outskirts of the field, attempting to creep up on The Chosen One's army. With stealth, they walked forward and straight onto the field of bombs, that detonated and exploded with huge fire flames. Debris and nails shot out - anything the agents could get their hands on in the castle had been plied into the bomb shells.

Huge numbers of demons and enemy agents were struck down, laying bloody on the field. The smell of burnt flesh and excrement hung heavy in the air. Then the fighting began in the centre, clashing swords, shouting, bullets, screaming of the wounded. Swirling lights of killing spells filled the thick night air and Polly's army were digging in, knowing that what they fought for was the right to be free of tyranny, free of evil and of keeping their own freewill. And they fought all the more ferociously for that dream and hope for all beings - they would not let the Black Dahlia rise again. They had all been told of the history, which was told as a fairy tale nowadays to frighten small children into behaving but none of them can forget what The Black Dahlia had done all of those centuries ago. It would end today and with them.

Kane led a charge from the woodlands and came on the enemy army from the rear and circled them in. Agents shot down enemy agents, that they once had worked alongside, and accepted their surrender, willingly. The demons, however, were not dissuaded from their evil purpose. There to commit acts of violence for the sheer enjoyment of it, as much as displaying their loyalty to the Black Queen. Nevertheless, their numbers started to diminish with each agile onslaught from the soldiers of the light, until eventually Polly had bludgeoned and struck her way through to the centre of the battle and was now face-to-face with the Black Queen.

The Black Queen looked around her and saw that her army had dwindled to barely nothing. The last few demons were on the ground. Tied up and on their knees. All is lost and this is when she is most dangerous.

The Black Queen shouts out "It looks like it is just you and me child. How it should be" she leapt from the horse made of cobweb, dead flies, and shadow, and pulls a large black sword from her saddle. Its sharpness sung in the chill of the night air, like harvest scythes slicing through cracking bones, and it is a sword chillingly named The Bringer of Terror.

Polly steps forward and holds her sword in both hands, closing her eyes, trying to not look at the body of Balan, as it stands there before her. Being used like a puppet by the cruel Black Dahlia. The Witch Queen smirks at her pain, the unwillingness to injure the body of her friend. The Witch Queen lunges forward and slashes Polly across the forearm. Her blood pulsates down her arm, making her hand grip slippery. Her arm shake.

Polly flinches back, she knows she will have to fight now, hoping that Toni would be able to complete the spell soon - ending the curse and the hold over Balan. The ferocity of the attack from the Evil Witch Queen is relentless, Polly is being pushed, slashed and pummelled backwards. Still she refuses to fight. The Black Dahlia jumps forward and spins round, lifting her legs up to kick out in mid-air at Polly and swinging her sword low to cut at the exposed parts of Polly's legs. Following through with punches swift and precise, landing blow after blow on the Chosen One's jaw. Wound after wound is being inflicted and Polly refuses to fight back. Eventually, the relentless attack leaves Polly collapsing in on herself. Broken, metallic blood in her mouth. Unable to heal rapidly enough against the assault. The Evil Witch Queen laughs aloud as she kicks Polly onto the floor, bent forward on buckled knees. The Chosen One slides across the floor, face down. Chris yells out to Polly in anguish "You've got to defend. I know its Balan, but she will not let up. Get up and fight. Fight now with all that you have. We need you. *I* need you. "

Polly lifts her head up miserably "Ahhh, the Chosen Child is hurt. Poor little baby. Poor baby who doesn't understand. Do you know why there are two Chosen this time? Have you figured it out yet, Child?" says the Black Dahlia with blackness of speech. Staring menacingly at Polly down on the floor.

Polly looked at the Black Dahlia suspiciously, wanting to hear, but equally cognisant that she may be toying with her, but she listened on anyway and replies "No, but I doubt you know either Bitch Queen".

The Black Dahlia delights in Polly's use of venomous vernacular and says "So sweet. She's trying to intimidate me with her words. You are naïve. The Chosen Ones' come forth in times of great peril and *is* what is needed to *be*. What this means is the stronger The Chosen, the greater the evil you face is. Your enemy is so powerful and there are two of you this time, and you are both destined to try to find the seven objects to bolster your powers even further. Think about what that means. He is hiding in plain sight and much more powerful than the two of you combined".

"Miles do you mean or *you*?" Polly hesitates, hanging back, wanting to know more.

"Not that buffoon and you only wish it was *me*. No, He is coming. Destroyer of the cosmos and killer of the maternal. I was the one He ordered to kill Her son, Krones. What I did, I did for Him" The Black Dahlia shrieks and rejoices "He is the Prince of Darkness, and I am but his servant. You shall see this in the end. The end of all and a complete darkness will blanket the whole, the universe, all dimensions. *Everything will be obliterated*".

While the Black Dahlia is talking, Polly is able to regroup her focus and strength. With a renewed sense of rigour, Polly jumps up and throws her axe in an arc and as she jumps forward, planting both of her feet in the stomach of the Witch Queen. She holds her arm up and the axe gravitates back downwards. Polly catches the axe in mid-air, smashing it down on to the shoulder of the Evil Witch Queen in Balan's body. The dull axe edge is used, lightly applied yet it still smashes through skin and bone. The Evil Witch Queen reels back and she is just about to cast a killing spell, when a lightning bolt. Blue of colour, comes streaking through the sky. Zigzagging its way down and landing before Balan. A seismic pulsating light shoots out horizontally, eerie in its brightness against the darkness of the night. The blue bolt lights up the surroundings giving off a strobing effect, which makes the crowd look like they are twitching and dancing in an odd convulsive way.

Polly holds the hilt of her sword up to her eye line, ready for what comes next. She hesitates. She is looking at Balan, expectantly. With hope in her heart. The blue streaks of lightning are surely a sign. Polly waits with bated breath.

Balan stands still for what feels like an age and then his hands trembles and flutters to rest on his heart and looking intently at Polly, he utters. In a cracking voice, he says, "You told me that my heart is precious to you" and he looks up at Polly with his own creamy brown eyes. Repeating the last words back to her that she had spoken to him, before the Dark Witch had taken hold of him in the cave, so long ago. Polly yelps out her feelings of relief.

And then, behind him, slowly rising, a tall black-haired woman arose. Her teeth were like knives and her eyes black, devoid of soul. The skin of the creature, who had been haunting Balan's steps, was stretched grotesquely over its face, as tightly as that of a snake. The Black Dahlia in her true form lunges forward, with her black sword in hand. Chris leaps at the same time and pushes Balan out of the way, taking the full force of the blade into him. Into his diamond hard skin. Polly screams and in her rage, commands a lightning bolt out of the sky and aims it at the Witch's head, while blindly leaping forward into the air at the same time. As she does so, the Black Queen without mercy, yanks the steel from Chris's broken ribs and thrusts it upwards, and sinks it deep into the belly of The Chosen One.


Casperian heard Polly's scream down on the battlefield below. With an almighty beat of his wings, he rose in the air. Intent on sweeping down to his Mother's aid. The beating of his wings are loud, as he wrenches and climbs through the air. Kane sees the young Dragon lift off of the battlements and shouts after him to go back, but the young Dragon does not listen nor heed his call.

Casperian the Dragon, circles the battlefield, sweeping low over the fallen looking for Polly. He sniffs the air, catching her scent and lands heavily on the ground, snarling and snapping his ferocious jaw and teeth. The soldiers on the field scream and yell, running for cover. Kane watches on in horror, as Casperian devours the remaining demons, and sets alight to the trees, in his agitated and heightened state. All is burning, all is chaos. Rampaging through the field, knocking people over with his horned tail and setting alight huge sways of grass and fields, in the dark.

The Dark With Queen stands clutching her detached skin to her head, hunched over and disfigured. Flesh dropping away. Barely able to hold up her black blade. Although her sword is drawn, she knows it is no match for a Dragon. Standing stock still, the Black Dahlia has been badly burnt by the

269

lightning bolt. Still hoping to call a portal unseen, but it is too late for her. Casperian's mighty gaze is upon her, the eye of the Dragon bearing into her soul and snapping his teeth at the Void that he will swallow whole and to her ruin.

He is Coming. Stalking her. Rearing up on the Dark Witch Queen, he roars out his anger shaking his magnificent head and neck. Siliva dripping from his exposed teeth and smoke curling from his slitted nostrils. The wildness in Casperian spirals in his chest and he roars into the night. He then stops, when he comes across Polly's broken and bloody form. There, beside her, he finds another Kaidaluminere, both injured by the Evil Witch Queen. His slitted eyes are wide with fizzing rage when he locks them upon the Evil Witch Queen once more. A look of horror is frozen on her crooked and blackened, blood-stained face. Turning weakly to run, but all is too late for her - she screeches in futility. The Dragon takes one large claw and pierces her stomach with a single sharp talon, pinning her to the ground. The Ancient creature swings his head low to place his face above her and looks directly into her eyes. She quells, pleads, and begs for his forgiveness. Casperian's scales expand and flex upwards in a display of his disdain and aggression. Dispenser of Justice is he. He then gives out one more deafening roar into the night sky, The witch's eardrums split open. The queen of old, faces something older, and she sees the furnace pulsating within his throat and a stream of molten fire shoots out, as wide as a river, poring over her and melting flesh from bone. There is none that can withstand Dragon fire, more powerful than any sword merely holding Dragon's breath - Casperian devoured her with molten flame alone.

Kane steps forward with purpose, "Easy Casperian, easy now. It's me. Its Kane" and he picks up the Sword of Hestia from the ground, where it had fallen, and he did cut off the remnants of the skeletal head of the witch and she was,

no                    more.

Casperian roars out a victory at the destruction of the black witch, but it is short lived. He is uncontrollable with rage; sensing Polly is mortality injured. The great Dragon is roaring out fire, spewing forth lava, as

270

rampant as flowing rivers, in his devastation. The flames from his great red belly catching everything alight. The landscape awash with red and amber floods and he continues ploughing huge furrows into the field, with his molten breath. All is a light, all is chaos and as he reigns down fire upon the land, he does not hear Kane calling to him - too mad in his grief.

. . . but then quietly, Polly coughs faintly, her throat filling with smoke. The great Dragon hears her over his swollen grief-stricken heart. He immediately goes to her and lands, swinging his head low to peer at her closely. He is blinking in the light of the fires he has set, all around. The dragon mother waves a hand at her beloved Dragon, and he heaves his body down, to lie flat beside her. Kane runs forward and picks Polly up.

"Casperian, we need to get them to the healers' quarters now. Through this wildfire you have set. Can you help me or are you going to continue your tantrum?" Kane says sternly. Casperian, The Adolescent, nods his great head and Kane lifts Polly, Chris and Balan onto his broad back and the Dragon beats his large wings, flying upwards, swinging round while in the air and heads towards the entrance of the castle.

Toni runs out of the Castle Gates to meet the great Dragon and with the help of the Professor, Esme, and Eleanora, they take turns to bring Polly, Chris and Balan into the Castle, where they are transported on stretchers, to the hands of those who can administer to their pain.

While this mayhem is occurring, Nuala transports herself and Miles to the battlements of the castle. Deep in a hidden crevice, cloaked by shadows, Kane has stored the bag with the broken horn of The Horned One. Nuala lifts it out, eyes heavy with the sickening need for greed and licks her generous lips. Miles goes to touch the ivory of the Horn of the Hunt not the hunted, and she clamps his hand shut and squeezes too tight. Wincing and shaking his fingers to let the blood circulate once more, glaring at her malice. Nuala's eyes glisten in relief that they have collected all of the items and then they both disappear from view. Cassadian is too distracted with worry and grief to notice the two thieves in the shadows behind her.

*** 

The Rite is being prepared. The Horn is placed in the sacrificium circle. The Crown of the damned demigod is placed on Miles' brow. A lock of the hair of Polly's mother is placed inside the spell ring, serving as a reminder of The Chosen One's pain. In His honour, a homeless shelter sponsored by Miles, was entered, earlier on this day. All one hundred inhabitants of the free house; run to greet Miles, their benefactor. To thank him for his esteemed generosity. The residents are herded into a room to meet him, and they find Miles standing in the centre, dressed in a long black robe. The doors are closed shut and locked from the outside. Miles pulled down his hood and those that saw his eyes knew what was coming, but silently stood still, too defeated by this world to struggle anymore. The futile screams erupted. They were just another one hundred souls offered before the Rite- three thousand and one hundred offered in total.

Miles stood in the middle of the Carven circle drawn on the floor by a priest with a piece of white chalk and he stood covered in the blood of the sacrificed. His blue piercing eyes look luminous against the crimson liquid of the fallen. The chanting of an ancient language began. The breath was taken from his body, and he slumped to the floor unconscious and when he arose, He arose within him. The Horned Champion had been born.

Nuala stumbles, as she walked out of the cold and greasy stone chamber, where the Rite had been performed. Still unsteady, walking along a stone passageway, lit by dozens of large wax candles. Eventually, Nuala came to a chamber that was hardly visited, as it only appeared to those that knew of its existence. On a simple wooden throne, without any intricate detail or impressive carvings, the oldest member of the Inner circle sat there humming to Himself.

"It is done" Nuala says this quickly and with a fearful glance at the throned man, not wanting to look around the room, not wishing to see the wide and terrified staring eyes of a young man, tied up and gagged, at His feet. Even though she does not look she knows that there are eyes, peeled back and silently pleading.

"Good, good. You can go now", The man born in Jerusalem says, while he drags the body up before him and drank of the young man's energy force. Casually tossing him aside, when he had finished. Nuala practically ran to the door to escape His presence. "Nuala, one last thing" He says while Nuala hesitates at the door "Make sure you capture an image of the Goddess when she is told her first born son is dead, I want to hang it on my wall" He points to an empty space where the stones are bare.

Nuala grips her shawl closer to her shoulders, visibly trembling and she nods, holding her hand over her mouth to stop a wretched scream. He smiles to himself and casually starts humming again, while Nuala swiftly exits the room. Behind her a portal to the underworld is being opened, and she can hear the screams of the innocent throbbing in her ears.

## Chapter twenty-three - The Beginning of The Age of Darkness for The Chosen....

**The members of the Inner circle are assembled.** The group had carefully selected an old and abandoned boat yard on the edge of some long-forgotten town in the Midwest of America. Most of the youth in these parts, enlisting in the army due to lack of employment options. There is a reek of despair. The name of the town is not important, it's the location that is - no one would expect a secret meeting of the globally powerful to take place somewhere like this. All of the members of the secret clandestine society are there apart from their founding member, Miles. He has never missed a meeting and his absence is being speculated in this creaking and dilapidated environment, where dead crunchie leaves and spiders balancing, on old twanging cobwebs, are the primary occupants nowadays.

A team of executive assistants had been sent forth to make the main areas of the site habitable and fitting for the Inner circle to meet, to deliberate their next move following the arrival of dragons into their crisp, clean and organised worlds.

Waiting patiently and sitting underneath a string of temporary twinkling ceiling lights - the original strip lights were deemed too harsh and unflattering by the team of assistants. After the meeting, every item would be thrown away. Cast out as an inconvenience - disposal like everything else in the inner circle's world.

The members are now seated in a circle. Perched comfortably on their favourite soft leather armchairs, transported here for this meeting. An expansive glass coffee table is in the centre. On the expansive glass sheet of the table, are tins of the finest matcha loose tea, ready to be served in exquisite hand-blown Japanese glass tea pots and matching cups. Jasmine tea pearls are currently spiralling open, for each member of the inner circle and the pretty flowers are drawing in the eye of all present, apart from the man born in Jerusalem - he is uninterested in trivia, as he calls it.

He is currently explaining to the other four billionaires that Miles has offered himself to The God of The Hunt. The Horned One and has killed Krones as a sacrifice to become the Chosen One of the demented God.

There is no outward or immediate response. The members of the Inner Circle look at one another curiously, but no emotions appear as expressions across their faces. Only one of them arches a manicured eyebrow and says, "What does this mean for us?" to The Man that is speaking.

He purses His lips "Well, our intelligence indicates that Miles has become deranged by using too much of the compound and he may be on his way here, to kill you all and take control of the bunkers and the resources, and ultimately take control of the plan".

A silence settles and throbs in the room like a silent bass vibration. Building tension, aching for the release that would come from the sound of a human voice.

Another man leans forward. Tall and lean, dressed in a natural-material, blue eggshell tunic suit "Hmmm, why would he do that? Miles cannot very well shape the world himself after the apocalypse. He has always been clear on this point. This does not make sense" The member of the group talking is called Te Huon. He practically owns the continent of Asia "This is not logical, and Miles is a person of logic. I wonder if there is more to this?" Te Huon continues, eyeing The Man with a deep look of suspicion and a shadow forms across his bright eyes. Looking around at the group for their views.

"Yes, this is very odd indeed, my friend" says the man that owns the continent of Africa who calls himself Viper. "Miles was the one that brought us together. He knew we needed each other to complete the plan, so why would he do this? We are not seeing all the picture, I would say." His deep brown eyes are fixed firmly on The Man and then his gaze draws in the Russian female member of the group.

The woman who owns Russia opines "Too odd. Too convenient. There is something else at play here, CIA or Federal Security Service, maybe?" she pouts and touches her platinum blonde hair and smooths down her creamy, butter soft leather midi skirt. She chose to dress in neutral shades with a white silk vest top. She calls herself Snow.

A tinkling, rolling voice breaks in "Are you doubting what I am telling you all, then?" The Man born in Jerusalem counters; he refers to Himself as Salem.

A visible tension spirals through the abandoned boat yard, a fission silently creeps under their collective skin. Acrimony nestles in the corners and whispers of the chaos starting to begin. There is something about Salem that the others have never wanted to look closely at. He is now in plain sight. He is cold. In truth, they are all cold and calculating but Salem is cold in a different way. Like he would peel the skin off of a human just to see what is underneath, while they watch him do it. He observes everything with a cruel keenness, eyes unblinking like a giant snake. His brain is quick, making him billions from the right investments at the right time, but he also takes a keen interest in funding wars of genocide. There is no other purpose to his meddling in the affairs of nations other than inflicting pain and suffering. He owns weapon manufacturing and missile development companies; he enjoys wielding fear and tightening of nooses around the worlds' neck.

They look round at him one by one, noticing too late what is being revealed, and not one of them wants to speak under his lizard like gaze - to be marked out by Him. But they are confident enough to operate billion-pound corporations so do not walk away from the uncomfortable situations in life - leaning in has gotten them this far. None of them will stand for intimidation or threats without putting up a fight and this was their first mistake and possibly the last they will ever get to make.

"Well, let's invite Miles to our next meeting and he can talk us through his motives" says Te Huon and he stares directly ahead.

"Yes, talking to him will give us clarity" says the Viper.

"Then we can consider the facts... for ourselves" says Snow.

He looks at them each in turn. Assessing the situation, weighing up all the different scenarios of how this exchange could turn out. They do not trust him; he should have calculated for this. Maybe? Or Maybe he is just not interested enough to have cared about how they would react. Salem coldly smiles to Himself and sighs "Oh well, I'll just have to do this the old-fashioned way". The Horde step forward, his servants made by Miles in the Labs of his science. The throats of the assistants, stationed outside are cut. Blood seeping out, onto the straw covered floor. Inside the meeting room, He began by lifting up his fingers and clicking them, summoning fire from his tips. The orb of flame glowed brightly in the iris of Te Huon's eyes and before his hand could lean on the arm of his chair to boost him up, his skin was consumed by fire.

The strangest thing really. The inner circle had carefully selected a meeting place not wishing to be observed, but it was selected as a desolate place where no one could also hear them scream for help either - chance is such a fickle friend indeed.

**Esme and Eleanora** take the long road of the Castle estate to get to the tunnel entrance, preferring to walk through the beautiful winter landscape. Upon reaching their destination, they both take care to remove their backpacks and place these in the tall grass to keep them hidden from view while they are visiting the High Priestess.

Entering the tunnel to the Goddesses kingdom, which is dark and ordinary apart from a whispering from within, they begin crawling along and downwards. After a while, the pagan witch sisters come across a strange sight, two baby fawns are nestling into one another and a venomous serpent is rearing at them - readying to attack. The fawns are watching the snake with an avid keenness. Their heads are following the undulating and rhythmic movements of the shimmering body of the snake. Yet, they do not show fear and are firm in their steadfastness, not running away. Esme raises her glass wand to intervene, but Eleanora holds her hand steady and shakes her head "We are seeing this for a reason. We must watch and try to understand" says Eleanora softly.

"A test?" Esme asks.

"An answer" says Eleanora gravely.

The snake jerks upwards and pounces forward and opens its mouth wide. Fangs gliding forward, dripping with venom and it clamps around the throat of the nearest fawn. The other fawn then bites at the head of the snake and when the snake turns to attack, the fawn bites off the head and spits it into the fresh earth on the floor of the tunnel. The fawn then proceeds to nudge at its injured sibling to try and withdraw the poison from its throat.

Esme looks at Eleanora, who is transfixed by the story being played out before them. The injured fawn wobbles around and lies down before giving out a final grasping breath. The other fawn lays its head down, bleating softly until a silence settles over both animals and the uninjured fawn weeps a tear of blood. The vision slowing evaporates and the outline of the fawns disappear into the interior of the tunnel, as if they had not been there at all.

Esme nudges Eleanora to move her forward, but she is not moving, unable to take her eyes away from where the two-baby deer had previously been. Her mouth clenched in an angry line and a steely gaze blazing across her stone-cold eyes.

Eventually, and after a while, the sisters both start moving down the tunnel to see the High priestess and to get the chance to ask about the two Chosen. As they go deeper downwards, into the subterranean parts of the tunnel, a sulphurous black cloud quickly spreads through the tunnel. It hangs with a heaviness over them and consumes all particles of oxygen. The smoke of it is leaking into their lungs, they are heaving and choking.

"Quickly Eleanora, get out now" commands Esme. "MOVE". The witches scurry down the last few yards of the remainder of the tunnel, as fast as their limbs are able to carry them. Reaching the cliff edge end within a matter of seconds. Before they attempt to hang drop down, out of the opening of the tunnel and onto the ledge below; they observe that they can hear the sound of a ferocious wind outside the entranceway. It sounds as powerful as a hurricane, and they can hear screaming coming from the outside of the tunnel. Cautiously, they drop down on the other side straight into a truly gruesome sight.

The place they are standing in has been desolated by volcanic ash. Huge meteorites are flying through the black sky, landing with seismic booms. Shaking the ground. Embers of bright amber ash are floating in lazy drifts, in the poisonous, sulphurous air. The mountains in the distance are spewing up into black clouds, tons upon tons of molten lava, even though they were not active volcanoes before, and pits of hissing steaming volcanic debris are everywhere. Nowhere can a blade of green grass be seen. Everything is blackness and ruin. The smell is of death and decay. Carcasses of animals and humans alike are strewn on the ground. Wailing from people and mewing of animals in pain can be heard all around. A loud humming, pulsating through their feet, can be heard in the distance. The most horrific sight emerges out of the horizon, as Eleanora and Esme walk through the apocalyptic landscape, the Willow Tree of Maternal Life is burning with a furious, red raging flame. The moon above is splitting open and half the large structure is dropping out of its own orbit, freefalling through space and coming towards earth at an accelerated speed.

The High Priestess is standing in full battle dress with her axe planted at her feet - she has been waiting for the Pagan Witch Sisters. The witches walk over to her urgently, with fear on their faces and a coldness piercing their hearts.

"What is happening here? Why is the world burning? Have we lost?" Eleanora demands.

"No, not yet. But this is a warning of what it could be like if you lose. I know why you come here. To ask why there are Two. There are two because you face the ultimate evil, The Prince of the Void, of the Nothingness, The Owner of the first Darkness. His plans are in motion, disease, famine, climatic crisis, war, vice, people treating other humans like objects and things. Self-centredness on the rise, hate and greed. His plans are delivered, Earth is not the only planet in this chaotic strife, and he will sit back and watch the universe burn. Covering the universe in his bitter blank darkness."

The High Priestess looks down at the small forms of the pagan twins and she stretches out her finger to point at the sisters "but you know of this already and you believe that the Chosen Two can defeat Him and you come for another reason. To ask if they can be saved at the end, is that right?"

Esme nods and Eleanora glares. She can barely contain the anger in her voice when she shouts "one of the fawns in the tunnel is killed and the other dies from grief. You were answering in the tunnel, so why did you bring us here, to this place?" Eleanora stands with tears dripping from her eyes.

The high Priestess swoops down to bring her gigantic face level with Eleanora "To show *You*, Eleanora, The Pagan Anarchist, what will come to be if you do not let this happen, if you try to stop the inevitable. To hold the mountain back is to watch the earth bleed. Do you hear me? You are unpredictable and it is you that must be shown".

"They have given enough. They have given enough to save the planet. The universe. This cannot be the way of it. There must be another way" Eleanora yells and covers her face with her blackened, smoke-streaked hands and slumps forward onto her knees - defeated and in melancholy. But she abruptly stops in her despair and sees a glinting star in the foreground of the cataclysmic landscape – it starts to glow brightly like the first Morningstar.

The High Priestess pats Eleanora's shoulder "It is what they were made for. To serve." and The High Priestess looks sadly on, as she watches the world burn, in the cosmic justice of a ruined kingdom, destroyed by its own people for nothing other than carelessness of not being guarded against corruption of the human spirit.


Eleanora and Esme climb out of the tunnel. Their smouldering and smoke drenched silhouettes appear alien against the beautiful back drop of the countryside that they are both surrounded by. Esme reaches forward and pulls back her sister's shoulder to bring her in for a tender hug. When her eyes look upon Eleanora's face they are greeted by an unexpected sight. Eleanora has a grin on her face. "Sister, I was not expecting to see you this happy. You seemed slumped over and defeated in that place. Eleanora what is happening? Please explain." Esme asks of her sister.

"Well, The high priestess went to such lengths to tell me not to try to save the Chosen. Which can only mean one thing, Esme. Can't you see?" Esme stared at her sister and shook her head at her pityingly. Eleanora felt exasperated but she carried on "It means that there is a way after all but it's a chance rather than a certainty. Thats why The High Priestess was warning me off. We must find the answer whatever it is and whatever the cost. We must do this." Eleanora says this with a happiness in her voice and then places her foot firmly on the path, and taking her first step forward, walks on, determined to set her own rhythm in this world.

Esme watches with her head held low, as her stubborn sister slowly starts walking back up the hill and through the golden valleys of Eleanora's own wild lands. Esme stands in the breeze, wondering if the High Priestesses' warning was given, as she has foreseen that Eleanora's actions may jeopardise the prophecy in some way. Esme sighs.

The wind swept through the clearing and tickled at Esme's face. There was a faint smell of spring in the air, and this was odd in October. Esme's face instinctively turned towards the smell of clover, of lilies of the valley, of snowdrops and of something else that she could not quite name. A bellowing braying sound floated down towards her from the top of the hill, where over the horizon a great White Hart was steadily walking into view. Its crystal eyes were glowing, and the first hint of sun beams of morning, were cresting over his large back, illuminating the great animal, as the flowers and birds burst forth behind him.

Esme stood staring in wonder and then tried to adjust her rucksack. It was heavily biting into her shoulder, but she realised this was easily remedied with an adjustment of the distribution of its weight. She gasped, it was odd how lessons are given in everyday situations and precisely when one needs to hear them - if only we paid more attention to the universe. Esme looked down at the rucksack and then gazed up at the silhouette of her sister that was moving out of view - she would not let her sister shoulder the burden of protecting The Chosen by herself.

Trudging now at a pace after Eleanora, Esme shouts "Hey, wait for me. You are not going to believe who has just arrived. Its…its well, the turning of the tide" and with these words Esme started to run towards her sister and into the unknown and onto adventure. The younger sibling twin chased her older sister, as they had been aptly doing since they were both small children. Bonded by love and the trust of the blood they share. Knowing that together they would be enough to help Polly and Balan remain whole in this great and magnificent world. The White Hart stood tall on the earth-mound, he occupied, and his great mane rippled in the high winds, and the sun brightly shone on his crown of antlers of brilliant silver birch. The sky overhead and the stars beyond all watched and listened, as he brayed and snorted into the clear morning air of the valley below, that holds life, continuously rolling on. We experience it in the blink of an eye compared to the journey of the great wide universe. But our time is precious, nonetheless.

**Chris** wakes up with a start, dripping with sweat from a dream where he could see Esme and Eleanora wandering in an apocalyptic landscape. They were distraught and covered with smoke dust. He had heard parts of their conversation and it alarmed him. He could've sworn the two pagan witches were discussing the demise of The Chosen with The High Priestess. Polly and Balan must die to save the universe was what he had heard.

His pounding heart is racing in his ears, but Chris rolls over on his bed and shoves the comfort of his soft pillow under his head and tries to fall back to sleep. It's the early hours of the morning. His thoughts are racing, and he admits to himself that his dream felt very real like as if he was there but was unseen. He looks down at his pillow and it is covered in a grey ash that is falling from his face. A dread falls upon him. His eyes prickle with tears. He squeezes his eyes closed trying to remember the end of his dream. A woman had appeared. She was unusually tall, with platinum blonde hair and striking violet eyes, and she was holding her pregnant belly. An enormous white gold crown was on her head and at the crest, a huge sparkling precious stone the size of a basketball. Just as he had been waking, the woman had lent forward and whispered a secret to him. Chris strained to recall her words, but he cannot seem to remember what she had said but whatever it was, he knows it is very important and that it may be enough to save The Chosen.

He looks out of the castle window and down at the fields below, that have been restored following the battle with the Black Dahlia. Chris absentmindedly touches the side of his ribs and the bones that had been shattered, as he recalls the battle, which took place two months ago. It is autumn now and the chill winds are picking up and battering at the sides of the castle. Icy rain is sheeting down against the hillside and the sky above is grey and drek. A knock on the door, but whoever it is does not wait for an answer and Toni comes bounding into his bedroom.

"What the hell are you doing here and how did you get into my apartment" Chis yells. She waggles her fingers playfully "Magic of course. Now, forget that and listen. I just had a dream, well more of a vision, I think. Esme and Eleanora were walking through a land that was covered in black ash and they start talking to..." Toni says.

". . .The High Priestess, who tells them that the Chosen must die and." Chris interrupted as Toni's looked at him in shock and then she picked up where he had left off "...Then the Goddess appears and whispered in my ear, but I can't remember what she had said to me . . ." Toni carried on and then they both say in unison, together "but I know it's a way to save Polly and Balan . . . ". They both stop talking, clamping their hands over their own mouths and stare at each other for a few minutes in shocked disbelief, realising that The Goddess has given them a mission.

"Okay, okay, is there a spell or an object that can recover our dream?" Chris says this in a panic.

"Yes, I've been looking up the Coin of Malvern, one of the sacred objects and it restores dreams. I think this means she wants us to find it and use it" Toni says with an astonished look on her face and continues "Can you do me a favour and pinch me? I can't quite believe that the Goddess appeared to us both".

"Erm, no thanks, you ask me to do the weirdest things sometimes, do you know that?" Chris says while shaking his head and finding his laugh even in circumstances, such as these. Toni laughed too. "Well, there is only one thing to do now" Chris says.

"What?" Toni replies.

"We get packed and find that bloody coin of course, any ideas?" Chris says raising his eyebrows.

"Well, the last known destination was the Himalayas..."

"Let's get going then, no time like the present. I have a feeling the Tome of Herne would come in handy too, so we'll have to steal it away from Eleanora before we leave... We'll have to sneak off..." Chris jumps up out of his bed, dressed in black pyjama's.

"Well, hang on. Let's get packed first and then a little breakfast and some make-up and I'm there", says Toni with a burst of laughter.

Chris looked at Toni with a sudden sadness in his clear green eyes and Toni mirrors this "I know. I know. Don't you worry. We will save her. This isn't over. Not while we both still live and breathe" Toni whispers, with a slight tremor in her voice, looking lost like a little girl waking up from a nightmare. They shake hands in the secret way they used to as children, both choked with the emotion of heaviness cloaking their hearts. They exchange a knowing look - that they would do anything possible to save their dearest friend whom they both love unconditionally. Then, they both walk out of the door, ready for whatever is presented to them, in the battle to save Polly and Balan – their friends, their family.

**The Chosen Ones** are walking through the forest, in a place familiar to Polly but not to Balan. She is showing him the way. Treading through knotted undergrowth and roots; and bobbing their heads under gnarled and entwined trees, until they come out into a clearing. Where Polly and Balan's feet kiss the grass of the open forest floor, tiny snowdrops spring up. Vast numbers of them in the wake of the Chosen two. The dense path of snowdrops look like glistening snow, so densely packed are they and the flowers leave a carpet of hope as they walk the path to the Willow Tree of Maternal life. The birds call, the bees hum, the squirrels chatter, and the forest comes to life even though it is the depths of Autumn, yet it feels more like spring here in the presence of The Willow Tree.

The Willow Tree appears before them, larger than any other tree in the woods. Tendrils of branches reach out to Balan and stroke his wetted, tear stained face. He rolls his shoulders back, the ever-present tension leaving his body for the first time in years. Balan The Chosen, reaches out, tenderly touching the bark of The Willow Tree, for the first time.

Afterwards, the siblings sit under the canopy of The Willow Tree and talk together, as they have been doing in the last couple of months, slowly recovering from their battle wounds - barely leaving each other's side. So very happy they are to have found a family in each other and in the dragons, of two.

"I wanted to ask you Balan, where were you when the Black Dahlia fully took over your body?" Polly says with a curiosity "The witch had told me you were dead. I could tell she meant it" Polly lowers her voice to whisper of death in that sacred of places.

"I was somewhere safe and warm" Balan replies whimsically and staring ahead with glassy eyes.

"There is more isn't there? More to this life and beyond the curtain. I felt the energy just out of reach when I lie there, presumed dead on the battlefield" she says.

Balan nods. He is whisked back in time, telling his sister of that time spent in a place far away from his body "I was in this rosy, warm, and safe place. I can't describe it. The place was made of nothing more than reflections of my memories of where I have felt happiness, where I have felt most at home here on earth. A space of scraping knees, skateboarding, laughing, beatboxing, and listening to terrible jokes...I could have stayed there, I know, but I knew that I am needed at the end." Balan says to his sister, Polly and then Balan continues, "but when I return there one day it will be so much more now that I have met you, Cassie, Casperian and the others. I will have experienced more happiness when I return there, next time. I know this to be true".

Polly replies "it sounds peaceful whatever it was." Polly reflects "people deserve for there to be something more. I'm glad for them all."

Balan reaches out and takes her hand, knowing his sister has the purest of hearts untainted by a world that once covered him in a void of despair.

"And what about you? What did you see in the chamber of the pentagram when you drank from the vessel." Balan asks with a curiosity.

"Love, I saw nothing but love, as I feel here and now, and in truth always. I've always had it in me. It was given to me by our mother, our father, my adoptive mother, by our group of friends and our dragons. It's always with me because it's what the very fabric of the universe is made from. We have just forgotten to look for it. I realise now that it's been with us all along."

They sat there together, hugging each other under The Willow Tree, maternal Tree of life. The dragons, laying their huge heads on the ground either side of the Chosen Two are pretending to be asleep but silently watching them out of their love for one another. This is as dragons do.


Polly rejoiced in her family, and she sat there under the comfort of The Willow Tree.

She watched. He eyes were caught by something on the ground. In the distance, the shadows of the branches of the trees from the other side of the clearing, started to stretch long, reaching, and clasping over the grass. When they had nearly touched at her feet, a despondency filled her. The shadows had appeared out of nowhere and were not facing the right way, away from the sun. Polly looked on in horror as she knew what this signified. The shadows were encroaching on her land. The end of the wholesome and the beginning of her family's life purpose was knocking at the door, declaring that destiny had arrived for her family - to do what is needed to be done, there is no end just the beginning of The End. The seeds of change swirl by her upturned face, floating through the sweet air that is blowing a little harder and a little chillier than before. The Kaidaluminere line sit there in that place, content to have one another. Holding onto this moment as if it was their last night on earth, knowing every moment is precious - given that they know what is to come.

The thrumming starts again and Polly and Balan both stir, and the dragons raise their great heads to sniff at the breeze of the coming of the storm, at long last. Standing, they draw their weapons.

The Father watched, unseen. Circling his young, to protect them all.

I will be there when needed he whispers. The full Kaidaluminere strength is present in the clearing and under The Willow Tree. Together at long last.

 I am watching my four children and as I look out over the world. Although, all is peaceful now, Destiny is coming into view like the first speck of a moving object, emerging over the horizon. A fierce breath of jagged air is inhaled through my demi-god nostrils. I could taste it on the wind. Destiny was moving, it would meet me and my children soon and, when it does it will be full on. I will make sure all are ready for the unfolding at **The End.**

Printed in Great Britain
by Amazon